IF I SHOULD LEAVE YOU

A Western Double

HARLAN HAGUE

WOLFPACK
PUBLISHING
— EST 2013 —

WOLFPACK
PUBLISHING
— EST 2013 —

If I Should Leave You

Paperback Edition
Copyright © 2021 (As Revised) Harlan Hague

Wolfpack Publishing
5130 S. Fort Apache Road 215-380
Las Vegas, NV 89148

Paperback ISBN: 978-1-64734-796-3
eBook ISBN: 978-1-64734-756-7

IF I SHOULD LEAVE YOU

A Western Double

SANTA FÉ MI CASA

Love is composed of a single soul inhabiting two bodies.
Aristotle

Love is a serious mental illness.
Plato

CHAPTER 1

"I'm telling ya', John Henry, I been making a survey of all the cantinas, and this one is different. They got the best-looking señoritas in the whole town. I mean, including the highfalutin' ones who walk the plaza of a Sunday. We'll just sit there and enjoy the scenery and have a nice drink."

"Or two."

"Or three." Brad grinned.

The two buddies, dressed in the uniform of the United States Army, strode down a Santa Fé lane that was lined with modest adobe houses. Brad occasionally reached back to pull his pard, John Henry, by the arm to hurry him along.

John Henry accompanied Brad occasionally on his cantina forays, not from any particular enthusiasm, but just to fill the evenings. Brad, on the other hand, seemed to have found his home and his calling. He spent most evenings in the cantinas, with or without companions. He was limited only by money, duty, or confinement for past excesses.

He caroused alone quite happily but he preferred company. Following an agonizingly dry six-day trial of duty and illness, Brad was determined to have John Henry's company and would not be denied. John Henry was happy to see his partner on his feet again and enthusiastic once more about something, even drinking, and agreed to go. Not without some apprehension. Brad was too eager.

Brad and John Henry were unlikely partners. Since John Henry's enlistment and posting to Fort Leavenworth, he and Brad had become inseparable friends. They were compatible but they were not alike.

Bradford was impulsive and excitable, quick to draw conclusions, the sort of person who can be swayed in a mob and be drawn back and forth as passions ebb and flow. John Henry weighed alternatives and pondered before acting to the point that, on occasion, others thought him indecisive.

John Henry Harris was a nice-looking fellow, though hardly handsome. Indeed there seemed nothing out of the ordinary about him. He was average height, muscular and hard. Without the severe life of a dragoon, he might have tended toward fleshiness. He had brown eyes with a hint of green. His hair was brown, straight and cut shorter than most. It was always neatly combed in the morning but, within an hour or two and for the rest of the day, it was unruly.

Unlike many of his comrades, John Henry did not sport a mustache. Aside from that, in a group of soldiers, he would blend, not standing out or apart. Yet, a careful eye would notice that his uniform was a bit neater, his body a bit cleaner, his manners and his speech a bit more polished. John Henry, if asked, would have acknowledged no difference and his fellows noticed none.

Anthony Bradford, like John Henry, a Missourian, was a shade taller and a bit leaner than his partner. He wore a neat mustache, had a quick wit and an infectious laugh. He was perpetually enthusiastic. About food, cantinas, pay, prospects in general.

Brad's ramblings on the prospects for sex embarrassed John Henry, to Bradford's delight. John Henry suspected that Brad's experience with sex was equal to his own, which was absolute zero, but he never responded to Brad's openings. Anyway, he didn't think any boy of nineteen was likely to have experienced such forbidden pleasures and Brad was only a year older.

Brad and John Henry, like most of the soldiers in the Army of the West, had been excited about the likelihood of a set-to with the Mexicans as the army approached Santa Fé. Like the others, they had been disappointed that it didn't happen.

The conquest of Santa Fé had concluded quietly. The defenders of the capital had melted away, much to the disappointment of the dragoons of the United States Army of the West who had hoped for some action after the tedious march across the plains. The only shots fired were a salute from American army cannon on a nearby hill that terrified the people and shook loose the few glass windowpanes in the town.

New Mexicans did not seem overly bothered by the American takeover here in the early stages of the war between the United States and Mexico. There had been some anxious moments when the women expected to be abused and branded on their cheeks, just as the Americans branded their mules. When they found that the newcomers were not the barbarians described by the government and the priests, they were more open and mixed freely with their conquerors.

The officers were wined, dined and otherwise feted. Stephen Watts Kearny had another cause for celebration. He had only recently learned that he had been promoted from Colonel to Brigadier-General. The now-General Kearny found time to set up a civil government and promise the new Americans that their customs, religion and property would be protected.

The dragoons were quartered in the old military barracks at the opposite end of the presidio from the Governor's Palace, which fronted on the plaza. The "palace" had long served both as the residence of the governor and a fortress. Its adobe walls were over four feet thick. The flat roof was a platform from which defenders could fire on marauding Indians. Windows were narrow to prevent the entry of attackers. The palace was part of a walled compound that included corrals as well as the barracks and officers' quarters.

Santa Fé was tranquil. Boring, if you were a soldier. The frontier farm boys had joined the army for some excitement and to escape the desperate life of the family farm. They wanted to fight Indians and shoot buffalo.

When the war with Mexico broke out in 1846, they looked forward to following the flag and enjoying a little kick-up with the Mexicans.

They were disappointed. Now they simply played the role of caretakers. Boring. Deprived of a fight, the soldiers looked elsewhere for their entertainment and reward.

Brad set a brisk pace. It was dusk and they met dozens of people who had come out of their houses a half-hour after sunset to enjoy the evening's cooling breeze. Walls of the adobe buildings, which bordered the dusty road, still radiated the sun's warmth. Doors, often resembling gates more than doors, were open to the flat earthen floors but revealed little of the dark interiors. Windows were small and framed by shutters that opened inward.

The people strolled casually, going no place. They stopped from time to time to talk in front of houses, some puffing contentedly on their cigarillos, then walked on. There were a few scowls at the two soldiers, especially from young men, but most of the Mexicans smiled and stepped aside, nodding deferentially.

The people moved to the side of the road, watching the Americans. This movement became a ripple that moved ahead until, a block away, strollers stopped, distracted from their conversation, glanced down the street, and then moved aside. They stood in front of houses on both sides of the road, watching Brad and John Henry approach.

The soldiers took no notice. They strode ahead, their boots raising little puffs of dust at each step, hurrying, talking and laughing about the evening's promise.

They soon left the townspeople behind. There were fewer houses now. The street was quiet, almost deserted, with only an occasional passerby.

A block ahead, a mounted vaquero emerged from between two houses. The soldiers saw him and stopped. His clothes were worn and dusty, his wide-brimmed hat tilted low on his forehead. The horse's bridle and saddle were lightly decorated with small silver stars and bars.

The vaquero rode slowly, directly across the road. The horse's hoofs raised spurts of dust, making no sound. The rider gazed at his mount's head, looking neither right nor left. He disappeared between adobe buildings.

The spell broke. "C'mon," Brad said. He beckoned to John Henry and stepped off. John Henry hesitated a moment, looking after the apparition, then hurried after Brad.

As they passed a small adobe in the next block, they saw a pretty little girl of eight or nine years, leaning against the frame of an open door. She smiled shyly at the soldiers, then darted back inside the house.

Another face immediately appeared in the doorway, an old woman, dark, leathery, wispy. She looked quizzically at the soldiers, then withdrew slowly into the darkness of the room.

John Henry suddenly felt depressed. Something's all wrong here, he thought to himself. Suddenly, he wanted to talk to them, the people of Santa Fé. He hardly heard Brad who continued to chatter excitedly, with some nervousness, about the cantina. Brad laughed and gestured and did not turn to see the somber face of his partner.

The cantina was no different from the others John Henry had seen. Maybe a little darker. Candles provided a soft illumination that hardly reached the walls. The only furnishings were a bar and a dozen plain square tables and stools. The earthen floor was smooth, clean and rock hard.

Patrons sat at tables, smoking, drinking from their tin cups and talking quietly. Three vaqueros and two women stood at the bar; three couples danced. Two guitarists and a violinist sitting in a dark corner supplied the music. An occasional guffaw added to the din.

John Henry and Brad sat on stools at a small table. John Henry's back was against the wall, and he was glad of the support. He was sipping his third fiery *aguardiente* and decided that it was enough. Enough for him to feel good, light-headed, a bit dizzy, but good. Brad must have had three drinks to John Henry's one and appeared to have every intention of widening the margin. He was smashed.

"Well?" Brad said, his head cocked to one side and smiling comically, his nose not a foot from John Henry's face.

"Well what, my friend?" John Henry smiled and drew back against the wall.

"Well, ain't this about th' greatest place in the whole American state of New Mexico? You haven't told me what you think about it."

"It's a dandy spot; you sure can pick 'em." John Henry smiled thinly. "But I think we've just about drunk the place dry." He wondered how his shoulders could be so heavy when his head felt so light.

"Not hardly!" With this, Brad raised his cup and brought it down hard on the table, sloshing the remaining liquid on the table, the floor and himself. The room was instantly quiet, every head in the room turned toward Brad.

Brad was beyond noticing. He drained the few remaining drops and raised the cup high. His head was down and he was oblivious of the eyes on him. John Henry felt pinned to the wall by the eyes. There was no merriment on the faces, no indulgent smiles. He had not noticed before that they were all Mexican faces.

A voice. Another. A laugh, conversation. Couples returned to their dancing and the din resumed. It had been only a moment, but to John Henry it was hours.

"Brad, what d'you say we get some air? It's blue in here."

"Ya havin' trouble breathin'? Look, if ya get down here close t' th' table" —Brad leaned over the table until his nose was flattened on the tabletop— "th' air is better." His arm remained stretched straight up, the empty cup waving in the air.

"All right, I'll try it. What d' you say we try another place? This place is getting crowded."

Brad sat up, turned on his stool to look toward the bar on the far side of the room. His arm was still in the air. He waved the empty cup.

"*Agardentee*!" he shouted at no one in particular.

The room was suddenly silent. Dancers stopped. Mexican eyes again glared at Brad. John Henry again shrank under their gaze. *Why*, he asked himself? *Brad isn't the loudest one here.*

"*Pinche gringo*," softly, from the shadows, followed by a murmuring from different quarters. Conversation gradually resumed but the din did not reach its previous pitch.

The bartender walked over and handed Brad a fresh drink. He took the empty cup and a coin from the handful that Brad offered him. The bartender pointed to John Henry who smiled thinly, raised his hand, palm outward, and shook his head.

Brad raised his cup and half emptied it in two gulps. He leaned across the table toward John Henry. "Now, what about th' señoritas?"

"What about them?"

"What d'ya think about 'em?"

"Well, there are sure some fine-looking women here," said John Henry, "I'll agree to that."

His eyes swept the room and rested on a girl standing near the wall on the left side of the room. She wore a loose-fitting brown cotton skirt and a white, short-sleeved, fitted blouse that was embroidered down the sleeves and around the low-cut neck.

She was listening to the cantina band. Her left arm was across her waist, the hand cupping her right elbow, her right hand on her cheek. She leaned against a table, and her shoulders swayed with the music. Her waist-length hair, pulled back and tied neatly, waved gently with the rhythm.

Her face was clean of the paint he had seen other Mexican women wearing. Her nose was small and John Henry swore that he saw candlelight reflected in her dark eyes.

Even at this distance, he could almost feel the softness of her cheeks. The lips of a perfect mouth were parted as if she were singing softly.

Shortly after they arrived—had it been minutes, or hours, or days?—he had caught her eye as she cleaned a nearby table and she had turned away quickly.

Later, as she worked across the room, he had stared until she looked his way. This time, she did not look away. She returned his stare, then as she moved away, smiled a little smile, looking at him from the corner of her eyes.

"Not that one, ya dummy, she's a servin' girl. I mean those!" Brad pulled roughly at John Henry's sleeve and gestured toward the other side of the room.

Three women were dancing with partners, and two others, sipping drinks, leaned against the bar. Their cheeks were blood-red, and their hair shone amidst swirls and combs. They wore dresses of thin, shiny silk. The dresses had no sleeves and were cut low in front, exposing most of their breasts. The women moved so gracefully that John Henry thought they could take flight.

"I've sure never seen nothing like that," John Henry said.

"See! Didn't I tell ya?" Brad beamed.

The numbers in the cantina diminished as patrons made the rounds, saying their goodnights. Those remaining just danced faster and laughed harder.

By midnight, few remained. Three men sat at a table near the bar, two couples danced, two men and three women stood at the bar, drinking and talking softly. Two or three sat in the shadows beyond the candlelight.

Brad emptied his glass, stood up, swayed backwards, then forwards and grasped John Henry by the arm. "C'mon, hoss, le's dance." He pulled at John Henry's arm.

John Henry slowly removed Brad's hand. His head was aching now, and his stomach was just beginning to rebel at the night's treatment.

"No, pard, I've had enough, and so have you. It's time to go." John Henry stood up, still leaning against the wall. He put his hands to his temples to stop the throbbing.

"Go?" Brad jerked upright. "Go? Hell, I hadn't done no dancin' yet!"

"Brad, I've got a terrible headache and my stomach's boiling."

"Okay, okay. Jus' one dance and we're on our way. Jus' one. Promise."

John Henry slid down the wall to his stool, his hands still on his temples. Brad weaved his way toward the bar, empty cup in hand. He collided with a chair, almost falling, and bumped into a dancing couple. He stepped back unsteadily.

"S'cuse me," he said politely and bowed deeply. The woman smiled thinly; the vaquero frowned.

John Henry closed his eyes and rubbed the back of his head and neck with both hands.

"*Le duele?*"

John Henry opened his eyes suddenly. The serving girl whom he had been watching was standing beside him.

"What?"

"*Le duele la cabeza?*" She touched his temple gently.

"Yes." He rubbed his temples.

"*Sí.*"

"Sorry, I don't speak Spanish."

"*Sí.*" She nodded her head and pointed at John Henry.

"Oh, *sí.*" John Henry smiled.

The girl smiled. She took his empty cup and wiped the table.

"Thank you," John Henry said.

"*Gracias.*" She pointed at John Henry.

"*Sí. Gracias,*" he said, imitating her pronunciation. John Henry removed his hands from his temples. She smiled and walked away. John Henry watched her go.

Brad finally reached the bar, after bumping every table, post, and customer at least once. He set his cup gently on the bar beside a pretty señorita who leaned casually against the edge.

"One for me and one for the lady," he said to the bartender. He turned toward the woman, supporting himself by holding the edge of the bar.

"How's 'bout this dance?" Brad gestured toward the dance floor.

The woman turned to face him. She saw his expectant look. "*No, señor, es muy tarde y además ya está muy borracho.*"

Brad took her arm gently and stepped away from the bar toward the dance floor. She did not move. "C'mon," he said softly, "le's dance."

She replied softly but firmly. "*No, señor, esta noche no. Otra noche, posible.*" She smiled and pulled her arm back, but he did not let go.

"What's 'is? I don't know Mex but I do know 'no'!" he said.

Conversation in the room ended abruptly. The dancers stopped while the musicians played on. Every eye was on Brad. Two vaqueros sitting at a table adjacent to the dance floor stood up slowly. They stepped up behind two other vaqueros who stood at the bar.

John Henry jumped up, upsetting his chair. He reeled momentarily as a sharp pain shot through his head. He stumbled past tables and chairs to the bar. He took Brad gently by the arm.

"Brad, we don't need trouble and you're just about to buy some. Let's just walk out the door quietly. Time to go."

"Fer chrissake, we cain't go yet! I hadn't even danced! I come here to drink and dance, and I hadn't danced yet!" Brad was shouting and his face was red. His grip on the girl tightened as she tried to pull away.

Another vaquero at the nearest table to the bar stood slowly.

The bartender hurried around the end of the bar and spoke to John Henry. "*No es la primera vez que viene aquí su amigo, pero nunca se ha portado así.*"

John Henry shook his head, squeezed his eyes closed and rubbed his temples. He wanted desperately to understand but he understood nothing.

The bartender motioned to the musicians and the music stopped. He put his hand lightly on Brad's arm that held the girl. "*Ya es muy tarde, señor. Estamos cerrando. Otra noche sería mejor.*" He applied the slightest pressure to Brad's arm, pulling it away from the girl.

"He-e-e-e-e-ey, hey, hey, what's 'is, what's 'is? I bin drinkin' yer rot'gut all night, ya never minded 'at, now I wanna dance, ya stop th' music and take away th' wimmin. No deal! No deal!" Brad's face was deep red, contorted.

It was a face that John Henry had never seen and he was shaken. "Let's go, Brad. It's not important. We'll come back another day. We'll go to another cantina now. We'll try to get into Tules's place. C'mon, you said you wanted to go to Tules's sometime to gamble with the big boys."

"No, by God! They got no right!" He released the girl and jerked loose from the bartender and John Henry. He stood spraddle-legged and weaving.

Five vaqueros faced Brad and John Henry. They

moved a step closer.

"Brad, if we don't go now, we've got real trouble," John Henry said softly. "It's not worth it. Will you go with me now because I'm asking you?"

"Leave him be."

John Henry wheeled around. The voice was soft and firm. The figure was at the edge of the candlelight. His face was obscured. John Henry squinted but could not make him out.

The figure stepped into the light. John Henry recognized Dougal. John Henry grimaced and his shoulders drooped.

Everyone in John Henry's unit knew Dougal and none called him friend. A model soldier on the post and in the ranks, Dougal, muscular and stoop-shouldered, had a reputation for brawling in town. He walked over slowly.

"Leave him be," he said again. "Th' greasers ain't goin' t' close this place if that's what they're aiming to do, not if an American soldier wants it open. We own this country and we're callin' th' shots."

John Henry had already tangled with Dougal.

On the long trail from Fort Leavenworth to Santa Fé, the troopers one evening were besieged by mosquitoes. "Here, pull up closer to the fire, John Henry." Eddy was a career soldier, a small man who was content to do his duty day by day and take whatever providence served him. He tolerated life and he was universally liked by his comrades. "We've decided this country is good for nothing but to grow Indians, gnats and mosquitoes, every one as pesky as th' others."

"Well, you said it, Eddy," John Henry replied. "This is their territory. Everything is fit for them and that's just the way they like it. They don't see many critters not like themselves coming through here. Right now, they're just coming visiting, to find out what you're doing here. You're sitting right in the middle of their parlor, you know. You can't expect 'em not to be curious. Maybe a little upset."

"What're we talking about here, muskeeters or In-dins?" said a voice from behind. The soldiers turned toward the voice. The speaker was sitting back from the campfire, at the edge of the circle of light. As the low flame waved and flared, the shadows played about the trooper's face. He had not taken part in the conversation until now. It was Dougal.

John Henry turned back to the fire. "Both, I suppose," he said, "they both seem to live where it pleases them and anybody who invades their territory better watch out."

The others nodded assent but Dougal responded, "You're not suggesting that In-dins have any claim on the land, are you?"

"They sure don't have a property deed paper if that's what you mean," John Henry said. He did not want to argue with Dougal. He had avoided so far being drawn into any of his frequent disputes. They were never useful. Dougal would admit no view contrary to his own.

"No, they don't have no paper and they don't have no rights. *People* have rights, and In-dins ain't hardly people. They're just part of the country that has to be whipped down before civilized people can take over. If a tree's in a farmer's way, he cuts it down. If a muskeeter buzzes 'round your head, you swat it. If a In-din gits in the way, you cut the savage down."

The others chuckled but Dougal's grim face told them that he was not making casual jokes.

John Henry did not reply. The conversation soon drifted back to the hard lot of the overworked, underfed soldier. After a minute of this, John Henry glanced back at Dougal and saw by the dancing firelight that his eyes were still fixed on him.

"Dougal," John Henry said, "you know damn well that if we don't walk out of here right now, we're going to get bloodied up and thrown out in a basket. What's right or not right doesn't matter at this point."

"Oh, it don't? I say it does," Dougal said, "and I say the three of us can handle the lot of th' greasers if it comes to that."

Dougal was looking at the half dozen vaqueros that now confronted them. He turned to John Henry and looked him in the eye. "Or is there only two of us standing here?"

Dougal stepped up beside Brad, who managed to look both resolute and confused. John Henry stood beside and slightly behind Brad. He looked at Brad, then at the vaqueros. It was too late.

The vaqueros stared at the soldiers. They glanced sideways at each other.

Then: "*No hay otro modo?*"

"*No lo que yo vea.*"

The Mexicans spoke softly to each other but their eyes were on the soldiers.

Lightning bolts pierced John Henry's head and the pain throbbed like it was alive.

"*Vamos a tener dificultades.*"

"*Ni modo, no hay otra.*"

"*No!*" said the bartender. The vaqueros ignored him.

"*Estamos de acuerdo. Cuando diga.*" The speaker paused, then . . .

"*Ahora!*"

The Mexicans charged the soldiers and all went down.

Brad wrestled with a heavy vaquero who had put a shoulder in his chest. Dougal sprang up, pulled a Mexican to his feet and promptly floored him with a punch to his jaw.

John Henry struggled to his feet, confused. A vaquero who had scrambled up beside him grabbed him from behind, pinning his arms to his side. John Henry felt a sharp pain in his stomach, then a sensation of falling slowly into a well that became wider and darker as he spun downward.

Señora Santa Ana,
por qué llora el niño?
—Por una manzana
que se le ha perdido

—Si llora por una,
yo le daré dos,
para que se duerma
como el Niño Dios.

The song was clear and sweet and surrounded him but where was it? It was beside him, then only faintly heard from a distance. Then it was gone and there was nothing but the darkness.

He closed his eyes, drifted and slept.

Later, how much later he could not say, John Henry opened his eyes. It was daylight. He saw a smooth earthen floor covered with a dark-colored carpet and a sideways doorway, the shade of a covered porch, and beyond, the glare of sun on the yard and an adobe wall.

He lay on his back on a low bed. No, it was a mattress on the floor. He rubbed his eyes. What is this place?

He closed his eyes tightly, squeezing the cobwebs from

his head. He pulled at the edges until he remembered. He opened his eyes and saw the same open door and sandy yard. There were patches of green at the base of the wall. One of the patches bore red blossoms. Roses.

He pushed off the light blanket that covered him. He was wearing what seemed to be white cotton pajama bottoms.

The room was cool. The expanse of the whitewashed wall opposite the door was broken by one small window. The only furniture besides the bed was a long, low chest against another wall. The sides and top of the chest were lightly carved but he could not make out the design. Otherwise, the chest was unfinished. A small crucifix on the wall over the chest was the room's only adornment.

He listened but not a sound could he hear. *Is this place lived in? Have I been abandoned*, he asked himself?

There! A bird song. A mockingbird! The sweet song of a mockingbird, the first he had heard since leaving Missouri. *Oh, what a heavenly song!*

He listened, staring at the ceiling. Then, mingling with the bird's call, that other song:

Señora Santa Ana,
por qué llora el niño?
—Por una manzana
que se le ha perdido.

Just as the song ended, he heard the regular pat-pat-pat that was now as familiar to him as a cock's crow. Someone was making tortillas. He rolled on his side to face the door.

"Ah!" A sharp pain shot through his chest.

The pat-pat-pat stopped. No sound announced her but he knew she was coming.

She stepped into the doorway and stopped. She smiled down at him. She was wearing the same cotton blouse and skirt she had worn last night. She was barefoot.

"*Pensé que ibas a dormir todo el día.*"

John Henry sat up, holding his side, and pushed back slowly to lean against the wall. He smiled as she walked to the bed.

Immediately, an old woman, wrinkled and angular, appeared in the doorway. She wore a limp black cotton dress and an expression to match. Her arms were folded across her chest. She glared at John Henry.

"*Te duele la cabeza?*" The girl touched his temple.

"No, my head . . . *Gracias*, no." He took her hand. "*Gracias* . . . for this.*" He touched the pajamas. She slowly withdrew her hand.

"*Bueno.*" She smiled at him. "*Tienes hambre? Seguro que tienes hambre.*"

"*Este no es propio!*" said the old woman.

The girl did not turn. "*Anda y cállate, tía. Tú, qué sabes!*"

John Henry glanced past the girl to the old woman.

"*No importa,*" she said. "*Voy a traerte algo de desayuno.*" She made signs of eating.

"Th- . . . *Gracias.*"

The girl turned to go and walked from the room. The old woman glared at him a moment longer, then withdrew from the doorway.

John Henry slid down on the bed and pulled the blanket to his chin. He smiled and closed his eyes.

"*Abre los ojos, ven a comer algo. De qué estás pensando? De qué viene esa sonrisa?*"

The girl stood beside the bed, holding a tray. John Henry opened his eyes and smiled. He sat up, slid backwards to sit with his back to the wall. He smoothed the blanket across his lap.

"Ah, what luxury, a beautiful woman and breakfast in bed."

"*Qué dices?*" She looked at him questioningly. "*No importa.*" She set the tray gently in his lap. John Henry took her hand and held it.

"You sweet thing. I wish I could talk with you."

"*Qué dices? No sabes hablar?*" Her tone was serious, but a smile played about her lips. "*Si no me dejas ir, nunca vas a desayunarte.*"

John Henry tried to pull her gently to him but she withdrew her hand, shaking her head slowly and smiling impishly as she backed away.

"*Ahora, come! Crees que se lo traje no más para que lo vieras?*" She paused as she passed through the doorway and looked back at him. The sunlight from the yard outlined her legs through the thin dress. She smiled and walked away.

He stared through the doorway where he saw her last and the shade of the porch and the dusty, glaring yard beyond with its scattered green patches along the adobe wall.

He smiled. She was singing again.

He turned back to the tray. He still gripped the sides. There were tortillas with meat and chili, a peach and apricots, and a cup of chocolate.

He was famished and ate as if he had not eaten in days. When he was finished, he held the tipped cup to his mouth to drain the last drops of the rich chocolate. He replaced the cup gently on the tray and set the tray on the floor beside the mattress.

He put his hands on his stomach, patted it with both

hands, and slid down on the bed, his arms extended and his head on the pillow. In less than a minute, he was asleep.

An hour later, the girl awakened him. She laid his clothes on the bed. The old woman stood stiffly at the door.

"*Adiós*," the girl said. "*Gracias*." She turned and walked out, followed by the old woman.

The next night, John Henry went alone to the cantina. He opened the door slowly and stepped in. He stood in the shadow near the door and looked about the room. Some vaqueros sitting at a table near the bar turned and glared at him.

The bartender saw him and saluted him gravely with a raised hand. He pointed to the table where he had sat last night. John Henry returned his wave and walked to the table.

He looked around. She was not there.

He stayed all evening. He stayed until every other patron had left but she did not come.

John Henry walked toward the door.

"*Adiós, amigo*," the bartender said.

"*Adiós*," John Henry said, "*gracias*."

The following evening, John Henry went again to the cantina. Brad had agreed to take his duty for him. When he arrived at the cantina door, he hesitated, reached for the door latch, stepped back, reached for the latch and opened it. He stepped inside.

She was standing across the room, looking straight at him. She smiled and walked to the table where he had sat the first night.

John Henry walked to the table and sat down. It was early. The *cantina* was empty but for two vaqueros who were talking softly with the bartender.

"Can you sit down?" he said. She looked blankly at him. He pointed at the stool beside him. She looked toward the bartender, who nodded, then sat down slowly.

"Why weren't you here last night?"

She smiled and shrugged her shoulders.

"*Por qué . . . antes?*" Why . . . before?

"*Antes? Quieres decir, anoche? Estuviste aquí anoche. Me lo dijo José.*" It was John Henry's turn to look blankly.

"*José, ese José.*" She pointed toward the bar.

"José!" she called. The bartender smiled and held up his hand in greeting. The vaqueros did not smile.

"*Por qué? . . . anoche. Anoche?*" Why? . . . last night. Last night?

"*Sí. Anoche. Estuve enferma.*" She rubbed her stomach, then turned her head to the side and put her arm across her forehead. She dropped her arm and giggled, putting her hand to her mouth.

"Oh, you were sick . . . *enferma?*" He pronounced it slowly, imitating her pronunciation. "Are you okay now? *Buena* now?"

"*Sí. Buena.* Okay." She smiled broadly.

They looked at each other a moment. She smiled.

"*Tus amigos están bien? Brad, se llama, y el otro?*"

"Brad? He's okay, banged up a little." John Henry touched his hand to his cheek, his nose, and his chest.

She smiled. They looked at each other.

"What is your name?" he asked.

She smiled a shy smile and shrugged her shoulders.

"My name," he said, pointing at his chest, "is John."

"John," she said. "John? *Juanito!*" She touched his

chest gently. "*Juanito.*"

He took her hand and held it.

"*Me llamo Morita.*"

"Morita," he repeated softly.

"*Tengo mucho que hacer.*" She pulled her hand back and stood up. "*Quieres una bebida?*" She made a drinking motion. He smiled and shook his head.

"*Y tú qué quieres, Juanito?*" What do you want, Juanito?

"Morita."

"*No Morita.*" She smiled playfully. "*Aguardiente.*"

"*Aguardiente.*"

He watched her walk to the bar. She leaned against the bar and turned to look at him as the bartender poured his drink. She brought the cup to him, put it on the table, took his coin and walked away.

John Henry sat alone at his table while the little cantina filled. His eyes followed her as she waited on other patrons, all Mexican, as she walked to the bar, as she waited for drinks, and as she took the drinks to tables.

She often glanced toward him and could not suppress a smile. Customers noticed and followed her glance to John Henry. They did not smile.

John Henry sipped his *aguardiente* slowly. His body floated, and his head spun. He closed his eyes and smiled to himself.

"*Otro vez te quedaste dormido, Juanito?*" Sleeping? John Henry started and opened his eyes. Morita stood by his side. She tilted her head and put her head in her hand.

"*Dormido?* No. *No dormido,*" he said. "No sleeping. Dreaming."

She shrugged. "*Otra?*" Another? She pointed at his glass. He gently touched her outstretched hand.

"Morita?" He held her hand gently.

"*Qué?*" What? She slowly withdrew her hand.

"*Otra.*" Another. He pointed at his cup. She smiled, took the cup and walked toward the bar.

The cantina was almost empty. John Henry was the sole patron. José, the bartender, Morita and another serving woman stacked dishes behind the bar. Morita walked to John Henry's table.

"*Hora de irte, Juanito. Ya puedes irte a dormir.*" She tilted her head in her hand and pointed at John Henry.

"Morita?" he said.

"Morita, Morita," she said, smiling, "*y qué tal Morita?*"

"Morita. Can I go with you to your house?"

She smiled and shrugged her shoulders.

"Morita and John . . . Juanito. Morita's house . . . *casa?*" John Henry pointed to Morita and to his chest, then pointed at the door.

"*Mi casa! Quieres venir a mi casa? Oh Juanito, me gustaría que vinieras a mi casa, pero . . . te quiero Juanito, pero . . . no, Juanito.*" She touched his hand tenderly. "*No, Juanito, lo siento.*"

"No." John Henry sighed. "Okay." He took her hand again, only for a moment, then released it. He stood up.

"*Adiós,* Morita." He walked to the door.

"For-ward, march!" shouted the sergeant. The squad stepped off in broken unison in the field that the army had commandeered for drill. John Henry kept his eyes front and walked woodenly.

Drill had never bothered him before. Sometimes, it had stoked his patriotic fervor; sometimes, it was even fun.

But now, it was irksome. He endured it and when it

was done and they were dismissed, he walked off the parade alone.

"Hey, Johnny!" Brad shouted.

John Henry continued walking, ignoring Brad's call.

He walked slowly to the upper end of Santa Fé and sat down on the bank of the acequia. He watched the life-giving stream splash and eddy as it flowed by, bound for the fields and homes of Santa Fé.

A half dozen patrons sat at tables and talked softly in the gloom. Morita set her tray on the bar. She put two cups on the bar and turned away. The door creaked and opened slowly. She started at the noise, smiled hesitantly and took a step toward the entrance.

A vaquero came in. Morita stopped. She glanced at José who had watched her with concern all evening. She turned away.

John Henry leaned against the corral, cradling his musket loosely on his arm. He stared at the shadows of corral timbers cast on the ground by the dying sun on the horizon behind him. His head lowered.

"Morita," he said softly.

John Henry stood in the deep shadow of an adobe across from the cantina door. For the last hour, he had watched patrons entering and leaving. He walked slowly across the road. He stopped at the door.

He pondered. He slowly slipped the latch and opened the door. He stood in the opening.

Morita was wiping a table across the room. She looked up and saw him. She straightened and smiled broadly. She dropped the towel on the table and walked quickly to the table where he had sat before.

John Henry hurried to the table. He felt light as a feather.

"*Buenas tardes*," good afternoon, he said.

"Hello," she replied. They laughed.

She frowned playfully. "*Buenas noches,*" good evening, she said, pointing at him.

"Ah, sí, Buenas *noches*," he replied.

John Henry sat down. Morita leaned against the table. John Henry touched her arm, traced his fingers down her arm and took her hand. Morita turned to look at José. He smiled.

"Morita?" John Henry said.

"*Sí. Juanito?*"

"*Sí. Aguardiente.*"

"*Sí. Aguardiente.*"

Morita walked to the bar and spoke to José. Two vaqueros and a woman who stood at the bar frowned at her. The woman looked quizzically at her and turned her back on her.

Morita glared at the vaqueros. She put her hand on the woman's arm and pulled her around to face her. Morita raised her chin to the three and turned back to José. Another woman who had just walked up to the bar raised an eyebrow to Morita and smiled.

When the last patron had left and the tables cleared, Morita and John Henry left the cantina together. In the dark street, John Henry took her hand and she turned to him. They kissed tenderly and embraced.

Morita pulled back. "*Mi casa?*" she said seriously but her eyes twinkled.

"*Sí.* Your *casa.*"

She laughed and they ran down the road into the darkness, hand in hand.

The days that followed were a dreamy idyll in which day was but an interval without substance between nights. John Henry performed his work dutifully; he was cooperative and he was happy, blissfully happy.

Evenings, he spent with Morita, a few nights also when he dared and when Brad agreed to share the risk by covering for him.

The risk was considerable. They knew—indeed the entire army and the town knew—what had happened to one troublesome fellow recently. A court-martial had sentenced him to six months' hard labor with ball and chain. That was to be followed by ten days of solitary confinement on a diet of bread and water at reduced pay. When all this was finished, he was to be dishonorably discharged from the army.

John Henry walked to his customary table. He waved to José, who saluted him. A vaquero waved and spoke to him. Others waved. He said a few words of Spanish to them. They smiled or laughed outright at his efforts.

Morita saw John Henry and hurried to his table. Patrons smiled at each other.

A vaquero called to Morita: "*Ey Morita, ven aquí! Necesitamos más aguardiente!*" Everyone laughed.

"Morita, *ayúdeme por un minuto!*" a woman behind the bar called. More laughter.

John Henry smiled.

"*Juanito, vamos a la cantina de Tules. Yo conozco las muchachas allá!*" another patron shouted.

"*Juanito, hay una muchacha que se llama Lupe. Estará buena para tí. Vámanos!*" from another.

"*Entonces, ven,*" Morita said. "*Tal vez ellá te enseñará*

algo. Necesitas ayuda." Loud laughter and back-slapping.

A woman at the bar responded. "*Morita, ven aquí, y te digo del amor—y otras cosas.*" Loud laughter.

"*Si tú sabes hacer el amor,*" Morita said, "*haz lo más que puedas porque pronto se te descolorar tu belleza y estarás vendiendo jabónes en el bazaar.*" Table-thumping laughter.

John Henry joined in. He laughed because he was happy. He understood nothing.

Each evening, except when he was on duty, John Henry went to the cantina, sipped his drink and watched Morita work. The Mexicans whom he saw there regularly, bartender, musicians, vaqueros, townspeople, had resented him at first, a gringo, part of the invading army.

But many of them had known Morita for years and they saw love in her eyes when she spoke to him. They came to know him and welcomed him with smiles and greetings that he began gradually to understand and to which he soon was able to reply. They would look at Morita when he came in, smile and exchange knowing glances.

Morita responded with a feigned haughtiness or real shyness. Sometimes, when there were only friends in the cantina, she replied with good-natured contempt, suggesting that a particular male tormentor was incapable of love or making love and that a female tormentor had better follow her example soon for her beauty was fast fading.

Taunts and jeers mixed with hearty laughter and good *aguardiente* and rapid-fire Spanish that John Henry knew was for his benefit since the speakers often gestured toward him.

John Henry was warmed by the *aguardiente* and their friendship and he felt secure.

Each night, John Henry and Morita walked together,

hand in hand, to her home. Morita was a pixie, full of life. She danced barefoot in the street, bathed in moonlight, swinging her sandals, forcing John Henry to frolic with her. Then they would stop and cling to each other and kiss softly.

In the coolness of her room, they undressed each other and went to her bed where they made love. Then they lay uncovered, whispering love in two languages, understanding nothing and everything.

The evenings always ended too soon. John Henry would get out of bed slowly, trying not to disturb her. Sometimes, when she had fallen asleep, she awakened and watched him dress in the moonglow that filtered into the room through the open door and window.

When he was ready to go, he would come to the bed. She would sit up, take his face in her hands and kiss him. Then she would get up and walk to the door with him and stand there and watch him as he walked to the gate.

He would turn at the gate to see her once more, her naked body dimly illuminated by the moonlight. Then he would go, her image burned on his memory, and it would remain there until he saw her again.

CHAPTER 2

"Morita! Morita!"

She was beside him, touching him! But now she was gone. John Henry felt frantically on each side of his bedroll but he could not find her in the darkness.

"Morita!"

Brad, lying next to John Henry, rose on his elbow. He reached over and grabbed John Henry's hand.

"Hey, Johnny," Brad said. "What's th' matter? Johnny! Are you okay?"

"Brad! Is that you? Where—?"

"You must've been dreaming. Are you okay?" Brad felt John Henry's forehead. "You're sweatin' all over."

John Henry was still now, half-sitting, taut, resting on both elbows. Then he relaxed and lay back until his head touched his blanket. He breathed deeply and exhaled slowly.

"Yeah . . . I'm okay . . . Thanks, Brad."

"You sure?"

"I'm okay."

Brad crawled back to his bedroll.

John Henry pulled the blanket to his chin and held it

there with both hands. He stared at the heavens. It was dark but presently pricks of light appeared and soon the sky was filled with stars, sparkling like so many gemstones.

John Henry tried in his mind to look beyond the stars and the expanding universe. He squeezed his eyes shut and shook his head. A gentle breeze cooled his moist cheeks.

He blinked his eyes, closed them again, and saw her. It was exactly a week since the army had left Santa Fé, seven anguished days. They'd had hardly four weeks together.

As time passed, he had learned more about her. Each picked up words and phrases of the other's language and they communicated in a sort of sign language as well. Sometimes when she could find no word or gesture to explain something to him, she would frown and become irritated, cross her arms on her chest and stamp her sandaled foot. This would amuse John Henry so much that he invariably laughed. Then she would laugh so hard that she would collapse weakly in his arms.

He learned that her family had once been wealthy landowners, holding ranches and farms around Santa Fé and Albuquerque. The family had fallen on hard times and the fortune melted away. All this happened before Morita was born.

The only home she had ever really known was the one where she now lived. It had been one of a number of residences owned by the family. They had stayed there during their frequent visits to Santa Fé, the capital and commercial center of New Mexico. When she was yet a small child, her father had lost the last of his lands and had moved the family to the Santa Fé adobe.

There were only three of them, her father, her mother and the young Morita. They brought with them only one servant, the old woman who lived with her still and who now was more companion than servant. Her father had died five years ago when she was fourteen. Her grief-stricken mother had died the following year, leaving her alone.

A coyote yipped somewhere in the distance. John Henry glanced toward the close-tethered mules that moved about restlessly. One whinnied. John Henry pulled the blanket up to cover his shoulders. The stars were less brilliant now, heralding the approaching day, though the darkness had not lifted.

John Henry closed his eyes and was in Santa Fé again. He remembered Morita's delight when she was finally able to communicate with him in their curious mixture of words and signs.

He remembered a particular night. They had just arrived at her house from the cantina and were sitting on the stone porch, facing each other, each leaning against a roof post, the bottoms of their bare feet touching. A bright moon cast sharp, deep shadows on the porch and yard.

"*Bonita*," said John Henry.

"Pretty," she replied. "You."

"No, you pretty." He pointed at her.

"Okay, I know, you pretty."

"No, confound it, I mean . . ." He saw in the soft moonlight that a smile played about her lips, and her eyes were sparkling.

"You little . . . you're making fun of me. I mean *you're* pretty!" With this, he raised a foot and struck her toes with his heel.

"Ay!" she said, surprised.

"Ouch," he responded, softly. Now he was smiling.

"Ouch you!" she shot back at him. At the same moment,

she pulled her legs under her and lunged at him, landing heavily on top of him. He lost his balance and they both fell off the low porch to the yard. They rolled in the dust as she tickled him. He tried at the same time to push away her hands and grab her, their shouts mixing with laughter.

At last, they lay still, panting. She was on her stomach beside him, with an arm across his chest. His arm was under her head, and her face was buried in the folds of his loose shirt. Their heavy breathing stopped and both were quiet. Finally, her muffled voice, softly, as if far away.

"Ouch."

Suddenly she sat stiffly upright: "*Juanito!*"

John Henry sprang to his feet and crouched, looking quickly from side to side. Morita exploded in laughter and collapsed weakly to the ground, rocking back and forth on her knees.

John Henry dropped to his knees before her. He grasped her shoulders and raised her to face him squarely.

"Did you do that on purpose?" he said sternly, with only a hint of mirth.

"*Qué?*"

"Why?" he asked and jumped, throwing his hands in the air, mimicking her.

She laughed lightly, covering her mouth.

"Come." She stood and dusted herself with both hands. When he did not move, she bent over and took his hand. "Come, come." She pulled him, grunting, until he stood. She helped him brush the dust from his clothes.

"Come where?"

"Come." She pointed to the house. "Look."

Inside her bedroom, Morita lit a candle and led him to the chest under the crucifix.

"Sit," she said and pointed to the floor beside the chest.

He sat on the dark carpet and she handed him the candle. She kneeled beside the chest and opened the top.

She reached into the dark interior and pulled out a *rebozo* of delicate Chinese silk. She unfolded it carefully and held it up for him to see, then handed it to him. She took the candle from him and set it on the rug. John Henry had not seen anything so fine as this at her house. He decided that it must have been her mother's. He folded the *rebozo* neatly and laid it in his lap.

He watched her admiring a comb. It was high, brown, with clear stones, like glass. She gave it to him and bent over the chest again. He deposited the comb in his lap. She showed him a book. The cover was rubbed and worn, leather it seemed. He traced a faded word on the spine with his finger in the dim light, "C-e-r-v-a-n-t-e-s."

She took a hand mirror from the chest. The glass was bright and he saw his image clearly in the candle's glow. He thought that the handle could be silver. She handed him a fine knife that clearly was silver, a table knife, he judged. And then a silver plate and a silver serving dish.

He realized what she was doing. She was showing him all that was left of her family possessions. She was showing him her past, the remnants of a proud, richer past, and at the same time, revealing herself to him.

Morita took more things from the chest. She examined each carefully, turned it, handled it gently, then passed it to John Henry. He took them mechanically and placed them with the other things in his lap.

He had stopped looking at them. Now he saw only her face, her eyes and her mouth, and the softness of her cheeks. She finally noticed.

"No . . . look . . . me. Look . . . this." She took his hand and lifted it to eye level. He held a leather belt with a silver buckle. She had just given it to him and he had not seen it.

He removed her hand gently and put the belt into the chest. He lifted the assortment of treasures from his lap and laid them gently inside.

"No," he said, "I . . . look . . . you . . . now." He leaned toward her and with one hand began slowly pulling her blouse from the skirt where it was tucked at her waist.

She tilted her head and smiled, tucking in the blouse as quickly as he pulled it out, her eyes fixed on his. He began working faster, with both hands now.

She slid backward on the rug, pushing his hands away as he grappled with her. She was laughing. "No look me, you!"

John Henry grabbed for her. "I look you as much as I like, *querida muchacha.*" He jumped to his feet, scooped her up and strode to the bed as she wriggled and pushed with her hands against his chest. Before they reached the bed, she was clinging to him and covering his cheek and neck with kisses.

A cold west wind whipped across the bivouac and blew the blanket off his legs. He pulled his legs up and kicked gently until the blanket covered him again. Then he lay back. A cloudbank had moved in and it was black as midnight. He stared into the void. Tears welled up in his eyes.

What has it been like for her these past seven days? She is alone again. The old servant is no company to her. She should not be alone. How different her life would be if she still had some family.

There had been more children. An older brother had been thrown from a horse and mercifully died after five days of terrible suffering. Two younger sisters had been carried away by Navajo raiders. Morita remembered all three of them and cried softly when she told John Henry their stories.

John Henry had taken her in his arms, encircling her shoulders and resting his cheek on the top of her head, breathing in her perfume. He smelled it yet. He had not known what to say but, after a moment, she drew back and, seeing his long face, she smiled a little smile, took his hand and led him out into the darkness. She stopped and looked up at the sky.

"Sisters," she said and waved her arm to encompass the starry sky. Then she had led him to the road where they walked arm in arm in the pre-dawn stillness. John Henry had understood then why he had awakened more than once to see her in the yard, looking at the heavens.

The army crossed the Río Grande at Albuquerque. The road they now took, running alongside the west bank of the river, was the best since leaving Santa Fé. As long as they were near the river, there was ample water, usually some grass and even firewood close at hand.

Nevertheless, fuel was a constant worry. Cottonwood groves on the river were all private property and were carefully watched. They were the only source of lumber for the country's carts. Woe to any dragoon caught with his ax buried in living wood.

General Kearny was so anxious to win the allegiance of these new Americans that he threatened soldiers with stiff penalties for molesting the inhabitants' persons or property. The dragoons grumbled that the commander favored the Mexicans over his own men and that it was a strange way to fight a war.

The river seemed to John Henry a thread of life in an otherwise barren land. In the evening, when camp was near enough to the stream, he enjoyed sitting on the bank, breathing in the scent of sagebrush and watching the flow of the stream and the birds that flew about the reeds and shallows. The ducks and geese were almost tame. He guessed they were not hunted.

When there was time, he fished, taking catfish mostly. This supplement to the monotonous army pork was always welcomed by his mess. He preferred the fishing to the nightly search for firewood, which sometimes required a ride of a few miles from camp.

On one notable evening, the fishing was spectacular. He caught a four-pound catfish, another of three pounds, and six respectable trout. The mess feasted as they had not since leaving Santa Fé.

When they were finished, they lay about on the ground around their fire, some smoking pipes. The evening was cool after an excessively hot march, and the air was perfumed with the fragrance of sage from the nearby hills. The troopers decided that it was a good end to a passable day.

"Now, if we'd only had a mess of hush puppies to go with th' catfish, I would'uv had to pronounce that just about the best supper I ever 'et," Eddy said. There was a murmur of agreement.

"Well, enjoy it. I hear we leave the Río Grande soon. No telling what kind of country we'll see then," John Henry said.

"This sure is strange country," said Russell. Russell, like Eddy, was a career soldier. He was convinced that his principal duty in the army was to complain about the army. "Nice enough at the river but go back a hundred yards and you might as well be in the Sahara Desert. Wouldn't support a goose to the acre.

"Somebody said yesterday that this would make wonderful cattle country. What in the hell would they eat? Six kinds of sand likely. The more I see of this country, the more I wonder why we're fighting Mexico to take it away from 'em. I thank we oughta pay 'em to keep it. I don't understand what this war's all about anyway."

"Well, Russell, didn't you hear Mr. Hall's lectures about the way the war started?" Brad said. "He held forth almost every evening as long as we were in Santa Fé. When he heard that he was elected a Congressman back in Missouri, I think he got all enthused and wanted everybody to know what they were fighting about."

"I heard him a couple of times but I'm still not clear on it," Russell said. "What do you think, Johnny?"

John Henry rose on an elbow and turned toward the speaker.

"Hell, they brought it on theirselves," Eddy said. "Poke sent a man down to talk to 'em and they wouldn't talk to him. They must've known that Poke would take that as a sign they don't want peace."

"That's not the whole story though," John Henry said. "When the Mexican government agreed to talk with Slidell—that was President Polk's man—Polk didn't tell them he had told Slidell to try to buy Arizona and California in the bargain. When Mexico heard about that, they weren't too happy and sent him packing."

"That's what I mean," Eddy said. "They didn't want to talk the problems out. They get upset over a little misunderstanding and throw a tantrum."

"Put it this way, Eddy. Suppose the King of Spain says to the President, 'I'd like to send my man over to talk about, say, a treaty of some sort.' Polk says 'fine,' and when the King's man gets here and they are talking about the treaty, the king's man out of the blue says, 'by the way, we'd also like to buy Florida.' How do you think Polk would react? He'd chuck him out of the country so fast he'd think he'd sprouted wings."

"Well, maybe, I don't know about that," Eddy said. "That's not the real reason for the war anyway. The real reason is the invasion. Mexico invaded our country and we had to defend ourselves. Mexico started the war. We didn't."

John Henry said nothing, staring absently over Eddy's shoulder.

"Well, ain't that right?"

John Henry hesitated, then: "Sounds reasonable."

"But you don't believe it."

"I truly don't know. I haven't made up my mind about it. Look. The President had General Taylor at the Nueces River. When the Mexican government refused to talk with Slidell, Polk sent Taylor down to the Río Grande. When the Mexicans crossed the Río Grande and shot at American troops, Polk called it an invasion, and Congress declared war."

"Well, wasn't that an invasion? The Río Grande is the boundary of Texas."

"The Mexicans don't think so. Mexico claims that the boundary between Texas and Mexico is the Nueces River, miles north of the Río Grande. So they said that Taylor was the invader when he moved his army to the Río Grande. And when Mexican soldiers crossed the Río Grande, they were just defending Mexican territory."

Eddy stared blankly at John Henry.

"It may be important in the long run," John Henry said, "whether the real boundary is the Nueces or the Río Grande but it has nothing to do with the beginning of the war."

"John Henry," Eddy said, holding his head in his hands, "you're beginning to give me a headache again."

"If Polk wanted to avoid war," John Henry said, "why did he send Taylor and his army across the Nueces? It's almost as if Polk was trying to provoke Mexico. You know, like if I was trying to bluff you or pick a fight with you, I would stick my nose in your face and say, 'I dare you.' Why should Polk do that? He wouldn't, would he?"

There was no sarcasm in the question. John Henry looked around at the half dozen soldiers who had been listening, looking for an answer.

Eddy shook his head. "I'll tell you for sure, Johnny, I don't know. What I do know is I gotta do something about this head." He got up to go. "You fret this one out and then tell me, will you?"

"Sure, Eddy." John Henry smiled. "I'll let you know."

Eddy walked away, shaking his head and mumbling. "Boy, you sure are hard to talk to. Ask uh simple question and ya git uh lecture."

John Henry lay down again, his hands under his head. The smile became a frown as he pondered his own argument. *I'm going to end by giving myself a headache.*

CHAPTER 3

"That's right, boys, the war in California is all over."

The speaker was Kit Carson, famous mountain man, Indian fighter and guide. John Henry had heard of him and was both awed and surprised as he stood in the tight circle of troopers who crowded around him.

The stories told about Carson made him seem a giant of a man but here he was, about five feet, four inches tall, stoop-shouldered, slight, longish reddish hair, with freckles and blue eyes. He weighed a hundred forty pounds, if that. John Henry thought he had an Indian look about him. He was altogether unimposing, except for his clothing. He wore buckskin pants and moccasins, a blue wool flannel shirt under a leather vest and a broad-brimmed hat.

The General had talked with Carson for two hours following his dramatic arrival. The mountain man and fifteen companions had galloped at breakneck speed toward the army column, shouting wildly and raising a dust cloud. John Henry had thought the whole Apache nation was about to fall on them. Soldiers had shouldered their weapons and stood ready for a fight. Now Carson stood placidly, finishing his coffee.

"The stars and stripes flies in every port, and the Californians are going peacefully about their business. I left Los Angeles twenty-six days ago today. Until an hour ago, I was bound for Washington to deliver the news to the President."

"What do you mean, 'until an hour ago'?" John Henry said.

"That's when General Kearny changed my plans. He says he needs a guide. That's true enough," he said, taking another swallow of coffee, "but I sure did want to see my wife. Our place is at Taos. I've been away a year. It looks like it'll be another year, at least, before I can get back this way."

John Henry was surprised again. He had not thought of Carson having a home and a wife. He moved closer.

"Are you sure it's all over in California?" Brad said. "We've walked over half the world, looking for some action. Any chance we can stir some up yet?"

Some of the onlookers laughed but others remained solemn. The dragoons, almost to a man, had been disappointed by Carson's announcement that peace reigned on the coast.

"Nope, no chance." He raised his cup and drained it. "In any event, the Californians won't fight. They do a nice job parading of a Sunday, and they are great horsemen, but fighters they are not.

"Nope, my boys, you must be content with a little exploring for the next few weeks. That'll have to do for your excitement. In fact, if you want to fight, you'll have a better chance if you stay right here in New Mexico. You might get to do battle with Indians or you might yet get to join a unit that's going down to Mexico."

Some of the dragoons indeed were going to stay in

New Mexico. Carson's news that hostilities had ended in California meant that General Kearny no longer needed an army to battle Mexicans. All he needed now was an escort force.

And he needed to get to California as quickly as possible since he had lately received orders, designating him the military governor. Therefore, he now trimmed his army to approximately one hundred men and ordered the others back to Santa Fé.

"Hell of a war this turned out to be," said a disappointed dragoon.

The camp was a beehive. Tents were struck and gear was stacked on the dusty parade. Wagons were assembled on the parade, ready for loading. Nearby, troopers carried harnesses to mules. Soldiers grumbled and swore as they performed all the tedious tasks of breaking camp. A boiling sun added to their misery.

John Henry and Brad each carried a load of gear toward a wagon. Brad hefted his load over the sideboard and dropped it in the bed. John Henry stopped beside the wagon. He turned to Brad.

"It had to be us! Of all the units!"

Orders had been read an hour ago. Their company was not one of those detached to return to Santa Fé.

"I thought you wanted to go to California," Brad said.

"That was before Morita. I don't want to be anywhere now but Santa Fé. I'm going to exchange with somebody. Most of the boys didn't care a damn about Santa Fé and they're dying to see California."

Sun-baked New Mexico indeed had begun to wear on the nerves of most of the dragoons in Santa Fé and the talk about the fabled land of California had increased.

John Henry stopped. He frowned and looked across the parade to a line of tents. He dropped his load of gear to the ground and strode toward Kearny's adjutant's tent. Brad started to speak but held his tongue.

Halfway across the parade, John Henry stopped again. He looked at the troopers, complaining and gesturing, loading wagons for the return to Santa Fé. He frowned.

What if Carson was right? What if the companies returning to Santa Fé were later attached to Doniphan's or somebody else's army that is marching to Mexico?

Do I really want to fight Mexicans? Maybe California is the best bet, after all, since the fighting is finished there.

Or what if the returning units are put to work fighting Indians?

He remembered a story he had heard and wondered about in Santa Fé. An Indian leader named Montezuma had grieved about the heavy yoke imposed by the Spanish on his people. He lit a holy fire and instructed the people not to let it go out until he returned to deliver them from their oppressors. He told them that he would reappear with the sun.

For generations, the fire was kept burning and the Indians, each morning, climbed to the roofs of their houses to await the sun and search the eastern horizon. Some said that the superstitious Pueblos believed that the arrival of Kearny and the Army of the West fulfilled the prophecy. *Are these the people I would be fighting?*

John Henry shook his head. *I'll take the risk. I must see Morita. Nothing else counts.* He headed across the parade to Captain Turner's tent.

"Private John Henry Harris requests permission to speak to Captain Turner," John Henry said to the orderly in front of the tent.

The dragoon disappeared into the tent, then reappeared and motioned John Henry to go in. Turner sat behind a folding table. He looked up immediately and laid his pen down. He leaned back in the chair. John Henry came to attention and saluted. Captain Turner returned the salute.

"What can I do for you?"

"Private John Henry Harris, sir. I would like to request a transfer to one of the units that are going back to Santa Fé."

"The reason?"

"I . . ." He hadn't thought about having to justify his request. He couldn't lie. He had always held honesty above almost all other virtues. Even if he could lie, what would he say?

"I . . . there is a girl there. I want to be with her." John Henry was startled by his own frankness.

"I see. How long have you known her?"

"The time we were in Santa Fé."

"And for this casual acquaintance of four weeks, you wish the War Department to alter its war plans?"

"No, sir, I'm sure I could find someone to exchange with me." John Henry was stung by the sharpness of Turner's response. He had always heard that he was a mild-mannered and reasonable man. He had never talked with him until now.

"That may be. You can imagine the chaos if we catered to every individual's whim every time an order is issued."

John Henry stiffened. "My request is not a whim, sir. I thought a lot about it before I came in. I'm not aware of anybody else who is requesting a transfer."

"That borders on disrespect, soldier."

"I'm sorry, sir, I didn't mean it to be." He hadn't but he was beginning to be irritated.

"All right," Turner said. He seemed tired. "Sit down,

Harris." He pointed to a folding chair. "I understand why you want to go back to Santa Fé. In fact, right at this moment, I can even sympathize with you. It's the hardest part of army life, this being away from the ones you love.

"Sometimes, I yearn for the life of a farmer. To say goodnight to your children and see them in their beds, to have your wife with you and to know that you are going to see all of them tomorrow and you are going to be in the same place tomorrow and the same bed tomorrow night. And to have your family around you every day . . ." Turner stared at his clasped hands on the table.

John Henry moved uneasily in his chair.

"But we cannot afford such luxuries at the moment, Private Harris," Turner said, straightening, his voice firm again. "Right now, we are escorting the Governor of California to his post. Yes, you probably could find someone who would be willing to exchange with you.

"However, I have found from much experience that this sort of exchange is not wise. I have done it in the past for men who desired it and then later been cussed roundly by both of them. It is impossible to foresee the future, so as a rule, we do not alter assignments unless the reasons are compelling.

"We have a job to do. There will be time later for home and hearth... and heart." Then, in a softer tone, "Harris, I do understand."

Turner picked up his pen, still looking at John Henry. John Henry knew he had been dismissed. He stood.

"Thank you, sir." John Henry saluted, turned and left the tent.

Outside, he stopped. He glared across the parade. He was fuming.

There was no good reason for not agreeing to my request. He can't see his wife, so I can't see Morita. That's what it amounts to.

It was both anger and love that made his eyes moist. He stamped the ground, raising spurts of dust, as he strode rapidly across the parade.

At least, I'll get this looking around out of my system. I would go back to Morita right now if I could but maybe the captain's right. In a few years, maybe I would wish I had seen California. At least, since I have no choice in the matter, I'll just have to make the best of it.

I'll leave the army as soon as I can and I'll take my money and go back to Santa Fé. Morita will be waiting for me on the porch. I'll take her in my arms and I won't let go for days.

The thought of her kiss and her smile and her body gave him such a warm feeling that he was smiling by the time he reached his tent.

He stood beside the tent, hands on hips and staring across the river and the rolling country beyond.

I will return to Santa Fé and marry my brown sweetheart and we'll have children who will grow up in this new American country. It will be all new to me but Morita will be there to help me.

"What th' hell you got to grin about?" Brad sat nearby on a rock, polishing his saber.

John Henry looked over at Brad, surprised at his voice. He had not seen him.

"Everything!" John Henry said. "This great day, this great country, and all these good friends. Don't you feel good about today?" He was only half jesting.

"By God, half an hour ago, you had a face longer than my mule's and now you think you're in paradise. I got news for you. This ain't paradise."

"Ah, but it could be. All it needs is people."

"People! What would people do? This country ain't . . ." —he waved his arms as if to include the entire land— "it ain't finished. When God was creating the world, by the time he got here, he must have been tired, and he sat down to rest and never got back to finish the job.

"It's back to Missouri for us, Johnny, or maybe California. I hear it's a great place with land for whoever wants it. Now that it's ours, a body could get a good piece of land for almost nothing."

John Henry was only half listening as he fussed around his mule gear. "Aren't you glad the General decided to switch to mules for the campaign, Bradford? They seem suited to the country."

John Henry had become quite attached to his mount since leaving Santa Fé. The dragoons had left Fort Leavenworth on horses but General Kearny, decided at Santa Fé, that mules would stand the journey to California better than horses. Many of the troopers had been indignant at the change but the hardy beasts had proved their worth on the trail and won the admiration of the soldiers.

"You're right on one count. Mules always did strike me as unfinished, or missing something, like brains. What do you mean, 'glad,' anyway? When the switch was made, nobody howled as much as you. 'Mules are for plowing, not riding,' you said."

"Well, I was wrong. Old Bell and I have become good friends. He'll do." John Henry smiled at Brad, picked up his bridle and walked away, his head in the clouds. Brad watched his partner go, his forehead furrowed, until he was out of sight.

"The Old Spanish Trail, you say?" Brad said to John Henry. "It's so damn old, I don't see much sign of it."

The Army of the West had just turned westward, leaving the Río Grande and pointing, at last, for California. Carson led them over a trail that had been used by trappers since the 1820s. Before that, it had been a road to rich copper mines that had been worked by Spaniards. Now, the mines were abandoned and the region was empty of settlers. The reason was obvious in the region's popular designation: "*Apachería.*"

The country became rougher. The dragoons had thought that the sandy trail along the Río Grande was hard going but they now had reason to complain.

The expedition had begun with wagons but these were now sent back and packsaddles were broken out. Carson had warned Kearny that it would take four months to reach the Pacific with wagons if they could be taken through at all. The General's wisdom in leaving the wagons was verified in the next few days as the country became more rugged and the trail almost vanished.

Four days after leaving the Río Grande, the army stood on the spine of the Rocky Mountains. A knot of soldiers stood beside the trail, holding the reins of their mules. From the high point, they turned in all directions, marveling at the spectacle.

"Major Emory said that this is the divide," Eddy announced to any who would listen. "Rainfall on this side," he motioned to westward, "flows to California. So, boys, it's all downhill from here!" A great cheer went up from all within hearing.

Carson, standing nearby, chuckled.

John Henry turned around and walked a few steps down the back trail. Brad watched him.

John Henry stopped. He stared eastward.

Leaving Morita was the hardest thing he had ever had to do. He had persuaded José, bartender and owner of the cantina, whom he learned had been an employee of her father, to let her go home early that evening.

José had assented, smiling, "*Como favor a mi amigo gringo*," as a favor to my gringo friend, and slapped him on the back.

They had dinner in daylight, a treat they had not enjoyed before. He had not told her that this day was any different from any other, only that he wanted to be with her longer.

Perhaps she suspected. It was well known that General Kearny's advance unit of the Army of the West was preparing to leave Santa Fé to carry the conquest to California but, until the last, only a few officers knew the date of departure.

She made the evening a festive occasion. A small table was set in the bedroom. It was covered with a fine lace cloth. It was dusk and there were slender candles in silver holders. The plates and bowls were the same pottery they always used but the utensils were heavy silver. He had not before seen the finery. He decided that it was probably borrowed.

Morita and the old woman worked in the kitchen for what seemed an eternity to John Henry. Cooking sounds mingled with Morita's child's songs. He sat on the bed, listening to her, eager for the night and dreading it.

Morita's singing stopped. John Henry waited. She came in and stood in the doorway. He sat upright and gaped, his mouth open.

She was wearing a brightly colored embroidered blouse and a black silk skirt. She wore black satin slippers and had a silk *rebozo* with stripes of yellow, brown, and black around her shoulders. A black lace *mantilla* covered her head.

John Henry was stunned. She was a beautiful woman, though the girl was still there.

John Henry got up from the bed and walked to her. He took her hand and, bowing, kissed it. She grasped his hand and pulled him to her. She put her arms lightly around his neck and kissed him. His arms slipped around her waist and he tightened them.

"Hey! No, no! You . . . you . . . trouble me!" She pushed him away, her face grim. She smoothed her dress.

"No . . . take . . . me!" and she shook her finger at him. "Eat now."

He helped her with her chair and sat down facing her. He smiled, and she could not suppress a faint smile.

"*Tía?*" she called over her shoulder.

The old woman came in. She was wearing a black dress of a fine material. John Henry had never seen her in anything but a loose dress of black or grey cotton. She nodded gravely to him and lit the candles.

She left the room and returned almost immediately to set a serving dish in the center of the table. She scurried, as fast as she could scurry, between the kitchen and the bedroom until the table was crowded with dishes. Morita watched, fidgeting. It was obvious that she was not accustomed to being waited on.

John Henry's eyes widened as the old woman brought in dish after dish. He had never seen such a variety since arriving in New Mexico. When she finished, the old woman stood behind Morita's chair. She and Morita beamed, delighted at John Henry's reaction. He stared at the table, speechless.

What a dinner it was! There were bowls of thin soup, roast chicken cooked with onions, a dish of boiled beef, rice covered with thin slices of boiled egg, tortillas and bowls of frijoles and red chili.

He remembered the first hot chili he had eaten. It had almost taken the top of his head off and tears had streamed down his cheeks. He had since acquired a New Mexican leather throat and he liked chili, which seemed obligatory at every meal.

At the edge of the table, there was a large bowl filled with peaches and apricots and bunches of small purple grapes. Beside it was a sponge cake.

Morita leaned toward John Henry and patted his hand. "No look food," she said. "Eat food." He looked up at her and smiled, embarrassed.

She returned his smile, then said over her shoulder to the old woman, "*Mira el muchachito tonto. No sabe que hacer.*"

The old woman looked at him. "*Mira como te ve, mi'ja, yo sí creo que sabe lo que hace.*"

Morita twisted in her chair and took a back swipe at her with her hand. "*Y tú, qué sabes vieja malcreada? Nadie te ha fijado en mas de un siglo! A tu cocina, o te pego!*"

The old woman had stepped back when she saw Morita turn, and her arm caught nothing but air. She cackled at Morita's discomfort and walked unhurriedly toward the door.

She stopped in the doorway and turned. "*Sé lo que veo, y se ve que está perdido por ti. Viene hambriento, pero no para frijoles.*"

Morita pushed her chair back abruptly and almost fell

when the leg caught on the carpet. Morita waggled a finger at the old woman.

"*Vete de aqui ahorita misma, vieja malpensada, o te echo a la calle! Malagradecida! No quiero verte hasta ma*ñana, o a lo mejor ni mañana!"

Morita was still shouting after the old woman had disappeared through the door, and the high, thin laughter could still be heard as she walked down the porch and into the kitchen. Morita pulled her chair back to the table, smiling shyly.

"What in the world was that all about?" John Henry said. He had caught only a word now and then. He could understand Morita when she spoke slowly and distinctly, using child's Spanish, but when she or anyone else spoke rapidly, which they ordinarily did, he was lost.

"*Qué?*" she said, wide-eyed, her head tilted slightly, as if surprised that he asked.

"No '*qué*' me. Trouble?"

"No-o-o trouble. Funny. Now eat. No like?"

"Me? Ye-e-e-s. I like *muy mucho.*"

She spooned a generous portion of chicken and onions onto his plate, then a serving from each of the other dishes. He watched her, knife and fork in hand. When she finished, he took a bite of each, slowly, as if tasting.

"*Bueno!*" he said, nodding his head, "*muy bueno!*" Very good.

Thus reassured, she served herself and began eating. Conversation was sparse during the meal. John Henry ate leisurely, stopping occasionally to watch her and enjoy her uneasiness when she noticed. She squirmed in her chair, told him to eat and once rapped his knuckles with a serving spoon when he continued looking at her.

It was dark when they finished dinner. Morita stood and gathered an armful of dishes. John Henry picked up a candle and some dishes and followed her along the porch to the kitchen. Two more trips and the table was clear.

On the way back to the bedroom, they stopped outside the door to look at the starry sky. He kissed her cheek lightly, her eyes, her nose, her lips.

They went inside. John Henry set the candle on the chest and walked to the bed. He undressed and sat on the side of the bed. He slumped forward, with his hands between his knees and was grateful that Morita could not see his face.

She blew out the candle on the table and undressed at the foot of the bed, silently, looking at him as he watched her. When she had removed her last undergarment and slipped her sandals off, she stood a moment, the light from the candle on the chest revealing the soft contours of her body, then she came to the bed and slid under the blanket.

They made love that night, desperately, consumed. When it was over, they lay quietly, their arms entwined. He leaned over to kiss her and found her cheeks wet. He pulled her to him and held her tightly.

"*Nunca te volveré a ver,*" she said softly, "*nunca te volveré a ver.*" He wanted to ask her what she was saying, but he could not speak.

It was just after midnight when he left her. He turned at the gate to see her once more. She was standing on the porch, leaning against a post. He could see her clearly, her naked figure outlined in the bright moonlight. She waved and smiled a little smile.

He tried to see her now but a shadow had fallen across her face.

The day after reaching the continental divide, the army had its first visit from the Apaches. Scouts had been trying to contact the Indians for days to try to trade for mules and to enlist guides.

About thirty Apaches came in, men and women, led by Mangas Coloradas. The chief welcomed the soldiers to his country. He swore his friendship to the Americans and professed eternal hatred for Mexicans.

Carson, standing next to John Henry, leaned over and said, with a twinkle in his eye, "I would not trust one of them." John Henry nodded his agreement.

The Apaches were clad in a colorful assortment of clothing, part Indian and part Mexican. John Henry shuddered when he saw that one warrior wore a jacket made from a Mexican flag.

John Henry took no part in the parleying or trading. He watched. They were the first wild Indians he had seen up close. He knew they lived mostly by raiding and that must mean killing. *That puts them just barely above the animal state*, he thought to himself. He looked at them now, moving about the camp, touching and examining. He thought of coyotes.

Some of the Apaches were on foot but many remained on their horses. They seemed uneasy unless they were mounted. On foot, John Henry thought them short, squat, bowlegged and knobby, awkward, ugly. Horseback, they seemed nobler, proud, confident, even haughty. They sat their horses as if they were part of them.

John Henry's attention was drawn to a woman who had not dismounted since the band entered the army's camp. She rode slowly about the camp, speaking occasionally to the other Indians.

When she passed nearby, John Henry noticed that her

arms and legs were severely deformed, being no larger than those of a small child. She had a fine horse and was well dressed. John Henry noticed also that wherever she happened to be, the Indians near her, whatever they might be doing, kept an eye on her. If she wanted for anything, they were immediately at her side. John Henry wondered at his earlier assessment of the Apaches.

John Henry was not the only one assessing the Indians.

"I've seen a lot of dirty savages in my day but this lot is the filthiest scum I ever seen."

John Henry turned to the speaker, who had walked up beside him, unheard. It was Dougal. John Henry avoided him whenever possible. He had been successful since the cantina incident. John Henry started to walk away but Dougal caught his arm.

"Listen to 'em talk. Their whole language is a bunch of grunts. Look at that one over there, the short one that's pawing the trade goods," he said, pointing. "Look at them long arms. I swear, he looks like he just dropped down outa th' trees."

Antoine Robidoux, one of General Kearny's mountain men guides, was walking by during the diatribe and had stopped to listen. He walked over to Dougal. He stood beside him a moment, watching the trading, then turned to face Dougal.

"Would it surprise you to know that they feel about the same way about you?" he said.

"What?" Dougal turned to face Robidoux. "These wretches? That's crazy as hell. They don't have the brains to make the comparison. You're crazier'n hell." Dougal turned aside in disgust.

The guide walked around Dougal and faced him. The old trapper was enjoying himself. "Do you know what they call theirselves? Not 'Apache.' That's a Pima word that means 'enemy.' That's what the Apaches are to all the peaceable Indians around here, the enemy.

"They call theirselves 'N'Dine'. That means 'The People'. You see what that means? The Apaches are 'The People' and everybody else is something else. You got that, hoss? Them savages over there think you're not people but something else. You got that?"

Dougal was incredulous, open-mouthed. He stood with feet spread and arms dangling, so mad he was speechless.

Robidoux doubled over with laughter. He turned and staggered away a few steps, then turned back, loath to leave such merriment. "I'll go ya one better," he said, almost choking. "You know the Cheyenne? They don't call theirselves 'Cheyenne'. That's a French word. They call theirselves 'Tisstissis,' which means 'The People,' or 'The Human Beings'. Do you get what that means? Only the Cheyennes are human beings.

"There're a few Indians who're their friends that are pretty close to bein' human beings," Robidoux said, "just a rung or two below the Cheyennes on the ladder. Like the Arapahoe and the Sioux. Farther down the ladder are the Shoshoni and the Rees. Way down there are their worst enemies, the Crows and the Comanches. The Cheyenne sure cain't stand the Comanches. They say the Comanches fornicate with their horses. Way below the Comanches are the Wasichus."

The guide bent over slightly, leaning toward the soldier, his head cocked to one side, grinning from ear to ear and looking him straight in the eye. The guide and the trooper were now encircled by a dozen soldiers who had been attracted by the mountain man's tale.

"Who the hell are the Wasichus?" Dougal said. He

had listened attentively but he was still furious. "I never heard of 'em."

"You want to know who the Wasichus are, do ya? I'll tell ya then. The Wasichus are th' *whites!* The Cheyennes say that since the Cheyennes are superior people, there has to be a lot of inferior people for it to make sense and that's where the whites come in. You see, hoss, to the Cheyenne, you don't even stack up to a dirty, disgustin' Indian who fornicates with his horses!"

The mountain man bellowed, threw his hands in the air, doubled over with laughter, stomped the ground with both feet and reeled away, roaring.

Dougal was furious. He puffed and snorted and stammered, "You . . . why, that . . ." but could say no more. He turned and stormed away in the opposite direction, fuming, mumbling to himself and menacing anyone who stood in his path.

The spectators hooted good-naturedly at the guide and laughed at Dougal's discomfort, though most shared his sentiments. John Henry approved of the whole episode.

CHAPTER 4

The Gila!

The troopers were as happy to see it as if it were the end of their journey. Carson had told them they would follow the Gila River to its junction with the Colorado, and beyond the Colorado was California. Their spirits lifted and their steps quickened.

At its headwaters, the Gila was a wild, tumbling stream. The soldiers took fish from the pools and drank the clear, cold water, so different from the brown waters of the languid Río Grande.

The troopers' elation at finally reaching the Gila soon evaporated. The trail that ran alongside the Gila was different from the one they had followed beside the Río Grande.

The earlier trail, level and sandy, meandered through the Río Grande valley. The army now made its tortuous way down the canyon of the Gila. The cliffs echoed to the creak and clatter of saddle gear, the metallic clink of fittings and mule shoes striking the rough, basaltic bed of the trail.

When the stream narrowed and rushed between perpendicular walls, the trail left the river and ran for miles through the even rougher mountains. Grass vanished and there was no water for man or beast. Dead and dying mules were left beside the trail. On one such detour, fifteen mules gave up the ghost. The dragoons named the trail the "Devil's Turnpike."

On the second day of one of these waterless traverses, John Henry suffered more than usual. There had been other, rougher trails, but he had taken them in stride. Today, he was exhausted. Every step his mule took jarred him from head to toe. His head was a mass of pain. He had had headaches before but only at the temples or at the back of his neck, near the hairline. Nothing like this. Beads of perspiration formed on his forehead.

Brad pulled up alongside John Henry. He looked ahead at the trail and did not notice his partner's condition.

"Great day, eh Johnny? Great country. Great to be alive and a part of it, eh?"

"Yeah, great," John Henry replied, wincing. He stared at his mule's head.

"This country sure does have a great future," Brad said. "I can just see a little farm growing corn and sweet potatoes, right here on this dome. Course, a body most likely will have to—"

"Did you ever know it to be so hot in October, Brad? Back home, it's cooling off by now, and the trees are starting to turn."

There was pain in the voice. "Hey, Johnny, what's the matter? Are you all right?"

"I don't know. I don't think so. I'm hot. Damn hot. Dizzy. Ringing in my ears." He shuddered.

"Here, you pull out of line. Wait there. I'm going to get Doc Griffin." Brad took John Henry's reins and pulled his mount off the trail. He dropped the reins and kicked his mule ahead at a fast walk, as fast as his jaded mount could negotiate the stony trail.

John Henry's mule stood where it was left, reins trailing on the ground. John Henry sat with drooping shoulders and head bowed. The end of the column passed him just as Brad and Doc Griffin reined in beside him.

Dr. John Griffin was a member of the expeditionary force by choice. When Carson's report that the war in California was over led to a division of Kearny's force, both of the army's doctors wanted to stay with the California contingent. They drew straws and Griffin won. The pugnacious Griffin had been devastated at Carson's news, but he still wanted to see California. He hoped Carson was wrong.

"Tell me how you feel, Harris."

"My head hurts like hell. I'm hot one minute and cold the next. I'm aching all over, 'specially in my shoulders. My arms feel like they're gonna fall off . . . I can ride."

"Are you sure? We'll hit the river in about two hours and we'll stop there. Can you make it?"

"I'll make it."

"Bradford, stay with him." The doctor moved off. When he reached the end of the column, he said something to the last two men and kicked his mule forward. The two men pulled their mounts off the trail. When Brad and John Henry passed them, they fell in behind.

The column moved farther and farther ahead. It was soon out of sight. The two dragoons in the rear looked nervously from side to side and behind them. Brad rode as close to John Henry as the trail and the jostling mules would allow. He occasionally reached out to steady John Henry when he swayed too far one way or the other.

John Henry squeezed his eyes shut, then opened them and stared blankly.

John Henry and Morita sat on the porch in the shade. They faced each other, each with legs crossed, knees almost touching.

"Now you sing, *Juanito.* Sing *'Naranja dulce limón partido'.*" She sang the phrase, then said: "You."

"*Naranja dulce lem-uhn partido,*" he sang, slightly off key.

Morita burst out laughing. "No sing 'lem-uhn,' sing *'limón'.*"

"*Naranja dulce lee-mohn partido.*"

"Bueno. Sing *'dame un abrazo que yo te pido'.*" She sang the phrase.

"*Muy mucho.*" Too much.

"Baby. *'Dame un abrazo'.*"

"*Qué, 'dame un abrazo'?*"

"Give me . . ." She leaned forward, threw her arms around his neck and squeezed lightly.

"Hug," he said.

"Give me hug."

"Okay, *un grande abrazo!*" He grabbed her around her shoulders and squeezed hard.

"No, no, Johnny, no hug now! Sing now!" She kissed him lightly on his cheek. "Big hug later."

"*Dame un abrazo,*" he sang.

"—*que yo te pido,*" she sang.

"—*que yo te pido.*"

"*Bueno.* Good boy. Now sing *'Si fueran falsos mis juramentos'.*" She sang the line.

"*Si ferr-uhn falsos mis juramentos.*"

"No, Johnny, dammit, no 'ferr-uhn.' Say *'fueran'.*"

"*Ferr-uhn.*"

She winced and frowned. "No, Johnny! Goddam no!

Say *'fueran'."*

He smiled. *"Fueran."*

"Good boy. Now we sing . . . *juntos. Juntos?*" She pointed at John Henry and herself.

"Together."

"Together. Now we sing together."

Naranja dulce limón partido
Dame un abrazo que yo te pido
Si fueran falsos mis juramentos.

"*Muy bueno, Juanito.*" She took his face in her hands and kissed him softly on the mouth.

"What?"

John Henry opened his eyes wide. He saw a stretched canvas overhead. He looked around at the bleak, rocky campsite. He rose on an elbow. He was rolled in his blanket. Brad stood over him, holding a plate of beans and biscuit.

"I said it's time to move. How do you feel?"

"What's this?" He looked at the plate Brad held. "Breakfast in bed? My, my." The voice was tired but firm. Brad handed him the plate.

"If you call this breakfast. You look better. You gave us a worry."

"I feel a little shaky but . . . okay."

"Hustle. We'll bring up the rear, in case you need to drop out for a rest. Glad you're feeling better."

John Henry watched him go. Could anyone have a better friend, he thought. He looked at the plate of beans and biscuit—breakfast—and shook his head. But he knew that it would be better than anyone else had that morning.

He put his hand under the blanket to move a pebble. The blanket was wet. He tried to remember the evening and night, but it was a blur. He remembered riding into camp and Brad and Doctor Griffin helping him dismount. They had laid him on his blankets and Brad had removed his boots and covered him. He remembered turning on his side, shivering and perspiring.

He had had wild, fantastic dreams. He raised the biscuit to his open mouth, then stopped, remembering.

In his dream, his mule's easy gait made riding pleasant on the sandy trail that ran alongside the Río Grande.

Ducks dropped down to skim just over the water's surface at dusk, their wings drooping and feet extended to splash down. Sunlight reflected on the water, sparkling, and highlighting the iridescent bodies. The sun dropped and it was dusk.

His mule stumbled down the flinty trail, hanging on the sheer face of a cliff, darker, darker until he could see nothing. The mule staggered on, colliding with the wall, the trail narrowing, descending, black. He lost his balance, swayed, careened and swirled, his mule still under him, bumping and scraping against the wall as the trail narrowed.

Then, ahead, no, to the right and up, he saw a point of light. It became larger. It was the mouth of a tunnel. The walls and floor of the tunnel just at the end were illuminated. A figure stepped into the circle of light. The light behind her outlined her body but her features were not visible. She appeared to be looking into the tunnel toward him.

Then she turned to look behind her. She started to walk away and was almost lost to view when she came back to peer into the tunnel. She did this again and came back, looking into the tunnel, then weaved side-to-side, uncertain.

"Morita!"

She stopped, listening, looking into the dark tunnel.

"Morita! Help me!"

His mule scraped against the wall, continuously now, his leg aching from the jarring, still descending, moving down, the circle of light moving higher.

Then Brad's call had awakened him. He remembered now that he had thought the sun brilliant when he first opened his eyes, though it had just topped the distant horizon.

The days that followed merged into one continuous experience, a routine without variation. Roll out at dawn, eat breakfast, mount up, jolt along the stony trail, a mule staggers into a cactus, a pack is upset, a mule founders. Noon stop. Mount up and ride, dust and sweat, the mule stumbles, dismount and walk, supper and bed. Trek through a country that was so strange, so wild, that not a single familiar feature could be seen. Sometimes, there would not be even one object off the trail—animal, plant or mineral—that bore any resemblance to anything known in the United States.

Every mile was agony and the agony of the day prevented sleep or tortured sleep at night. There was no yesterday, no tomorrow, no back trail, no trail ahead, only a succession of todays and the trail and the mule and the heat and the weariness of body and mind.

And the thirst, especially the thirst. John Henry began to suffer increasingly when water was short. When the trail left the river, and water could not be carried or located, his want was quick and virulent.

During the dry treks, he had recurring thoughts of water. Crazed by sun and thirst, he seemed to be suspended between consciousness and sleep.

He dreamed of buckets of cool well water, a tin dipper brimming and running over, splashing in the green grass; a morning mist, wetting the green leaves and forming drops on his upturned face; rain falling and running off the roof and splashing on paving stones, sending up a spray; rainwater running down the center of the road, cutting little channels, filling the ditches; waterfalls, lakes and rivers, and the spring at the lower end of the meadow at the farm, so clear you could see the pebbles at the bottom of the pool, ice cold . . .

Some days, John Henry simply survived, eating supper automatically and collapsing, exhausted, into his blankets, his body throbbing with pain. He awoke some mornings, after sleep but not rest, and the day became another trial.

Those were the bad days but they were out of the ordinary. On most days, John Henry suffered no more than anyone else in the column. Most days, in spite of the usual fatigue, John Henry found nourishment for the spirit in the clear skies, broad vistas and the newness, the mystery of the land.

He especially enjoyed the days when he was permitted to accompany Lieutenant Emory on his explorations. William H. Emory was a natural scientist, an officer in the United States Army Topographical Engineers.

John Henry thought he looked like neither an engineer nor a scientist. More like a leader of cavalry. He sported red whiskers and had a temper to match. At the same time, he was gracious, even a bit haughty, and seemed to be the superior of the other officers in intelligence. Unlike every other man in the Army of the West, he seemed actually to enjoy the march.

Emory delighted in forays up streambeds and side

canyons, with frequent stops to identify a new plant or to describe an interesting landform. John Henry had watched Emory's comings and goings and had asked, in an uncharacteristic moment of confidence, if he might go along sometime. Emory was agreeable. He needed some assistance and, he told John Henry, he would rather have a kindred spirit of any rank rather than one of the other officers who thought his interests a little silly.

John Henry's superior officer had given his permission, under the condition that it did not interfere with his duties. John Henry figured that since his sole duty seemed to be to keep moving toward California, he should make the moving as interesting as possible.

Emory showed John Henry things the Missouri farm boy had looked at but had never seen. He told him how to distinguish volcanic rock from sedimentary. He pointed out different rocks and minerals and described their properties: feldspathic granite, red sandstone, feldspar, quartz and basalt, agate and obsidian. He showed him a conglomerate formation and explained its origins.

Emory customarily explored in stolen minutes before departure in the morning, during rest stops and after encampment in the evening.

During one notable evening walk, Emory and John Henry came upon five tarantulas in the path. John Henry drew back; he had heard that they could spring ten feet and that their bite was sudden death. He brought the shovel down from his shoulder and raised it high, preparing to dispatch them.

Emory stepped in front of him and crouched in front of the little cave-homes of the tarantulas where they had scampered and now stood in defiance. He tossed some small pebbles toward them. John Henry could almost feel their rage.

Emory stood up and the two men walked on their way, John Henry with a new sense of respect for the big, furry spiders. He had never felt anything before but revulsion and fear.

John Henry knew cottonwood, willow, and cedar. Emory showed him how to identify mesquite and acacia. He pointed out wild sage and a rarely seen sedge.

Emory excitedly showed John Henry some grasses, native to the region but unknown to him and, he suspected, to science.

"Look at this, Harris!"

John Henry looked up from the burrow he was examining.

Lieutenant Emory was standing beside a gigantic saguaro, at least six feet in circumference. Emory reached as high as he could with his saber and still did not reach half its height.

"Look up there," Emory said, pointing with his sword up the canyon they were exploring. "There is a grove of the cereus and those are more massive and more heavily branched than this one. Imagine! Remember the little barrel-chested fellow we saw a few days ago? What a contrast!"

Emory had called it a "vegetable curiosity." It was about eighteen inches high and the same in diameter. Emory had told him how the cactus, split open, would provide enough liquid to save a life. Later, they had found several of the cacti beside a dry streambed. They had been ripped from the ground and opened by someone unknown, proof of their usefulness.

Another evening, they walked over a low ridge behind the army's camp, then across a grassy flat where the army's animals were grazing. Emory bent as they walked and occasionally stopped and picked up something, a stone it seemed, and examined it. Then he would toss it aside and move on, talking animatedly about the good and the bad of army life.

They had walked a couple of miles from camp when Emory stopped and turned to face their back trail.

"Amazing," he said. "Absolutely amazing!"

"Sir?"

"Do you know what this is, Harris?" Emory held up what appeared to be a small gray stone, about an inch thick. It was the same sort of stone that the lieutenant had been picking up the last half hour. This one he had picked up right where they stood. He handed it to John Henry.

"Well, I'll be . . ." John Henry exclaimed. The fragment was not a stone at all. One side was lightly pitted but the underside was smooth. It was a piece of pottery, slightly curved. John Henry turned it over and over in his hands.

"What do you suppose it is? It doesn't look like the pottery pieces we saw in the canyon a couple of days ago," John Henry said.

"Look here," Emory said. He pointed across the open flat where they had walked. "You see the mesquite tree there that is a bit taller than the rest?" John Henry nodded. "We came through that thicket just to the left of that tree. From there, we walked in a straight line here. I was following the shards. I suspect," he said, taking the fragment from John Henry and holding it up between them, "I suspect that these are pieces of a pipe used to transport water."

"A water pipe? I didn't know Indians were that smart."

"My good man, you have just voiced a popular misconception of the ancient inhabitants of this land. Savages and heathen they were but stupid they were not. I believe these Indians were irrigating land right around us before

Columbus was born."

They walked on, through a mesquite thicket and along the bank of a dry streambed, about twenty feet wide and three feet deep. They walked through the loose sand of the bed and climbed out on the other side. There on a wide bench between the stream and a low ridge about a hundred yards away, they found evidence to support Emory's speculation.

"What sort of place do you suppose this was?" John Henry said.

"No question about it," Emory replied. "It was a village of farmers."

They walked among the unmistakable foundations of buildings. They were rectangular, some sides a full hundred feet long. Building materials were mostly unworked stone and cedar logs. Some of the timbers were remarkably well preserved.

Emory looked at the sky above the walls of the canyon. "We'd better get moving. It's late."

The sun had disappeared behind a distant range of hills and the land was darkening. The sky was still bright, though the line of orange at the western horizon was growing, and the land was graying rapidly.

"Let's head back to the river this way," he said, climbing up a water-cut path in the wall of the gully. "We'll be about a mile from camp once we hit the river." They set off at a brisk pace.

They had walked fifteen minutes when they saw the Gila in the distance. "We may yet make it before complete darkness," Emory said. "I hope so. We're downstream from camp, so there won't be a trail unless we pick up a scout's track. I'm counting on it."

They were hardly fifty yards from the river when

John Henry stopped.

"Lieutenant Emory? I hate to tell you this but look over there." John Henry motioned toward the left side of the trail.

They were walking in a corridor bordered by stands of mesquite. Through a break in the thicket, Emory saw the low wall to which John Henry pointed.

They walked through the break to look at the wall and saw the ruins of an extensive settlement, four times as large as the village above that had so impressed them.

They examined the remains of a circular wall with a circumference that Emory guessed was two hundred seventy feet. Beyond that, they found another circular wall that they agreed must be four hundred feet in diameter. Probably a defensive wall, Emory explained.

John Henry was dumbfounded. *If the lieutenant is right, these villages, with their pipes, irrigation works, and fortifications predate the castles and knights and battles in the old world that I have read about. How I wish I could know about these people! If only there was someone who could tell their story!*

Who were they? Who was it that touched this very stone I am touching and put it in this wall? What was his life? Why did they leave this place, their home? Where did they go?

John Henry walked from the ruin, following Emory who was already disappearing into the gathering gloom. He rubbed the caked dirt from a rounded fragment of pottery, his head so full of questions rocketing around that he felt it must burst.

CHAPTER 5

"I'll be glad when we're free of these blessed mountains," Brad said.

A dozen dragoons sat around a cooking fire. Fatigue was written on their faces and they ate listlessly. Some leaned against rocks, others sat cross-legged and slumped forward, their empty plates lying on the ground or in laps. The stony walls of the canyon loomed darkly above the camp. The red ball of the sun rested lightly on the saddle between two peaks.

"I know what's happening, boys," Russell said. "We're not going to leave these blessed mountains. Remember at Fort Leavenworth when the General said he was going to make soldiers of us if he had to kill us? All you hard cases been grumbling so much lately, he decided that he's failed so far.

"So each night he has a detail that moves all the tents around. You're sleeping so sound from all that hard work bellyaching, you ain't even aware what's happening. Next morning, you don't know that the tents are facing a different direction, so you don't kick when the General leads you back around in a circle. He's just toughening us up so we'll look right smart when we march into California."

Eddy suggested that he might go straight to hell if he wanted to but most were too tired even to respond.

"I never saw such a lot in all my days!" Carson had walked up and heard the end of Russell's story. "What would you boys do if the Apaches rode in here, right now, yelling for your scalps?"

"I'd suggest they stop all the racket because it's disturbing my rest," said Brad.

Russell responded, "I'd simply remind them that the part's on the right side and please don't disturb it."

"I'd point out politely that the best head of hair is Dougal's," said Eddy, "and I'd direct 'em to the right tent." Eddy grinned and pointed a seat to Carson. They liked the guide and enjoyed hearing him tell about the country and recollect the old days.

Carson squatted, sat down lightly on the ground and crossed his legs. "You think this is tough, do you? This is the best season. Try traveling this country in August. You'll know what hot and thirsty is."

For the next half hour, the soldiers questioned the mountain man about his life in the Southwest that began in the 1820s. He told of dry marches, parched and starving, the hard labor of fur trapping, always on the alert, danger and death a constant companion.

"Actually, the season don't matter a lot, boys. I never knew any party to leave these mountains that wasn't starving."

"What about the people who live here all the time? How do they make it?"

"It's a hard life for the ranchers and farmers. They're fighting two wars all the time, one with the Indians, and the other with the weather. I've done a bit of farming myself around Taos."

"Town life is safer around here, isn't it?" Brad asked.

"That's true," Carson said, "and we don't travel too much between towns unless we have a number of well-armed friends with us."

"But town life is better than the country, isn't it?" said John Henry.

"You're right there. You saw Santa Fé. That's our best."

The troopers exchanged glances. They remembered all right and most had not liked what they saw. Most of Kearny's soldiers were raised on the frontier and the life they knew back in the United States, their farms and small towns, they judged far above anything they had seen in New Mexico. John Henry remembered and was warmed by the memory.

"If it's so all-fired dangerous and hard to scratch out a living in this country, why do you stay?" Eddy asked Carson.

"Now, that's a hard one," Carson said. He drew slowly on his pipe, staring into the fire. The others sat waiting for his answer. He puffed, concentrating on the dancing flames.

One by one, the troopers drifted away to their bedrolls. Carson stood up, stretched, said good night, and left. John Henry sat a minute longer, until the flames became embers, then turned in.

Later, wrapped in his blankets, on the edge of sleep, he heard the distant honking of geese. He searched the sky but a dark cloud had drifted across the full moon, and he could see nothing.

A cheer went up from the entire column. The line of troopers had just topped a ridge, and there below them laid a broad valley. It was unmistakable. They were leaving the mountains.

Their sagging spirits lifted. Even the mules sensed the change, the loose ones frolicking about like colts. The pace quickened and the soldiers talked more animatedly than they had in weeks.

The column reformed and marched slowly down the trail to a flat where the noon stop was called at a patch of good grass.

"What sweet relief to leave those mountains." Brad sighed as he sat down heavily in the shade of a huge saguaro. Troopers standing nearby nodded. The joy on seeing the plain for the first time had not subsided.

"Mr. Carson, you don't seem to be sharing in all this jollity about leaving the mountains," said John Henry. The guide was standing near his mule as it cropped grass. At Carson's name, a half dozen soldiers standing nearby turned to listen.

"Oh, I'm just as happy as anybody that we're closer to the end of this expedition than we were yesterday," Carson replied. "But that ain't California you're looking at, boys."

"He means reaching the flat country," Brad said. "Traveling is going to be so much easier on the old bones. My old mule is going to feel like a yard swing here on out."

"Well, that may be. If he can stay on his feet. You might notice that in spite of the sores and patches and scars on those pore animals' backs, they aren't in too bad shape. However, you better hope your mule will learn to eat twigs and cane because from here on, he'll find precious little grass. I'll agree that mountain trail was tough but it was solid footing for your mules. Now, they're going to have a sand trail."

Carson looked around at the lounging soldiers. "Did you like that road along the upper Gila?"

The troopers groaned.

"That was a turnpike compared with what's ahead," Carson said.

Carson glanced around, smiling. "One other thing. Some of you boys seemed to be uneasy about the Indians we saw occasionally and about those we didn't see. There's still Indians ahead. There's also Mexicans. See that mountain over there?" He pointed southwestward across the dry flats toward a peak.

The soldiers nodded.

"Tucson is right near there and there's always been a Mexican force at Tucson. That's three days' ride from right here."

The troopers looked around at each other.

"I thought you said the Mexicans wouldn't fight?" Brad said.

"I said the Californians wouldn't fight. The Mexicans might if they have strong leaders. They might not fight either but hell, they might throw a ball or two at you before they start running. If you step in front of a ball anywhere, it's going to hurt." Carson smiled.

"What do you think are the chances that we'll meet a Mexican force around here?" John Henry said.

"That I can't say." The levity was gone. "I told you that General Castro high-tailed it out of California in a hurry. The story was that he was going to Sonora to recruit an army, then come back to California.

"I didn't tell you this. A few miles back, we saw a fresh trail that had been cut by a lot of horses. Might be Castro coming back with his new army. It would be a feather in somebody's sombrero to capture the American governor of California.

"Or might be Indians. Whoever it was, maybe they've seen us. Maybe they haven't. The General will be posting a few more guards than usual and we'll be doing a bit more scouting."

"Let 'em come," said Brad. The soldiers murmured their agreement and walked toward their mules.

It was a sobered troop that mounted and moved off. Not that they were fearful about the prospect of a fight. Most longed for a fight. It was the odds that worried them.

True to Carson's prediction, scouting parties now were sent out in advance and to each side of the army's route. They looked not for water or grass, not even for Indians. They looked for Mexicans. John Henry hoped fervently that they would find none.

It seemed to John Henry that the patrol had left camp that noon in another life. The five scouts had to cut their midday halt short in order to move out ahead of the army. The corporal led the unit two miles on the army's projected route, then turned off the trail, heading about forty-five degrees leftward through a sagebrush-studded plain.

The land began to tilt gently upward. Riding in single file, the troopers looked back and saw the thin column miles below, entering the flat from a patch of willows.

A moment later, the patrol topped the rise and lost sight of the army. Ahead lay a rolling plain, gashed by erosion, with sparse vegetation, in hues of gray, tan and purple, still, empty. The sky was a soft blue and absolutely clear.

A strange, beautiful land, John Henry mused.

After another hour of steady riding, the corporal called a halt. He rode alone to the base of a hillock and dismounted. Tying the mule's reins to a stunted mesquite, he crawled to the top of the hillock. He peered over the top with his telescope, moving from right to left and back again. After two minutes of this, he inched backward down the hill, retrieved his mule and walked to where the four dragoons waited, still mounted.

"There's a plain up ahead, slopes downward, lots of washes. 'Bout three or four miles out, there's a line of what looks like willows, so that means water—unless it's dry. Anyway, it's the only place in the country that looks like it ought to have water, so if there's anybody about, or if anybody has been about, we should find some sign there. I didn't see any evidence of an enemy force but we will have a look nevertheless."

Corporal Jackson, a member of General Kearny's personal guard, was an intense soldier. Muscular, ruggedly handsome and well clipped, his military bearing was faultless and always impressive. He was well liked and respected by both officers and men. There were no doubts in his mind about this war. In fact, he did not think about the war. He concerned himself with duty and carrying out orders. John Henry envied him.

"We'll fan out. Stay in the washes if you can and out of sight. If you get in trouble, fire your carbine, and yell like hell. If we don't root out anybody, when you reach the willows, turn to the right, and we'll re-form where the willows end.

"I'm on the right. Fredericks next to me. Then Edwards, Dougal and Harris on the left, in that order. At a slow walk." He mounted and the five spread to their assigned places. They were shortly lost to each other's view.

John Henry rode a considerable distance to the left before dropping into a gully that ran down the slope toward the thin line of willows at the bottom of the flat.

The wash ran almost straight for a mile, then turned sharply to the left. After fifteen minutes in the cut, John Henry decided that he was spreading the fan too wide and determined to climb out. But the wash had become a shallow canyon with steep sides, devoid of vegetation. He continued.

The line of the wash eventually turned gently to the right and—John Henry sighed with relief—undoubtedly toward the willows. At least, he assumed so, for the cut was so deep he could not see over the top. The rocks in the bottom of the sterile gully were now so large that his mule was having a hard time of it, skirting the huge boulders, and stumbling and sliding on the pebbly stone pavement.

John Henry dismounted. He removed the strap from his carbine and pulled it from its bucket. He checked the weapon, then took the reins in his other hand and began to pick his way down the wash.

He walked carefully, alternately searching ahead and glancing down at the floor of the wash. He heard no sound but his own footsteps and the hoofs and blowing of his mount. He stopped momentarily to listen. Nothing. His anxiety grew as the shadow climbed the canyon wall.

The others must have regrouped by now. Will they be looking for me? Embarrassing. He picked up the pace, sliding often on the pebbly footing.

The gully finally opened and the walls dropped. There was a cut in the wall ahead and John Henry turned to climb out. *Probably a game trail. Game? In this country?* He smiled.

Either that or . . . He stopped abruptly and looked closely at the ground in the cut. Tracks. But not game tracks. They were horse tracks. He wasn't good enough at trailing to know how old they were.

When his head was level with the top of the wall of the wash, he stopped. He looked around anxiously and saw nothing unusual. But then he saw the willows, not a half-mile away! He sighed deeply and climbed quickly out of the wash.

I don't mind admitting I'm glad to get out of there, he said to himself. He looked at the sun. The red ball floated just above the horizon. *There's no time to waste, mule. Let's get out of this rock patch and I'll give you a bit of exercise.*

He made his way through a chaos of room-size boulders toward what appeared to be an open flat. He was hurrying now. *I can just hear Brad. "First patrol you go on and . . ."*

He froze! He dropped the reins and brought his carbine up sharply. He shook his head and felt the sweat burning in his eyes but he dared not wipe them.

It can't be! It's happening again!

But the apparition did not go away. There, not thirty paces away stood a soldier. A Mexican soldier. The Mexican held his musketoon at the ready, crouched and taut.

He was looking straight into John Henry's eyes, his mouth open. He had no hat and no other accouterments, only his weapon. His mount was nowhere in sight. They stared at each other, both motionless, each ready.

John Henry thought of the first time he had seen a deer. His father had sent him down a game trail with instructions to walk down to a large oak they both knew and to wait for him there. The trail ran through heavy brush, so high the twelve-year-old could not see above it. But he carried his gun at the ready, as his father had taught him.

"You never know when you'll see your buck," his father had told him.

He had turned a corner and came face to face with a three-point buck, fifty feet away in the middle of the trail.

The deer had heard him but had stood to verify the

sound. The boy stared wildly and in wonder at the animal. *How beautiful it is!* He was in shock—"buck fever," his dad called it later—but his training was thorough, and the rifle went automatically to his shoulder, fired, and the deer went down.

He raced to the animal that lay on its side. The boy was ecstatic. *I shot a deer! A buck! By myself! Daddy isn't even here!*

He watched the deer as all four legs pumped, and the body quivered. The thrashing stopped, the legs stiffened straight out, and the body trembled all over.

"Daddy!" he yelled, "Daddy! I got a deer! Over here!" The quivering subsided. He looked at the deer's head—the liquid brown eyes unmistakably were looking directly into his own eyes—and turned away.

"*Agua*," the soldier said softly, slurring his words, "*por favor . . . agua . . . tiene agua?*"

John Henry started at the sound of the voice. He gripped the carbine stock tighter with his right hand, and his finger gently rubbed the trigger.

"*Agua*," the soldier said again. He pointed with the index finger of his left hand toward John Henry's mount. His left hand held the forestock of his weapon, and the motion brought the muzzle up slightly.

Instantly a shot cracked behind John Henry and to his right. He spun around, crouching, carbine at his shoulder. He saw a dragoon, fifty yards away, just lowering his own carbine.

John Henry whirled around to see the Mexican sink to his knees. He dropped the musketoon and extended his hands toward John Henry, his eyes wide in terror. His mouth was open as if to speak.

John Henry ran to him. The soldier did not move. Only his eyes followed John Henry.

A red circle on the soldier's breast widened. John Henry was horrified.

"*Agua . . . por . . . el . . . amor . . . de . . . Dios*," the Mexican said weakly. His eyelids fluttered and closed and he fell forward, brushing against John Henry's leg and sliding off to lie on his back.

John Henry and Carson sat at a cooking fire. The other members of the mess had wandered away in the darkness to their tents or to visit at the other fires. John Henry and Carson stared into the dancing flames. John Henry stirred the coals with a stick.

"He looked me right in the eye. I'll never forget it. It's been so long since I heard any Spanish and he was hurting."

Carson stood and stretched. "Yep, it surely gets thirsty out there," he said and stepped into the darkness.

"*Agua, por el amor de Dios.*" Water, for the love of God.

He remembered the face clearly. It was not fear alone he had seen. There was also agony. *When he pointed at my mule, the movement that killed him, he was pointing at my canteen. He asked me for water in his very last breath. My God, my God.* John Henry closed his eyes and shook his head.

John Henry sat down slowly, holding his tin plate out in front of him. He leaned against a rock, set the plate in his lap, and breathed deeply. He looked at the sunset. The sky was colored in ten shades of red and pink. Any other day, he might be overwhelmed. Not today.

He was exhausted. The food had little appeal for him

and he began worrying the beans with his fork. Another trooper walked over and sat down stiffly on a rock, grunting as if in pain. John Henry looked up, saw Dougal, nodded, and returned to his plate.

After a moment, the time it took Dougal to clear his plate, he said, "That was a close call out there, hoss."

John Henry moved the beans on his plate with the edge of his fork.

"I almost didn't take that path," Dougal said. "I might've missed you."

For a long moment, John Henry said nothing, then: "You shouldn't have shot him." He stared at his plate, avoiding Dougal's eyes.

"Shouldn't have shot him? What're you talking about? Hell, he was about to kill you."

"I don't think he was going to shoot me. He was as scared as I was. He didn't want to kill me. Anyway, I could have got away." John Henry continued to push the beans around the plate with his fork.

Dougal looked sharply at John Henry. "Got away? What th' hell are you talking about? What do you mean, 'got away'?"

"I mean, I could have got away. He wouldn't have come after me. He didn't want to shoot me. And he would be alive now."

"Hold on, hoss, hold on. It's one thing to be scared. It's something else to run. You mean, you would've run?"

John Henry turned to look at Dougal.

"I mean I would have got away, backed away, walked away, run if that's what it would take."

Dougal slowly set his plate on the ground beside him. He stood and faced John Henry, hands on hips. He dropped his head and shook it.

"Now look here, Harris." His voice was calm but his eyes squinted and he spoke more slowly than usual. "In this man's army, we got to depend on each other. I saved your life out there. You might be in a position one day to save mine. And I want to know here and now whether I can count on you. I admit I've wondered a bit about you, hoss, but I never took you for a coward."

"A coward. So that's it. A coward." John Henry looked at his antagonist, for so he had become. "What's a coward, Dougal?"

By this time, a dozen troopers had taken an interest in the conversation and a loose circle had formed around the two.

"For Christ's sake," the heat rising in him, the agitation showing clearly in his face, "a coward is somebody who won't stand and fight!"

"Do you mean that you would always stand and fight, even if you could avoid getting yourself or the other man hurt, or worse, killed, by getting away?"

"Harris, you keep saying 'getting away.' What you mean is 'running.' No, by God, I won't run."

"But that makes no sense, to hurt somebody or take a life when it's not necessary. You'd have that man's blood on your conscience the rest of your life."

"My conscience? Sweet Jesus! Man, I'd be doing my duty! I'd be defending myself!"

"That wouldn't be self-defense, not if you could have gotten away. That'd be murder."

"By God, that's nonsense and that's personal, and I won't stand for it!" Dougal advanced a step toward John Henry who kept his seat. Dougal waited, fuming.

"Dammit, Harris, get up!" More troopers had joined the circle, which now pressed in on the two. "I want no cowards beside me if it comes to a fight with the greasers. I'm going to brand you here and now!"

Dougal stepped toward John Henry. He bent down, grabbed him by his shirt and pulled him to his feet. John Henry dropped his plate and struggled to gain his balance, his feet slipping on the gravel. He wrenched free and backed away.

"Dougal, I didn't mean all this personally. I thought we were just talking in general. I apologize if you thought I meant anything personal."

A murmur rose from the circle of dragoons who pressed in closer.

"By God, you are a coward and I'm going to brand you!" Dougal moved toward him.

John Henry backed away until he bumped against the stone face of a hillock. The dragoons now formed a tight semi-circle around the antagonists.

No escape.

Dougal rushed in, his shoulder plowing into John Henry's chest and his arms encircling his waist, his legs churning. They crashed into the stone wall and fell together.

John Henry clawed at Dougal's back, trying to grab something to steady himself, as his feet went out from under him. He fell heavily with Dougal's full weight on his chest. He saw flashes of black and silvery sparkles and could not get his breath as they rolled on the ground, grappling.

John Henry was on his feet first, braced, but unsteady.

"Dougal . . ." he said weakly, but that was all, for Dougal, rising to a crouch, charged again. His shoulder caught John Henry at the waist. As John Henry recoiled from the blow, Dougal straightened and threw his right arm, grazing John Henry's chin with his fist. His weight was forward and he stumbled as John Henry sidestepped.

John Henry had his wind back now. Dougal whirled around and threw another right at John Henry. He dodged and Dougal's fist brushed his shoulder. Dougal drew back, ready to charge again. His face was red and distorted.

John Henry was shocked. Dougal never had been a likable person but here was a figure altogether unrecognizable, transformed by rage.

They faced each other. John Henry glanced from side to side. *No. No way out.* The circle of troopers had pressed in closer. Dougal stepped slowly toward him.

All right, thought John Henry, *if we must.*

Dougal lunged forward, swinging a right at John Henry's jaw. John Henry ducked and stepped aside, at the same time slamming his right fist hard in Dougal's stomach. Dougal doubled over and almost fell.

John Henry waited as Dougal gasped for breath. When he recovered, Dougal turned abruptly and charged, catching John Henry in the chest with his shoulder and grabbing him about the waist. John Henry fell backward but grabbed Dougal around the neck as he fell. He arched his back and pushed Dougal's head down. Dougal released a muffled grunt as his face ground into gravel.

John Henry released his hold and rolled quickly away. He scrambled to his feet. Dougal rose to his hands and knees and got up slowly. Blood streamed from his nose. His chin and cheeks were reddened from a dozen cuts, the blood mixing with the dirt that covered his face.

"Let's call it quits, Dougal, we've both had enough."

"Enough? . . . damn you!" He lunged, connecting with a left to John Henry's jaw, which sent him reeling. John Henry recovered in time to fend off Dougal's right and to connect himself with a right to Dougal's head.

Dougal began throwing both fists, blinded with blood and rage, connecting mostly with air. John Henry managed to land a punch often enough to infuriate Dougal and hurt him.

Dougal bled steadily now and his shirt front was flecked with it. His right eye was swollen almost shut and he was breathing heavily, gasping for breath when he threw a blow and recovering more slowly after each effort.

"Enough, Dougal!"

Dougal stood, shoulders forward and arms hanging. His breathing was labored.

"Damn you, Harris! Stop whining and fight!" Dougal swung and landed a hard blow to John Henry's head.

John Henry stepped backward and shook his head. He licked his lips and tasted blood and sweat. He raised his fists and advanced slowly. Dougal, gasping, put up his fists, and they circled. Blood ran down Dougal's cheeks and dripped from his chin.

John Henry feinted with his left and punched Dougal hard in the mid-section with his right. He followed with a blow to Dougal's jaw, staggering him.

John Henry stepped back and watched Dougal reel. He admired him as he despised him. *I'm not fighting a man anymore*, he thought, *I'm fighting a dumb brute and he is forcing me to treat him like one.*

Dougal stumbled to the attack and flailed with both arms, seldom connecting and exhausting himself in the process. John Henry punched him at will now, landing blows to his body more often than his head, not wishing to do him serious injury.

John Henry finally buried his fist hard in Dougal's stomach, sending him to his knees.

"Okay, Dougal? Give it up!" John Henry shouted.

Dougal struggled slowly to his feet. "Go t' hell!" he said, between gasps. He swung wildly at John Henry. John Henry dodged easily and landed a blow to Dougal's head. His head snapped back sharply and he almost fell. He reeled drunkenly, his legs spread apart.

He gathered himself, swallowed with difficulty, crouched and lunged at John Henry. John Henry deflected the blow and as Dougal brushed by him, struck him hard on the back, sending him heavily to the ground.

Dougal lay still, face down. His face and neck were smeared with blood and his shirt hung in ribbons. John Henry fell to his knees beside him, gasping.

"Okay!" he shouted in Dougal's ear.

Dougal did not move. After a long moment, he turned his face slightly toward John Henry, his eyes slits, glazed. He inhaled slowly. "Okay."

John Henry helped him stand and others supported him as he stumbled toward his tent.

Brad walked over to John Henry and they walked away together through the circle of dragoons that was thinning now.

"John Henry, by God, I'm proud of you! You gave old Dougal a proper whipping. I thought at first that I should take a hand, I figure I'm more his size. Thank God, I didn't. Are you all right?"

"I'm okay." But he did not feel okay, in body or soul.

The next evening, after supper, Dougal sat down on the ground by John Henry. John Henry looked at him uneasily. Dougal smiled. They talked about how hard the going had been that day and agreed that, on the whole, the mountain trail had been better than the desert.

Dougal finally got to the point. "I don't understand

you, hoss," he said, "but if you ever do decide to fight again, let's be on the same side." He slapped John Henry on the back and walked away, strutting. His broad shoulders were thrown back.

John Henry had won Dougal's respect but on Dougal's terms and he found no satisfaction in it.

CHAPTER 6

The column was halted and each man was ready, his carbine unslung. All eyes were focused on the single figure approaching them on foot, dead ahead in the trail.

Carson sat with General Kearny at the front. "He's no Apache," Carson said. "Apaches are too timid for that. They're curious but they know that curiosity can get a body killed. This fellow is either careless or friendly."

Carson rode toward the Indian. They met about fifty yards from the head of the column and Carson dismounted. They talked a couple of minutes, then both walked briskly to the head of the column.

"He's Pima," Carson said to Kearny, "out looking for his cattle. We're only about eight or ten miles from the Pima villages. He says there is a good patch of grass ahead."

"Good," Kearny said, "we'll camp there. We can do our trading in the villages tomorrow morning."

Camp was pitched that evening with more enthusiasm than usual. Every member of the army had heard at Santa Fé about the Pimas and their friends, the Maricopas. These native farmers had provisioned explorers and armies since Spaniards first entered the country over one hundred fifty years ago.

With camp set up, John Henry and a few others sought out Carson to ask about the Pimas.

"These Indians," Carson said, "are different from any others you will find in the entire West. You'll see tomorrow."

They did not have to wait until tomorrow. They had hardly encamped when six Pimas came riding at full gallop. They had come in to verify the identity and intent of the strangers. They had been out scouting and, seeing the column from a distance, thought they were Apaches. Approaching, they decided that they were either Mexicans or Americans.

They were delighted to find the latter. The leader of the scouts immediately sent a message to the village.

In less than three hours, the army camp was filled with Pimas, weighed down with packs of produce that they wished to trade. There were beans, corn, clay jars of molasses made from cactus fruits, and, a wonder in November, watermelons. Major Swords, the quartermaster, was in charge of the trading and offered red and white cloth, beads, and blankets.

All of the Pimas who had produce wanted to trade but they were neither anxious nor impatient. Some set their packs down and wandered about the encampment to satisfy their curiosity.

"Look at that," Carson said to John Henry and two others who were watching the trading. "Those two packs right there" —he pointed—"belong to those bucks clear on the other side of the square. Nobody's watching the packs."

The soldiers watched. Other Indians walked by the packs and ignored them. One passerby brushed against one of the packs and upset it. He bent over and lifted it upright, leaning it against the other. Then he walked on.

After fifteen minutes, the owners strolled back, picked up the packs, and walked casually over to the awning where Major Swords was still buying.

"I'll be damned!" Brad said. "I didn't think any Ind-in could resist a little easy plunder, even from his own kind."

"I told you they were different. Theft is unknown among them. And they assume other people have the same high morals they do." Carson winked.

The next morning, the army moved to the village and set up camp in a cornfield that had been harvested. This chore done, the soldiers not on duty wandered about, amazed at what they saw.

Fields were fenced and leveled for irrigation. Individual fields were subdivided by ridges where the lay of the land required smaller units for irrigation. Huge feeder canals drew water from the Gila. The unused water was returned to the river.

The principal crops were corn, wheat, and cotton. All crops had been gathered, and the evidence was clear that the harvest had been plentiful. Cotton in the pod was arranged on the tops of arbors for drying, and stubble fields stretched for miles.

Houses were the shape of cones or large loaves about six feet high and twenty to fifty feet long, thatched with willow branches and straw or corn stalks. *What could be more practical*, thought John Henry, *in such a moderate climate?* Dogs lay in the shade of the arbors and chickens scratched in the dry grass.

John Henry was profoundly impressed with this savage pastoral. All seemed order and beauty. He thought of Morita. *She is my order and beauty.*

She had been much on his mind lately. The more

fatigued he was, the hungrier from the bland and meager rations, the colder he was at night when the wind blew his blankets, the hotter he was at noon, the more he thought of her.

His headaches had returned, throbbing during the march, at night preventing sleep and exhausting him as he rolled about. When he was racked with the pain, which coursed from his brain to every joint, he tried to focus on Morita.

He remembered one night in Santa Fé when he had drunk too much and his head pulsed with pain. She had helped him sit up in bed, with his legs pulled up and his head resting on his knees. She massaged the back of his neck, rubbing and squeezing gently until the pain subsided.

Another time, when he had been with her during the afternoon of a rare day when he had no duty, the sun on the adobe placita had given him a severe headache that settled in his sinuses. She had sat on the floor with her back against the wall. He lay beside her, his head in her lap. She gently rubbed the bridge of his nose, massaged his forehead and temples, and bent over to kiss his closed eyes.

Walking back into the Pima village, John Henry saw that trading was still brisk. Indians brought dried and fresh pumpkins, beans, corn, flour, honey, cactus molasses, and more watermelons.

"Harris, come over here." John Henry turned and saw Lieutenant Emory. "Taste this and tell me what you think of it."

"What is it?"

"Just taste it and tell me if you like it."

John Henry took the cup hesitantly. The last mysterious beverage that had been offered to him, when he happened to be very thirsty, was Apache mescal, and it almost took off the top of his head. But, a good life is a collection of experiences, his Pa used to tell him. He raised the cup and tasted it. Another taste, then he emptied it. *Good. Very good.*

"That's very tasty. What is it?" John Henry said.

"It's called '*pinole.*' It's made from the heart of corn. They bake it, grind it up, and mix it with sugar. Very nutritious. They eat it as is or dissolve it in water for a beverage. Major Swords is trying to decide whether to buy some." Emory raised the cup in a gesture of thanks or goodbye and walked toward Swords's awning.

Major Swords was able to purchase adequate supplies of beans, corn, and wheat. He bought only three cows, though he bargained for more. They simply were too valuable to the Pimas as draft animals. The Indians traded for them from Mexicans and the source was unreliable.

Horses and mules the army needed most and they were not able to purchase a single animal. The Pimas had few and prized them highly. They were absolutely essential to protect the villages from Apaches.

The Indians seemed also to be quite attached to their horses. John Henry was amused—after almost being run over—by a Pima who raced his mount into the heart of the army's camp. The horse shied at the unfamiliar sights and seemed to go out of control. The rider, a young man with flowing black hair, was unconcerned and was in such rhythm with his mount's movements as to appear part of it. He had no saddle and no need of one.

He pulled the horse to a sliding stop in the middle of the square, enjoying the stares of dozens of soldiers and Indians. An officer immediately walked over to him and made him a generous offer for the animal.

The Indian leaned forward and put his arms around his

mount's neck, resting his head on the mane and shutting his eyes. The officer smiled and walked away.

John Henry looked around him. *I like these people.* He watched the Pimas as they wandered casually about the army's camp, mixing easily with the soldiers. *They're happy and comfortable and hardworking. They laugh easily. They are self-sufficient and they take care of themselves. They're heathen all right, but they top most Christians I know in farming and they top them all in honesty. I haven't heard of a single case of theft since we've been here, against their own people or the army. These are good people, people I'd like to know. Good people aren't much different, no matter who they are or where they live.*

He smiled, remembering an incident the previous evening. One of the first Indians to arrive at the army's camp was the interpreter for Juan Antonio Llunas, the Pima chieftain. Governor Llunas, the interpreter called him. He was appointed to his post by the Mexican government.

The interpreter stood with Emory, Captain Turner, and Carson. Passing the group, John Henry overheard Emory questioning the interpreter about the ruins that Emory and John Henry had investigated, and he stopped to listen.

The Pima's tongue was loosened by Emory's *aguardiente*, and he replied at length.

"Those are the homes of the first people, our ancestors. Long, long ago, before the beginning, a beautiful woman lived in a green valley in the high mountains over there." The Pima pointed. "She was a very good woman and she was a virgin.

"One day when she was lying naked on her back, a drop of water fell on her womb. She conceived and gave birth to a son. He was the first man and was the founder of a great people who farmed in these valleys and lived in the buildings that you saw."

"Very quaint," Turner said when the interpreter was gone. "Primitive peoples throughout history who have not received the blessings of the Lord have always tried, and always so pathetically, to explain their beginnings with these fanciful legends."

"I don't know, Captain," Carson said, a twinkle in his eye. "Sounds like a pretty good story to me."

"Oh, interesting, but naive, like all of them. A drop of water? And a man who was the founder of a whole race of people? Without a wife?" Turner chuckled. He watched the two Indians.

Emory turned toward Carson and John Henry. They exchanged quizzical looks.

Emory turned back to Turner and said soberly: "Well, Captain, I don't recall that the Virgin Mary had the benefit of even a drop of holy water. And just as a matter of interest, who was Cain's wife?"

Turner stared into the distance. "Christians believe on faith what they cannot know by experience."

"So do the heathen, Captain," said Carson, "so do the heathen."

John Henry remembered that Turner was unshaken but the others had been embarrassed for him.

When the army was ready to be on its way and mule packs were made, General Kearny gave Governor Llunas a letter, directing all United States forces that might follow to respect him, his people and their property. It declared that Llunas was a good man. The letter was read to the assembled dragoons before it was delivered to the chief. John Henry thought it an exceedingly strange document.

"General, at this point, you have two choices." Since leaving the Pimas the previous day, the army had ridden alongside the Gila. Now the column was stopped while Kearny and Carson talked.

"Just up ahead, the river turns to the north to pass around that range of hills to the northwest. Then it turns back to the south before heading west again. We can follow the river and have water and a little browse all the way."

"Or?"

"Or we leave the river here and head due west. This cuts off the horseshoe bend of the river and saves all told about sixty miles. However, this means a march of forty miles across that ridge there," he said, pointing. "The trail is hard and there is positively no grass or water for the whole stretch."

"What do you recommend?"

"I'd take the cutoff. I took it last time across here."

"So shall we," said Kearny. His impatience had been growing visibly lately. He turned in his saddle. "Captain Turner, have the men fall out and water the stock well. We have a two-day dry march ahead."

The dragoons in the front ranks had heard the whole conversation. John Henry did not know what to make of it, whether to be happy with cutting off sixty miles of the journey or worried about the waterless stretch.

Carson's forecasts about trail conditions had not always proved accurate in the past. He had said that there would be no grass along the Gila once they left the mountains but grass had been found often enough, and sometimes of good quality. Maybe he was going to be wrong again.

"Mount!"

"Move! Move!"

"Fall in, right smart now!"

Sergeants shouted at the dragoons who were taking an unusually long time to water their mounts and get back into marching order.

The soldiers were as anxious as the General to reach California but the thought of leaving the river now made them uneasy. They traded for as many water gourds as they could afford, and at high prices, from the Maricopas who had been riding along with the column since last night's encampment. Their village was only a few miles downstream and scores of Maricopas had come to the camp for trading.

Carson led the column away from the river and turned in a southwesterly direction toward the low pass in the range of hills in front of them. The trail was deceptive. The surface looked hard but the animals broke through the light saline crust. Beneath was deep sand as fine as powder. The trail was a gradual climb with no plateaus for resting. Horses and mules that had been refreshed with corn and rest at the Pima village began to wear down quickly.

Mid-afternoon. The army column moved slowly on the trail that rose gradually in a waterless, sterile moonscape. The blistering sun reflected off rocky surfaces and assaulted the troopers from all sides.

John Henry's head throbbed. His eyes were shut, and he began to rock forward and backward in the saddle.

"Headache?" Brad said.

"Yep, it hurts something bad."

Brad rode close by, anxious and ready to help.

That evening, Brad had John Henry bedded down ten

minutes after stopping. Brad unsaddled their mules and tied them to a stunted mesquite tree. He tried to give John Henry supper but he would take nothing.

John Henry lay like a mummy, with eyes closed and a fixed, tortured expression on his face. His jaw was clenched and he breathed slowly and evenly. Doc Griffin could only tell Brad to watch him and let him know if he took a turn for the worse.

Brad stayed awake all night, wiping the perspiration from his partner's face and listening to his groans and his repeated "Morita . . . *mi amor* . . . Morita . . . *mi vida* . . . Morita . . ."

Brad felt the sides of the tent pressing in on him. He burst outside and stood, his arms folded tightly across his chest, breathing heavily, his eyes moist.

John Henry sat bolt upright.

"Easy, hoss, it's okay."

"Brad?"

"Yeah. You all right?"

"Fine. Are you up? I can't see you."

"I'm up and rarin' to go."

"What woke me? Why are you up?"

"Well, I s'pose the bugle roused you. And I'm up because the bugle just sounded to horse."

"To horse? It's the middle of the night!"

"Right you are. You may not remember this . . . sure you're okay?"

"Little shaky but I'm okay. What's up?"

"You may not remember this—I don't think you were too attentive the last couple of hours yesterday—but we're in the middle of a godawful march, so we're going to ride in the cool. The poor mules have been bawling all night.

There was no water or grass for 'em. I just hope they can make it to the river. They're in terrible shape."

John Henry threw back the blankets and reached for his trousers. The blankets and his drawers were damp. He struggled into his trousers and picked up a boot.

As he drew on the boot, he tried to remember the dream that the bugle had interrupted. He was with Morita at her house. But something was wrong. He stopped, the partially booted foot suspended in midair, trying to recall the images.

Yes. It was evening, and we were sitting on the porch, watching the sun go. I turned to look at her. Her profile was perfect. I never understood perfection until I knew her. She turned toward me and smiled. The sun was soft on her cheek and her hair shone. She said something that I didn't understand. That was it! There wasn't any sound. She was talking but no sound came out. I couldn't hear what she was saying!

"Are you about ready, Johnny? We need to get the tent down." Brad held the flap open.

"Right smart, sergeant!" John Henry pulled the boot on and crawled from the tent. Brad smiled and John Henry could see in the bright moonlight fatigue written on the face.

I don't suppose you slept at all this night, old friend. I'll make it up to you one day.

By sunrise, the column crossed the spine of the ridge, and the troopers saw the thin green line across the plain that meant the river. The downhill trail and the promise of water comforted man and beast but the journey had already taken its toll on the animals. Worn-out mules had been left along the trail that morning, dead or dying.

John Henry worried about his own mount. The mule's head drooped almost to the ground, and every step, even on the down trail, was labored. Every pebble in the trail was an obstacle and, when stepped on, almost tumbled mule and rider.

"C'mon, pard, we'll make it," John Henry said softly.

John Henry's concern about his mule had grown with the column's progress. He had been strong, almost frisky, on the trail along the Río Grande. He had slowed a bit on the trail from the river to the headwaters of the Gila but he was still strong.

In the mountains, when the trail left the river, there was little grass and water, and the mule lost weight. The flesh seemed to melt away and his bones pushed against the slack skin. John Henry had nursed him along, walking often and talking to him, encouraging him. Grass and water just ahead, he would say.

Once John Henry fed the mule a biscuit that was supposed to have been his own breakfast. With his hat, he dipped water from potholes too deep for the animal to reach.

When John Henry's head throbbed and he rode with clenched teeth and eyes shut, only half conscious, his reins were slack and the mule moved on, stopping when the column stopped, moving ahead when the column moved and stopping again when a halt was called, standing quietly until someone came to rouse John Henry and help him dismount.

The mule's pace had slowed so much that other riders passed each time the trail momentarily widened. Each step sent a shudder through the animal and he stopped every few steps to blow. His muzzle almost scraped the ground when he walked.

John Henry looked ahead and saw a wide spot in the trail, just around a rock outcropping, where he could dismount.

John Henry was looking ahead when he was suddenly jolted hard and almost lost his seat. As usual, he had been riding with a loose rein. The mule had failed to follow the trail around the outcropping and instead had collided headlong into the rock face. The poor animal recoiled and staggered a step backward, then stood quivering, his legs spread wide and feet planted.

John Henry slid from the saddle and stepped in front of the mule. He stooped to look at the animal's head where he had hit the wall. He tried to pull his head up but it was a dead weight.

"What is it, Bell?" he said aloud.

"Move it, John Henry! You can make polite conversation with your mule when we hit water." The troopers were piling up behind on the narrow trail.

John Henry walked ahead, coaxing the mule toward the wider spot in the trail. He watched his mount pick up each leg and set it down as if it were stepping amongst eggs, trying to pick a safe spot. Each step was cautious, tentative, and painfully slow.

"C'mon pard, c'mon, just a little more," he almost whispered.

When he rounded the bend, he pulled his mount close to the wall and the dragoons moved past. John Henry stroked the mule's neck, wet with sweat and caked with grit. *Poor old fellow. As if you hadn't been through enough, now this.*

He was blind. John Henry had heard of the condition. Old troopers said it was temporary and strong mules could recover.

"We'll make it," John Henry murmured. By this time,

the entire column had passed. He began walking slowly down the trail, turning often to watch his mount. The mule's eyes seemed fixed on the ground, as if to pick the best trail, but John Henry knew he saw nothing.

The army reached the Gila at mid-morning. Bell stopped at the bank. There was a sharp decline of three steps that led to the wide streambed. John Henry stepped down into the bed and pulled on the reins. The mule obediently stepped to follow, but finding no level ground to plant a foot on, he drew back.

"You smell that water, damn it, you know it's there. Now, just a few steps and you'll be standing in it."

Other mounts and pack animals, thirst-crazed, slid down the bank or jumped to the bed, wading into the shallows and drinking deeply. No amount of tugging and coaxing would move John Henry's mule. He stood on the bank, shivering.

John Henry dropped the reins and walked to the stream edge. He dipped his hat into the water and carried it up the bank to the mule. The animal's head was almost touching the ground, so he slid the hat under the muzzle and lifted it. When the water touched the muzzle, the mule jerked his head slightly upward, then relaxed. His muzzle was in the water, but he did not drink. The mule turned aside and browsed on some cane and tender willow branches.

"Okay, pard, we'll take it easy. You'll want the water later."

"All right, the General has said that we will lay over two nights to let the animals recruit!" John Henry looked up at the sergeant who was riding along the bank of the stream and shouting at dragoons who were beginning to climb from the streambed.

"Fall in now! We're moving about five miles down-stream where there's good grass."

John Henry instinctively started to tell the sergeant that his mount needed rest and why didn't they just lay over right where they were but he caught himself, realizing how ridiculous his protest would sound. *We'll make it, Bell, but at your own pace. The hell with forming up.*

John Henry watched the ragged column move off, slowly, with no apparent order, in no hurry. He walked at a snail's pace, the rein held loosely in his hand. The mule followed, moving stiffly and stepping heavily in the sandy trail.

It was mid-afternoon before John Henry saw the dragoons again. They had encamped in the unexpected shade of an acacia grove.

John Henry led the mule past some soldiers who were scattered along the riverbank, lounging and chatting, enjoying the luxury of inactivity. One of the dragoons nudged a friend and pointed at John Henry. The other turned to look. They both grinned.

When he reached the bench where the stock was grazing—*good grass, you could almost call it a meadow*—he released the girth and slid the saddle off. He slipped off the bridle.

That's it. We made it. Now you've got two whole days just to rest, eat and get fat and happy. You'll have more to eat than I will, pard but I surely will enjoy the rest. My bones do ache almost as much as my head. John Henry went to the supply wagon to borrow a bucket.

The water from the bucket sloshed on his trousers as he climbed from the river's edge to the bank. In spite of his fatigue, he was lighthearted. He almost felt like whistling. Almost. He hardly thought about the headache any longer;

it seemed always with him. He noticed it only when it became worse and now he was becoming slightly light-headed, a little dizzy. It's only the sun, he thought, and decided that he would ignore it.

The mule had not moved. The animals that had surrounded him when John Henry removed the saddle and bridle had moved on and now grazed thirty yards away. John Henry's mount had neither grazed nor followed.

John Henry slipped the bucket under the mule's nose and pushed his muzzle into it. The animal left his muzzle in the water a moment, then pulled back.

"It's all right, Bell. In your own time. There's plenty of time." He set the bucket on the ground and patted the mule gently on the neck. Then he walked toward his mess where he was sure he would find coffee.

Now, where is that mule? John Henry, at first impulse, was annoyed that he could not locate his mount among the grazing stock but then he breathed a sigh of relief. *By damn, he made it.*

The animals had been left unfettered during the evening and night so they could move about and graze and water at will. There was little grass beyond this wild meadow. They would not wander far. Most were cropping the same patch they had grazed the previous day.

John Henry glanced toward the river. There was not a single animal there. They would have watered earlier, he guessed. He walked to the edge of the herd and stopped. He looked in all directions, down the wash on his left, into the mesquite thicket on the right, and he scanned the gently rising slope in front of him.

No sign of Bell. John Henry moved up the slope and to his right, skirting the mesquite. *That mule's not dumb.*

He's found his own private patch somewhere back here and . . . there he is!

John Henry strode quickly to where the mule lay on his side at the back of the mesquite. He dropped to his knees and laid his hand on the animal's neck. At his touch, the mule raised his head a few inches off the ground, then dropped it heavily and lay still. John Henry watched the mule a moment. The breathing was weak but steady. John Henry jumped to his feet and ran toward camp.

"Hurry up, Manny! Come on!" The sergeant of dragoons walked straight through the herd with long, unhurried strides. John Henry was ten steps ahead, turning often, and beckoning.

"What do you think, Manny?" The sergeant examined the mule. He looked at his eyes and bent over to listen to the animal's labored breathing.

"Manny?"

The sergeant stood up, hands on his hips and looking down at the mule.

"Well, Johnny, if the beast was stronger, I'd say we should try to git 'im on his feet but he's too bad for that. We might's well save our energy."

"Damn it," John Henry said, shaking his head. "I should've been out here last night. I knew how bad he was. If I had been here last night when he came to and started walking around, I could've got some water in him and he would be better now.

"I'll just have to keep coaxing him. If he's not fit by the time we march, we'll just have to leave him. The Pimas will find him. Or maybe even the Mormons. He might make it to California yet."

The Mormon Battalion, a unit of the Army of the

West, left Santa Fé three weeks after Kearny's departure. The General had ordered Lieutenant-Colonel Philip St. George Cooke, the commander of the Mormon volunteer force, to follow his trail.

"What I mean is, he won't last th' day."

John Henry said nothing. He had expected nothing else. "Are you sure?" he said quietly.

"I've seen a lot of mounts die in my day, Johnny, quite a few on this march. This animal ain't gonna make it."

John Henry turned around and looked up the hillside. The constriction in his throat was so painful that he could hardly breathe. Neither man spoke. The sergeant had turned and was watching John Henry.

"What do we do?" John Henry said.

"Well, we can walk off and let him die . . . but what we oughta do is shoot him right now." John Henry winced at the sergeant's bluntness.

"I suppose that's what we should do?" It was more a question than a statement.

"Yes, that's what we should do. You go on back to camp. I'll take care of it."

"No, Manny. Thanks, but that's my responsibility. I'll do it."

"Th' hell you will. You shoot that mule and he'll haunt you the rest of your life. Gawdamighty, I never saw anybody git so close to a mule. Hell, Johnny, it's not as if a favorite maiden aunt passed on to her reward. It's only a mule. Now, git on back to camp so I can take care of this."

The sergeant's tone invited no protest. John Henry turned and started down the hill. He had hardly reached the grazing animals when he heard the pistol shot. He did not look back.

CHAPTER 7

"Did you hear that, John Henry?" Brad said over his shoulder, wide-eyed. "We're only one day from California!" The news was being passed from man to man down the column. "Carson was wrong. He told us at noon that we were three days' march from the Colorado."

"Bully."

"Buck up, Johnny." Brad stepped out of line to let two troopers pass. When John Henry came up, Brad walked beside him. "It means we're near the end of this damned *jornada*. It means we're gonna make it and I'm gonna see the ocean!

"I've dreamed about it three times this week. It's the same each time. I'm standing in the water up to my ankles with my pants rolled up. There's this pretty little señorita standing next to me, real close, holding her skirts up to her knees and kicking at the water with her feet. She turns her head and flashes me a smile and starts running along the beach.

"I run after her, she's laughing and running like hell, and me right after her. I'm gaining on her and just about to grab her when a big Mexican guy steps out from behind a rock and starts coming for me."

"Then what?"

"Then I wake up. Damned frustrating."

They fell silent and plodded along, side-by-side, in the heavy sand.

The ranks were afoot now. Only the staff still rode their mules. The men were strung out in single file for three hundred yards behind the officers. Even the General's pampered bay had failed and he had been forced to take to his mule.

The few mules beside those of the staff were used for packing and to pull the howitzers. The little cannons had taken a fearful toll on the poor mules, resulting in considerable grumbling among the soldiers and not a few of the officers.

John Henry kept his eyes on the trail before him. His gloom had deepened the past few days. *It's not just the mule. Brad's news was good news. I want to see this march end as much as he does. The more distance I put between Morita and me, the sooner I will see her.*

He wanted her so much, to hold her and smell her perfume that he felt he could not bear it. *Oh God, take me back to her.* He realized that he was praying, for the first time in years.

Only one day to California. Let's see. He looked up at nothing and calculated. *That should put us there just about Thanksgiving Day. Thanksgiving. Giving-Thanks.* He bowed his head and his dark mood returned.

I wonder how Ma and Pa are doing. They'll be getting all anxious about the kinfolk coming. Pa has his turkey by now and it'll be hanging under the eaves. Ma will be making pies today, three pumpkin and two mincemeat, like always, no more, no less, no matter how many are coming. He smiled to himself and his eyes blurred.

Telling his folks about his decision to join the army had not been easy. The memory of that day was still vivid, a deliciously warm day in early March. He told his father as the two walked toward the barn, just after breakfast. His father had registered no surprise. It was not his way. They stopped beside the barn and talked, warmed by the sun reflecting from the weathered boards of the barn.

"Things are gonna get better 'round here," his father said. "Another good crop and we're gonna get us a hand. That'll ease the load."

"It's not the work, Pa. I've never minded the work." The older man was leaning against the barn, hand-hewn planks that he and his son had produced from their own woods, hands in his pockets and looking at his feet.

"And what kind of help would you get? My pa, a slave owner? You buy a slave and you'd let 'im go in a week. You couldn't stand to hold him, and you know it." The father glanced up and smiled briefly and dropped his gaze again to his shoes.

"I know. I know." After a pause, "We'll hire us a man." He looked up expectantly. "How about that?"

"Pa, it's not the work. I just have to get away. I just want to have a look."

"Your mother'll miss you. Have you thought about her?"

"I'll miss her too. I'll miss both of you. It's not as if I was gonna die. I didn't say I wasn't coming back. A lot of people look at the world before they settle down."

Settle down. Here. This little spot. The thought of it terrified him. But the decision to go had still been hard. *Twenty years from now, how will I feel about what I've got to decide right now? Better that I try than never make the effort. How would it feel to reach old age, never having looked? How would it be to reach the end of life and in the twilight, realize that you had never lived?*

After a long moment, his father straightened. Hands still in his pockets, he stretched and turned to face his only child.

"You're going then. Go with my blessing, and God watch over you. I hope you find what you're looking for. I do. I suppose I had to lose you someday. You've got too much for this place. You've learned everything I can teach you about farming and you must have learned something from those books that you care so much about.

"You've got more brains than all your forebears and kinfolk combined. At least you've got more chance to use them. Do what I didn't do. Keep on looking, and don't stop until you find what you're looking for. Don't stop too soon. Don't be satisfied too easily."

The father put his arm around the boy's shoulders and they walked off slowly toward the house, the boy now telling his father all that he planned, his excitement rising, the father listening and smiling.

His mother had taken the news quietly, with no visible emotion, as if she had expected it. She had gone about her chores as usual but, at supper that evening, she was more attentive to her son and after the meal, she sat with the two men before the fire and talked, a pleasure she had always said she had no time for.

John Henry was gone in a week. His father at the parting was cheerful and encouraging but the son knew he was hurting inside. Johnny kissed them, waved goodbye and promised to see them at the end of his enlistment. His mother smiled and told him to write as often as he could and to be a good boy. He knew she was too proud to cry and shame her men.

What will Thanksgiving be like in Santa Fé? Morita has probably never heard of it. Come to think of it, she will know nothing of Independence Day either, even of the Revolution. I'll have a whole history to teach her. And, come to that, she'll have one to teach to me. How rich we're going to be! Two pasts and a whole life ahead of us. Together.

He shivered. He closed his eyes and could almost feel her smooth, soft body against his.

"Hey, watch it. Are you in a hurry all of a sudden?" John Henry opened his eyes suddenly. He had quickened his pace and collided with Brad.

"Sorry, Brad. I just decided that I've got a long way to go and I need to get moving."

"Not so long now, John Henry," Brad said. "California in a day and it can't be more'n a few more days to the coast."

"Oh, I'm not going to California, Bradford, I'm going to Santa Fé."

Brad smiled thinly, shifted his carbine, and moved back into line ahead of John Henry, trudging ahead, each step raising little puffs of fine dust.

The straggling column marched through a valley bordered by sand hills. Mesquite dotted the hillsides, and thorny brush in the flat plucked at the soldiers' clothing. The sandy trail lay along the bank of the Gila. The stream that the army had followed for so many weeks was beginning to look more like a river. It was over a hundred yards wide now. The flow was slower and there were more sandbars.

Some bathers at the noon stop had said that it was an average of about four feet deep away from the shallows and even deeper in the channel. Captain Turner, standing on the bank, heard this report and said to no one in particular that four feet of water was more than enough to float a steamboat.

John Henry thought the remark odd, for he could not imagine what a steamboat would carry here. Mesquite beans? Sightseers maybe, standing on a lower deck in the shade. Worn-out dragoons, more likely.

He looked up at the sky. Crystal-clear. *No, there's a hawk!* He watched the bird circle, higher and higher until it was only a speck. He turned to look behind. Tired troopers in single file moved sluggishly but kept to their pace and the line had not lengthened.

Facing forward again, John Henry saw that the General and his staff had pulled far ahead of the leaders of the column and were just at the crest of a low ridge where the trail momentarily left the river. John Henry estimated that the party was easily a quarter-mile away but he was able to identify every person before the group disappeared over the ridge.

John Henry looked to his left at the sand hills, then scanned to his right past the river and across the flat to the line of mountains beyond. It was as if he were just awakening.

He realized that he could hardly remember the past few days. But every day is too precious to be lost, he pondered, and he tried to recall those days before they faded completely.

He remembered the drawings and strange symbols the dragoons had seen scratched on a mound of rocks near the trail. Lieutenant Emory explained that ancient Indians had made the drawings hundreds of years ago, perhaps thousands of years, by rubbing a hard stone against the rock, wearing away the black coating, to reveal the light-er-colored rock beneath.

The soldiers had wandered about, calling out when they recognized an image: a man, a dog, a lizard, a horse.

There was a drawing that looked like a sheep, but everyone had agreed that the ancient Indians would not have seen sheep, though the image looked very old. Then, a few days later, Carson had killed a wild mountain sheep whose ancestors had roamed the land before the arrival of the ancients.

A few days after seeing the Indian pictographs, Carson showed the dragoons some rocks just off the trail with names carved on them. He explained that most were American trappers who had passed this way in the 1820s and 1830s. John Henry had also seen Spanish names that were even older.

The following day, the trail had left the rocky, broken country and entered a flat where the valley of the Gila widened to six or eight miles, and the soil was excellent. They had seen much broken pottery, smooth grinding stones, and other evidence of ancient settlements.

All these wonders had made no mark on him when he saw them but now they fired his imagination. He vowed never again to lose a day, be it good or bad, but to draw as much from it as he could find in it.

He remembered sitting in camp last evening, listening to the gunfire at the river, a hundred yards away and hidden by willow and cottonwood. Soldiers were blazing away at rafts of ducks that covered the quiet pools of the Gila.

It was just after sunset and the muffled gunfire had reminded him of home when he would sit on the doorstep at dusk and listen to the rumbling of a storm just beyond the horizon. He could tell exactly where the storm was by the rolling thunder and black line at the horizon that expanded and merged with the darkness overhead. He had shivered at the memory but now he remembered those chilly evenings with a joy that was both nostalgic and anticipatory.

He remembered being awakened last night by the sound of geese overhead. The sound of geese in flight, a hauntingly beautiful sound, as if from another age and another world, had always thrilled him to the very depths of his soul but last night he had just turned over in his blankets and closed his eyes. Now, he shook his head and vowed to himself that would never happen again.

"Headache, John Henry?" Brad had dropped back and was walking again beside him. Lost in his reverie, he had not noticed.

John Henry looked at his friend. "No headache, old buddy. Soul-ache."

"What's that you say?"

"Nothing." John Henry smiled. "I'm fine. In fact, I think I might venture to say that I feel good!"

"Who th' hell . . .?" Russell, who was walking in front of John Henry and Brad, turned around.

"John Henry. I might'a knowed it'd be you. You're th' biggest oddball I ever seen. One minute, you got such a long face, you're kickin' your own chin and th' next minute, you're prancin' around like a fairy pickin' daisies and sprinklin' moondust. What th hell're you made of?"

"Well, Russell," John Henry smiled broadly, "don't you relish the thought of reaching the Colorado? We'll just take a swim, then it's just a hop, skip and a jump to the ocean."

"Th' hell you say. It's this hop, skippin' and jumpin' that's about t' be th' end of me. I didn't join this man's army to hop, skip and jump, even t' walk, fer that matter."

"I'll agree with those sentiments," Brad said. "This

country is tough on people and worse on mules."

"Hell, my mule's doing better'n I am," Russell replied. "At least, at the moment. But I wouldn't bet on his future. He's hitched to one of them damn cannon. Damn cannon've killed more mules than th' damn country. But do we leave th' damn cannon? Hell no, we don't leave 'em and we won't leave 'em."

"I expect we'll leave them when the officers have to give up their mounts to pull them," said John Henry.

"That may sound reasonable but I wouldn't take no bets if I was you. Nope, they'll keep their mules and we—meanin' you and me—we'll pull th' damn cannon." Russell turned to face ahead, his pace quickening, seemingly content.

John Henry and Brad exchanged grins.

"Move it! Move it! Catch up! Double time!" The soldier was spurring his mount down the ragged column as fast as his jaded mule would carry him. He had burst onto the trail from a mesquite thicket ahead, shattering the calm and frightening the leaders out of their wits. Now every trooper to a man stopped in his tracks to stare back down the column at the rider. In fifteen seconds, he had reached the end of the column and was trotting forward again.

"What're you gaping at? Move!" It was Corporal Jackson.

"Jackson, what in the world has got you and that mule so lathered about," Brad asked.

"Trouble! There's a large Mexican force ahead! All you hot-bloods who been frettin' for some action just might get your chance. It looks like we do battle tonight! Now move out fast!" He spun his exhausted mount around and spurred him hard back down the column.

"Mexicans?" John Henry turned to Brad. "I thought the war was over."

"You got me, Johnny. I thought so, too. Maybe the Mexicans hereabouts don't know that." Brad was talking between gasps.

They weren't exactly running. It was more like a fast shuffle but the column was in motion. The soldiers, so worn with fatigue a moment ago, had found a new reserve of energy.

"This is it, John Henry! Finally!" Brad threw this last over his shoulder and quickly moved ahead of John Henry.

Brad was more aware than the others about John Henry's growing doubts about the war. John Henry had confided to no other person. Nevertheless, Brad could not contain himself. He had so looked forward, like most of the other troopers, to battle with the Mexicans.

John Henry remembered how depressed Brad had been at Carson's news that California had fallen to American arms and that there would be no fight there.

What went wrong? A Mexican force on the Gila? How? Why? Am I yet going to have to fight? Oh Lord, no. He tried to clear his mind and think of nothing but whether he would survive to the end of this mad rush.

After what seemed a succession of eternities, John Henry and some others emerged together from a mesquite thicket into a little hollow, hidden on all sides by mesquite trees and sheltered by a chain of sand hills.

The earlier arrivals were setting up camp. Those who had come in just before John Henry's group still stumbled around the clearing, gasping for breath. Little knots of men formed about the camp.

John Henry saw Brad and walked over to him. He was

standing alone, leaning on his carbine, the butt resting on the ground.

"What's it all about?"

"Seems the trail up ahead is beat down like the whole Mexican nation passed by a few hours ago. The General is over there conferring." He motioned with a nod of his head. "He said he would give us the word as soon as everybody is in." Brad did not look at John Henry. He was staring at the officers. John Henry was surprised by his tranquility.

John Henry looked in the direction indicated by Brad and saw Kearny about thirty yards away, huddled with Carson and his officers. Brad had not taken his eyes off the group. Carson was pointing down the valley and gesturing with his hands. They returned to their talk, glancing occasionally toward the mesquite thicket. Stragglers were still coming through.

After five minutes had passed since the last man appeared from the mesquite trail, General Kearny and Carson moved toward the center of the clearing, still talking. They stopped abruptly when they saw a dragoon appear from the thicket, stumble, then walk with a determined stride straight toward the General.

It was Corporal Jackson. The scattered troopers, who had begun moving toward Kearny, stopped in their tracks and fell silent, watching Jackson. When he came up to the General, he talked animatedly, in spite of his obvious fatigue, gesturing occasionally toward the back trail. John Henry strained to hear but he could make out nothing.

After two minutes of talk, the corporal stepped back, and Kearny moved alone a few steps forward. The men moved closer and formed a loose semi-circle in front of him. The officers moved up behind Kearny.

"Men, I want to tell you all we know about the situation

and give you some idea of the night's work. Some of you have seen the trail ahead and the rest of you have no doubt heard about it by now.

"There is evidence of the passage of a large number of horses and mules, perhaps as many as a thousand." A murmur arose and men glanced nervously at each other.

"All right, all right," the General said, with his hand upraised. The talking stopped immediately. "Now, Corporal Jackson has just come in and told us that he saw two Indians off the trail about five miles back. This could mean that the tracks up ahead were made by a horse herd stolen by Indians in Sonora or California, and now they are trailing the herd to their homes. That's still a possibility.

"It seems more likely, however, that we have fallen onto a large Mexican force bound for California. We know that General Castro was commanding the Mexican army in California when the war broke out. We also know that he fled to Sonora. We think that he has recruited an army in Sonora and is now on his way back to California to try to recover it by force of arms.

"Carson believes that Castro is at the crossing of the Colorado, just ten miles below us here. He does not think it likely that they will have detected our presence. If they do, it may go badly for us. We are only one hundred ten men. We are too few to be attacked by such a large force.

"Therefore, I have decided that if we can locate their camp, we shall attack them. Tonight. We will have the advantage of surprise and, in the darkness, they will not know the size of our force.

"The future of California may lie in the hands of this little band." He swept the camp with his arm. "We will not falter. We will win."

The excitement of the men had risen with every word

and at the end were on the point of cheering but the General's raised hand was enough to remind them that they must be still. The Mexicans might be near.

"Ready your weapons and your equipment. Be as quiet as possible. No fires. We will keep you posted. Dismissed."

The men hurried to their packs. They pulled gear out, cleaned, oiled, sorted, repacked, preparing for this first battle of the campaign. They talked in hushed tones. Their fatigue was gone. The tension in the camp was almost audible.

John Henry sat quietly on the ground, rubbing his carbine mechanism and barrel slowly with an oiled cloth. His gear was packed and stowed. He had checked the carbine over thoroughly and lubricated it. He had drawn his full ammunition ration. He was ready for the baptism that he had prayed would not come but down deep expected. At least, as he looked around him, he was ready physically. Otherwise, he was still not sure.

As he sat pondering this, still rubbing the barrel absent-mindedly, he glanced up at the horizon to catch the end of day. The sun had just disappeared behind the sand hills and the sky was beginning to color. No matter how tired in body and spirit, no matter how much he hurt, he had always gloried in the desert sunsets. If anything could convince him that God existed and had a hand in things, it was desert sunsets.

As he watched, the silver and pink at the horizon began to form layers. Then the layers broke into pastel shades and thin dark slivers of colors.

A movement caught his eye. He sat up. *There it is again!* He watched as the movement enlarged and became a horseman at the crest of a sand butte not two hundred yards away.

He reached over and touched Brad's arm. When Brad turned toward him, he pointed at the figure, noticing at the same time that other dragoons were looking at the butte. The horseman's features could not be made out but silhouetted against the bright sunset, the sombrero and the serape waving in a light breeze were unmistakable.

What a magnificent sight! John Henry shivered. The figure, man and horse, remained perfectly still for a minute then whirled suddenly, the serape catching the wind, and they were gone.

"So much for the Indian horse herd theory," Brad said, still looking at the butte.

"Yes . . . What?" John Henry felt himself being pulled back and turned to face Brad. "Why do you say that?"

"That was a Mex scout for sure. Now they've spotted us. There's gonna be hell to pay."

John Henry returned to his polishing. He had not thought about that. Strange. From the first sight of the stranger, he had not thought: "Enemy."

The dramatic appearance of the horseman had conjured up memories of stories he had read, about lonely heroes and brave deeds, dreamy romantic stories that had always transported him to another time and another place, far from the Missouri farm. Now the story had materialized as: "Enemy."

"Harris! Bradford!" They turned sharply to see Corporal Jackson striding rapidly toward them. "Be ready to ride in five minutes!"

"Ride? Ride what? Where?" Brad called after him as he passed.

"Your mounts will be ready in five minutes, right where you're standing! See that you're ready!" he threw over his shoulder and was gone.

"Hell, corporal, I'm ready now," Brad said aloud but to himself. He still looked at Jackson, striding away.

Brad turned to John Henry, "I wonder what this is all about. Probably a patrol. Jackson's not rousing the whole camp. It appears, John Henry, that we have been selected once again because of our strong bodies and quick wit." John Henry smiled in spite of himself.

"On the other hand," Brad said, "it might be just because we happened to be standing in Jackson's line of sight. Hell, I don't care, I'm delighted. Maybe the General wants us to capture old Castro and the devil take the greasers that get in our way." He grinned at John Henry, then sobered when he saw that John Henry, his jaw clenched, peered off into the distance.

"I'm sorry, Johnny. I know how you feel about all this. But you have to admit that the boys don't agree with you. We joined the army to do our duty and to have some fun. So did you. That's what you told me back at Fort Leavenworth. Remember? You've changed. We haven't. I've tried to accept how you feel, and I'm sorry when I forget. I hope you'll accept how we feel. I'm not saying which is better, just that we have to understand each other and accept the difference."

John Henry looked aside. Leavenworth. It seemed a hundred years and a million miles away.

Everything had seemed so simple at Leavenworth.

He sat his horse quietly. The animal seemed to sense that this was no ordinary parade and was skittish but John Henry held him in check with little difficulty. His grim expression was matched by that of the soldiers on either side of him.

The line of horsemen undulated continuously but always reformed smartly. Other units of cavalry and light artillery were positioned in front of and behind John Henry's line. Waiting. The troopers were boot-to-boot and tense.

It was strangely quiet. John Henry had never seen it so quiet on parade. Nor had he ever seen so many people at the fort. Family, friends, well-wishers and idlers, all had arrived the last few days to say their goodbyes and Godspeeds and to enjoy the wonderful spectacle of men under arms. Now all the speeches had been made and the banners and flags presented. The crowd of men, women, and children stood motionless at the edges of the field, waiting for the start.

The only movement was that of the restless animals and flags that fluttered gently in the light breeze. The squeak of saddle leather and the metallic clink of sabers and horse gear were the only sounds.

John Henry's mother and father had not come. They had wanted to come and said so in their last letter but they simply could not be away from the farm the two weeks it would take to make the trip. There were no other hands at home now that John Henry was gone.

John Henry turned his head slightly to his left and studied the faces of the spectators at the perimeter of the field. He re-read the letter in his mind, the last contact he would have with his parents for months, perhaps years. Perhaps ever.

The band struck up "Yankee Doodle." Tension began to build. The horses became restless. Spectators shifted and moved to get a better view. John Henry had not permitted himself to think much about this moment, the leaving. It was to be just another day, another patrol.

The reality now struck him. He was part of an army

that was about to set out to march a thousand miles across the prairie, not just to see a foreign country, but to attack it and seize its territory. This Missouri farm boy had come some distance.

The breeze quickened. Guidons and flags whipped in the wind, and the stirring music increased in volume. John Henry raised himself slightly in his stirrups, eased back and sat stiffly. He shifted his hold on the reins.

He was ready. You've got the best gear in the world, his sergeant had repeatedly told them. His heavy saber, U.S. Model 1840—"old wristbreaker," they called it—was the dragoon's principal weapon. And it was a beauty, with a heavy, white leather knot and a blade of polished steel.

His platoon had only recently been issued the new percussion .54 caliber pistols to replace the old standby flintlocks. The dragoons were fortunate to have had some instruction from a manufacturer's representative in their use since the manuals still said nothing about their handling.

There were rumors that the army was considering the adoption of a pistol that had a revolving cylinder and would fire a number of times without reloading but Fort Leavenworth had seen nothing of that wonder.

The regiment's carbine was the latest Hall breech-loader, also a .54 caliber. Unlike his comrades, John Henry preferred the carbine to the other weapons. He had spent considerable time at target practice, sharpening his eye and adjusting the trigger pull to a light touch.

John Henry knew he made a fine figure this day. He was well mounted and he was satisfied with his horse equipment. Some of the recent recruits had hoped that the new Grimsley saddle would be issued before the regiment went out but he was as superstitious as the old hands and was happy to stay with the Ringgold.

His greatcoat was tied to the pommel, and he expected it to stay there during this march. The two cartridge boxes on his saber belt held twelve pistol rounds and thirty carbine rounds. He wore blue wool pantaloons and a shirt of gray wool flannel. He had taken care that his uniform was crisp and clean.

His hat was low-crowned and broad-brimmed. His carbine dangled from a wide white leather sling across his left shoulder. He was prepared to impress Mexicans, renegade Indians, or the admiring public.

"ATTENS-HUT!" He started at the shouted command and involuntarily pulled his horse half out of line before regaining position.

Colonel Kearny and his staff and the engineers rode in front of the line of guests. The colonel, riding tall and straight on his fine bay, waved to his wife and children who stood on the steps of his quarters.

Colonel Stephen Watts Kearny was well known for his service on the frontier and was almost universally admired. He was a competent leader, respected by both officers and men. He was known to be kind and polite, a firm disciplinarian, but fair. In short, he was both a gentleman and a soldier of the first rank.

Physically, he was impressive. He stood five feet, ten inches tall and was ruggedly handsome. His blue eyes could flare fiercely when he was angry but he was rarely angry. Generally, his manner was mild, and he was a most pleasant conversationalist.

The light artillery with its polished twelve-pound bronze mountain howitzers moved noisily into line. Last was John Henry's detachment of First Dragoons. Guidons snapped and the crowd cheered, and the band played "The Girl I Left Behind Me".

John Henry turned toward Brad, who rode at his side, to share the glorious moment, but his comrade sat ramrod stiff with eyes ahead.

"It's been a long time since Leavenworth, Brad. That was in another world. . . Look! Here come our mounts. Look at this! We're getting the staff's mules! This must be important." Brad was wide-eyed and grinning.

"Choose your mounts and stand by." Corporal Jackson held the reins of his mule while the dozen dragoons took the reins from the soldiers who had led the animals from the corral.

"What's 'is all about, Corporal?" John Henry turned to see Russell behind him. Russell winked at him. The low murmur of conversation stopped abruptly.

"We'll know soon enough," Jackson replied, looking past the group into the gloom from where he had emerged minutes before. John Henry turned to look in the same direction and saw nothing. It was almost dark. The conversation began again.

"Just as I thought," Russell said softly to John Henry. Russell had moved up noiselessly beside him and now leaned toward him, conspiratorially. "He don't know as much as I do about what's goin' on. In fact, my mule knows more'n he does." He smiled and winked again.

"Sure, Russell." John Henry returned his smile and turned his attention back to Corporal Jackson. Jackson was still looking into the darkness.

"Your mule?" Brad had been listening to Russell and now moved over beside him. "I thought you said your mule was with the cannon."

"So I did." Russell turned his fixed grin on Brad. And waited.

"All right, dammit, Russell. I grant you know something I don't. Now, out with it."

"All right, since you ask so politely," Russell said. "I was back at the latrine when I heard the cannons comin' in. I followed 'em in and talked with one of Hammond's boys. A ways back up the trail, they saw a big fire on th' north side of th' Gila, 'bout five miles away. Hammond hustled right over to th' General soon as he got in. I figure Hammond's news on top of that greaser we saw on th' hill decided th' General to send out 'is patrol."

"All right, quiet now," Jackson said softly. Lieutenant Emory walked briskly past the group and stopped beside the corporal.

"Are we ready to ride, corporal?"

"Yes, sir."

Emory turned to the waiting soldiers. "You men know by now that the enemy is about. At least, we think there is a sizable force quite near us. You heard the General say that if we can find them, we plan to attack. Well, we are going to find the enemy camp." John Henry wished he had half of Emory's confidence.

Emory turned to Jackson. "Let's go, then." Emory took the reins of his mule from the soldier who had followed him from General Kearny's tent. "Ride as quietly as possible. We want to find them. We do not want them to find us." Emory swung into the saddle.

"Mount!" Corporal Jackson said, with a fraction of the energy he would have spent had he not suspected that the enemy might be waiting in the nearest mesquite thicket.

The soldiers mounted and fell into a column of twos behind Emory and Jackson. The darkness that followed dusk had given way to bright moonlight and the leaders found their way, without difficulty, through the scattered creosote bushes. Scrubby mesquite and ironwood trees were black shapes and the sand hills, formless silhouettes.

Ominous, John Henry thought. *And cold.* But the ride was almost pleasant after the heat and footslogging of the day. Even the weary mules had revived in the cool night air.

No more than a half mile from camp, Emory reined in. Corporal Jackson dismounted and knelt to examine the ground. The two leaders had been riding about fifteen feet ahead of the group and their hushed conversation was inaudible. Jackson remounted and rode back until he was in the middle of the patrol.

"We're crossing here. We've cut the trail of the Mexicans and this must be where they crossed. It appears to be a ford. It's wide here and should be a slack current. It's probably not swimming but take care. Single file. Stay in line."

Jackson turned and rejoined Emory. A word to the Lieutenant and Jackson moved ahead. Emory fell in behind him and the column moved toward the river.

The line of animals entered the water, nose to tail. *Not too bad. Hardly up to the mule's belly, and he doesn't seem to mind. Must be a hundred and fifty yards wide. Thank goodness, we're not crossing at high water.* Soft moonlight sparkled on the water and highlighted the dimples produced by the wading mules.

John Henry turned to look at Brad who was just behind him. Brad seemed to be studying the water in front of his mule, moving his head from side to side at each step.

John Henry smiled. He remembered that Brad had told him with no shame that he had a deathly fear of any water whose bottom he could not see. He wanted to say something to Brad to reassure him but he did not dare.

John Henry faced front and squeezed his knees to catch up with the rider ahead.

"Oof!" John Henry whipped around to see Brad's terrified face. His mule had stepped into a hole and water lapped at Brad's knees.

"Johnny!" Brad said softly, stifling a yell. He had hardly called when his mule stepped from the hole and found solid footing on the ford.

"Whoo," Brad said, exhaling. He grinned. "You okay, John Henry?" John Henry smiled and faced front.

On the opposite bank, the party regrouped where Jackson was kneeling, feeling the ground. Emory was standing beside him. A heavy cloudbank had drifted across the moon and it was dark again. John Henry, still mounted, was close by.

Jackson stood up and looked westward, downstream. "I can't say for sure, the ground's like rock here, but I'd say the trail cuts down here along the bank."

"Lead off, corporal," Emory said. Both mounted and the Lieutenant fell in behind Jackson.

"Single file!" Jackson threw back softly to the dragoons.

The line moved slowly along a mostly open bench near the river's edge, brushing in the dark against the sparse cover of creosote bushes and low bur sage. After ten minutes at this cautious pace, the land seemed to close around them.

The sand buttes and low ridges, dimly outlined against a sky that was beginning to show some cold stars, lay nearer the trail, and the mesquite grew thicker, forcing the troopers to push their mounts through the prickly branches that tore at clothing and flesh.

John Henry leaned right and left to avoid the branches that reached out for him. When the foliage choked the trail, he raised a hand to avoid a slashed cheek. He began to think that they surely would have to turn around and retrace their path.

Then a branch that he had raised his arm to ward off brushed him so lightly that he touched it with his hand and let the leaves run through his open fist. *Willow. Must be a slough nearby.*

"Harris, is that you?" Emory asked, hardly more than a whisper. John Henry had not realized in the darkness that he was riding directly behind the Lieutenant.

"Yes, sir."

"Pull up here. I'm going to test your tree-climbing."

John Henry reined in beside Emory.

"Corporal Jackson has just told me that up ahead there are some willows that appear to be taller than anything else around here. We're getting nowhere in this brush. Find the heaviest tree you can and shinny up it. See what you can see."

"Yes, sir, which way?"

"Corporal!" Emory called softly.

"This way, Harris," Jackson said. The voice came from the gloom ahead. "Leave your mule and come straight on."

John Henry dismounted and walked back to Brad. He handed his reins to him. "Hold my mule, Brad. I'm going after a possum."

"You're gonna what?"

"Just hold my mule." *That'll give him something to think about.* John Henry smiled to himself as he walked past Emory. He had been puzzled at first at Emory's comment about tree-climbing until he remembered telling Emory during one of their exploring forays weeks ago that he had been one of the best tree-climbers on possum hunts at home before he had given up the sport.

John Henry moved from tree to tree, feeling the trunks.

Selecting a willow that seemed larger than the others, he climbed the trunk until he cleared the tops of the adjacent trees. The moon shone through a thin cloud cover and dimly illuminated the treetops.

He strained to see. The line of the ridge was faintly outlined. Beyond the willow grove, scattered mesquite trees were black shadows on a gray landscape. He saw nothing more. No fires, no movement. He leaned back in the crotch of a branch and relaxed.

How peaceful it was. Clean, soft, cold, sterile, and peaceful. And lonely. *What would it be like, to be alone in the world? I'd like that, for a time at least, to sort things out. As long as I knew that I wasn't completely alone. I don't think I could handle the solitude unless I knew that Morita was waiting.*

It can't be long now. We're almost on the Colorado. California is on the other side and the coast is only a few days' march. I do dearly hope that the war is over. I hope we find only a bunch of thieving Indians here. Then, they won't need me. I'll get back to Santa Fé somehow.

Maybe Carson will finally persuade Kearny to let him go. If he does, maybe I can be detached to go with him. I can carry dispatches. Kearny will have a cartload of messages to go to the rest of the army in New Mexico and to Washington.

What if I'm sent to Washington? I'd have only one night with Morita. Or what if I'm sent by the northern route? I wouldn't see her at all. It would be months before I could get back to Santa Fé, maybe not even until the end of my enlistment. That wouldn't do. I'm going to have to . . .

What was that? He sat upright sharply and listened, turning his face slightly away from the direction of the wind. *Was it my imagination? I could have sworn . . . there it is again! Horses neighing!* He was looking due north.

Again! The light breeze brushed his face. *And louder this time! Many horses! Unmistakable!*

He moved rapidly down the tree, stepping quickly from branch to branch, slipping, sliding, losing his foothold on the lowest branch and falling the last six feet to the ground.

"For God's sake, Harris, what's got into you? I thought you'd gone to sleep up there. I was about to send somebody up after you! Quiet now, did you see anything?" John Henry had fallen almost on top of Emory.

"No sir, yes sir, lots of horses!" John Henry gasped.

"What are you talking about? Did you see the fires?"

"No! But there are plenty of horses! I heard them neighing and they must cover a lot of ground! They're there, all right, right where Lieutenant Hammond said they were!"

"No fires. Strange. Well, let's have a look. Harris, lead off." Emory turned to the others who had bunched up behind them. "Single file. No noise." Emory motioned Harris ahead.

John Henry moved off on foot. Emory and Corporal Jackson followed, still mounted. The patrol fell in behind.

John Henry pushed deeper into the willow thicket. After about ten minutes of hard going, pushing branches aside, backing, and going around, the cover opened slightly.

Presently, John Henry straightened. *Neighing!* He turned toward Emory.

"Yes, I heard them," Emory whispered. "Go on."

The heavy willow stand gave way to scattered palo verde and ironwood. Now the neighing was occasionally punctuated by the sound of horses' hoofs on hard ground. Following this sound, John Henry led the column around the point of a ridge.

A bright fire blazed about a hundred yards ahead, softly illuminating the hillside and casting dancing shadows along the base.

CHAPTER 8

"Softly now," said Emory. "Corporal, leave the animals here. We'll move up a bit for a better look."

Jackson pointed to two men and then pointed to the mules. The other dragoons fell in behind Emory and the corporal.

They crept almost to the edge of the circle of light. There were no horses to be seen. A vaquero stood alone before the fire. He cradled a carbine in his arm.

Emory held up his arm. The line of dragoons stopped. "Londeau, Martínez, you come with me. We're going ahead. The rest of you stay here. Look lively!" he whispered. "If I signal, corporal, bring the men up quickly but as quietly as possible. The fire will be beyond me, so you'll be able to see me. Watch carefully. If you can see me, so can they."

The three men moved up, crouching, staying in the shadow. John Henry had wondered at first why Emory had singled out Martínez and Londeau, but as the two men moved past him, he knew the answer. They were members of Emory's topographical party. They were not soldiers and therefore not in uniform.

John Henry's guess was shortly confirmed. When only about thirty yards from the fire, the three disappeared into the shadow of a house-size boulder. Presently Londeau and Martínez emerged from the shadow, walking nonchalantly toward the fire.

The startled guard stepped backward almost into the fire. He brought his carbine up and took a step toward the intruders.

Martínez and Londeau walked to the fire and warmed themselves. The guard watched them. Martínez apparently was talking with the Mexican now, gesturing with his hands. The guard lowered the carbine and cradled it in his arm.

Two figures stepped from the darkness on the far side of the fire and stood there, ten feet from the fire, watching.

"Let's go!" Jackson whispered. "Off to the left, stay in the shadow." John Henry had seen Emory's wave just before Jackson ordered the advance. The dragoons crouched and ran noiselessly to the Lieutenant's hiding place.

"Harris, Bradford!" Emory said quietly. "Move up behind our men. Don't start anything. I don't want to scatter the Mexicans. I want to find out what's going on here. Go!"

John Henry and Brad stood upright in the shadow and walked boldly out of its protection and toward the fire. They carried their carbines loosely cradled in their arms.

John Henry's mind raced. *Is this the way it happens? This is what the army says all the training is for. Discipline. The Lieutenant says, "Go," and you go. You don't think about it, you don't weigh reasons or consequences, you just do it.*

The vaquero at the fire straightened when he saw them. He did not bring his carbine up. He shot a glance at Londeau and Martínez and then looked nervously over his shoulder at the other two men.

At once, two more Mexicans stepped into the light. One was a tall, craggy man, better dressed than the others. The man who had advanced with him stood slightly behind and the other two vaqueros stepped aside when he appeared.

John Henry and Brad arrived at the fire. They warmed their hands.

Hardly had the two Mexicans appeared when John Henry heard a step behind him. Without looking back, he knew that two more dragoons had moved into the firelight.

"*Quiénes son ustedes? Qué quieren? Qué uniforme es ese?*" It was the tall man speaking.

Martínez replied so rapidly in Spanish that John Henry understood not a word. The Mexicans listened without taking their eyes from Martínez.

"*Arrímense a la lumbre,*" said the tall man. "*Hace mucho frío. Un café caliente?*" He pointed toward the huge coffee pot in the embers at the edge of the fire.

The tension eased as if a spring wire had been released. Martínez talked animatedly with the vaqueros. Weapons were lowered and some were placed on the ground on saddles and blankets.

Lieutenant Emory and the rest of his party moved out of the shadow and walked to the fire. Three more Mexicans appeared. They went to the fire and warmed their hands. They were not armed.

Emory sipped the weak coffee that one of the Mexicans gave him. He stood beside Martínez.

"What did you learn, Martínez?"

"He," Martínez nodded his head toward the tall man, "he says he is a poor man, says he works for some rich men in Sonora. Says he got these horses in California. He is taking them to Sonora for his employers to sell."

"Do you believe him?"

"Sir, he is no *peón*."

"Right. How many horses do they have?"

"About five hundred." Martínez threw a quick sideways glance at Emory.

"I suppose they know who we are by now but explain it to them so there will be no misunderstanding. Tell the tall man—he seems to be in charge—that I want him and his three top men to go with me to our camp. I intend to leave a guard here to prevent anyone leaving until we're ready to let them go. The herd is to be kept under close guard. Be sure he understands."

John Henry stood nearby and heard Emory's instructions and now watched the faces of the Mexicans as Martínez addressed the tall man. The vaqueros looked nervously at each other and talked softly.

When Martínez was finished, the tall man turned and spoke to the men standing near him. Three stepped forward to stand beside the leader.

"There are your men, sir," Martínez said to Emory.

"All right. Tell him we will ride in five minutes." Then Emory turned to face the dragoons who had bunched up near the fire.

"Do any of you speak any Spanish?" Emory said.

"John Henry speaks Mex, Lieutenant," Brad said. John Henry's jaw tightened and he turned to look at Brad, but Brad, sober-faced, was looking with studied concentration at Emory.

"Harris?" said Emory.

"Well . . . I speak a little, Lieutenant. But I'm sure there must be—"

"Good," Emory said. "You six men," Emory motioned with his hand, "stay with Harris. You are to guard this camp. You are to be sure no one leaves—there will be six Mexicans here after we leave—and be sure the herd is kept quiet and close in. I expect we will be finding a few mounts from among them tomorrow." He smiled. "We, or somebody, will be returning either tonight or tomorrow morning. Is everything understood?"

The soldiers nodded.

"Harris, you are in charge." Emory turned to walk away from the fire. He motioned to Martínez and the Mexicans to follow. The dragoons fell in behind.

John Henry caught Brad's arm as he passed. "Damn you, Brad, why did you do that?"

Brad showed mock surprise. "Did what, Johnny? Oh, that. You're so modest, I knew you'd never volunteer, so I decided I'd just have to look out for you. You got to seize your opportunity in this man's army if you expect to get ahead. It's your first command, Johnny! Hell, I'm proud of you!" With this, Brad straightened and marched off quickly to catch up with the others.

"I'll get you for this, Bradford!" John Henry called softly after him.

The last of Emory's party stepped into the darkness. John Henry watched another moment, then turned to face the dragoons. They stood where they had stood, watching him. He searched their faces. He recognized all of them but he did not really know any of them. They were about his age, or younger. They did not move. They just watched him.

My God! John Henry started. *They're waiting for orders! What in hell do I do now? I don't want this . . . no part of it.*

The dragoons waited. They did not tease or laugh. They did not seem to sense his terror. They seemed not to comprehend anything unusual. They simply awaited orders. Discipline.

I . . . I suppose we should do something to show the Mexicans that we are in control. . . . Let's see. How many Mexicans did the Lieutenant say would be left here? Six, it was.

There were four vaqueros at the fire. Waiting. The terror rose again in him, and he fought for control. He addressed the dragoons who had pulled together into a tight knot.

"There's supposed to be six Mexicans here. Has anyone seen the other two?" The dragoons shook their heads.

John Henry turned to the Mexicans. "*Dos vaqueros,*" he said, "*dónde?*" Two vaqueros, where?

The vaqueros looked at each other. "*Aquí estamos todos, señor,*" we are all here, señor, one replied, with a sweep of his arm that included the four. The man speaking was older than the others, graying at the temples. John Henry had noticed that the young vaqueros had deferred to him after the departure of their comrades with Emory.

"No, señor," John Henry said, "I mean . . ." He closed his eyes and searched for the word. "I mean, *dos otros vaqueros,*" two other vaqueros.

The men looked at each other again. They're nervous, John Henry observed. "*Dónde?*" Where? He raised his carbine and cradled it in his left arm with his right hand at the trigger guard. He took a step toward them. "*Pronto!*" Quickly!

"*Bueno, bueno, señor. No se moleste. Allá; están atrás,*" said gray hair, quietly, motioning over his shoulder toward the darkness.

John Henry did not understand the words but he realized now that there were at least two men—enemies?—somewhere beyond the firelight.

"*Usted . . . dice . . . dos hombres . . . vengan*." You . . . tell . . . two men . . . come, John Henry said, haltingly, pointing to the ground at his feet.

"*No, señor, no pueden venir*," gray hair said. The reply was firm and without hesitation.

John Henry gripped his carbine firmly and rested his finger on the trigger. He did not understand all the Mexican said, but the "no" was clear enough.

"Be on your guard," he said softly to the dragoons, without taking his eyes from the four vaqueros. "There are two more men around here somewhere and we don't know what they're up to. This man has just told me that they won't come in. Spread out a bit to my left and right. Don't bunch up."

He marveled that he was actually preparing his troops for battle. He was actually doing this. But he marveled more that he had actually communicated with the Mexican. It was the first time he had communicated, after Morita and her friends at the cantina, with someone who spoke no English and he smiled inwardly.

The soldiers moved away from each other, their carbines at the ready, glancing right and left into the darkness, and squinting through the flames at the vaqueros.

"*Señor, todo está bien, no hay problema*," gray hair said. "*No queremos dificultades. Ellos no pueden venir pa' aca, pero nosotros podemos ir pa' allá*." The vaquero took a couple of steps backward and motioned for John Henry to follow.

"*Jefe, venga conmigo. Está bien. Le doy mi palabra*." Gray hair motioned again for John Henry to come.

"He wants me to go with him. I don't know what's going on," John Henry said to the dragoons. "Watch these three. If I'm not back in ten minutes . . . shoot them." He walked around the fire and followed gray hair into the darkness.

John Henry stumbled along, colliding with creosote bushes until his eyes adjusted to the darkness, then he picked his way easily through the brush, softly outlined by moonlight. They had not walked a minute when a dim light appeared ahead. They were almost on the tent before John Henry saw it. The light was a bright spot on the thin material.

"*Un momento, señor.*" Gray hair opened the flap and disappeared inside. John Henry heard an exchange between two men, spoken softly. After an interval of silence, the flap opened. "*Entre, señor.*"

John Henry stooped and stepped inside. The sloping sides of the tent prevented his standing erect, so he stood, bent, beside gray hair. The interior was lighted by a candle lantern hanging from the peak rope.

Sitting on the floor at the old vaquero's feet was a young man of seventeen or eighteen years. He looked anxiously at John Henry. The candlelight made dark shadows of the furrows in his brow. He's terrified, thought John Henry.

Then John Henry heard a sound, like a muffled cry, whether from inside or outside the tent, he could not tell.

"*Qué?*" What? he asked gray hair. Gray hair looked down at the boy who leaned back to reveal the face of the girl who lay on the ground behind him.

John Henry started. He had seen the blankets but had not dreamed that the mound under them was anything but more blankets. The girl looked at John Henry. The candlelight was reflected in her eyes, and her wet cheeks glistened. She was a pretty little girl, no more than fifteen or sixteen years old, John Henry guessed. What's happening here?

At that moment, the girl cried out and gripped the boy's hand tightly. She moaned softly, and the tears rolled down her cheeks.

"*Qué?*" John Henry said again to gray hair.

"*Ella va a dar luz,*" he replied. "*No la deberíamos haber traído. Va a ser muy dura para ella. Tengo miedo que vaya a tener complicaciones.*"

"*No comprendo,*" I don't understand, said John Henry.

"*Niño, bebé,*" he replied with emphasis, turning to John Henry and gesturing with his hand to draw a full belly over his own ample paunch.

Oh, my God! She's going to have a baby! "Now?" he said. He searched for the word. "*Ahora?*"

"*Sí, señor. Creo que ahora!*" Yes, señor. Now, I think so, he replied, nodding his head. He did not take his eyes from her. "*Ella es mi hija, mi única y adorable hija.*" He turned to face John Henry. "*Comprende usted, señor, mi hija?*"

"*Sí, comprendo,*" John Henry replied softly, "*su hija.*" Yes, I understand, your daughter.

"*Tenemos miedo. No sabemos nada de esas cosas. Podría ayudarnos, señor?*"

John Henry understood only one word, "*Ayudar,*" help. Help? Me?

Now what, John Henry Harris? I can get out of this mess just by walking away. But I probably do know more about what's going on than these stupid men. Why in the hell would they bring along a woman whose time had almost come on such a hard journey? No, not a woman, she's just a child herself. And this has to be her first baby.

Maybe I can do something. I've helped birth a few calves and foals and watched the midwife deliver a couple of cousins when Mother and I went to help out.

He remembered how his father had been shocked the

first time when he learned that John Henry had been permitted to watch.

A man is what he has experienced, his mother had said and his father had agreed, remembering that he had said the same thing himself more than once. His father had raised no protest the second time.

The girl gasped, uttered a sharp cry, and clung to her husband's arm with both hands. The distraught boy held her tightly.

"*Puede ayudarla, señor?*" The boy was trembling.

John Henry drew a long breath and exhaled slowly. "*Sí. Yo trato.*" Yes. I try.

A distant shot rang out. John Henry's head came up sharply.

"Oh, my God!"

John Henry ran from the tent, tripping on a guy rope. He scrambled up and ran headlong toward the campfire, stumbling and crashing into and through creosote bushes, kicking up sprays of sand at every step.

"No! Stop! Don't shoot! Stop!"

He arrived at the campfire, gasping for breath. The dragoons stood in a ragged line at the campfire, carbines at the ready.

A vaquero lay on the ground on the opposite side of the fire. Two other Mexicans knelt beside him.

John Henry ran to place himself in front of the vaqueros. "Don't shoot! I'm okay! I forgot!" John Henry ran around the campfire and bent over the downed vaquero. The Mexican's eyes fluttered open.

"He's alive." John Henry looked up at the vaqueros. "*Está bien. Un error. Ayudar su amigo.*" It's okay. Mistake. Help your friend. John Henry pointed at the wounded vaquero.

John Henry turned to the dragoons.

"Put your carbines down!" The soldiers obeyed and breathed easier. "I'm going back. I'll explain later. Do what you can for him." John Henry ran into the darkness.

First light. John Henry sat cross-legged by the fire, sipping the hot, bitter coffee. Old gray hair sat across the fire, smoking his pipe and staring into the flames. Three vaqueros slept nearby, rolled in their blankets. Two others watched the herd. They had just relieved the lone vaquero who had been with the herd when John Henry had tried earlier to take a count of his charges. He marveled at his innocence.

John Henry stared into the campfire, studying the embers and tongues of flame as they rose, colored, waved and vanished.

How long ago was it that we came into this camp? Seems like days.

I thank the good Lord that it was a normal birth. Normal, he smiled thinly, meaning that she hurt terribly, but that she will heal, and the baby is fine, and everything will be all right. When he and gray hair had returned to the campfire and gray hair told the vaqueros what had happened, they had shaken John Henry's hand and smiled and slapped his back.

John Henry looked behind him at the soldiers, sound asleep in their borrowed blankets. He remembered with wonder and shook his head at the instruction he had given them as he walked away from this same fire only a few hours before.

Stupid! Stupid! What could have possessed me? My first command! Brad's words. God have mercy.

He looked across the fire at gray hair, still pulling slowly at his pipe and studying the flames, and at the sleeping vaqueros. He thought of the exhausted girl, holding her baby at her breast, and her husband, almost a man, tears in his eyes. *These are not my enemies.*

John Henry glanced past gray hair to the thin silver line at the eastern horizon. He looked up. Cloud edges showed a hint of color and he fancied that he could see a million miles. He stood up and stretched.

What a day! What a country!

CHAPTER 9

"Everything under control, Harris?" Lieutenant Emory and his party had just ridden into camp.

"Yes, sir," John Henry said. "Everything's peaceful." He noticed Emory glancing about the camp at the sleeping soldiers. "I told them they could catch a little sleep, Lieutenant. No sense in all of us staying up to watch one man."

The vaquero was pulling apart a brittle length of mesquite and tossing the pieces on the flames, scattering sparks that rose and danced in the breeze.

"All right, rouse your guard, Harris. We'll get them to camp and I'll leave this party here to relieve them." Emory turned to Corporal Jackson. "Take Harris's men back to camp and report to the General that this camp is secure and that the night passed without occurrence." Jackson started to leave.

"Lieutenant Emory, there is this one thing," John Henry said. Emory turned and looked over his shoulder at John Henry. Jackson stopped.

"Yes?"

"You remember last night we counted six Mexicans here?"

"That's right."

"There's more we didn't know about. I helped birth a baby girl last night."

Emory's jaw dropped. "You what?"

John Henry grinned from ear to ear. "Yes, sir! I helped birth a baby last night!"

"Be damned! You do have hidden talents, Harris."

"The mother's no more than a girl herself. They had no sense in bringing her along on a trip like this. She could have died. Thank goodness, there were no problems. She might have been able to handle it but I'm not sure I would."

"She's all right now? And the baby?"

"They both seem to be fine. The tent's just a ways over there." He pointed. "I walked that way just before you came in, and I didn't hear anything from the tent. Her husband's with her. He's not much older than she is."

Emory turned to speak to Corporal Jackson.

"There's one more thing," said John Henry. He told Emory about the events that led to the wounding of the vaquero. "It was my fault. It was dumb. It was on my orders. I was at the drovers' camp too long. My fault. He seems to be okay. He's over at the drovers' camp now."

Emory frowned. "Harris, you do break the routine."

Emory turned to Jackson. "After you report to the General, talk to Major Swords and see what he can come up with for the woman and her baby. And ask Dr. Griffin for some field dressings. Send the stuff back with the next unit that comes this way."

"Yes, sir." Corporal Jackson saluted and walked to his mule. Emory turned back to John Henry.

"Sir, I'm really sorry."

"Harris, you don't apologize for command mistakes. You note mistakes, remember them, and file them away.

Mistakes are building blocks, just like successes."

"Yes, sir. Thank you, sir."

John Henry's guard were on their feet now, stretching and yawning, running fingers through tangled hair and tucking shirts in trousers.

John Henry and the dragoons walked over to the mules where the incoming guard had tied reins to mesquite branches. John Henry slipped the muzzle of his carbine into the saddle bucket and snapped it to the sling. He checked the cinch.

"Harris." John Henry turned. It was Emory. "Stay with me. I may need to send a message to camp."

"Yes, sir," John Henry said. He stood beside the mule, waiting.

Corporal Jackson mounted and moved off. The guard fell in behind him in a column of twos. John Henry watched them go. In a minute, they rounded the ridge.

John Henry walked back to the fire. The new guard stood and squatted around it. Emory stood near the fire, chatting with Lieutenant Warner and Mr. Stanley, both members of his topographical party. Emory gestured with his hands, pointing occasionally to the west and south. John Henry could not hear the exchange.

Three vaqueros walked to the fire and warmed their hands. John Henry waved a greeting to gray hair who smiled and returned his wave. John Henry walked around the fire and spoke to the vaquero whose shoulder was bandaged.

"*Lo siento, amigo. Un error. Un mal error.*" I'm sorry, amigo. A mistake. A bad mistake.

"*Está bien*," the vaquero said. "*No importa.*" It's okay. It's not important.

John Henry nodded and smiled. He turned and warmed

his hands, staring into the fire.

"Let's go," Emory said, loud enough for all around the fire to hear. He pulled on his gloves and began walking toward the mules. Stanley, Warner, and Martínez followed. John Henry hurried around the fire and joined them. The five mounted and set out on the back trail. John Henry and Martínez fell in behind the other three.

"*Dónde?*" Where? John Henry asked Martínez.

"*Quién sabe?*" he replied. Who knows?

Crossing the ford on the Gila, Emory led the party westward. They followed a faint trail along the south bank of the river. The sky had darkened and rain threatened. A brisk, cold north wind had come up. The men hunched their shoulders and pulled their coats about their necks.

The river entered a canyon with steep walls and the trail left the river. The track ran through a flat that was so sterile that it might have been a thousand miles from water.

After about a mile on the flat, Emory turned his mount to begin a gradual ascent of a cut in the canyon wall. The others fell into single file behind.

Ten minutes later, they reached the top, and Emory disappeared over the rim. The two other officers then cleared the rim.

John Henry heard a sharp shout from above. It was Emory. Then two other cries, these from Warner and Stanley. John Henry and Martínez kicked their exhausted mounts up the trail and over the rim.

John Henry gasped. There it was. The Colorado. These past weeks, he had wondered if he would ever see it. But there it was.

From their lofty vantage point, a granite butte about fifty feet above the plain, they looked out over the confluence of the two rivers. Along the eastern horizon, they saw the line of hills that lay along the north bank of the Gila. Northward, the Colorado was obscured by the rolling landscape but its course was marked by a cloud of sand blowing from its banks.

At the foot of the butte where they stood, the blue-green water of the Gila entered the brown Colorado almost at a right angle. The waters mingled and the clear Gila was lost in the silt-laden larger stream.

John Henry dismounted and stood holding his mule's reins, transfixed. The sharp wind whipped the bottom of his coat and pressed the trousers against his legs.

"Quite a sight," Emory said. He had walked over from the edge where the others stood, still talking.

"Yes, sir, it certainly is."

"Just think, Harris. Someday, this junction of these two great rivers," here he swept across the scene before them with a wave of his hand, "this is going to be the site of a great city. Steamboats will come up the Colorado at least this far. Small steamboats should make it as far as the Pima villages at high water and flat boats at all stages of water.

"This will be the commercial and shipping center for the whole region, once it is opened up. This country can't help but be a great mineral producer. And good stock country. It's got a future."

It would be exciting to be in at the beginning, John Henry thought to himself, *one of the pioneers to open up a country. But after the newness was gone and the country settled, would the memory be enough? It would be a new American town with no history. I'll take Santa Fé,* he decided and smiled.

John Henry noticed that Emory was watching him. "Are we crossing today, sir?" John Henry said.

"No, General Kearny ordered a day's layover for the animals to recoup and the men to rest." Emory looked eastward.

"We'd best be on our way. We've got to meet the hostlers at the Mexican herd tomorrow. We're going to pick enough fresh animals to get the command mounted. There's still rough going ahead and we want to be at full strength when we reach California. After all, we are escorting the new governor and we do want to impress our new American subjects," Emory said, smiling.

Emory turned toward the others. "Let's go," he shouted into the wind. The five mounted and began the descent from the butte, Emory in the lead.

They were halfway down the slope when John Henry shouted.

"Lieutenant Emory!"

Emory turned in his saddle to see John Henry pointing toward the plain. A rider about three hundred yards distant angled away from them at a slow lope. They caught glimpses of him as he passed through stands of mesquite and ironwood. He wore a colorful serape that flapped in the wind.

Emory raised his arm and reined in sharply. The others stopped. Emory pointed at the rider. The party watched a moment, then Emory leaned toward Warner.

"One of ours?" Emory said.

"I don't think so. I haven't seen any of our Mexicans wearing a serape."

"I want to see what he's up to," said Emory.

He turned in his saddle. "Harris!" John Henry rode down and stopped beside Emory.

"I want you to intercept him. Head down that wash," Emory said, pointing to his left at a gully that appeared to parallel the rider's direction and about two hundred yards from it. "I don't think he'll hear you. He hasn't seen us, I think."

"Warner, you and Stanley move off that way." He pointed to the right in the direction of a mesquite thicket. "Pick up his trail and follow it. If he heads back on his trail, pick him up. I'm going to head down the middle straight for him. Martínez, you go with me."

"Okay?" Emory said to the four. They nodded. "All right, go!"

The riders began to make their way down the slope, gradually opening into a fan. At the bottom, Warner and Stanley set out at a fast walk. John Henry kicked his mule into a lope toward the wash. Just before dropping into it, he looked back toward the butte. Emory waved and he and Martínez moved off at a walk.

The bottom of the wash was loose sand and his mule was slowed to a walk. John Henry reined the mule to a narrow bench on the sloping side of the gully. Looks like a game trail, John Henry thought. At least, the footing will be better than the sand. He kicked the animal into a steady, easy lope.

After five minutes, John Henry realized what a predicament he was in. *How am I going to know when to get out of this wash? How do I know whether this thing is not running completely away from his track? We're probably heading in opposite directions by now.*

He glanced over his shoulder at the sun and over the other shoulder, looking for the butte, trying to get his directions. But he couldn't see it. The butte was hidden by the side of the wash and the mesquite trees on the edge above.

He decided that he would have to get out of the gully to

take a sighting on the butte. But the gully walls were too steep at this point to climb.

He looked ahead. About fifty yards away, there appeared to be a cut in the right bank that might be a way up. Before he reached the cut, the bench dropped back into the bottom and the mule slowed to a plodding gait in the deep sand.

He came up to the cut. It was just an erosion channel but it would do. He turned the mule into it and drummed his flanks with his heels. The head of the cut was so steep, the mule hesitated, but he had some momentum, so John Henry kicked him hard to get him over the top before he could stop. The mule responded and in two leaps burst over the rim and directly into the path of the Mexican rider.

The Mexican was not ten feet away when the apparition exploded from the earth into his path. He uttered a sharp cry as his terrified horse shied, almost unseating him. He grabbed the saddle horn and instinctively pulled back on the reins.

The horse twirled and reared, the rider's hat was sent flying, and his serape fell over his head. He lost his reins and grabbed the horn with both hands as the horse bucked wildly around the little clearing in the mesquite.

John Henry had seen the oncoming rider the instant he cleared the rim of the wash. He reached quickly for his carbine, but before he could clear the boot, he was convulsed in laughter.

The Mexican's horse whirled, hopped stiff-legged across the clearing, bouncing its burden on the saddle, twirled again and propelled the Mexican, his head still wrapped in his serape, in a graceful arc into a clump of prickly pear cactus.

John Henry guffawed loudly, then stopped abruptly.

The rider was lying where he had fallen. He had not moved. It was deathly quiet all of a sudden.

John Henry dismounted quickly and ran to the Mexican. He laid his carbine on the ground and knelt beside him.

The rider was lying on his back, cradled in the thick cactus. John Henry unwound the folds of the heavy serape from his head. His face was a grimace and his eyes squeezed tightly shut, but he was alive.

He was no older than John Henry. His eyelids fluttered and opened. He jerked backward when he saw John Henry, then relaxed and grimaced again, closing his eyes.

"*Bien? No lastimado?*" Okay? Not hurt? John Henry asked.

"*Estoy bien, señor, creo que sí,*" Okay, señor, I think, he replied, wincing.

"Let's see if we can get you out of there, amigo." John Henry stood up, bent toward the Mexican and took his hands. He pulled gently. "*Bien?*" Okay?

"*Sí.*"

John Henry pulled harder. The rider dug his heels in the sand and stood upright. John Henry braced him as he swayed and shifted his feet uneasily to get his balance.

"*Perdóneme . . . mi risa.*" Sorry. . .my laugh, John Henry said.

"*No importa,*" never mind, the Mexican replied, smiling thinly. He had a handsome face marked by a scar on his right cheek.

"*Dónde . . . tu caballo?*" Where. . .your horse? John Henry asked.

The rider looked at him blankly. He shrugged his shoulders.

John Henry remembered that he was still wrapped in the serape when he was thrown. John Henry looked around and saw the horse a short distance away, cropping mesquite beans. John Henry walked over and took the horse's reins and led him back. He handed the reins to the Mexican.

"*Gracias, señor . . . y su mula?*"

"*Qué?*"

"*Mula,*" he said again, smiling and putting a fist to each temple with the index finger extended.

"Ah, my mule. I don't know. I forgot about him."

"*Allí!*" the Mexican said. The mule was standing quietly in the shade of a palo verde at the edge of the wash. As John Henry walked over to recover him, the rider picked up John Henry's carbine from the ground. John Henry returned, leading the mule. The Mexican handed John Henry the carbine.

At that moment, Lieutenant Emory and Martínez appeared from behind a rock where the trail turned. Warner and Stanley were a few steps behind. The rider froze. John Henry took a few steps in their direction and waited.

"*Señor,*" the Mexican said.

"*Sí, señor?*" John Henry turned toward him.

"*Sus amigos?*" Your friends?

"*Sí señor, mis amigos.*" Yes, señor, my friends.

Emory and the others reined up. "What the devil is going on here, Harris?" Emory said. "I saw the Mexican had the drop on you. The next thing, I see you holding your carbine."

"Everything's okay, sir, we were just having a little fun."

"*Juego,*" fun, John Henry said to the Mexican and they smiled. Emory shook his head.

"Ask him where he comes from, where he is going and what is his business."

John Henry looked at the rider, then at Martínez. Both

looked at John Henry. No one spoke. John Henry looked at Emory, who was looking intently at him.

"Well?" Emory said to John Henry.

John Henry realized that Emory had been talking to him. "Lieutenant, I . . . Martínez . . ."

Emory smiled and turned toward Martínez. "Ask him, Martínez."

John Henry's embarrassment did not prevent him from trying to listen to the interrogation. He strained to understand but he caught only a word now and then. He moved closer to the two Mexicans who talked rapidly and gestured with their hands. John Henry cocked his head and squinted.

Emory watched John Henry. "What are they talking about, Harris? You understand all that, don't you?"

"No, sir, I don't." He straightened and turned toward Emory. He had not realized that he was being watched.

"I'm surprised." They both turned back to listen to the Mexicans. Emory turned again toward John Henry. "You like this country?"

"Yes, sir, I do."

At length, Martínez walked over to Emory. "Well?" Emory asked.

"He says he goes to hunt horses. He says his friends wait for him and will worry if he does not go soon to meet them."

"A horse hunter, eh?" He glanced toward Lieutenant Warner, who stood by him. "Not likely. Not in that outfit." Emory gestured toward the Mexican with a nod of his head. The rider's garb was wrinkled and coated with layers of dust but the clothing was clearly too fine for horse hunting.

John Henry was standing near enough to overhear Emory's comment. He had already seen the neck of a water bottle peeping from a saddle holster and the food sack on his croup, such as one makes for a journey, not for a horse-hunting expedition with a party. He assumed that the sharp-eyed Emory had seen them.

"Martínez, tell him he is going to our camp with us."

"*Tiene que acompañarnos a nuestro campamento,*" Martínez said to the rider.

The Mexican's eyes widened. He glanced nervously at John Henry. John Henry shrugged and made a face. *Sorry pard, nothing I can do for you now. I'm afraid you're in the soup. And I suspect you know something that you don't want to tell.*

The rider said something, urgently, to Martínez.

"Lieutenant Emory, he says that his friends will worry. He wants to go see them now and he will come back here then."

"I'll bet he would," Emory said to Warner. "No," this to Martínez, "tell him we must go now. His friends will just decide that he is on the trail of the best wild stallion in Mexico, and they won't worry about him. Tell him we won't detain him long."

Martínez translated. The rider walked wearily to his horse.

"Harris, put him between you and Martínez. He's your responsibility."

Emory and the others mounted and set out toward camp. John Henry and Martínez, their charge between them, followed.

The rider glanced anxiously from side to side as they rode. From time to time, he spoke rapidly to Martínez who responded with a grunt or ignored him altogether. The rider turned to John Henry and spoke in the same manner, in rapid-fire Spanish.

"What's he saying," John Henry said to Martínez, "I

can't get a word of it."

"Same thing he said before. He says if we will just let him go see his friends for a few minutes, he will come right back to us."

The rider fell behind and looked over his shoulder at the back trail. John Henry moved close beside him and kicked the horse in the flanks.

"Martínez, tell him to keep up with us, or I'll have to take his reins. He wouldn't like that."

Martínez translated. The rider slumped in his saddle and appeared finally to accept his fate.

"*Yo* sorry, *amigo*." John Henry said to the rider.

The rider looked at John Henry and smiled weakly.

CHAPTER 10

"Lieutenant Emory, I do believe you have struck gold."

General Kearny was the speaker. He and a half dozen other officers crowded around his camp table. On the arrival of Emory's party in camp around noon, the General had ordered the Mexican's belongings and saddlebags searched.

John Henry had dumped the contents of the bags on the table and stepped back to stand beside Martínez and the captive.

It was the mail from California. Kearny shuffled slowly through the stack, picking up an envelope, looking at it, tossing it back on the table.

"These are addressed to some of the most important men in Sonora," he said to no one in particular. "Ah, what have we here?" Kearny picked up a letter. "For General Castro himself. Altar. Now what are you up to in Altar, General?" Kearny said as he tapped the envelope by the corner on the tabletop and stared off in the distance.

For God's sake, open the letter! John Henry resisted the impulse to yell at the General.

As if he heard, Kearny tore open the envelope, suddenly

in a hurry. He showed the sheet to Carson who stood beside him. They talked in low tones and John Henry could not make out what they said.

"Let's have a look at all these letters." He spoke to Turner, Johnston, and Emory. "Go over these with your interpreters and we'll see what we can make of them. I think we'll find a bit of news."

The officers sat down on folding camp chairs that were brought hurriedly by orderlies. Interpreters stood around the table, reading passages and answering questions. Martínez was beside Emory. John Henry stood a few steps away with the rider.

Emory leaned back in his chair and turned toward John Henry. "Harris, get him something to eat." He gestured toward the Mexican.

"*Comer*?" Eat? John Henry asked. The rider shrugged his shoulders. John Henry motioned for an orderly to watch him. John Henry walked over to a tent and brought back two plates of salt pork and beans.

John Henry and the rider sat on the ground in the lacy shade of a mesquite. The Mexican's earlier indifference to the prospect of eating did not square with his appetite. He ate ravenously. John Henry ate slowly, alternately watching the officers opening mail and studying the rider.

The Mexican's clothes were covered with trail dust but they were made of fine material with colorful stitching. His boots were in good condition, showing no evidence of long, hard use. His hands were almost delicate, strong but not calloused from hard, outdoor work.

John Henry looked at the scar. It ran from just under his right eye almost to his lip. It was distinct but light and not disfiguring. He wondered what had caused it. He thought about asking the Mexican about the scar but decided that it would be rude.

The Mexican scraped his plate with the spoon until it was clean. He glanced at John Henry. John Henry dropped his gaze abruptly, then recovered.

"*Dónde . . . tu casa*?" Where . . . your home? John Henry asked.

"*Mi hogar? Monterey,*" he answered.

"*Usted . . . tu casa . . .ahora*?" You. . .go home . . . now? John Henry pointed toward the south.

"*A casa? No, yo voy a Sonora. México. Mi casa es allá.*" Home? No, I'm going to Sonora. Mexico. My home is that way. He pointed toward the northwest.

John Henry was puzzled. Back at Leavenworth, when he learned he was going to war against Mexico, he had done some reading at the post library. He was pleased with himself that he remembered that Monterrey was one of the principal towns in the northern part of Mexico.

"But Monterrey is there," he said absentmindedly and pointed southward. Then he caught himself. "*Monterrey, allá.*" Monterrey, there. He assumed that the rider had just lost his sense of direction.

"*No, mi casa no está al sur. Mi casa, Monterey, es para allá. Yo no soy Mexicano. Yo soy Californio.*" The Mexican pointed again to the northwest.

John Henry did not understand all he said but he did comprehend that a distinction was being drawn between being Mexican and Californian. Which just confused him more. Just then he saw Carson striding by.

"Kit, could you help me with something?" he called.

Carson stopped, then walked over. "I expect I can."

"I've gone just about the limit of my Spanish, trying to sort out something here. This fellow says he is from Monterrey but says his home is to the northwest. I think he's saying that he isn't Mexican but Californian. Aren't Californians Mexicans? And isn't Monterrey in northern Mexico?"

Carson squatted down on his heels beside John Henry. "You remember, don't you, how disappointed the boys were that they didn't get to shoot anybody when they marched into New Mexico?" John Henry nodded. "The main reason is that New Mexicans have little love for Mexico. For a long time, New Mexicans have felt that they've been neglected, even ignored, by Mexico City. They especially don't think the capital gave them enough protection from Indians.

"For the last twenty years, since trade over the Santa Fé Trail has been going on, they have felt closer ties on many counts with the United States than with Mexico City. When General Kearny pronounced New Mexico American territory and New Mexicans American subjects, I suspect that most of 'em weren't too unhappy with the change. Remember that?"

John Henry nodded.

"Californians are about the same way. In fact, Californians in the past few years have just about been governing themselves and Mexico be damned. If th' big guns in Washington had just been patient, the Californians would likely have declared their independence from Mexico. They might've been able to prove up on it. More likely, they would have been made part of somebody's empire, British or American.

"Larkin—Thomas O. Larkin, that's the United States consul in California—had some of the most important Californians convinced that they had best go with the Americans. Understand?"

John Henry nodded.

"Course, patience, you know, is something that politicians and generals ordinarily have in small store."

"And Monterrey?"

Carson smiled. "There's two Montereys. There's Monterrey, in Nuevo Leon, in northern Mexico. And there's Monterey, the capital of Alta California. Beautiful town. Passable harbor, I'm told. It's got a great future."

Carson turned to the Mexican. "*Hermosa ciudad, Monterey*," a beautiful town, Monterey. The rider raised his hand in agreement, smiled and nodded.

"And by the way," Carson turned back to John Henry, "don't call a Californian a Mexican. They're '*Californios.*' They think they're about two rungs above Mexicans." He stood, grunting from the effort, and walked on his way.

John Henry turned back to see the Californian watching him. "*Yo comprendo,*" I understand, John Henry said. The other nodded.

"*Dónde está su casa?*" where is your home? the Californian asked.

"Miss—" He stopped. His head came up. An epiphany. It was so clear. So easy.

"Santa Fé," he said.

"*Santa Fé? Su casa?*" The Californian, wide-eyed, stared at John Henry.

"*Sí,*" John Henry replied firmly, leaning back and resting on an elbow. "*Santa Fé. Mi casa.*" My home.

"All right, men, your attention now. I want to tell you what we have learned about affairs in California."

The officers had finished with the letters and put their heads together for another quarter hour. Kearny then had the entire force assembled in the center of the camp. A hundred men crowded the clearing in front of him.

"We have talked with the four Mexicans from across the river." He motioned toward the drovers' camp. "We have read the letters that were carried by the courier brought in by Lieutenant Emory."

He paused long enough to announce silently to even the dullest in the throng that what came next was important.

"It seems that we have a fight ahead of us, after all. Since Mr. Carson brought us the happy news that California had fallen, the Mexicans have risen, if we can believe what we read and hear.

"The Mexicans have retaken some areas, rather important areas, in fact. The Mexican flag flies now in Santa Barbara and Los Angeles. There seems to have been a sizable battle near San Pedro and the Mexicans claim to have won it.

"We have also learned that the horses across the river are for General Castro in Sonora who has plans for returning to California to assist in the counterrevolution. How much of this is true and how much we can discount to the Mexican tendency to exaggerate, it is impossible to say. Since we learned it from two separate sources, we must believe that things have taken a turn in California."

The soldiers were unsure how to react to the news. Kearny and the other officers were not smiling. The soldiers were excited but subdued.

"There's one more thing," said Kearny. The murmuring stopped, and all turned back toward the General. "This information dates from the middle of October. That makes it about five weeks old. Much could have happened in California in those five weeks."

The murmuring rose again until the buzzing sounded like a hundred beehives.

"Tomorrow," Kearny shouted, then paused for the

talking to stop, "tomorrow we will pick remounts from the Mexican herd and we will march. Look sharp! We have our work cut out for us!"

With this, he turned on his heel and walked toward his tent. The officers followed him. A cheer went up from the knot of soldiers, then individual yells, lusty and primitive.

Emory walked over to John Henry and the Californian. John Henry jumped up; the Californian rose slowly.

"Harris, tell the Mexican that he is free to go."

"Yes, sir."

John Henry watched the Californian adjust his saddle. That done, the rider gripped the saddle horn and swung up lightly into the saddle.

"*Muchas gracias, mi amigo*," said the rider. "*Hasta la vista*." Many thanks, my friend. Until we meet again.

"*Adiós. Vaya con Dios*." Goodbye. Go with God.

The Californian spurred his horse and galloped away.

"Look at that one, John Henry! Ain't he a beauty?" Brad and John Henry stood in a line of troopers near the herd of milling horses. Vaqueros rode about, cutting out animals that had been selected by two dragoon sergeants. Brad pointed to a buckskin, larger than the rest, with fire in his eye, stamping and rearing and defying any to approach him.

"There's your remount, Johnny," Brad said without looking at John Henry. John Henry turned toward his friend, expecting his customary grin but Brad was straight-faced.

"Think you can ride 'im?" Brad said.

John Henry stared at Brad's profile a moment, then turned back to look at the buckskin. "It'd take a bit of learning but I could ride him, yes."

Their attention was diverted by an unintelligible exchange in Spanish between two mounted vaqueros. The riders slouched in their saddles. Their horses stood perfectly still. As the men talked, each took a coil of rope from his saddle.

They walked their mounts slowly toward a group of five horses, still talking softly and nonchalantly shaking out their ropes, enlarging the loops. The space between the vaqueros widened.

As the riders neared their quarry, the five bunched-up horses became increasingly nervous. Then one trotted stiff-legged away from the group. The vaqueros simultaneously squeezed gently with their knees and touched their mounts' flanks with their spurs. The mounts slipped to the right and loped ahead to intercept the horse.

Both riders twirled their ropes slowly over their heads. Suddenly, the ropes shot out simultaneously. The lead rope settled around the horse's neck and rested on the shoulders. The second rope fell to the ground under the horse's belly.

"Missed!" Brad said.

Both riders stopped their mounts, abruptly. The ropes drew taut and the horse was thrown violently on its side.

"What th' hell!" Brad shouted. "Did you see that?"

At the instant that the lead rider had begun to tighten his rope around the horse's neck, the horse had stepped into the second rider's loop on the ground. Instantly, the vaquero jerked his rope up and tight around the horse's hind legs.

The horse had no sooner fallen to the ground than the lead rider was loosening his loop. Two soldiers ran up to hobble the horse and slip a halter over his head. The horse lunged to his feet and was led away, not quite subdued.

"What's the matter? You boys never see the lasso before?" Carson said to Brad and John Henry, who still stared, wide-eyed and open-mouthed. Carson was standing nearby with a knot of soldiers. He walked over.

"Not me," Brad answered, "I never saw stock handled like that! That rope was alive!"

"That was really something," John Henry said. "Can all Mexicans handle a rope like that?"

"Not Mexicans, hoss. Californians. Remember? A Californian can throw the lasso better with his foot than a Mexican can with his hand."

The three watched as more horses were caught and led away by dragoons, remounts for the army.

"Stir yourselves, soldiers, we gotta get outta here." The dragoons turned to see Corporal Jackson who was just dismounting. "We're to be back in camp by half past ten. Then it's off for the Colorado by noon. That is, if you boys can set your saddle. From what I seen in just the past two minutes, you're gonna have old Billy gettin' a saddle on these devils. I'm sure glad I got a mount." The corporal grinned from ear to ear.

"I'd rather have a live devil than that crowbait you're riding," Brad replied.

"He may be that but he's got his feet on th' ground, and he goes where I point him. And I expect I'll be on top of him when we see th' Pacific Ocean." He was still smiling.

"You boys better hustle up and get yourselves back to camp quick as you can and turn in your borrowed animals. If you're first in line for remounts, maybe you can find yourself a plow horse in the bunch. You might but I don't think so."

He climbed slowly into his saddle and kicked his

mule in the direction of the river.

Brad and John Henry watched him a moment, then turned back to the herd. The vaqueros were moving the horses and mules that had just been cut out to a patch of grass where the army's remounts were being held.

Major Swords, with two dragoons and an interpreter, stood near the smoldering ashes of last night's fire, talking with two Mexicans. The Major waved toward the bunch of army mules that he had brought that morning from the army's camp. The animals huddled together, their bodies touching.

"So they won't fall down," Brad said.

There were twenty or twenty-five mules, the most forlorn-looking creatures imaginable. They stood with heads down, walking unsteadily, when they moved at all. Their ribs were visible and rump bones appeared ready to break through the hanging skin at any moment. Most had raw, red saddle sores. They were jaded, used-up, worn-out creatures.

"Poor, dumb beasts," John Henry said, "I hope they make it."

Brad turned to John Henry. "Don't worry about it, Johnny." There was no mirth in his tone. "They're just that, dumb beasts. Mules reach the end of their usefulness, just like people."

"True enough but we did that to them."

Brad dropped his head and shook it, just slightly. "Besides, they'll come back. They'll be put with the Mex herd and they'll have a slow walk to Sonora, grazing all the way. When they get there, each one of 'em is going to be given to a little girl who will feed 'im green grass and clover and ride 'im to church every Sunday morning."

"Go t' hell, Bradford." John Henry looked at his friend

from the corner of his eye and started walking toward the line of saddled mules they had ridden from camp that morning.

"I'm telling you, Johnny," Brad shouted, "I got it from the head Mex hisself. He plans to turn these U.S. Army mules into pets!" Brad hurried to catch up.

"All right, Bradford, if you say so. We'll say they'll recover." He turned to look back at the men around the campfire as they walked.

"I wonder how much extra Swords is paying for the remounts?" John Henry said. Even at this distance, a hundred and fifty feet or so, he could see coin changing hands.

"I'll bet they're surprised as hell to be paid at all." Brad said. "The General sure is taking pains to please the Mex. Hell of a way to fight a war." They walked together toward the tethered mules.

"By the way," said Brad, "since you love mules so much, I should tell you that we still got a passel. The General figures that these fresh mounts might wear out quick and we'll be back riding mules."

The soldiers reached their mounts and began to untie reins that were tied to mesquite branches.

"*Señor! Momentito.*" The two soldiers turned to see the new grandfather, gray hair, hurrying toward them. He was leading a horse.

"*Buenos días, señores,*" gray hair said. He shook Brad's hand quickly and turned to John Henry. He took John Henry's hand, shook it firmly, and held it.

"*Buenos días, señor. Cómo . . . niño?*" How is the baby? John Henry asked.

"*La niña está bien, y también su madrecita, mi hija.*" The baby is fine, and also his mother, my daughter, he replied.

"*Bueno,*" John Henry said. Then, solemnly, "*Nos vamos*

ahora. Adiós. Buena suerte. Vaya con Dios." We go now. Goodbye. Good luck. Go with God.

"*Sí, yo entiendo. Pero, primero, quiero darle esto.*" Gray hair put the reins of the horse he was leading into John Henry's hand and closed the hand around them.

"*Qué?*" What? John Henry said, puzzled.

"Even I can understand that, Johnny. He's giving you his horse."

John Henry had told Brad about the baby and had pointed out the young father and the grandfather earlier as they worked the herd.

John Henry was stunned. He stared at the horse. It was a beautiful chestnut stallion, well-muscled, long-legged, with a finely formed head. The saddle, embossed and well rubbed, was lightly trimmed with silver buckles, slides and stars. The bridle was similarly, but more richly, decorated.

John Henry looked at gray hair who smiled benevolently. "*Muchas gracias, mi amigo, pero . . . es mucho.*" Thank you, my friend, but . . . much. John Henry wrinkled his forehead, searching. "*Muy mucho.*" Too much.

"*No, señor, no es demasiado. Yo estoy muy feliz, y quiero dárselo. Es buen caballo. Se llama 'Remolino'.*" He pointed at the horse. "*Remolino.*"

"*Pero usted . . . necesita . . . su caballo.*" But . . . you . . . need . . . your horse.

"*Tengo muchos!*" I have many, gray hair said, smiling and sweeping his arm toward the departing herd. "*El General Castro no lo echara de menos. Yo escogeré el mejor de la manada antes de llegar a Altar, y comerá de mi mano!*"

Gray hair sobered and took John Henry's hand again, closing it tighter on the reins.

"*Favor de aceptar mi regalo, mi amigo. Hoy, yo tengo una nieta, de mi carne y sangre, y de mi única hija. Le debo más de lo que puedo pagarle. Somos hermanos.*"

The Mexican pointed to John Henry, then to himself. "*Hermanos.*" Brothers.

John Henry was profoundly touched as he had never been touched before. He struggled to control his emotions.

"*Yo comprendo.*" I understand, John Henry said softly. He took the old vaquero's hand in both of his and held it tightly.

"*Muchas gracias,*" John Henry said. "*Adiós. Hermano.*" Thank you. Goodbye. Brother.

Gray hair smiled broadly. "*Qué Dios los acompañe, mi amigo! Hasta la vista!*" May God accompany you, my friend. Until we meet again.

The entire command gaped at this first sight of the Colorado. The soldiers lined a ridge, facing the river, about a mile away. Their mounts were tied to bushes nearby. The bone-dry sandy plain they had traveled through since breaking camp made the spectacle that much more impressive.

The broad valley below, twenty miles across, was choked with mesquite. Nearer the river, there was a heavy growth of willow and an occasional cottonwood marking the water's edge. The river was about a quarter-mile wide.

"Quite a sight," said John Henry. "The other side, that's California." John Henry and Brad sat on rocks, apart from the other dragoons.

"Quite a sight, all right. I've been dreaming about this damn river the past few nights. And I'll be right happy to cross it. Just as soon as they throw a bridge across."

John Henry smiled and knew that Brad said it with more humor than he felt.

"Damn Mex horse of yours will probably just tiptoe all the way across without you getting the seat of your pants wet. This runt animal I'm riding will have to swim and I'll be lucky if I don't get eat by a crocodile.

"Speaking of your horse, you better stay out of the General's line of sight. He's not very happy about you parading around with a better animal than his own. I hear he don't care much for the non-reg gear either."

John Henry had, in fact, been riding high since they left camp and he was enjoying it. The dragoons had been green with envy when John Henry rode into camp earlier that morning. They had crowded around, admiring the horse and the saddle and bridle. John Henry had cantered about the camp, showing off. The chestnut reined beautifully, with the movement of a show horse.

He was ashamed now, as he remembered, that he had been so vain. But he had never sat such a horse, much less owned one, and he was proud of Remolino.

John Henry had noticed General Kearny standing in front of his tent, watching. Disapprovingly, John Henry assumed. John Henry had pulled up abruptly and dismounted.

"Peters told me that Kearny said that since everything's in such short supply, I can use the gear until we reach the coast," John Henry told Brad. "He'll play hell getting me off Remolino even then. I'm going to ride this horse, with this gear, right up to Morita's door."

Brad fussed with his saddle fittings. When Brad did not respond, John Henry turned to look at the river—and California.

He had thought little about California lately. The past two days, since he helped deliver the baby, he had thought constantly of Morita. Her smile and her peculiar perfume, the softness of her cheek on his. The sheer ecstasy, at the end of the day, walking from the cantina to her home, finally having her to himself. The warmth of her body beside him when he awoke in the night.

He remembered one particular evening. After leaving the cantina, they had walked hand in hand. She swung her sandals and hopped lightly about as though she had not just finished ten hours' hard work.

"*Yo no trabajar mañana,*" John Henry said. "*Yo me quedo a su casa . . . todo mañana.* Okay?" I'm not working tomorrow. I'm staying at your house all day.

Morita stopped abruptly and took his hand in both of hers.

"*Qué? Todo el día? Qué bien!*" All day? That's wonderful! "Sunday . . . tomorrow . . . We go . . . *iglesia. Iglesia . . .* church?"

"Church. Church? That's not exactly what I had in mind for my free day."

"*Qué?*"

"Yes, we will go to church. *Dese o . . . ir . . . iglesia . . . con usted.*" I want . . . go church . . . with you.

"*Contigo. Gracias.*" With you. Thank you.

"*Apúrate! Vámonos! Apúrate!*" Hurry! Let's go! Hurry!

Morita jerked the blanket off John Henry and shook him. John Henry opened his eyes and squinted sleepily at her. She was fully dressed.

"*Apúrate, Juanito.*" She squeezed his shoulder.

"Hurry? Why? It's still dark."

"*Iglesia! Apúrate!*"

"You said noon . . . *mediodia.*"

"Yes, yes. Change . . ." She pointed to her head. "Church now. Hurry."

She held out his trousers and shirt. John Henry fumbled with the clothes as she helped him, laughing and scolding. "*Apúrate! Apúrate!*"

John Henry sat on the edge of the bed and pulled at his boots. Morita stood at the door, impatiently shifting her weight from foot to foot, repeating softly, "*Apúrate! Apúrate!*"

"Aren't we going to eat something?" John Henry said.

"Eat? Eat? No eat now. Eat . . ." She looked impatiently at the ceiling. "*Después.* Church now. *Apúrate!*"

Morita crossed the room, pulled John Henry from the bed, and tugged him out the door.

It was a brisk ten-minute walk to the church, just off the plaza. The town seemed deserted at this early hour on Sunday but for the few women and fewer men hurrying toward the church. Morita ran a few steps, then stopped to look back at John Henry. He was half-asleep and lagged.

Morita pled. "*Apúrate, Juanito, Apúrate. Por favor.*" Hurry, Juanito, hurry. Please.

They reached the church and Morita hurried to grab the door, just as it was closing behind a couple who had scurried through. She held the door open for John Henry. He stepped into the church and she followed. She slowly closed the heavy door.

A few steps inside, John Henry stopped as his eyes adjusted to the dim interior. He was surprised to see so many people, having just passed through the almost empty plaza.

Morita walked a few steps farther, then turned to see whether he was coming. He walked up beside her. She loosened the black *rebozo* about her head and crossed herself. Then she knelt on the floor.

There were no pews. Women were on their knees, praying with bowed heads. Most of the men stood, though some also knelt. Morita looked up at him. He smiled at her and she returned to her prayer.

IF I SHOULD LEAVE YOU | 177

John Henry had heard about Catholic mass but he had never attended a service and was fascinated. An orchestra of violin and guitar was playing. The melodies seemed familiar. Were they the same he had heard in the cantinas? Surely not.

Morita looked up at him again, smiled, then crossed herself and bowed her head.

John Henry looked around. A statue of Christ covered with a protective net stood at the altar beside a larger statue of a priest holding a cross. Some faded paintings hung on the walls. A priest walked back and forth at the altar, speaking in Latin.

John Henry knelt beside Morita. She opened her eyes, looked at him and smiled, and returned to her prayers. He bowed his head and watched Morita's hands on her beads.

After church, John Henry and Morita strolled in the market set up along the walls of the palace compound. Stalls not under the palace porch were protected from the hot sun by white canvas canopies. Vendors shouted to passersby, proclaiming the high quality and low prices of their wares.

There were dressed turkeys and chickens, chunks of beef and venison, live poultry, lambs and pigs, dried beans, apples, apricots, onions, myriad varieties of chili and stacks of firewood.

The rich smells of garlic, simmering cooking pots, and sweet cakes clashed with that of spoiling meat and the stench of live animals, blending into a single fragrance that John Henry was already coming to recognize as Santa Fé.

John Henry watched Morita make her small purchases of chilies and fresh vegetables. It was a Morita he had never seen. She was efficient, combative, friendly, and in complete control.

John Henry stopped at a stall where small balls of soap and face powder were stacked in little pyramids.

The female vendor smiled broadly, picked up two balls of soap, one yellow and the other pink, and thrust them under John Henry's nose. They were lightly scented and had a smooth texture unlike anything John Henry had ever used.

He took the balls and put them under Morita's nose. She inhaled and smiled.

"For you," he said and put the balls in her hand.

She looked wide-eyed at him. "*Para mi? Son demasiado caros, demasiado elegantes*," she said softly. For me? They are too expensive, too elegant.

"Yes, *para* you." He closed her hands on the two precious soaps and paid the seller. Morita started to protest again but he took her arm and moved away from the stall.

"Thank you," she said, without a trace of accent, and squeezed his hand. They walked to the last stalls. John Henry bought tamales and sweet cakes. They crossed the road to the plaza and sat on the ground in the cool shade of a huge cottonwood.

John Henry liked the plaza. It was the heart of the town. People came to stroll, to buy from the stores and stalls, and simply to pass time. There was never a sense of urgency, even during market, always an air of serenity and peace.

John Henry glanced around the plaza. The palace fronted on one side. Opposite were some fine houses and a church under construction. The two other sides of the square were filled with stores and houses. The buildings on all four sides of the plaza had walkways covered by roofs supported by round, whitewashed pillars to protect pedestrians from sun or rain.

Men with striped serapes folded over their shoulders

lounged in the shade of a porch. They watched three women wrapped in dark *rebozos* walk by, talking softly, animatedly, bending toward each other.

All turned to watch a file of oxcarts, the wooden wheels screaming, and a dozen loaded burros moving slowly across the plaza. Dust rose about the wheels of the oxcarts and the animals' hoofs. Then they were gone and the dust settled.

They ate in silence. John Henry looked at Morita. She was watching some children playing in the road. She held a sweet cake daintily, brushing the crumbs from her dress as she ate.

He marveled at her perfect features, the dark eyes, the contour of her nose, her delicate mouth. He felt in his mind the softness of her cheek as she pulled back a strand of black hair from her face.

A gentle rustling overhead distracted him. He looked up to see the leaves of the cottonwood move gently in the light wind. The breeze had the slightest hint of coolness that made him think of autumn, his favorite season. He looked through the treetops to the clear blue sky. The mountains seemed close enough to touch.

I could live here.

John Henry stared at the new flagstaff in the center of the plaza. It flew the flag of the United States. John Henry frowned. He had always been thrilled by the sight of Old Glory, waving in the breeze, rousing patriotic sentiments and a call to duty. Why not now?

The breeze quickened and a few drops of rain fell. Morita scrambled up. "We go *apúrate*. Rain now," she said.

She gathered up her small purchases and reached down to pull John Henry to his feet. Large scattered raindrops pelted them. John Henry looked up and saw the dark cloud moving overhead. They ran for the shop porches.

They stood under cover, watching the rain and the shoppers and strollers running for cover, serapes and rebozos over their heads.

John Henry smiled. He turned and saw Brad, grim, watching him. Brad turned away. John Henry turned back and looked at the Colorado and the desert beyond. The road to Santa Fé.

He frowned. Was he remembering Santa Fé, the real Santa Fé, or had a fantasy replaced the reality?

He remembered when he first entered the town. While still on the trail from Fort Leavenworth, he and a few others had been detached from the Army of the West to serve as a guard for Captain Philip St. George Cooke and a trader who knew the governor.

Cooke and the trader were going ahead under a flag of truce to parley with the Mexican governor. Their charge was to convince the governor that resistance was futile, suicide really, and that he should surrender the town peacefully.

John Henry's excitement had grown as the advance unit approached Santa Fé, his first foreign town. He had read a little about Spain and Mexico and, at Bent's Fort on the trail from Leavenworth, he had talked with Santa Fé traders.

Growing up in Franklin County, Missouri, he had been stirred by the stories of two old men who claimed they had trapped in New Mexico in the 1820s. They talked about Taos, the Gila River, a Spanish mission they called San Xavier, a Sky City, cantinas, cool nights and soft, brown *señoritas*.

The oldsters scratched a living from a creekside farm

near his daddy's that showed little promise and they, and talked incessantly about going back to New Mexico. Sitting for hours, with his chin in his hands, listening to the old partners, New Mexico had seemed the most wonderful, mysterious, desirable place in the world.

The reality of Santa Fé had stunned him. Green corn fields foretold human habitation but all John Henry saw in his first glimpse were piles of earth-colored bricks.

No, those are not brickyards, the trader had told him, they are houses. "Then this is the poor fringe of the town," a trooper said. "No," the trader smiled, "this *is* Santa Fé."

Their spirits sank lower as they continued their ride to the town center. The houses were hovels, the people mean, the city a cesspool instead of an oasis.

The magic returned with night. John Henry had drawn guard duty outside the governor's palace on the plaza where the talks were held.

From a bench on the porch, he watched the night come. The plaza was soon deserted. He listened to the whispering sounds from the tops of the cottonwoods and watched the moon shadows dancing on the stone walls and pavements.

John Henry stared at the land across the river. California. Almost home.

The dragoons were unusually quiet as they watched the sun setting. Tomorrow, the army would cross the river, leaving New Mexico and entering California.

They would march toward the coast, and if all they had learned in recent days proved true, they probably would engage the Mexicans in battle.

A plan began to form that John Henry never thought he could harbor, even in the deepest recesses of his mind.

CHAPTER 11

John Henry stared at the darkening river. He turned to Brad.

"Brad, you've been a good friend. I've got to tell you something. I didn't sleep last night. Thinking about Morita. And this war. This damned war. The whole thing makes no sense. Only one thing makes sense to me now. Morita."

Brad looked hard at John Henry. "I know what you're thinking, Johnny. You'd best put it out of your mind. You've got a duty to your country and to all of us. And to yourself."

"I'm telling you as a friend. I can't stop thinking about Morita and that little adobe house. Remolino was a confirmation, don't you see? And that order that I gave the guard. My God, Brad, I was thinking like a soldier."

"I know how you feel but you can't do it. It's almost over. That's California, Johnny, right there." Brad pointed at the land across the river.

John Henry shut his eyes and rubbed his temples and the back of his neck.

Camp was laid out on a sandy clearing near the ford. Horses and mules cropped the tender shoots of young willows that fringed the campground. Patches of good grass were found nearby but since stock would wander and be hard to recover in the dense thicket, grass was cut by the dragoons and brought to the animals.

"Be sure your mounts get all the feed they want," Corporal Jackson told the dragoons who shuttled between grass patches and the tethered animals. "And when you get through feeding 'em, cut some more to be taken along behind your saddle. Carson says that tomorrow we begin a march of some ninety miles without feed of any kind. Unless your mule has learned to eat sand and scorpions."

"Doesn't sound very promising, John Henry. Damn the people who planned this march anyway, saving the hardest for last, when we're the tiredest. Why couldn't they have put the hard part at the start where we could have fairly pranced through it? Damn poor planning, I'd say."

John Henry smiled and continued sawing at a clump of dry grass.

John Henry lay awake, staring into the heavens.

It would be easy. I could go back to the Mexican horse camp. Gray hair would let me go with them to Altar. They would help me find the way to Santa Fé. Or I could just go back to the Pima villages and get supplies there. This would get me . . . home . . . faster.

It's not as if I would be doing something wrong. Surely it's not wrong to refuse to do something that you know is wrong. It's the war that's wrong. The United States has no right to make war on Mexico. The Mexicans are not my enemies. Right is on their side. How can it be wrong if I simply refuse to fight? Just withdraw. I can't stop it but I don't have to take part.

Just before daybreak, John Henry had drifted off into a

fitful sleep. He awoke with pulsing temples and a throbbing in the back of his neck, wet with perspiration. As the day began, he fell into the familiar routine.

Gradually, all thoughts of desertion evaporated and the throbbing in his head subsided. Later, he marveled that what had been so clearly right in the middle of the night was as clearly unacceptable at midday.

He knew that desertion was alien to his sense of responsibility and obligation. Obligation, if not to the United States of America and its war of conquest, then to himself and his comrades. He wanted no dark memory that would eat at his vitals with the passing years. He would finish this campaign, though he would not fight. He would find ways to avoid fighting. At the end of it, he would be clear of the army. He would have no regrets.

He would see the ocean and the end of the war. Then he would ride Remolino back to Santa Fé and Morita and live in that little adobe house the rest of his life. He had begun today's march impatiently, remaining in column only with difficulty. He had an impulse now to break into full gallop. He knew now that every step taken away from Morita brought him closer to her.

The dragoons were in single file, winding down a track into the mesquite thicket. The trail was narrow and the soldiers had to weave and duck to avoid the thorny branches. An occasional profane cry was heard when a rider did not move fast enough or when a tired mount did not answer the rein fast enough.

"I doubt that you'll get your bridge on this trip," John Henry said to Brad who was riding just ahead of him, "but the crossing shouldn't be too bad. Carson said there is a good ford and we should get across in no time at all. If that doesn't suit you, I suppose you could put up at the hotel until the ferry comes along."

"Hotel? Ferry? Is there . . ." Brad twisted in his saddle to look at John Henry, then jerked back to the front and spurred his mule.

John Henry smiled.

The mounted dragoons lined the bank that sloped gently about four feet down to the surface of the river. The chocolate-colored water flowed lazily, with little eddies and whirlpools and quiet places along the sculptured bank.

John Henry watched a piece of driftwood about twenty feet from the bank float by. About two miles an hour, he guessed. The sun was pleasant at this time of the morning and he enjoyed its warmth, remembering other times and other rivers.

". . . on the ford. Just follow the tail of the beast in front of you and you'll have no trouble." John Henry was brought back to the present by Carson's voice. "If the bottom has washed away anywhere, it will be just a few feet, so don't worry. Your animal is a strong swimmer and he'll want to get back on the ford as much as you.

"Our route crosses those three sand islands." He pointed. "But don't stop. Keep right on going. If you stop, your mount will like the idea of the solid ground and he'll balk at going back into the water. So kick him right along."

"If my brute has that much sense, I think I'll agree with him and we'll just take up residence on the island," Brad said to John Henry. "Do you think they'll grow corn?" Brad looked anxiously at the river. "I don't like this a little bit, I tell you for sure."

At that moment, the column started moving. John Henry moved off and Brad fell in behind.

Carson led the file to the water's edge. He did not pause but urged his mount directly into the stream. He moved steadily, turning in the saddle to wave those immediately behind him to catch up. The animals found good footing and soon the column stretched across, rising at the islands, then descending again beyond.

"Stay close, Johnny." John Henry had just entered the water and turned back to see Brad kicking his mount into the stream.

"Okay Brad, just stay in my track as close as you can." Remolino plunged ahead and the water rose to John Henry's knees.

On the far bank, the riders at the head of the column already were leaving the water. They collected in a knot at the bank but soon moved away and were lost to view behind a sand hill.

"Johnny, they're leaving us! Look!"

"No, they're not. They're just moving so they won't bunch up at the edge. They'll be waiting a little farther on." John Henry heard the terror in Brad's voice. He didn't look back.

The first island. He looked back at Brad as he urged his mount from the water. Brad smiled sheepishly.

"What do you say we blow a bit, Johnny? We could—"

"Straight on in, Brad. Stay with me." John Henry moved ahead, entering the water, his horse's nose almost touching the hindquarters of the mule ahead. He did not look back, knowing Brad would follow.

The second island. Then the third. As they entered the water for the third time, Brad shouted, "Ho for California!"

John Henry turned in his saddle to see Brad raise a clenched fist in triumph. He smiled and faced forward. Remolino plunged ahead and the ford dipped. The water level rose to John Henry's hip.

A moment later, mid-way between the last island and the riverbank, John Henry heard a cry behind him that sent a shiver up his spine.

"Johnny-y-y-y-y!" John Henry turned around sharply and saw Brad, out of line and drifting. Only the horse's head and neck were visible, bobbing as he swam, his ears laid back and eyes bulging. The water lapped across Brad's chest. Brad was paralyzed, his face a mask of terror.

"It's all right, Brad! Stay where you are! Stay in the saddle! He's swimming!" Then, more calmly, "he knows what he's doing, stick with him."

The current was stronger here than between the other islands and Brad's mount, swimming frantically, drifted farther from the ford.

"I'm going! I'm going!" Brad shouted.

"It's okay, you're making headway." John Henry spoke calmly, fighting his own terror.

And Brad was making headway. John Henry's horse had continued plowing through the water on the ford. Brad's horse, still trying to follow Remolino, pointed his head at him and, though the current prevented his recovering the ford, he was now making forward progress, parallel with the ford.

A minute later, an eternity, Brad's mount found footing in the shallows. John Henry and Brad left the water simultaneously, twenty yards apart. They rode up the gradual incline of the bank together and to the plateau where the army was gathering. They reined in and dismounted.

"Okay?" John Henry asked.

"Yeah," said Brad, a quizzical look on his face. "Oh, you mean that back there." He motioned with his head toward the river. "I was just testing your reflexes, Johnny.

You'll do okay in a clutch. You did get a little excited, though. You're gonna have to work on your self-control."

Brad emptied the water from a boot and squeezed the cuff of a trouser leg. John Henry wiped his face on his sleeve and smiled thinly.

"Hey, Johnny, hold up there! Where you going?" Brad dropped his mount's reins and stumbled in the deep sand, following John Henry who had veered off the trail. John Henry swayed from side to side, head down, shuffling rather than walking. Remolino followed obediently.

"Johnny, wait for me," Brad called softly.

John Henry stopped. He turned back toward Brad. He squinted.

"I can't see you, Brad. I can't see! Is that you, Brad?"

"Yeah, hold up." Brad shuffled up beside John Henry. "You okay?"

John Henry looked at Brad through half-open lids. "I can't see," he said softly. "What's wrong?" He closed his eyes and lowered his head. "Is this camp?"

"Not yet, pard. Come on, let's move up here and set and blow some."

Brad took John Henry by the arm. They walked to a mesquite where Brad gently helped him sit in the lacy shade. Brad sat down heavily. John Henry's head was down and his eyes clenched. He rocked slowly back and forth.

"Hurt?" Brad said.

"Yeah." John Henry rubbed his temples and the back of his neck. He continued to rock. "I don't think I can take much more of this, Brad." He pressed on his temples as if to contain the pounding that threatened to shatter his skull.

"Hang on, pard. We're almost there. Kit said that we'll reach a stock ranch tomorrow and San Diego's only three or four days further."

John Henry took a deep breath, rubbed his eyes and opened them. He looked at Brad and squinted.

"Better?"

"A bit. Looks like you're swimming under water but I can see you. Whew. That was scary."

John Henry looked around. He squinted in the dazzling sun. A waterless, barren, sterile desert.

Dragoons shuffled along single file in the loose sand, leading their exhausted mounts, the intervals between men lengthening. Abandoned equipment and dead and dying animals lined the trail.

John Henry looked down the back trail and guessed that the last man—that would be Corporal Jackson—must be a mile below.

"Ready?" Brad stood up.

John Henry did not move. He sat with legs extended and spread, gazing down the slope to the desolate flats.

"You know, Bradford, what I really need is to sit on Morita's porch and have her rub my shoulders the way she does while I eat old Tia's *frijoles* and drink her chocolate. That's what I really need."

Brad followed John Henry's gaze eastward. After a long moment, he said, "That's not possible."

John Henry looked up at Brad. "Tell me why not. You know how I feel about all this. You don't want me beside you if it comes to a fight, Brad. This is not my war. I won't fight. There's nothing for me west of here. My life's there." He pointed down the back trail, eastward.

"I know what you mean but we've got to do what we came to do. Hell, it might be over already. All we'll have to do in California is wade in the ocean and lay on the beach." Brad smiled.

John Henry rubbed his eyes, straightened and shook his head. "Well said, Bradford." He sighed. "Help me up."

Brad took John Henry's outstretched hand and pulled him up. They walked slowly back toward the trail where their mounts were tied to a mesquite. John Henry walked unsteadily but without assistance.

"What I want to know," John Henry said, "is where's all the fat sheep and cattle we've heard so much about? Where's all the green? This is not the California we've been hearing about." John Henry waved his arm as if to take in the whole landscape.

It was a land of sand and mesquite, with scattered thickets of sharp-pointed century plant and ocotillo and an occasional palm. Grass was sparse and of the coarsest kind. The craggy mountains of granite and quartz, seamed with volcanic debris, were bare of vegetation.

The day before, the soldiers had, with difficulty, prevented their mounts from drinking from salty pools. Shortly after, the earth had quivered three times within a minute, the last tremor sending more than one man in the column to his knees. It was as if the army's trail lay along the very rim of hell.

"I've been wondering the same thing, John Henry. But Carson knows this trail and he says that that California is just over that ridge." He pointed to the pass toward which the column headed. "Warner's place should be just on the other side."

Since the day, a century ago it seemed, that Carson had told them about Warner's Ranch, every soldier had longed to reach this oasis that to them meant the end of suffering and the ascent into paradise.

"All right, Bradford, if you promise it's just on the other side, I believe I'll make it."

John Henry untied Remolino's reins and stepped into the track of the slowly moving column. Brad fell in behind him.

I'll make it, all right. It's on the road home. He suddenly had a warm feeling for Juan José, born Jonathan Trumbull, Warner, who had himself trekked from Santa Fé to California over fifteen years ago.

The seven days since leaving the Colorado had been a nightmare. Though it was late November, the sun had been scorching. Water was found occasionally by digging in dry streambeds but it was never enough.

The poor animals were reduced to eating mesquite beans and dry sticks. Their cries during the night had affected even the most calloused campaigner.

Horses and mules staggered under their loads. Equipment was abandoned and the command was still on foot. The trail was marked by valuable military equipment and dead and dying animals.

A heavy fog one day brought welcome relief from the sun and light snow was seen on nearby mountaintops. The weakened troopers were soon shivering in their wet blankets and greatcoats that were broken out for the first time since leaving Fort Leavenworth.

An abundant spring finally was found near the trail and men and stock drank their fill. But then the heat returned. The trail melted to deep sand and turned upward. The animals, bloated on water and cane, failed by the score. Packs of wolves, which had shadowed the column since daybreak, now moved in and tore at the carcasses.

Warner's Ranch proved, if not paradise, at least salvation. General Kearny requisitioned enough mutton and beef to satisfy his hungry army. The soldiers did justice to the supply, none having had enough to eat since leaving Santa Fé. That agreeable chore finished, they were free to wander about the ranch. The General had decreed that they would move no more this day.

"Bradford," John Henry said, "this day will be recorded in history as one of the most notable. I don't recall that I have ever eaten so much or so well." They were strolling leisurely toward the huts of the ranch's Indian laborers.

"I don't know, Johnny. It was pretty flat eatin' without salt and bread."

"Wha-a-a-t? Flat eating! I didn't notice that the lack of salt and bread prevented you from eating a whole hind-quarter by yourself."

Brad, John Henry, and five others indeed had consumed an entire fat sheep at a single meal.

"It was filling. I'll grant you that," Brad replied. "I've eaten better."

"No doubt you have," John Henry smiled, "and no doubt you'll eat better again. Tell you what. You come to Santa Fé two months to the day after my enlistment ends and I'll serve you a meal you'll talk about the rest of your life."

Brad stopped walking and looked at his partner's back as he continued walking slowly.

"What's he talking about, Kit?" John Henry had stopped beside Carson who was talking with some half-naked Indians standing in front of their mud and thatch huts. Brad joined them.

"They're just groanin' about bad times. They say they lived pretty good when they lived at the missions. But when the Mexican government took the mission lands away from the good padres and gave them to the ranchers, the Indians were caught in the middle. They had forgotten the old ways, so all they could do was sell their labor to the ranchers. This is the way they live now." Carson motioned toward a hut with his head.

John Henry and Brad glanced inside. There were but few personal possessions lying about the mud floor. Though the temperature was near freezing and dropped well below freezing at night, there was no fire or coverings of any sort except a few well-used sheepskins.

"Poor devils won't fare any better in an American California," Carson said as he walked away.

At dusk, General Kearny had the army assembled before the main ranch house. They were a different lot from the derelicts who had stumbled into the same yard just a few hours ago. They had eaten their fill and their faces were no longer drawn with fatigue. Kearny climbed upon a watering trough and faced the gathering. They fell silent.

"Men, I want to tell you what we have learned about the state of affairs in California and my immediate plans. First, you may have been wondering why you have not met the famous Mr. Warner. He is, in fact, away in San Diego. We have his foreman, Mr. Marshall, a New Hampshire man, to thank for his hospitality." Kearny motioned toward the man who stood at the corner of the house.

Marshall blushed and nodded shyly as a shout went up from the soldiers.

Kearny held up his hand, and the shouting died. "If our information is correct at this moment, the Mexicans are in control of the entire province of California except the ports of San Diego, Monterey, and San Francisco, which our forces hold.

"Now, we have a job to do. We will prevail but it will not be easy. It will require the utmost from every man.

We have made a magnificent march. Your training and your courage have brought you through." The soldiers shouted in unison. "We set out to secure California for the American nation and to give its people the blessings of liberty and democracy.

"Now we must finish the job. We will lay over here tomorrow. Rest and prepare yourselves and your weapons. The following morning, we march for San Diego where we will join forces with Commodore Stockton, the American naval commander. That is all."

The dragoons cheered loudly as Kearny stepped down from the trough and walked away, followed by his officers and Marshall.

Corporal Jackson watched four Mexicans who were packing saddlebags on their mounts and tying blankets behind saddles. Their mules stood quietly where they were tied to the hitching rail. One of the Mexicans reached down to tighten a cinch.

John Henry and Brad strolled over. "What's going on?" John Henry asked Jackson. "The General said we weren't moving ahead today."

"True enough," Jackson replied, "but these Mex ain't the army and they ain't moving ahead. They're going back to meet Colonel Cooke and lead him here. Cooke's Mormon Battalion is on our trail and the General's afraid he'll get lost."

"When are they leaving?" John Henry asked.

"You see 'em getting ready. They're leaving as soon as they finish. Half hour or so. I'm here to keep 'em busy."

"Just the four of them going?"

"Yep."

"Isn't that a bit risky? They could decide soon as they

get over the first rise that they're on a fool's mission and just head south."

"I suppose that could happen."

"Wouldn't it make sense if a dragoon or two went with them, just to be sure Cooke gets the word?"

"S'pose so."

"Shouldn't someone bring that to the General's attention?"

Corporal Jackson turned to face John Henry. He frowned. "Somebody maybe but not me. I'm not gonna do it. The General might agree that it's such a good idea that I should go with 'em. I seen that desert once and I don't intend to see it again." He turned away and strolled over to the Mexicans.

John Henry turned excitedly toward Brad.

"Brad—"

"Forget it, Johnny."

"But Brad, what a chance—"

"Goddammit, John Henry, I said forget it!" Brad turned on his heel and strode away.

CHAPTER 12

Morning came slowly. The sun's rays did not penetrate the heavy gray cloud. The army had hardly taken the trail when the rain began. It was soon falling in torrents.

Their route lay through a narrow valley between high, barren hills. Dragoons plodded along, soaked through, heads down, blending with the sodden landscape.

Night brought no relief. Attempts to kindle fires failed. The water-soaked wood would not light or it would flicker briefly and die. In the end, the troopers bedded down on the cold, wet ground in blankets already soaked.

Daybreak was little different from night. Yesterday's overcast had lowered and darkened. Dragoons awakened from a fitful sleep. They rolled from their blankets more slowly than usual, stretching and groaning, rubbing stiff joints. A few poor fires had hardly begun to radiate warmth when the call to horse sounded.

John Henry climbed woodenly into the saddle. He had not slept, shivering, hurting, thinking. He sat silently, staring into space, waiting. His eyes were slits. He had not shaved for days and his hair hung in wet strings over his forehead and ears. His hat was dirty and wet, his coat soaked.

The heavy ceiling dropped, gathered, and became a dense fog. A column of twos formed and moved off down the narrow canyon. Dark oaks covered the hills that became walls and closed about them. Fog obscured the landscape and the antlike army that disappeared into it. A light rain began to fall.

John Henry dozed in the saddle. Awake, he could see no other living being, in front or behind. He heard no sound save the muffled steps of Remolino.

Asleep, he was in Santa Fé, sitting on Morita's porch, barefoot, leaning against the wall, the sun warming the white canvas shirt and trousers that were hot when touched, eyes closed against the glare, Morita sitting on the porch, leaning against a post, facing him, the cotton dress pushed above her knees in the heat, revealing soft, brown legs, their legs touching, her arm and hand resting on his bare leg, watching him, unsmiling . . .

He jolted upright. Remolino had bumped into the mule in front. The column was stopped. He heard voices ahead. Excited, unfamiliar voices. He rode up beside the trooper in front of him. It was Brad.

"What's going on, Brad? Can you make out what they're saying? Who is it?"

Brad held up his hand to quiet John Henry. He leaned forward in his saddle, openmouthed, trying to hear. After a minute: "Nothing. I can't see ten feet ahead and I can't make out a thing."

The fire burned brightly but it was a pinprick of light in the deep canyon where the army had pitched its camp. The rain had stopped and the fog had thinned and lifted to the tops of the huge black oaks. The trees towered above them and took on grotesque shapes as the firelight danced among the branches.

John Henry sat in front of his tent, a short distance from the fire. Two of his messmates squatted on the other side of the crackling fire, talking excitedly, but he was not listening to them. He stared into the flames. His thoughts raced and he could feel his heart pounding.

He glanced down the canyon at the other tiny fires of the army. At that moment, the cloud cover parted and moonlight filtered through the thin fog, flooding the canyon camp with a silvery glow, making indistinct, gray shadows.

The little, two-man tents were white slabs on a black lawn. The cloud closed and the vision vanished. John Henry shuddered.

His eyes adjusted to the darkness. He looked around. His messmates were gone. He stared into the fire. The flames burned lower.

So there would be a fight after all. Not perhaps. For sure. Not "when we get to California," or "if we contact the enemy." Not some undetermined time.

Tomorrow. Not some shadowy, faceless enemy. A group of flesh-and-blood Californians who were camped nine miles ahead in the middle of the trail the army must take to reach San Diego.

The commotion that fog-shrouded afternoon was the result of the arrival of a party of thirty-seven sailors and volunteers under Marine Lieutenant Archibald Gillespie, sent from San Diego by Commodore Stockton to rendez-vous with the Army of the West.

Gillespie had brought with him the rumor that an en-emy force was moving into the army's path below. After making camp that evening, Kearny had sent Lieutenant Hammond with a small party to scout out the enemy. In the dark, the troopers almost stumbled into the middle of the Californian bivouac.

The Americans escaped and now both Americans and Californians knew of the presence of the other. Each would prepare for the battle that they knew must come and could not honorably avoid.

On Hammond's return, General Kearny had announced that the camp would be roused at two a.m. They would march at two-thirty a.m. They would attack the enemy at first light.

John Henry got up. He walked to the fire and stood there, hands in pockets. He watched the last flame wave, flicker and go out. He turned, walked back to his tent.

Stooping, he crawled into the tent. He removed his pants and boots and slid into his blankets, careful not to disturb Brad. Hands under his head, he lay, staring in the dark at the tent wall.

"Brad," John Henry said softly. The tent flap was open and the bright moonlight dimly illuminated the interior and John Henry kneeling beside Brad's bed.

Brad's face was toward the tent wall. He breathed evenly and deeply.

"Brad," John Henry said again. He gently touched his partner's shoulder.

Brad rolled over slowly. He opened his eyes and frowned when he saw John Henry. He rose on an elbow. He blinked and shook his head.

"Is it time?" He rubbed his face. "Damn, that was a short night." Brad started to throw the blanket from him, but John Henry caught his arm.

"It's not time yet," John Henry said in little more than a whisper. "I wanted to tell you that I'm leaving."

"Leaving!" Brad sat sharply upright. He was wide-awake. "You can't do that! We've got—"

"There's nothing more to say. I can't take part in that fight tomorrow. I'm going to Santa Fé. If I don't go back right now, I'll go mad."

Brad sat up. He rubbed his face vigorously with both hands. He took a deep breath and exhaled slowly.

"Johnny. You said it. We've been through all this before and you admitted that you have a duty. To your country, to every man in this army, and to yourself. You admitted it."

"That's changed. I know now what I've got to do."

"You'd never make it. The Indians or the country would do you in. Your horse is worn out. You'd be afoot in no time. And what about yourself? You're not well, John Henry. What if you have one of your spells?"

"I've thought about all that. Brad, I haven't slept. I've been awake, thinking. I felt like boulders were being piled on top of me to the point of crushing me. My head was so full and hurt so much I thought—I actually thought—that only my death would give me relief.

"My death—or Morita. Do you see how simple it is? When I decided to leave, the weight pressing me down vanished and my head cleared. I have never felt better, physically or mentally."

"But you can't make it. Have you completely forgotten these past weeks?"

"I haven't forgotten. That's the point. I'll follow the back trail. I know where the water is. I've been squirreling provisions, in case it came to this, and I can buy supplies from the Maricopas and Pimas."

"You'd be a deserter. The army'll be after you. They'll make an example of you."

"The army will forget me. There'll be no roll call

before marching. After the fight, I'll simply be missing in action. If not, I'll not worry. The army is going to be too busy to worry about me."

"Don't go, Johnny."

"Don't you understand? There's nothing for me here. The war has nothing for me. California has nothing for me. I can't make it unless I go back to Morita."

Brad slumped and withdrew into the shadow.

"You can't go back," Brad said softly.

"The time for talking is finished, old buddy. My kit is packed and time is getting on. I must—"

"There was some trouble."

"Trouble? What do you mean, 'trouble'?"

"Some trouble at the cantina, just before we left. Morita may not . . . be there."

"Oh, come off it, Brad. I'm going now. When all this is over, you come—"

"She was hurt bad."

"What?"

John Henry jerked around to face Brad but he could not see above the line of shadow across his chest. John Henry froze, but instantly relaxed. He bent down to lift his pack.

"It won't work," he said. "I saw her just before we left Santa Fé." He picked up the pack.

A hand reached from the shadow and rested on the pack.

"Johnny," Brad said softly, "you spent the night with Morita that you thought was our last night in Santa Fé. You got back just before dawn and the watch caught you. Remember?"

"Yes." John Henry set the pack down.

"Remember we didn't march that day. Our departure was delayed a day and you had to march in circles all day with a full pack. You were confined to the post that night. I went to the cantina alone. Remember?"

"I remember. You told me next morning that you'd told Morita that we were leaving the next day and you told her why I couldn't come. You said she cried."

"That's true. That all happened," he said.

John Henry was frozen. He waited.

"There was a bunch of no-count volunteers there that night, no better'n hogs. They raised hell all evening. At closing time, one tried to get Morita out the door with him. She tried to pull away from him and I got up to help her.

Before I got there, he hit her with the bottle. He was so drunk, he didn't know what he was doing, but I killed him anyway, Johnny. Me and th' Mexicans killed him."

John Henry grabbed handfuls of Brad's shirt and held him at arm's length.

"What happened to Morita!"

"The Mexicans carried her into the back room. She was unconscious. She might have been . . . they wouldn't let me see her. They were confused and angry. They threatened me and made me leave."

"My god, Brad . . . why didn't you tell me?" The voice was forced and unnatural. "Damn you, Brad!"

John Henry lunged forward and connected with a blow to Brad's jaw. John Henry fell on him.

Brad grabbed him and held him tightly.

"Hang on, Johnny! Hang on."

John Henry relaxed. He sobbed.

Brad released him.

John Henry rolled off Brad to the ground to lie on his back. He was still. He stared at the dark peak.

"I wish I had told you, Johnny. I was sure you'd never go back to Santa Fé. I was sure you'd get to California and the end of this goddammed war and your enlistment would be up and you'd be anxious for home and your folks and New Mexico would be a million miles away and you'd never go back.

"I didn't want to see you hurt. I wanted Morita to be something good that happened to you. That's how I reasoned it out when I decided not to tell you. I was wrong, Johnny, and I'm so sorry."

John Henry sat up. He stared blankly at the tent opening.

"What're you going to do?" Brad said.

John Henry shook his head. He reached for his pack. "I told you. I'm leaving. Nothing's changed." He pulled the pack toward him. He picked it up and held it to his chest.

"Damn you, Brad," John Henry said softly, as tears streamed down his face.

John Henry crawled backward on his hands and knees toward the tent opening.

"Roll out! Roll out! We march in fifteen minutes! Make your packs and leave 'em! Step lively! Fifteen minutes!"

John Henry's head came up sharply. "What? It's not time yet!" He backed hurriedly from the tent on his hands and knees.

Once outside, he stood quickly and almost collided with Corporal Jackson. John Henry grabbed Jackson's arm.

"It's not two o'clock yet! What's this call about?"

Jackson jerked loose from John Henry's grasp. "The General has decided to get an early start. Move!"

John Henry started to object but the corporal was gone.

Soft moonlight illuminated the camp. The huge leafless trees cast ragged black shadows over the campground. Soldiers stood before their tents, fussing nervously with packs and weapons. Brad checked his carbine and cartridge boxes, and then he checked them again. He adjusted his saber and stuffed gear into his pack.

John Henry's carbine hung on his shoulder, his saber at his hip. His pack rested at his feet. He stood motionless and waited, staring blankly. He was reminded of drills at Fort Leavenworth.

What games we play.

A subdued call to horse sounded. Brad motioned toward the corrals. He looked anxiously at John Henry. They walked away together.

There was a scurrying about in the darkness, the creaking of leather and metallic clinking as dragoons mounted, settled, and moved into a column of twos. After a minute, all was quiet.

The march began, without signal, as they moved off into a light, silvery ground fog.

An advance guard of twelve soldiers, including John Henry and Brad and led by Captain Johnston, took the lead. They were mounted on the best horses the army could muster. General Kearny and a few officers rode behind the advance guard. The rest of the force followed.

John Henry weaved in the saddle. He squeezed his eyes shut and rubbed his temples. Beads of perspiration appeared on his forehead, collected and rolled down his cheek. His joints ached and his sagging shoulders rocked back and forth with Remolino's steps. His head was racked by waves of pain that were becoming unbearable and a comfort.

The sky lightened with the first hint of dawn. Darkness still covered the land like a blanket. The army's trail wound among low hills covered with brush and shadowy trees that were outlined against the rose-colored sky.

Hoof beats ahead brought the column to a halt. The rider rounded a point in the trail and slowed to a trot. It was Carson. He passed the advance guard and pulled up at General Kearny's position, five ranks back.

"They're there," Carson said.

John Henry didn't turn in his saddle but he heard the scout distinctly.

"The trail ahead drops down gradually about half a mile, then it opens into a narrow valley, not much more'n a ravine. The Californians are drawn up about a half-mile further on. A ways behind them, there's a little Indian village, name of San Pascual. Beyond that, the valley widens out.

"I got pretty close to 'em. They're well mounted, that's for sure. Some have carbines. They all seem to have lances, willow lances. It's a good weapon in the right hands."

"Did they see you?" Kearny said.

"I don't think so. Wouldn't make any difference. They know we're here."

"You said the Californians won't fight."

"The Californians like a good show, General. Show 'em a little steel and they'll decide real fast that the party's over."

"Good. I trust you know your Californians." Kearny turned to the front.

"All right, Captain Johnston."

The column moved forward. Rounding a point, the trail began a gentle descent. At the same time, the fog began to thin and lift. John Henry weaved and bounced in the saddle as Remolino picked his way down the stony path.

He was dizzy, the same feeling he had when he had fallen from the hay wagon and banged his head on the hard ground. No, it was the same feeling he had when he had drunk too much at the cantina and Morita helped him walk to her house. *My house. Home. Mi casa.*

Abruptly, the jostling stopped. John Henry numbly realized that Remolino was walking now on level ground and on sod instead of rock. He shook his head and tried to focus. The column had emerged from the canyon into the head of the valley.

Dawn. The ceiling had lifted but still obscured the sun. Patches of fog lay near the ground.

The column halted. There was a sudden buzzing of conversation, which ended abruptly. Absolute silence. The dragoons stared down the valley. John Henry squinted through bleary eyes in the same direction.

There they were. The enemy. A line of horsemen, about three hundred yards away, blocked the trail. They sat quietly. Waiting.

Members of the guard began talking softly. Their excited talk revealed both an eagerness for combat and apprehension. John Henry's head was down and his eyes shut.

"Yeah, I got here just in time. Colonel Cooke sent us ahead to scout trail and we ran into your camp last night.

"Say, do you know somebody in your unit named 'Juanito'?"

John Henry's head came up slowly. His eyes opened, fluttered and squinted. He tried to focus, still facing forward.

He shook his head. He turned around in the saddle to face the speaker in the rank just behind him. John Henry didn't recognize him.

"I was supposed to give him a message but I couldn't find him last night. I was—"

"I'm Juanito," John Henry said, suddenly clearheaded.

"What's the message?"

"You don't look like—"

"I'm Juanito! What's the message!"

"Okay, okay. It's from a Mexican girl. All she said was to tell Juanito: '*Apúrate*'." Hurry.

John Henry stiffened. His eyes opened wide.

"How was she! How did she look!" John Henry was oblivious of the other soldiers' stares.

"She was fine." The soldier grinned. "She looked damn good to me."

John Henry turned abruptly to the front. He jerked his head right and left. His body was suddenly taut, coiled. His hands tightened on the reins. He glanced quickly at Brad on his right.

Brad had not taken his eyes off him since the new arrival started speaking. He betrayed no emotion now.

John Henry snapped back to the front. He jerked Remolino's reins, almost causing him to rear, then suddenly wheeled the horse leftward out of line and collided hard with a passing horseman, almost unseating him.

"What the hell are you doing? Get back in line! By God!" It was Captain Johnston. At that precise moment, Johnston was riding alongside the guard toward the front. He settled his horse and continued forward.

John Henry pulled Remolino slowly back into line beside Brad. John Henry closed his eyes and rolled his head back. He slowly faced front, eyes still closed, and sat quietly. Brad watched him but said nothing.

Captain Johnston took his place at the head of the advance guard. He drew his sword slowly and pointed the blade skyward.

John Henry had heard the sword being pulled from its scabbard and opened his eyes to slits, seeing the naked blade through fevered eyes. Dragoons in front and around him drew their swords and came to the carry. The blades shone in the morning light and waved gently as horses shifted from side to side.

John Henry drew his sword mechanically and brought the guard to his right hip, the blade against his shoulder. Discipline.

The only sounds were those of swords being drawn from scabbards, creaking leather and clinking of metal fittings and horses stamping.

God in Heaven, it's going to happen! Oh God, let me wake up from this bad dream! Oh God, before it's too late!

John Henry looked back, over the heads of the dragoons, to the trail where the army had left the canyon.

"Charge!" Captain Johnston's shout shattered the calm.

The dragoons in the advance guard shot forward, their swords held high. John Henry almost lost his seat when Remolino lunged ahead, following the other horses. He regained his seat and tightened the slack rein. He heard sharp cries behind as General Kearny's party and other units joined the dash.

The entire command charged at full gallop directly for the line of Californians. Order vanished as the column widened and became a ragged mass of individuals. The crash of hoofs and the jangling of bits and equipment, punctuated by primitive yells of troopers, attacked John Henry's ears until he thought he must cry from pain and anger.

John Henry turned to look at Brad who returned his glance sharply, then turned to the front, sword held high, spurring his mount and yelling loudly.

A puff of smoke lifted from the enemy line. Captain Johnston rose in his saddle, as if to listen, then settled back. His body relaxed and he slid slowly from the saddle and dropped to the ground.

John Henry was riding not more than fifteen feet behind Johnston and had seen his hat fly off and the back of his head open when the bullet struck him. Remolino swerved to avoid colliding with the tumbling body.

After firing the single volley at the charging Americans, the enemy line broke. The Californians turned their horses and galloped down the valley. The dragoons shouted and spurred their mounts after them.

John Henry rode as if in a trance. He tottered drunkenly in the saddle. He blinked his eyes to clear them, to watch the Californians, fleeing for their lives—God with them!—then his eyes filmed over and he saw only a translucent, shimmering mass. He winced as thunderbolts pierced his brain.

How strange that I didn't hear the shots. Didn't I scream when Captain Johnston was hit? Why don't I hear the horses now and the men? They're all around me. It's so peaceful now. So quiet.

John Henry shook his head, blinked rapidly, and recovered his vision in time to see the Californians pull their horses to a skidding halt, wheel about and charge the Americans, lances lowered.

They are brave men, he thought to himself, placidly, detached, an observer, *but foolish to sacrifice themselves. Do they think to preserve their liberty, these few?*

A glance from side to side changed his mind. His fevered condition did not prevent his seeing that the advance guard had run away from the rest of the army and was alone.

The charging Californians outnumbered them and they were better mounted. He remembered that Carson had called them the best horsemen in the world. They and their mounts were fresh and they were armed with the long willow lances against the dragoons' swords.

So, I am to die. He shuddered, and his vision blurred. *It's so quiet. How will it feel, the lance? Where will it enter my body? Will I feel it? How deep will it go? Will it break? Or will he let it go after it has penetrated far enough to kill? How does it kill? I never thought about that.*

John Henry was calm. He dropped his sword to the ground.

The dream-trance broke and the sight and sounds of violence gradually returned. The pounding hoofs, rattling of saddle gear, shouts in English and Spanish, all mounting, blending to a roar in his head that obscured his vision.

He closed his eyes to make it stop, they fluttered open and saw the white horse, eyes bulging and ears laid back, the Californian leaning forward, the lance held tightly aimed at John Henry's chest, a shaft of lightning, a sparkling point, the soldier's face a calm mask, a handsome face marked by the scar on his right cheek, their eyes locked a moment and John Henry was light and spinning. The roaring diminished and ended as he was lifted, drifting, spiraling upward. Black.

Naranja dulce limón partido
Dame un abrazo que yo te pido
Si fueran falsos . . .

CHAPTER 13

The bird's song awakened him. It came from a distance but, unmistakably, a mockingbird's song. Each note was sharp and distinct. A pause, then the song again, closer.

He lay on his back, with his arms and legs extended, quiet and still. His eyes were closed. He stared upward into a black void. He felt a pebble under his left hand and moved it with his index finger. He lay still again.

He became conscious of lying on something sharp. Just below his right collarbone. He moved his shoulder slightly and the pain eased.

A breath of air cooled his cheek. He felt something on his neck, then his ear, but he dared not move, even to open his eyes.

After a long moment, he extended the fingers of his left hand, gripped the pebble in a fist, then released it and relaxed.

His eyelids fluttered open, slowly, tentatively. He saw blue sky, nothing more. Clean, clear, light blue sky, a million miles of it. His mind was as clear as the sky. He closed his eyes and concentrated. He did not hurt.

He opened his eyes. Something moved in his peripheral

vision. He turned his head slightly leftward and saw leaves overhead, swaying gently in the light breeze. Brown leaves, and dull green leaves, others with a hint of yellow. Oak.

He rolled his head slowly to the right. He saw a line of low bushes, a type that he did not recognize. He remembered that he had seen masses of them the morning of the battle.

The battle. He tried to recall the battle. The charge, the sounds, the feel and the field. But he could not. He closed his eyes and scoured his memory but found only shadows.

He opened his eyes and saw blue sky again. A bird flew across his view. He stared at blue sky a long minute.

He must do something. He was afraid but he knew that he must try.

He pulled his legs together slowly, then brought his arms to his sides. He rolled gently to his right until he was on his side.

Then he stopped, waiting for the pain. Nothing. Stiffness, but no pain. He pulled both knees upward and, pushing with his left hand on the ground in front of him, he rose on his right elbow. And waited.

Nothing. He sighed heavily. *I do seem to be in one piece yet.*

He looked around. He was lying in a small clearing bordered by brush and an occasional oak. A snap behind him brought him around sharply.

It was Remolino. The horse was standing at the edge of the clearing, about twenty yards away in a lush patch of grass. He was saddled and the reins trailed on the ground as he cropped grass.

John Henry realized that he was sitting up. And he felt all right. In fact, he decided right then that he had never felt so good, in body or soul. A sense of euphoria flowed through him that he made no attempt to examine.

He drew his legs under him and, pushing on the ground with his right hand, stood slowly upright. He stretched and breathed deeply, relishing the sharp, clean air. He scanned the horizon. The heavens, the land, and his soul were without blemish. All was pure.

He walked slowly toward Remolino. The horse stopped grazing, looked at him, and tossed his head in recognition, the reins flying.

John Henry laid a hand on the horse's neck and gathered the reins with the other. He put a foot in the stirrup and swung lightly into the saddle. He closed his eyes and faced the warm morning sun. He opened his eyes and patted Remolino on the neck.

Squeezing gently with his knees, he pointed the horse toward a break in the brush. The break opened to a dry wash that meandered down toward the valley. John Henry rode slowly down the wash.

He pulled Remolino to a stop more than once, simply to listen and to look. The morning sun filtered through the thin cloud layers, drawing soft circles and rectangles of light on the valley floor. All was quiet, serene, and peace.

Near the base of the wash where its course entered the flat valley, John Henry stopped. He scanned the valley, from the copse at the head where the army had left the canyon to the opposite end.

Near the foot of the valley, slender smoke spirals rose and merged with the lacy cloud layer. John Henry watched for a minute, then turned Remolino off the wash and rode through the tall heavy brush along the edge of the valley.

Nearing the smoke spirals, John Henry reined in and dismounted. He tied Remolino's reins to a bush, then moved quietly through the brush to the edge of cover. He crouched behind a low bush.

The army's camp lay a hundred yards away. Equipment was strewn about the campground. Some soldiers wandered idly about. Others stood talking, cleaning weapons and working on horse gear. A few soldiers crouched at cooking fires. Some lay on blankets near the fire. The wounded.

A few troopers wandered about the perimeter of the camp, collecting firewood. A soldier walked in John Henry's direction, bending from time to time to collect dry sticks and adding them to the stack cradled in his arm. When he was about thirty yards from John Henry, the soldier straightened up, facing the brushy hillside, and flexed his back.

It was Brad.

John Henry watched him readjust his load. John Henry slowly lowered the branch that hid his face.

Brad saw him. Brad stared, grim. After an eternity, he smiled broadly. John Henry and Brad looked at each other for a long moment.

Then Brad stooped and picked up a stick and added it to his load. He turned and walked back toward the camp, his small collection of firewood cradled in his arm.

John Henry watched him go. Releasing the branch slowly, he backed up until he could stand upright.

He walked back to Remolino. He untied the reins, mounted, and turned the horse back the way he had come, toward the morning sun.

"*Adelante, Remolino. A casa.*" Home.

APPENDIX

Origins of The Mexican War

When Texas won its independence from Mexico in 1836, the United States recognized the new republic and the already strained relations between Mexico and the United States worsened.

Fearing that they would have to fight a perpetual battle with Mexico to preserve their independence, and quickly accumulating a debt, the Texans applied for admission to the United States, an action that seemed to justify Mexico's assumption that the United States had sponsored the rebellion.

Most Americans favored expansion but the Texas application was not an immediate success. Northerners did not relish the acquisition of a territory that could be divided into four or five new slave states. Many Americans feared war with Mexico, which had not acknowledged the loss of Texas. Mexico had promised war if the United States should annex the northern province, part of Mexico's sovereign domain.

The tide, nevertheless, ran for Texas. Sam Houston, the shrewd president of the new republic, informed

Washington that if the United States turned a deaf ear to the Texan entreaties, it would have to look elsewhere, to Great Britain or France.

Britain certainly was interested. British merchants saw an independent Texas as a lucrative market for their manufactured goods. Texas cotton would serve as a price-dampening competitor to cotton from the American South.

Leaders of the British anti-slavery movement were overjoyed at the prospect of British influence in Texas giving them a foothold in the young nation. If the crusade could weaken the abominable institution in Texas, it could then strike at slavery in the United States.

Washington was not unaware of the danger of Great Britain or some other European nation pulling a weak Texas into its orbit. The Monroe Doctrine was dusted off and quoted as justification for annexing Texas. The issue was settled in 1844 with the election of James K. Polk.

The virtually unknown Polk had sensed the expansionist mood of Americans and rode the swell to the White House. We will have Oregon, California, and Texas, he had said in his campaign. The voters agreed that he was their man and elected him. Annexation soon followed, even before he was sworn in.

The winds of war quickened. Commodore John Drake Sloat commanded a squadron of American warships off Mexico's west coast. Mexicans knew why he was there. His predecessor, Commodore Thomas ap Catesby Jones, in 1842, had sailed into the bay of Monterey, the capital of Mexican California, and took possession of the town.

Jones had believed a rumor that war had broken out between the United States and Mexico. He soon realized his mistake, apologized and withdrew, but the Mexicans were not reassured.

While Sloat hovered off the coast, Thomas O. Larkin, an American merchant in Monterey and also the United States consul to California, had secret orders to encourage the rebellious spirit of the Californians who had no great love for the distant national government in Mexico City.

At the same time, Lieutenant John C. Frémont, United States Army Topographical Engineers, was in California with a party of sixty-two well-armed men, a small army in frontier regions. On being challenged by the authorities, Frémont explained that he was surveying. But why in Mexican territory, they asked?

Since the annexation of Texas, new disputes had arisen to divide Mexico and the United States. American citizens had claims of something over $2,000,000 against the Mexican government, largely for damages to property during Mexico's tumultuous civil disorders following 1821 when its own revolution against Spain ended. Mexico had agreed in 1843, to pay the claims but defaulted after three installments.

There was also heated controversy over the boundary of Texas. Texans claimed the Rio Grande as their southern and western limit. Mexico claimed the more northerly Nueces River.

Polk would fulfill his campaign promises by peaceful means if possible. He proposed negotiation of the claims and boundary disputes. Mexico City agreed to talk but because of turmoil within Mexico and an unexpected attempt by the United States to purchase California, an overture that Mexico considered insulting, the American emissary was rejected. Polk responded by ordering General Zachary Taylor to march deep into the disputed territory.

As relations between the two countries worsened, Polk became impatient and decided on war. He prepared a message for Congress, a delicately worded message, for he was going to ask Congress to initiate war by authorizing American forces to fire the first shot.

The message was never delivered. Three days before he was scheduled to deliver it to Congress, word arrived from General Taylor that a Mexican force had crossed the Rio Grande and fired on American dragoons. There were casualties.

Polk revised his message. Mexicans had shed American blood on American soil, he said. The members of Congress were outraged and declared war on Mexico.

A new force, the Army of the West, was formed at Fort Leavenworth, Kansas, to carry the war to Mexico's northern frontier. Fort Leavenworth had been patrolling the frontier since the fort's establishment in 1827 and sending out columns over the Santa Fé Trail to protect merchants and up the Oregon Trail to convince Indians not to molest emigrants.

Following the declaration of war on Mexico, Fort Leavenworth was a beehive of activity as volunteers poured in from the Missouri countryside, full of the flag and ready for adventure. Noncommissioned officers swore and sweated in their labors to turn the free spirits into soldiers while officers despaired of their success.

The Army of the West, nevertheless, took shape. It was made up of a number of units. There were the two regular companies of First Dragoons under Edwin V. Sumner, two batteries of six-pounder artillery commanded by Major Clark, and a small group of topographical engineers under Lieutenant William H. Emory.

The rest, the bulk of the army, was composed of volunteer units. There were the first regiment of Missouri Cavalry under Colonel Alexander W. Doniphan, an infantry regiment from Missouri led by Colonel Sterling Price, and an infantry battalion of Mormon volunteers enlisted by Captain James Allen who had been dispatched to meet the Mormon migration at Council Bluffs. Colonel Philip St. George Cooke assumed command of the Battalion at Santa Fé.

It was in this Army of the West that dragoon John Henry Harris cast his lot.

IF I SHOULD DIE

CHAPTER 1
Roots and Kin

I have a ranch on the west Texas plains. I do a fair job running it but I didn't build it. It was a gift from a long line of hard-working forebears with grit and imagination.

It all began in a foreign country a long time ago. This is their story and mine.

I'm reluctant to invite people, even good friends, into my study. They see nothing but chaos here and they tell me. I smile at their ignorance. Where they see chaos, I see order.

Piles of original letters and photocopies, a box of yellowed, brittle newspapers, a bunch of fat folders filled with all manner of documents, six stacks of books ranging from old volumes with worn leather edges to new paperbacks. And five journals with pages chipped at the edges and puffy with decades of humidity.

The top of the desk is completely covered with the stuff, save a small workspace before the chair, ample room for the computer and a document or two that I'm working on. The books are arranged neatly in stacks on the floor on each side of the desk.

I know precisely the location and identification of every

item in view and something of its contents.

I picked up a journal and was immediately distracted by the musical whistle of a meadowlark somewhere outside. Pushing my chair back, I stood and walked to the open window, still holding the journal.

There it was in the yard, facing me, its bright yellow chest inscribed with a black V. I swear it looked me right in the eye. I could almost hear it saying: "What now?"

The bird did a pirouette and strutted slowly toward the corral, tail feathers flicking open and shut.

I returned to my desk and sat in the high-backed oak chair. I don't much care for this chair. But Donie liked it. That is, she liked it since it was long in the family, it was old, and it matched the desk. She never sat in it, so she didn't know how uncomfortable it is. I never complained to her and I wouldn't part with it now.

I laid the journal on the desk, pushed it aside, and reached for a stack of letters. I thumbed through them, not really sure what I was looking for. I've been working on this thing over a year now and I'm still learning. Before I became obsessed with it, family history had been a great bore. It's who's here that counts, I always figured, not who's gone on.

Now, history in general I like. I majored in history at Texas Tech, figuring I might want to teach someday. That would get me off the ranch and into town. Somewhere not too far away. I had never been out of Texas at that point and my world was pretty small. I hadn't even been to New Mexico and it was only a few miles west.

That changed with my Navy service. I had requested sea duty and was disappointed when I was assigned shore duty in Okinawa and Japan. It was the best thing that could have happened to me. Living there almost three years cracked the insular barriers in my soul and my mind began to open.

I was fortunate to serve between wars. Too late for Korea and too early for Vietnam. The only combat I saw was a ruckus at Teahouse August Moon in Naha.

Four airmen in uniform who had consumed an abundance of sake thought the serving girls should dance with them but the girls didn't think much of the idea. The airmen squeezed butts and breasts and laughed at the girls' attempts to push them away. The servers were accustomed to some playful attention from airmen and sailors but this was getting out of hand. They were scared.

I got up to defend the girls. The airmen wouldn't likely do violence to an officer. I forgot that I was wearing civvies. I was alone that evening and I had had a few cups of sake myself. I didn't impress the airmen who turned their attention to me. The leader of the lot pushed me in the chest. He ignored the mama-san who pulled at his sleeve.

The outside door opened and a couple of Marines in uniform walked in. They looked over the field and quickly took charge. They didn't actually hurt the airmen, just convinced them real fast that the party was over.

After escorting the rowdies through the exit, the Marine sergeant came back inside and bowed sharply to the girls. Then he turned and bowed to me. He smiled ever so slightly and walked to his waiting companion. They sat at a low table against the far wall. Three girls hurried over, knelt before the table and poured sake into their cups.

By the way, that's Teahouse August Moon, not Teahouse of the August Moon, the abominable movie featuring Marlon Brando as a clown of a Japanese. I get angry every time I think about that damn movie. Donie watched the film with me and she kept patting me on the shoulder and saying, "Olin, it's only a movie."

Anyway, back to *Teahouse August Moon*. The sergeant had recognized me and I him. Only last week, I had driven up island to the Marine brig to visit a sailor who had been sent there after a Navy summary court martial had found him guilty of petty theft. The sailor accepted the finding and he was sentenced to two weeks in the brig.

Three days after his admission to the brig, the sailor complained of being mistreated. I was delegated to investigate.

When I entered the visitor's room, the sailor was standing ramrod straight, butt and back of his head against the wall. He looked straight ahead, eyes fixed on the opposite wall. The Marine sergeant stood behind me. Ramrod straight.

I asked the sailor to explain his mistreatment. He replied loud enough to be heard by ships at sea: "No mistreatment, *sir!*" I reminded him that he had complained of mistreatment. "It was a mistake! *Sir!*"

I turned to the sergeant. "Is that true?"

"Yes, *sir!*" he said. Loudly.

"Carry on," I said to the sailor.

He didn't move. The sergeant nodded to him and the sailor bolted for the door. I nodded to the sergeant.

"Sir!" he said. Loudly. He saluted sharply.

I returned the salute and left. We both knew that the greatest deterrent to wrongdoing on the Navy base was the prospect of spending time in the Marine brig.

I took my release from the Navy in Japan and traveled six months solo in Asia, North Africa, the Middle East, and Europe, in the process, proving that the world was round. My universe enlarged enormously.

But returning to Texas, I knew what I wanted. I wanted to return to my roots. I wanted to return to the ranch and raise cows. I had enjoyed my sortie into the larger world but I knew what world I wanted to inhabit and make my way.

Graduate study in animal husbandry at Texas A&M followed. I knew a little something about cattle and range management but I figured that I could learn a bit more before settling down. I finished my master's degree and returned to Sweetwater. That was 1962. I've been here ever since.

I enjoyed sitting with Daddy in our rocking chairs on the covered front porch in the evening, sipping our G&Ts, watching the sunset. We talked about cows, corrals and fencing, the beef market and the neighbors.

We talked a little about politics. As little as possible, that is, since we had different opinions on most issues of the day. Living in the same house, we both knew that the less said on that subject, the better.

Daddy was content to let me do the worrying and making the hard decisions on running the ranch. Well. I realized later that he was a master in letting me think I was making the decisions. He's long since gone and I miss him terribly. My mama, too. She passed on to her reward a year after he died.

My sweet wife, Donie, died these two years ago and I thought I would never get over her being gone. But I did, though sometimes memories creep back, and I am caught between smiling and crying.

Now I rattle around in this big old house. Six hands drive in each day to help with ranch chores. There's a bunkhouse that used to be home to as many as eight cowboys but it's generally empty now except when one or more of the hands need to get up early in the morning or get chased inside by a late hard rain.

Barbara comes in once or twice a week to clean, get the dishes washed and pass the time with me over coffee in the kitchen or out on the porch. We know that everybody thinks that she stays over at night and it gives us a chuckle over our coffee.

Barbara is fifteen years younger than me and a lot better looking. That doesn't make her any spring chicken since I'm eighty-five. She's a sweet woman and she was Donie's best friend.

She did stay over one night when I refused to let her drive home in a furious storm. "People will talk," she said. "Yeah," I replied and we both laughed out loud.

"I can just hear 'em now," she said. She sat up stiff-backed in her chair. "Olin Harris! You let that woman—they would call me 'that woman'—stay at your house overnight? Well, I never!" We had another good laugh.

We sat on the porch in our rocking chairs at dusk, drinking coffee and listening to the heavy rainfall on the corrugated tin roof, watching the lightning bolts on the horizon and listening to the booming thunder.

I have thought of replacing that roof a bunch of times but each time I pondered out loud, the kids would have none of it. They liked it, even when they moved away. They said it was one of the happiest memories of their childhood. I must admit that I like it too, a hard rain drumming on the tin roof in this dry country, sounding like a loaded freight train racing down the track, out of control.

The rain slackened and the thunder rolled away, at the end sounding like water in a kettle boiling on the stove. Lightning flashed like an electric short, illuminating the yard and barn as bright as midday.

Barbara slept in the guest room and I enjoyed a better breakfast the next morning than my usual toast and tea.

Son Paul didn't take to ranching. He's an attorney in Houston and likes to sail more than he does lawyering. Keeps his boat at Galveston. He must be a good attorney since he and Mollie are off right now on a six-month sail in the south Pacific. They have no children, on purpose, so there's no problem with working around the school year. I get an email or text from him now and then from countries I never even heard of.

I'm also enjoying his occasional postings to Facebook and pictures on Pinterest. I taught him how to use all this social media stuff. My kids marvel that the old man is about as computer-literate as they are. I think it bothers them.

Now my daughter, Cindy, two years younger than Paul, shows more interest in the ranch than he does. She teaches third grade in Seguin, near San Antonio. She and her sweet girl, Gail, come up for a visit occasionally and seem to like the place. Gail loves to ride a little mare I keep for her and she likes to sit on the porch in the evening, talking horses and cows and all sorts of ranch stuff.

Gail might be the future of this ranch. She's going to follow in her granddaddy's and her mama's footsteps and enroll at Texas Tech next fall. So she'll be close and I'll see more of her.

I like their visits and always hope they'll come again soon. They're good reminders of what family is all about. Before Cindy shucked her good-for-nothing husband, their visits had been a bit of a chore since he didn't like the ranch and was bored stiff.

Best thing that ever happened to Cindy was when he ran off with the kindergarten teacher at her school. I mean they ran off. She got a teaching job in Houston and he found work at a car dealer. When all that soured and he wanted to come back, Cindy told him to get lost. I don't say too much since Gail still sees him every now and then.

These days, when I'm alone, I think too much. I mostly take my daily G&T alone in the same rocking chair on the porch, watching the same sunset, listening to the same warm summer breeze in the cottonwoods.

I remember sitting out here evenings as a boy, swinging slowly in the porch swing that hung from the ceiling on thin chains, closing my book and looking out past the corrals to the pasture, yearning almost painfully for a time and a place that probably existed only in the minds of writers like Will James. I read *Sand* four times and never quite got over it.

People have told me that I have come to terms with Donie's passing but I'm not sure about that. Sometimes when I'm trying to sort out why I'm feeling like I do, I seem to be searching for something, some family to hang onto.

It's in these solitary evenings that I began to fill the empty places by populating my past with my forebears. Not just my mama and daddy but their parents and their parents and beyond.

I often wondered about the Indian. There's been a persistent family legend about an Indian ancestor. Every real Texan wants a horse thief and an Indian in his background, specifically a Cherokee princess or a Comanche warrior. Never had any great interest in looking for our horse thief but I was interested in the Indian.

I had DNA testing done by 23 and Me and ancestry. com. I wasn't surprised that the results declared that my ancestors came mostly from Western Europe, largely

England, Northern Ireland and Germany. I was surprised that 3% of my ancestors were from the Middle East. I was delighted to learn that I have Neanderthal ancestors. But, alas, no Indian.

Well, maybe. The results did show 0.2% Native American. The genealogy web sites say that a percentage that low can be dismissed as a testing error. But when both tests showed the 0.2% reading? I think I'll have DNA testing done again. The techniques are better today than when I had it done years ago. Maybe I'll find the Indian yet.

Cindy has shown some interest over the years in family history but only sporadically. She'll get all excited and do some research on the genealogy web sites but the interest fades.

Why did my kids move so far away? I've often wondered whether it was to get away from us or for employment. I've put the question to both of them and they simply frown and don't answer. I hope the frown means, don't be silly, rather than, you finally noticed.

Sometimes at family gatherings, we'll talk about our forebears. Paul just looks sort of glassy-eyed. He listens, smiles and nods, but he's not really interested. Nor Mollie, his wife.

Both Cindy and I got pretty excited when a black guy in east Texas wrote on the ancestry.com web site to say that it appeared that he was my fourth cousin and would we be interested in comparing notes. I wrote back to him through the web site and said that we sure would like to correspond, but didn't get a reply. I think it was a glitch on the web site. Cindy tried with the same result. Then she lost interest. I guess he lost interest too.

I became increasingly intrigued by one particular ancestor who was not a legend, one that I knew something about: John Henry Harris.

John Henry was a soldier in the Mexican War. He was an exceptionally bright Missouri farm boy who, if he had lived at the opening of the twenty-first century, would have been a professor or a scientist or a governor.

He joined the army early in 1846, for adventure, to shoot buffalo and fight Indians. And to escape the desperate life of a Missouri frontier farm. At twenty years of age, he feared that he had reached the end of the road. The army would give him another chance.

When war was declared on Mexico only a couple of months after he enlisted, John Henry cheered along with all his fellows. Here's another adventure. Now he would get to wave the flag and fight greasers.

He was a member of the United States Army of the West that marched out from Fort Leavenworth, entered Mexico's frontier province of New Mexico in August and conquered it without firing a shot. The Mexican army had melted away.

In Santa Fe, the provincial capital, this country boy's universe was fixed for eternity. In Santa Fe, he met Morita and nothing would ever be the same again.

John Henry spent every free hour with Morita. Unless duty prevented, he stayed nights in her little adobe where she lived with no one but the old woman who had served her parents when the family had land and cattle.

On one morning, still in darkness, they stood on the porch. He was fully dressed, ready to begin his stealthy return to the post. She wore her nightdress. He asked her about her family. Her parents had been among the largest landowners in the region. A dozen vaqueros had worked the cattle and sheep. She was a child of privilege, wanting for nothing, ahead of most of her friends in education.

There had been more children. An older brother had been thrown from a horse and mercifully died after five days of terrible suffering. Navajo raiders had carried two younger sisters away. She never saw them again. Morita remembered all three of them and cried softly when she told John Henry their stories.

John Henry had taken her in his arms, encircling her shoulders and resting his chin on top of her head, breathing in her perfume. He had not known what to say but, after a moment, she drew back and, seeing his long face, she smiled a little smile, and took his hand. They walked to the adobe wall at the far end of the courtyard, away from the candlelight in the adobe. She stopped and looked up at the sky.

"Sisters," she said and waved her arm to encompass the starry sky. Then she had led him to the road where they walked hand in hand in the pre-dawn stillness. John Henry had understood then why he had awakened more than once to see her in the yard, looking at the heavens.

Morita was nineteen when they met and she had already seen more hardship than most adults many years older.

When he stayed overnight, John Henry left the adobe before dawn and stole back onto the post before the sun was up. Once he was caught and spent days in detention and marching on the parade ground carrying a full pack.

On the first night after his release from detention, he went to the cantina where she worked, walked home with her and spent the night.

A few of his army friends, those he trusted, knew of his overnight trysts but they said nothing. They envied him and covered for him.

John Henry met Morita's friends at the cantina and the markets on the plaza. Her friends soon became his friends.

He was surprised to find that they were like people he knew back in Missouri. Good folks who had the same hopes and worries as friends back home.

John Henry found no enemies in Santa Fe. This led him to begin thinking about the nature of this war. He asked questions of anyone who would listen about the war's origins in Texas and took part in discussions about the progress of the war in Texas, New Mexico and Mexico.

He attended talks by Lieutenant Willard Hall who held forth almost every evening as long as the army was in Santa Fe. Hall was a patriotic political activist and wanted everyone to know what they were fighting for.

John Henry reached conclusions contrary to what Lieutenant Hall intended. He began to wonder whether he could support a war against a people and a country that he decided had not wronged him or his own country.

The idyll, the time with Morita in Santa Fe, ended. John Henry was part of a force under General Stephen Watts Kearny that marched out of Santa Fe in September to carry the conquest to California.

He meant to tell her, but he was unexpectedly confined to the post the night before the army's departure. He was devastated that he did not say goodbye and wondered whether she would be there when he returned.

During the march, John Henry worried about the war. He struggled to sort out conflicting passions of patriotism and justice. He confided his feelings to his buddy, Brad, who reminded him that he had an obligation to his country and his comrades. John Henry agreed but was that enough when his country was fighting an unjust war?

It wasn't only the war that troubled John Henry. He longed for his sweetheart in Santa Fe and suffered recurring bouts of severe headaches, dizziness, blurred vision and occasional blackouts. A modern doctor would have diagnosed his malady as chronic migraine.

The army reached southern California without mishap but there, near the Indian village called San Pascual, they were confronted by a force of Californian lancers, determined to defend their country.

John Henry decided that he could not take part in the battle and prepared to leave, to return to Santa Fe and Morita and her little adobe. But an officer stopped him and John Henry, delirious with fever, committed to the battle. He blacked out during the cavalry charge on the Californians.

He awakened in a mountain wood, clear-headed and refreshed. He found his horse and headed east, toward Santa Fe, *a casa*. The headaches never troubled him again.

All this I got from John Henry's journal. His prose showed him to be intelligent and eloquent in his description of events and his deepest thoughts. He left quite a variety of documents and Morita added to the collection.

The documents were passed on, mostly unread, from father to son, until they ended in my granddaddy's hall closet where they remained until he gave them to me the year before he died. He had offered them to my father but he had declined. Daddy was interested in his lineage but he enjoyed hearing what others knew. He was not interested in adding to what was known.

Now the papers are mine, spread over my desk and floor and worktables. They appear a hopeless mess and more than one visitor has cluck-clucked and said why don't you get organized. I smile and go on about my business. I am organized. It's all in my head. Ask me what you want to see, I tell them, and I'll go right to it.

I have sorted through the documents many times, digesting and taking notes. Two stories are emerging. There's the account of my ancestor's coming of age and his love affair with a woman and a place. And there is John Henry's role in the larger story of the first widespread opposition to war in the history of the United States.

I picked up the journal.

CHAPTER 2
Camino a Casa

Following the cleansing battle at San Pascual, John Henry rode back over the same trail that the army had followed westward from Santa Fe. The army's tracks were still visible except on the rocky stretches but John Henry remembered. The journey had been etched on his troubled mind as he rode westward with the army, farther and farther from Santa Fe where he had spent the happiest month of his life and where he finally decided he must return.

Now on the eastward journey, he rode in winter and the days were tolerable. He wore his greatcoat in the cold dawn. By mid-morning, he had shed the coat and tied it behind the saddle. By afternoon, he was comfortable and almost enjoying the ride. Before sundown, he found a campsite where he gathered anything combustible and built a fire. He slept near the fire, covered with his greatcoat and awakened often, shivering, to toss more wood on the fire.

John Henry found the small bundles of food that he had cached during the march westward. He had not made up his mind during the early weeks of the march toward California but he was being prudent. If he decided that this war had nothing to do with him, he would need supplies on the ride back to Santa Fe.

He had often ridden out with Lieutenant Emory in evenings after camp had been struck. William Emory was a topographical engineer who had an obsessive interest in the ancient cultures of the arid country and took every opportunity to examine ruined sites along the route. When he became aware of John Henry's interest, he invited him to join him on the evening forays.

It was during these explorations that John Henry cached the food bundles. He often wondered whether the Lieutenant had seen him hiding the packages.

John Henry crossed the Colorado at the same place where the army had forded on the westward march. He remembered that first crossing well.

There had been three sand islands between the banks. Follow the horse in front of you and head for the island ahead, said the guides. I cain't swim, said more than one of the country boys. Don't worry, said the guides, the ford is shallow. Even if your horse loses footing, stay with him. He's a good swimmer and knows where he's going.

Kit Carson was the chief among the guides. The soldiers had heard of the famous mountain man and took him at his word. Still, most of the soldiers were apprehensive or outright scared but they made the crossing and felt pretty good about themselves on the other bank. Brad had been terrified when his horse lost the bottom and had to swim but with John Henry's coaxing and encouragement, he made it. John Henry smiled, remembering.

This time, heading eastward, the river was up from rains in the north. One of the islands had disappeared, and John Henry's horse had to swim most of the distance. He worried not at all. He trusted his horse and he let him have his head.

Across the Colorado, he rode alongside the Gila which flowed into the larger river. The tracks of the army were clearly visible as if they had passed the week before. He camped one night where he had acquired Remolino. The site still showed the footprints on footprints where hundreds of horses had been pastured and worked.

On the westward march, scouts had reported to General Kearny that they had come across a trail that was trampled by hundreds of horses. Kearny concluded that a Mexican army was in their path.

The General had prepared for a surprise night attack on what he thought must be a larger enemy force. The darkness would hide the number of the American attackers and perhaps spook the Mexicans.

Instead of a hostile army, the Americans found a small group of vaqueros driving a large horse herd. The leader of the vaqueros said that the animals were not meant for the Mexican army. Kearny accepted the explanation, though he assumed the opposite. He arranged an exchange of the army's worn-out animals for fresh mounts. The vaqueros were puzzled that the Americans did not seize the entire herd.

John Henry was among the soldiers sent to the drovers' camp to prevent the Mexicans from trying to move the herd until the Americans had picked their replacement mounts. Much to his surprise, John Henry was put in charge of the American detail. His superiors had been impressed more than once with his intellect and attention to duty.

During the night, he was shocked to be led by the anxious Mexican leader to his tent where his fifteen-year-old daughter was in labor. Can you help, he asked? The man wrung his hands, rocking back and forth, tears welling up in his eyes.

The young woman's husband, who looked no older than she, stared at John Henry, open-mouthed, tears rolling down his cheeks. John Henry suppressed his panic and pondered. He had witnessed two births, to the dismay of his mother, and decided that he knew something more about birthing than these terrified vaqueros.

That night, he helped deliver a healthy baby girl.

The next morning, the new grandfather gave John Henry a gift, Remolino, his own horse. John Henry protested but the vaquero insisted. He took John Henry's hand in both of his, his eyes misty.

"*Somos hermanos*," he had said. We are brothers.

Through eastern California and across the Colorado River, John Henry had been able to avoid contact with Indians. He saw a few and he was fortunate to see them before they saw him.

He had an advantage over the sharp-eyed Indians. He had a spyglass. When he had ridden from the hill above the valley of San Pascual where Kearny's force camped after the battle, he followed the trail eastward that would take him through the site of the army's last bivouac. He had approached it carefully but the site was deserted. The grass was trampled right up to the edge of the scrub timber.

Determined to leave no tracks, John Henry was riding in the tall grass under the scrub when he saw a glint on the ground beside the trail. He dismounted and found the spyglass. Some unlucky officer had dropped it in the chaos of the early morning departure.

During the ensuing ride, every time he topped a rise or rounded an outcropping, John Henry stopped and scoped the country. When he saw Indians in the distance, he either holed up until they passed, or he altered his route.

But his luck ran out or so he thought. Across the Colorado, he rode alongside the Gila on the army's trail. Rounding a dune, he came face to face with an Indian who stood at the water's edge, looking directly at him. The Indian was neither frightened nor aggressive, curious rather. Then the Indian smiled and raised his arm in greeting.

John Henry relaxed, smiled. He raised his arm in greeting. He recognized an Indian with whom he had dealt when the army visited the Pima villages on the westward march. The Pima mounted and bade John Henry to follow him.

At dusk, John Henry and the Pima made camp in a streamside stand of willows. They hobbled their horses nearby in a patch of grass. Building a fire, they sat and chewed on strips of dried meat the Pima took from his pack.

The Pima explained in rough Spanish that he was out hunting horses that had scattered when Apaches had stampeded the tribe's herd. The villagers had chased the Apaches off and, now, Pimas were riding out in all directions to retrieve as many horses as they could find.

John Henry was delighted with the fortunate meeting. On the march toward California, the army had visited the Pima villages on the Gila and traded with them. This had not been a chance encounter. The peaceful Pimas had been welcoming and provisioning travelers for hundreds of years. First Spanish, then Mexican, now American. The army had counted on resupplying at the villages.

John Henry told the Pima that he would help him hunt for his horses and then return to his village with him. The Pima was pleased with the prospect and added that John Henry would be happy to know that there were American soldiers in his village at this moment. The soldiers had helped the Pimas chase the Apaches away.

He was stunned. American soldiers? They would not be Kearny's force. The General would have led his battered troops westward from the battle site. Washington had ordered the General to take his force to the southern California coast to assist American naval forces there in the conquest of that Mexican province.

John Henry stared at the river, pondering. Then he remembered. A battalion comprised of Mormon soldiers under Colonel Philip St. George Cooke was following Kearny's force.

The Mormons had been recruited only a few months ago at their encampment at Council Bluffs in Iowa and mustered into the Army of the West. The Mormons in recent years had suffered repeated expulsions from the towns where they lived and were on an organized trek to new settlements in Utah when the army recruiters rode into their camp.

Many of the young men had resisted recruitment since they would be leaving their families who would need them during the trek westward. But Mormon leaders intervened and said that the money and arms that the soldiers would receive from the United States would be invaluable.

So the Mormon Battalion was formed. The new recruits marched across the plains on the Santa Fe Trail and had hardly arrived in Santa Fe when the Battalion was ordered to follow Kearny's force. These would be the soldiers at the Pima villages.

John Henry was devastated. He had counted on buying and trading for food with the Pimas. Now he could not visit the villages.

The Pima watched John Henry. He had not asked why this solitary soldier was riding in a direction counter to the westward march of the American army. Nor did he ask why this solitary soldier did not want to meet other soldiers.

The Pima said that he would help. He told John Henry to cross the Gila and ride along the northern shore of the river. The scattered horses were forgotten. When he had passed the village, he should cross to the southern side and wait at a place he described. Meanwhile, the Pima would ride to his village and collect the provisions that John Henry needed. He would join him at the designated meeting place.

John Henry watched the Pima as he rode ahead alongside the Gila toward his village. He pondered. If the Pima reported him to the army commander in his village, all was lost.

He rode on the riverbank, found a ford and eased Remolino into the stream. Climbing up the bank on the northern side, he kicked Remolino into a gallop eastward.

The Pima performed as he had promised. John Henry had decided on the westward march that the Pimas were among the most trustworthy, honest and industrious people he had ever known. That opinion was now confirmed.

"Thank you for your help," John Henry said. "You have saved my life."

"I understand," the Pima said. "I think you are a good man. I think you would do the same for me."

*****

John Henry rode for days in an open plain of widely scattered sotol and century plants and milkweed, surprisingly green in the dry landscape. It was a beautiful and, at the same time, forbidding country.

The tracks of the army were still clearly imprinted on the sandy landscape, except where hard rains had obliterated all signs of the column's passage. Campgrounds were easy to spot. In any event, he was not concerned. He frequently recognized landmarks, and the morning sun always drew him eastward.

Since beginning his ride toward Santa Fe, John Henry had easily found the caches he had left on the westward journey. He had taken great care when placing the bundles. After making a cache, he had faced the four directions and imprinted on his mind the scenery in each direction.

But now the caches were finished. He had opened the last one two days ago. He had not begun to hide the supplies on the march westward until the army had crossed the continental divide. Only then had he begun seriously pondering the possibility of deserting and returning to Santa Fe.

Now he sat Remolino at the crest of the divide. The eastern foothills below flattened to a rolling country that stretched to the horizon, broken occasionally by lower mountains that rose from the plain. Though it was February, heat waves shimmered on the plain, blurring distant landforms.

Rather than being discouraged by the certainty of suffering ahead from fatigue and lack of food and water, he was elated. He was almost to Santa Fe. Home.

Reaching behind the saddle, he pulled the spyglass from his pack. He scoped the hillside and plain below. Nothing moved in his view but heat waves. Replacing the spyglass in the pack, he rode down from the crest, determined to follow the trail of the Mormon Battalion all the way to the Rio Grande and Santa Fe.

I laid the journal on the desk and picked up a book on southwestern trails that included the marches of the American forces between New Mexico and California during the war. I opened the book to the map that traced the routes of

Kearny's unit and Cooke's Mormon Battalion.

John Henry, you got it all wrong. You're not following the Mormon Battalion trail at all. On the westward march, both Kearny and Cooke had marched south from Santa Fe along the banks of the Rio Grande. Both units left the Rio Grande at just about the same place.

Kearny turned westward past the Santa Rita copper mines and hit the upper reaches of the Gila River. But Cooke marched southward into Mexico. Then the Battalion turned westward to hit the San Pedro River. They marched northward along that stream, crossed it and headed westward toward Tucson where they expected a set-to with the Mexican garrison there.

They were surprised to find no enemies in Tucson, soldiers or citizens. The Mexican force had withdrawn and the Americans were able to trade and enjoy a peaceful interlude with a friendly population.

From Tucson, the Battalion marched northward and hit the Gila a few miles above the Pima villages.

John Henry, you've actually been following Kearny's trail all the way from California, the same trail that you rode on the march westward. The Mormons had added their tracks to the trail west of the Pima villages but, east of the villages, it was all Kearny's force. The trail was still visible after all that time.

There's nothing in John Henry's journal later that would suggest that he learned about the Battalion's route. It's not important, of course. The point is that he wasn't lost or wandering. He knew where he was going and he knew how to get there.

Not that it was easy going. I suspect that for one very tense moment he thought that his luck had run out. That was when he saw the Apaches.

John Henry left the hillside trail and rode into a rolling plain. The sun was high and he sorely needed water. The last semblance of refreshment had been the previous morning when he had broken open a short barrel-shaped cactus, dug out the pulp and sucked on it. It had not quenched his thirst.

His eyes had begun to blur and he thought it was a mirage that moved above a long sand dune fifty yards on his left and parallel to his path. He shook his head and looked again. The three images in a line continued to bob gently up and down and move forward, at the same pace as his.

His trail and the path of the images moved toward a convergence ahead. He was too confused and dehydrated to react.

The images rode from behind the dune and materialized as three mounted Indians. It was their heads and shoulders he had seen bobbing and advancing behind the dune. The Indians stopped in the middle of his trail, looked intently at him. John Henry pulled Remolino up. The Indians stared, their faces blank.

"Americano?" said one of the Indians.

"Sí," John Henry said.

"Dine'e," the Indian said. John Henry recognized the Apache name for themselves. He raised his arm in greeting. The Indians responded in the same fashion.

John Henry relaxed. He remembered the peaceful meeting with a Mimbreño Apache band on the army's westward journey. Kearny and his officers had traded with the Indians for mules. The General was not pleased that some of the soldiers traded trinkets for mescal but he hadn't prohibited the exchange. The soldiers were most content that evening, lubricated liberally with the fiery alcoholic beverage.

John Henry and his escort rode into the center of the Apache camp. They reined in before the chief, Mangas Coloradas. The Indians and John Henry dismounted. Mangas smiled, opened his arms and shook hands with John Henry.

"You are welcome," said Mangas. "All Americans are welcome in the villages of the Dine'e. We are friends of the Americans. It is the Mexicans we hate. You are army. The Dine'e and the American army should fight the Mexicans together. We hate the Mexicans."

The Apaches had been fighting Mexicans for centuries. Both sides had committed atrocities and the Apaches welcomed the Americans as allies in their conflict against a common enemy.

Mangas said something to a man behind him who ran to a tent and returned with a skin bag. He handed it to Mangas. Mangas dug into the bag and pulled out a sheet of paper.

"See," he said. "Look." He showed the paper to John Henry.

The document was a writing in English that declared the friendship of Americans for the Apaches and mentioned Red Sleeves, Mangas Coloradas, by name. It was signed by General Stephen Watts Kearny.

John Henry looked up to see Mangas beaming and nodding his head. John Henry returned the paper to him.

"I am glad to be friends with the Apaches," John Henry said.

The Indians fed him and cared for his horse. They showed him to a tepee where he was to sleep. Mangas offered him the companionship of an Apache woman for the night. He said that she had lost her husband last year and had asked Mangas if she could share the American's bed. The comely woman, who appeared to be in her mid-twenties, stood behind Mangas, trying not to smile.

John Henry declined with all the diplomacy and will power he could muster. Both Mangas and the woman were as surprised that he declined as John Henry had been with the offer. That night, he dreamed of Morita.

The next morning, John Henry was again fed, and again assurances of friendship were exchanged. Two warriors rode with him until they saw the Rio Grande in the distance. John Henry thanked them and the Apaches set out westward at a lope.

From here, the road to the river and along its banks toward Santa Fe was well traveled. He was almost home.

CHAPTER 3
Quién es?

John Henry rode at a slow walk into the outskirts of Santa Fe. The cloth tied around his head covered his lower face. Riders often wore neckerchiefs to protect against blowing dust but they also could serve as a mask to hide an identity.

The barrio hadn't changed much since he rode away with the army column five months ago. The adobe houses and walls, the small shops, the occasional cantina, they were the same.

The streets were almost deserted. An old woman, wearing a long dress and rebozo wrapped about her head and carrying a small bag, walked across his path. She glanced up at him, walked on.

He turned Remolino into a dusty side street and rode slowly to the last house but one. The high adobe wall hid the house from passersby. Pulling up, he dismounted stiffly, flexed his back and tied the reins to the post beside the gate of vertical slats. He pushed the gate open and stopped.

It looked the same. The little adobe, the covered porch, the two doors leading off the porch to the kitchen and a bedroom, the large cottonwood that shaded most of the roof, the eroded patch on the far adobe wall that he had never gotten around to repairing. He took a step inside the wall and closed the gate behind him.

"*Hola!*" He waited.

The kitchen door opened, and Morita stepped out to the porch. She looked at the stranger at the gate. She wore the simple yellow cotton dress that she had worn that day he said goodbye and rode away, his heart breaking.

His head filled, his eyes misted. She was barefoot, holding a cloth, perhaps a dishcloth. The day before he left Santa Fe, he had sat with her on the porch, their legs stretched out and backs against the wall of the adobe, the dress pulled up above her knees to warm her legs in the autumn afternoon sun. She would shift position, lie in his lap facing him, he would touch her breast lightly through the thin material, and they would kiss.

From the first time he saw her in the cantina, he knew that she would be his. Was it only six months ago? It seemed an eternity.

She stepped off the porch into the yard and stopped. She shaded her eyes with a hand.

"*Quién es?*" she said.

He simply stared, unable to speak. She stepped back. He remembered that his face was covered. He pulled the neckerchief down, revealing his bearded face.

"*Quién es?*" she said.

"What do you mean, '*quién es,*' *muchacha!*"

Morita's eyes and mouth opened wide. She dropped the cloth.

"Juanito!" She ran and collided against him, forcing him to step back to regain his balance. She held him tightly around his waist as he encircled her shoulders with both arms, his face in her hair, breathing her familiar perfume.

They pulled back and kissed lightly, then embraced

again.

"I knew you would come," she said softly, her head pressed against his chest. "I prayed every day at the church and I knew you would come." She leaned back, rubbed his cheek. "You look like a bear or a big squirrel."

He took her cheeks in both hands. "Then I hope you like bears and big squirrels, *bonita*." He put his arm around her waist and moved her toward the kitchen. "Now do you have any *frijoles* and *tortillas* and *chocolate*? I'm mighty hungry."

John Henry and Morita sat on the covered porch. They leaned against the wall, their legs extended, their favorite place and favorite posture. The late February sun warmed their legs while their upper bodies were in shade. They looked at the sandy yard that was enclosed by the high adobe wall. A few rose bushes along the base of the wall showed tiny green leaf sprouts, a sure sign of spring.

They both started at the sound of pots banging in the kitchen. This was followed by a muffled "dammit!"

Morita flinched, smiled. "It's the only English word Tía knows. She would never say it around me or anyone else. Certainly not around you."

Tía was the old woman who lived with Morita. She had been a servant of her parents and had more to do with raising Morita than her own mother. She had always been with Morita and was more companion now than servant.

John Henry rarely saw Tía except on those evenings when he arrived at the adobe in time for a late supper. Tía would prepare the meal, serve it and withdraw to her room off the kitchen, closing the door. Occasionally, she would leave the adobe without a word and walk alone in the dark streets.

Another clash of bouncing pans and another soft "dammit!" Morita frowned and started to get up. She stopped when Tía appeared at the kitchen door with two cups. Dressed in a severe, shapeless black dress and an expression to match, Tía handed the filled cups to Morita and John Henry.

John Henry took his cup in both hands. "Ah, *chocolate*," he said, smiling. *"Perfecto! Gracias, Tía."* She nodded gravely and returned to the kitchen.

They sipped their chocolate in silence, staring at the yard and the thin clouds that hung just above the horizon.

John Henry took a swallow, lowered the cup to his lap. "What's my name?" John Henry said, staring at the horizon above the far wall.

She looked at him, puzzled. "Juanito."

He frowned. "Morita."

She turned to him. "Well, John Hen—"

He took her chin with his hand and pulled her head around sharply. "No, sweetheart." He paused, kissed her lips.

"Oh, yeah," she said. "Jed Weber. But I like Juanito better."

"You can call me Juanito, softly, in my ear, in bed, after we've made love. He squeezed her chin again. "But not in public where somebody else can hear. John Henry Harris was killed in a battle in California with a lance driven halfway through his body. Or he is wandering around in the California mountains, holding his head and muttering to himself."

She pouted, looked up at him. "Not funny, Juanito."

"Or he deserted. Whatever happened to the poor fellow, he cannot be spotted in Santa Fe." He took her cheeks in both hands. "You're right. This is not funny. It's dead serious. If we are to stay in this town, we must let John Henry go his way and get used to Jed Weber."

They watched the dust swirls at the far end of the courtyard. Above the adobe wall, in the distance, the lacy clouds had thickened and darkened. They looked up at the sound of soft rumbling thunder. A single lightning bolt shot from the cloud toward the ground.

He stared at the dark cloud. "Tell me something about Jed Weber."

She pondered. "He was with some men that brought a bunch of wagons to Santa Fe in 1846. They—"

"Before that."

She looked puzzled.

"Missouri."

"Oh, yeah. He was a farmer from Missouri."

"Where in Missouri?"

She squirmed and pulled on his arm. "Juanito."

"I'm sorry, sweetheart, but people are going to ask. You need to know everything about Jed. You sleep with him. You know all about him. He told you all this and often talks about his past. He mentions places and people."

"Uh, near, uh, tell me again," she said. She squeezed his arm.

"Franklin."

"Okay, he worked on a farm near Franklin with his daddy and mama."

"What did he do on the farm?"

"He worked with cows, and they grew some corn, and they had chickens," she said.

"Was he happy working on this farm near Franklin, Missouri?" He leaned down and bit her ear.

"Ouch." She hit him on his arm.

"Well? Was he happy on this farm?"

She frowned. "He was happy because he loved his mama and daddy but he wanted to look at more of the world than he could see on the farm near Franklin, Missouri." She gathered her legs under her and started to get up. He grabbed her and pulled her down.

"So what did he do?"

"Juanito, you make my head hurt."

"C'mon, sweetheart. We need to leave Missouri. What did he do?"

"Okay. One time when he was going to Franklin to buy supplies, he saw a bunch of wagons outside the town that some men were loading and he wondered who they were and what they were doing. They said come over here and sit with us and have coffee, and we'll tell you."

"Ah, now this is something. What did they tell him?"

"They said that they were getting ready to go to Santa Fe. They were traders. They had made money trading with Santa Fe. This was their fourth trip."

"And what did Jed Weber do then?"

"He got all excited and asked when they were leaving. They said they were waiting for some more traders to show up and they would probably leave in two days."

"What did Jed Weber think about all this?"

"He got all excited. And they said, well, you seem a bright young man. Why don't you go with us? We need a good hand."

"And so?"

"He told his mama and daddy that he was going to become a Santa Fe trader and he was leaving in two days. His mama and daddy were very sad but they said that if he wanted to see more of the world, they would not stand in his way. His daddy drove him in the wagon to Franklin the next day and the caravan left the day after."

She wriggled and pushed him on his shoulder. "I'm tired, Juanito. I'll make some more chocolate." She pulled her legs under her and started to get up. He pulled her down.

"We're almost there, *muchacha*. Did anything interesting happen on the drive to Santa Fe?"

She pouted, pushed him away from her again. "Okay. The wagons were stopped at Bent's Fort by the army. The army was marching to Santa Fe because war had started. After the army left, the traders went on to Santa Fe."

She looked up at him. He kissed her lips.

"And what did these *gringos* do in Santa Fe?"

"When they got to Santa Fe, Jed and the others he was with sold their things and—"

"What kind of things?"

"Juanito. I'm tired!"

He looked sternly at her, frowned, softened. "Morita, the more you can tell, the more likely they will believe you."

"Okay. Jed and the six other men he was with sold their, uh, cloths, mostly calico and flannel, and needles, buttons, knives, axes, that kind of stuff."

"Is that all they sold?"

"They sold the wagons and the oxen."

"What did they do with the money they got for the goods?"

"They bought some mules and packs to carry silver coins and a bunch of mules they were going to drive back to Missouri to sell there."

"And Jed?"

"He liked the look of Santa Fe and decided to stay."

"And what else did he like?"

She smiled, slid her hand inside his shirt to his chest. "He liked *cantinas*."

He reached around her shoulders and pulled her to him, almost nose to nose. He caressed her breast through the thin cotton dress. "And did he like young Mexican women?"

She kissed him. They stared into each other's eyes, stood and kissed again. Arms entangled, they stumbled toward the open bedroom door. Behind them,, scattered large raindrops silently pelted the dry courtyard, sending up tiny eruptions of dust.

John Henry and Morita hurried at dawn down a side street toward the plaza. The smells and sounds of breakfast from adobes bordering the road reminded him that they had not eaten this morning. Morita had pulled him out of bed and handed him clothing, piece by piece, and was not at all sympathetic with his complaint.

"*Apurate!* Hurry!" She liked to be among the earliest shoppers at the market. When he had protested that he was hungry, she had cocked her head and pursed her lips. Okay, he had said. Later.

They left the side street and entered the plaza. Merchants' tables arrayed along each side of the plaza bore an abundance and variety of vegetables, nuts, dried beans, onions. Beef and venison were offered, sliced and in chunks. Pork and lamb were available in slabs and on the hoof. Live poultry set up a din from their cages. Firewood was stacked beside tables, ready to be carried away.

John Henry remembered that Morita was a careful shopper and he anticipated a long morning. Not that it mattered. Nothing pleased him more than watching Morita at work or at play. On this rare off-duty day, he would not let her out of his sight.

They strolled down the line of vendors. She stopped

and walked to a table that displayed pine nuts, bread and slices of beef. John Henry stood a few paces behind her.

She pointed to a piece of beef and said something to the vendor. He smiled, responded. She frowned, replied sharply, setting off a furious exchange, seemingly heated, until a price was agreed on, money and package were exchanged, and merchant and buyer parted, happy and smiling.

Morita walked back to John Henry, smiled and placed the package into the bag he carried. Taking his arm, she pulled him along until she stopped, pondered another table that featured pyramids of squashes and stacked rows of ears of green corn. She released him and walked to the table, spoke to the merchant.

John Henry watched as the bargaining began. He smiled. The merchant saw the smile, waved, turned back to Morita, frowned and protested her last offer.

John Henry looked around. He liked the plaza. It had not changed since last September and he felt he was home. The government building, called the Palace, occupied the entire north side of the plaza. The other three sides were lined with a great variety of shops. Merchants displayed their wares on tables and blankets spread on the ground at the edge of the covered walkways. Shoppers bent over the goods, examining and pondering, stopping often to chat and laugh with strollers and other shoppers.

The plaza appeared to be in constant motion as people entered from side streets, and others, their shopping done, walked from the plaza. From two streets, strings of burros laden with packs of foodstuffs and firewood entered the plaza to replenish merchants' stores.

"John Henry!" He looked aside sharply and saw Manuel striding toward him, grinning broadly, his arms widespread. "Is that you?"

Only a few days after returning to Santa Fe from California, John Henry had started to shave off the beard but Morita said she liked it, so he trimmed it and kept it. His friends, on seeing him for the first time since his return, still had some difficulty seeing their old friend through the beard.

Morita spotted Manuel. She held up her hand to the merchant before her as if to say hold it right there, and hurried toward Manuel, balancing her last purchases in her arms, running a few steps, striding again. Her arms loaded, she nudged and pushed and guided him across the road toward the center of the plaza. Manuel, confused, looked back over his shoulder at John Henry.

Morita stopped in the shade of a large cottonwood, leaning almost into his face. As Morita spoke, Manuel took some packages from her, looked back at John Henry. Frowning, she grasped his arm with her free hand and turned him away so he was looking in the opposite direction.

As she continued talking, explaining John Henry's rebirth as Jed Weber, Manuel nodded, comprehending. He nodded again. She smiled. He nodded once more. She took her packages from him and he walked away in the opposite direction from where John Henry stood. He did not look back.

Morita walked to John Henry. She handed him two parcels to carry, took his arm, and they strolled. She spoke softly, her head down.

"He said to tell you that he was happy to see you here and that he will see you at the *cantina*. He said he would tell everyone about his new friend, Jed Weber."

The *cantina* had not changed much in the five months since he left Santa Fe. A dozen small square tables were encircled by stools and a few chairs. The floor was earthen, flat as a griddle and stone hard. The bar had been enlarged a bit and the bottles of spirits more varied.

In addition to *aguardiente*, Taos whiskey, sometimes called "Taos Lightning," was becoming more widely consumed. Wine from El Paso del Norte, though more expensive, was now more popular than the local Rio Abajo wines.

Morita still worked at the *cantina*. When John Henry first visited after his return, Morita met him at the door. She held his arm and walked him to the bar and around the room. The two dozen patrons that evening were all Mexican and all friends. They greeted their new friend, Jed Weber, and a few could not avoid a broad grin or a snicker. Morita playfully but firmly chastised any who saw mirth in the situation.

John Henry found work on a ranch just three miles outside Santa Fe. The owner, Antonio Espinosa, had been a close friend of Morita's parents. Antonio had known them during the happy days when Morita's family had been among the largest landowners near Santa Fe. Espinosa had recovered from the hard times, particularly the prolonged drought that had ruined many large ranchers, including Morita's father.

John Henry rode out each day to the ranch. He found the work satisfying, inspiring even, and he began to think of the day when he would have his own place. In the saddle and back at Morita's adobe, he daydreamed about this ranch where he and Morita would live, prosper and raise a houseful of children.

No one on the ranch spoke English, so he was forced to improve his Spanish. He was glad because, since his return from California, Morita insisted that they speak only English when they were alone. She improved so quickly that he was sure that her English soon would be better than his.

Evenings he spent in the *cantina*, sipping *aguardiente* or wine, watching Morita, and then walking back to the adobe with her after closing. She frolicked in the dusty road, swinging her sandals, forcing him to play with her, as if she had not just finished hours of hard work.

On one memorable evening, they had a light supper in the kitchen that was illuminated softly by two candles. When they were finished, they stacked the dishes in a small tub. Then each took a candle, walked outside. They set the candles on the porch against the wall, sat on the edge of the porch, and looked up. There was a quarter moon and the sky was perfectly clear. The array of stars was brilliant.

"Magnificent, like you, *bonita niña,*" he said.

"Niña bonita."

He turned to her, puzzled.

"Don't say *'bonita niña.'* Say *'niña bonita.'* "

"Oh. What else can I say to tell you what a pretty girl you are and how much I love you?"

She smiled, ducked her head. "You can say *'mi amada'* or *'mi bonita.'* "

He took her chin, pulled her head around, and leaned toward her. "What else can I say?"

She smiled. "You can say *'mi preciosa.'* Or *'mi amour.'* "

He kissed her lips softly. "And what else can I say?"

She slipped a hand inside his shirt to his chest. "You can say *'mi hermosa'* or *'mi guapa.'* "

He kissed her again, touched her breast through the dress. "And what else can I say?"

She pushed her hand to his back under the shirt, smiled. "You can say *'mi angelita,'* and you can say, 'I love you, sweetheart.' "

"I love you, sweetheart, with every bone and fiber in my body." He wrapped his arms around her and pulled her tightly against his chest.

"Ow, too tight, *guapo!*"

He smiled, stood and pulled her up. They picked up their candles and walked through the bedroom door. There they undressed each other, blew out the candles, crawled under the covers and made love.

Afterwards, when they lay apart and she slept, he lay on his side facing her, listening to her deep breathing and an occasional soft sound, almost a whimper, wondering whether it was possible to be happier than he was at this moment.

On an evening that began like any other evening, everything changed. Three soldiers came into the *cantina* and walked to the bar. They ordered *aguardiente* and looked about the room that had gone silent at their entrance. The *cantina* was at the edge of town and was patronized almost entirely by Mexicans who feared and resented the American soldiers.

The intruders leaned against the bar and talked to each other, ignoring the patrons who stared at them. Gradually, the locals returned to their drinks and talked softly, glancing occasionally at the *gringos.*

The soldiers had consumed a few glasses of spirits before coming to this *cantina.* One sloshed his drink as he swayed with the music produced by the orchestra of two guitars and a violin. The soldier stepped aside when Morita came to the bar to pick up a drink for a patron. He looked her up and down and smiled.

"My, my, ain't you a purty little piece," the soldier

said. Morita ignored him. He bowed slightly. "How about a dance, little purty?" He set his glass on the bar and took her arm, moving her away from the bar, intent on having a dance.

Morita pulled away from his grasp. *"No Señor, estoy ocupada. Vaya y busque a ver si encuentra una puta que aguante su mal aliento."* No, señor. I am busy. Go find yourself a whore, if you can find one that can stand your filthy breath. She smiled. She knew that he didn't understand a word she said.

He smiled and took her arm again, more firmly this time. "We're going to have us a dance, little purty. That's what 'is place is all about, ain't it." He pulled her away from the bar. She jerked away again.

"Vete al Diablo, gringo mal criado!" Go to hell, you badly-raised *gringo!* She glared at him.

"I don't understand the rest but I do understand *'gringo.'* You're a feisty little bitch. I like that and I'm gonna have a piece uh you." He grasped her arm hard and pulled her toward the outside door.

The other two soldiers laughed. One took her other arm and helped move her toward the door. She struggled and swung at both soldiers. They laughed and held her tighter. The second soldier found her breasts with his free hand.

"Hey, look out," the first soldier said, laughing, "that's mi—"

The first soldier, the one who began it all, was thrown violently sideways by a blow to the head. The broken bottle spewed glass shards, wine sprayed in all directions, and the soldier collapsed to the floor.

John Henry dropped the neck of the bottle and grabbed the second soldier by the arm. With his free hand, he punched him hard in the belly. The soldier collided backwards against the wall, gasping for breath. The third soldier backed away as a half dozen vaqueros bunched up behind John Henry.

The Mexicans and John Henry stood quietly as the two soldiers, one still wheezing and gasping, dragged their unconscious comrade toward the outside door.

When the soldiers had passed through the door to the outside, the soldier who John Henry had punched in the stomach leaned back inside and pointed at John Henry.

"I know you," he said softly and he was gone.

Two days later, the *cantina* was closed. An American civil servant, standing in the open doorway, told Miguel, the owner, that he must appear at the mayor's office on the following day.

"Why am I closed?" Miguel said. "What is the charge against me?"

"You must appear," the official said. He handed Miguel a sheet of paper on which were written instructions for his appearance. On the outside door, the civil servant tacked a paper, which stated in Spanish and English: THIS CANTINA IS CLOSED UNTIL FURTHER NOTICE BY ORDER OF THE MAYOR.

I looked at the paper. It was brittle and it still showed the two tiny holes at the top corners where it had been tacked to the *cantina* door. I laid the paper on the desk and stared at the window.

John Henry must have realized that he had a decision to make. I think at this point that he did not consider himself a deserter. Sure, he had abandoned his unit in California before riding back to Santa Fe but he was firmly convinced that he had done what was right.

Now he had to decide whether to remain quiet and live happily in the little adobe with Morita, hoping the soldier was too drunk to remember what had happened at the *cantina*. Would this be enough, just to let it rest and hope it would go away? Or should he make an issue of his view on the war and risk arrest? Or should they leave Santa Fe forever?

The *cantina* was allowed to reopen after a week. There was a rumbling among a great number of the Yankee residents of Santa Fe that the administration was too easy on the Mexicans, a carryover from General Kearny's policy of treating the defeated populace leniently, even kindly, respecting their customs, religion and lifeways. Kearny thought it the best way to work the gradual transition from Mexican province to American possession.

Most of the Americans who had lived in New Mexico before 1846 thought this a wise policy. Many of these had totally assimilated and were as Mexican as the Mexican nationals. Some had not gone quite that far in accepting the Mexican lifestyle but they still understood the Mexican mentality and sympathized with them. It was the newcomers who would rather the Mexicans be treated as a conquered people.

While some of John Henry's and Morita's friends believed that all was well, John Henry knew otherwise. He had heard the rumor going around that an army deserter had been seen in the town. The soldier from the cantina probably started the rumor. The beard would give the soldier some pause to declare firmly that he had spotted a soldier he knew, a deserter, but the suspicion was sufficient to fuel the rumor.

Morita and John Henry had risen late this morning. They sat on the porch, leaning against the wall, their breakfast plates beside Morita.

"What are you going to do?" she said.

"Jorge told me that the administration has sent a letter to General Kearny, asking for any information he might have about a suspected deserter." Jorge, a friend, worked in the office of the governor. He told John Henry that a Mexican trader to California was carrying the dispatch.

John Henry was not overly concerned. How could Kearny conclude that the absence in his force of a certain soldier was due to desertion rather than simply being killed and lost in the confusion of the battle at San Pascual and its aftermath? Yet, he knew that the army could reach its own conclusions based on suspicion, if not on fact.

Maybe he should disappear for a while. If he were not around to be discovered, perhaps the rumbling about a deserter would dissipate. Morita agreed that he should go away for a time.

"Where will we go?" she said.

"Not you, sweetheart. You must stay and carry on. Only our friends know that a gringo lives with you and you must remind them that they should not tell. If any official goes to the *cantina* to investigate, no one there will have seen this strange foreigner for a long time. Perhaps he was passing through."

"But I want to go with you. I want to be with you," she said.

He put his arm around her shoulders and pulled her to him. "It will not be forever, *mi querida.* Just till the talk goes away."

He stared at the sandy yard, the adobe wall, the cloudless blue sky. Was he taking the coward's path? Shouldn't he act on his convictions? Shouldn't he speak out, telling anyone who would listen that this was an immoral war against a people who had not wronged the United States? And, in spite of the administration's lenient policy, weren't the *Mexicanos* bearing the burdens of a conquered people? Shouldn't he speak out now?

"I have talked with Antonio," he said. "I have told him everything. I trust him. He has a friend who runs a big ranch in northern Mexico, a few miles south of El Paso del Norte. Antonio said he could arrange for me to go there and stay as long as I wish. He said I would be welcomed. This friend has not been touched by the war but he is very angry about it. Antonio said that traders who travel between Chihuahua and Santa Fe call often at his ranch and I can send messages to you with people he trusts."

"I would rather be with you. But I will do as you say." He squeezed her shoulders, leaned down and kissed her.

He also would rather she be with him. He had thought at first that they should leave Santa Fe and go to Colorado. He had heard that there was empty land there, claimed by no one, that was perfect for raising cattle.

Or they could go to Chihuahua where they would live as free people, begin again, with no fear of capture and imprisonment.

But leaving now, going to Colorado or Chihuahua permanently, would be the way of the coward. Someday, somehow, he must speak.

For the moment, he would keep silent. To speak out now might appear to put him in sympathy with the Taos insurgents.

CHAPTER 4
Rebels or Patriots?

Many *nuevos mexicanos* had not accepted the change of sovereignty gracefully. Their discontent simmered and boiled over in January, hardly a month before John Henry's return to Santa Fe.

When Kearny left Santa Fe with his force in early October to join American naval forces in the conquest of California, he left Colonel Alexander Doniphan in charge of the army in Santa Fe. Doniphan was to remain until the arrival of Colonel Sterling Price who was leading the Second Missouri Mounted Volunteers to the provincial capital. On Price's arrival, Doniphan was to turn over control of American forces to him. Doniphan then would lead his army to Chihuahua.

For the top civil post in the new American province, Kearny had appointed Charles Bent governor. This was the same Bent who had operated the trading fort on the Santa Fe Trail.

Bent had been associated with the New Mexicans long enough to know that they had a history of chafing against any sort of government interference in their daily lives. Now they complained bitterly of the American soldiers' insults and deprivation of their rights.

The Governor appealed to Doniphan to control the soldiers. Bent predicted serious consequences if he were not able to control them. Apparently, Doniphan was not impressed or at least was not able to rein in the soldiers.

There were also rumblings from New Mexicans who worried that their land titles would not be honored under the change of sovereignty. Dissent escalated to rumors of resistance in some form.

Bent had not taken the rumblings seriously and traveled from Santa Fe to his home in Taos without military escort. The miscalculation cost him his life.

In Taos, a group of Mexicans and Taos Indians broke into Bent's house and killed him, along with members of his family and some Taos government officials. The insurgents then proceeded to attack and kill other Americans in the north, including Simeon Turley, whose distillery was the chief source of Taos Lightning.

Flushed with success, the rebels marched southward, intent on liberating Santa Fe from the Yankee invaders. Colonel Price, who by this time commanded the American army in New Mexico, met the insurgents on the road and scattered them. Price marched his force north to Taos.

The rebels withdrew to the Taos pueblo and Price followed them. When they retreated to the pueblo church, American cannon blew holes in the wall and set the church on fire. The fleeing insurgents were either killed or captured.

The next day, some of the captives, including one of the leaders, Pablo Montoya, were summarily executed in the plaza. Other leaders were jailed and awaited trial.

John Henry leaned on the bar, holding his wine glass and watching Morita. She stood at a table talking with two *vaqueros.* The three exchanged smiles and quips, glancing at John Henry. One waved to him and John Henry returned the wave. He felt good, among compatriots, safe.

The outside door opened, and an American stood in the doorway. Grizzled and unkempt, he looked around, closed the door and walked to the bar, weaving a bit en route. John Henry nodded to him and he returned the nod.

"What would you like, *Señor?*" said José, the bartender.

The man turned to John Henry. "You're American, I think."

"I am."

"What are you drinking?"

John Henry looked at his glass. "Well, most locals drink *aguardiente* but I drink wine. Good El Paso del Norte wine."

The stranger turned back to the bartender and pointed to John Henry's glass. José nodded. He set a glass on the bar, poured wine into it and pushed it to him. The man dug in his pocket, extracted a handful of coins, selected one and handed it to the bartender who took it and nodded.

The man glanced at John Henry, glassy-eyed, and looked at his drink on the bar. He picked up the glass, tipped it up and drained it. He got the bartender's attention and pointed to the glass. José came over, poured another glass and took the proffered coin.

The stranger took a long swig. He looked at John Henry. "It ain't right," he said.

John Henry waited. When the man continued to stare at his glass, John Henry motioned to a table against the wall.

"Let's sit." John Henry said.

They walked to the table. The stranger weaved, sat down heavily and slumped against the wall. He straightened and leaned across the table in John Henry's face.

"I'm Lewis Garrard. Who are you?"

"Jed Weber."

"What do you do, Jed Weber?"

"I'm a *vaquero.*"

"What brought you to Santa Fe? Not cows."

"I was a trader. Came here on the trail from Missouri."

Garrard straightened, looked at John Henry, frowned, squinted, shook his head. "Be damned. I did the same. Didn't count on the damned war to interrupt."

John Henry waited. Garrard, obviously, had something he wanted to say.

"You hear about the trial of the leaders of the Taos business?" Garrard said. "You know, the uprising?"

"I did. Everybody is waiting to hear about the result."

"I know the result! I was there! Damned if I waren't." Garrard shook his head, emptied his glass. He held the glass up, looked at the bar.

"José, El Paso del Norte wine, please." John Henry called. José waved, walked over and poured into Garrard's empty glass.

Garrard looked up at José, nodded. *"Gracias."* He raised the glass and took a swallow. He set the glass on the table.

"Damnedest thing I ever saw. You know, the rebels— that's what they called them, Mexicans and Navajos, *rebels*—killed Governor Bent and some other American officials. Price, you know, the army commander, set up this military court in Taos to try the leaders. He appointed th' judges, a close friend of Bent and another who was th' father of somebody Beaubien, an American who was killed in the rising. Yeah."

He weaved, opened his mouth to speak, took a drink instead. He set the glass on the table, looked up. "The foreman of th' jury was Governor Bent's brother. The jury included a brother-in-law of Beaubien and a bunch of friends of the Bents. Yeah.

"So what do you think was th' outcome? Damned right! They found the Mexicans guilty of murder and treason. *Treason!* Citizens of uh foreign country, tried in uh court of th' winning country, found guilty of treason for defending with their lives the liberty of their country.

"I left the courtroom sick. This is justice? I'm just plain sick, *mi amigo.* Just plain sick." He slumped, raised his glass, drained it.

Garrard brightened, weaved, leaned toward John Henry. "Say, Mr. St. Vrain would like t' talk t' you. Ceran St. Vrain. He's an old Santa Fe trader. He likes to talk with any trader who's been down the trail. He'd love to talk to you. He was the interpreter at the trial. I'm staying at his house. He'll want t' talk t' you."

John Henry looked aside. "He wouldn't know me. I'm nobody. I was just an employee. Nobody."

Garrard stood, flexed his back. "Well," he said. He weaved, almost fell forward. John Henry put his hands up to catch him. Straightening, Garrard touched John Henry's shoulder and walked a circuitous route to the door. He opened it and went out. The door swung shut.

*****

Four days after Garrard and John Henry's conversation, the six convicted leaders were hanged in the Taos plaza. Two weeks later, five more were executed. In all, twenty-eight, all Mexican citizens, were executed for their part in the revolt. Traitors, as in treason.

I re-read a page of my notes, headed "Central Authority Headaches." It was the best title I could muster at the outset. It included accounts of decades, centuries actually, of opposition to edicts of the Santa Fe government by people who lived outside the provincial capital.

Pueblo Indians in 1680 rebelled against their Spanish overlords and expelled them from the province. The Spanish reestablished their rule and the Pueblos rebelled again in 1696. In 1837, New Mexicans revolted against oppressive financial measures of the central government. The Taos uprising was just the latest attempt by New Mexicans to oppose a government that they felt did not represent their best interests.

John Henry, you didn't know all this, but you're right in the middle of a ruckus that's going to make the history books.

John Henry sat with three friends on the bank of an acequia, watching the languid flow of the life-giving water and exchanging reports that they had heard about the Taos rebellion. A few of their friends had an active part in the hostilities but most were involved only by their agreement with the motives of the insurgents and their grief at the result.

In spite of the eyewitness revelations of Garrard, John Henry was still baffled at the outcome of the trials and executions. Treason? The leaders were convicted and executed for treason? How can citizens of a conquered country be accused of treason for defending their country? How can foreign nationals be tried in a court of the victor, found guilty and executed for treason?

He also wondered what meaning the trial held for his own circumstances. If he carried through on his determination to make his case, would he receive a fair hearing? Would he even be permitted to explain?

John Henry, you would have been even more confused if you had known about another Mexican who had been hauled up before the authorities for treason. I thumbed through the pages of a biography of Manual Antonio Chaves.

Chaves had earned quite a reputation for fighting Indians in the 1830s and early 1840s and was a leading citizen of Santa Fe. Now, like other notable locals in the aftermath of the American takeover, he either became implicated in the plans for a December uprising or his enemies planted the rumor that he was.

Whatever the truth of the matter, Colonel Price had him arrested and held for trial. The charge, yep, was treason.

Price had him interrogated in jail. Chaves admitted that he had indeed been prepared to defend his country against the American invaders but when Governor Armijo disbanded the army, he accepted the result. He was not now part of any movement, he said, to murder anyone in cold blood.

Price was unmoved and Chaves was brought to trial in January before a military tribunal. The charge of treason was based on General Kearny's pronouncement on entering New Mexico in August 1846 that residents were now to be considered citizens of the United States and that any opposition to his government would be considered treason.

My, my, General, that's pretty thin. You surely knew, or you should have known, that the question of citizenship of the conquered Mexicans would be settled only in the treaty ending the war. But victors in war don't ordinarily have to resort to reason in their deliberations. So, treason it was.

Happily for Chaves, he had good counsel. Captain William Z. Angney had been a Missouri lawyer before joining Kearny's Army of the West. Angney argued before the tribunal that Chaves was still a citizen of Mexico. Any action he took in these troubled times was in defense of his country. Far from branding him a traitor, Angney said, we should be calling him a patriot for having the courage to defend his country against great odds. The United States would henceforth be disgraced if it executed a man for defending his country in its time of need. Surprisingly, the court was persuaded by this reasoned argument and Chaves was acquitted and released.

I had to shake my head. Since I began this journey into my New Mexican past, I have looked at a lot of court records. Angney's argument was one of the most reasoned and logical I have seen. Yet, in the climate of the time and the place, that he won the case is phenomenal. Man, I would like to have Angney represent me next time I'm hauled into court.

Point is, I'm not sure John Henry had even heard about Chaves. Chaves's trial took place before his return to Santa Fe from California. Surely some of his friends were aware of the trial but it seems nobody told him. Too bad. It might have given him some hope to counter his depression over the charge of treason brought later against the leaders of the Taos uprising.

There is nothing to suggest that John Henry knew about Chaves until the good man later came to John Henry's defense.

The talk of the Taos uprising left John Henry troubled. He regretted the loss of life on both sides but he sympathized with the native New Mexicans who were willing to risk their lives to defend their country and resist subjugation by the invaders.

When he learned in February that the resistance was

still alive, that conspirators still talked of rebellion, he counseled his friends not to get involved. The Americans have won, he said, they are strong, and they are not going away. Nor will they be evicted by force or appeal to reason. He had heard too much talk, even before joining the army, about the inevitability of American expansion westward to believe that the annexation of New Mexico would be anything but permanent.

Accept the change in sovereignty, he told his friends, and work peacefully for a life in the new order as good as you can make it. The government promises that you will be treated fairly and your property and religion will be sacred.

That's what he told his friends but he wasn't sure that's what he believed. He wondered whether the native New Mexicans would ever be equal with the Americans in the new American province, even if they accepted the offer of United States citizenship.

I looked up from the journal, stood and walked to the window. The sun at noon was brilliant. Nothing moved in my view, from the yard to the corrals and beyond to the meadow and the hill.

I suddenly felt depressed. John Henry, John Henry. What you might have accomplished with only an ounce of opportunity! You had greater insight into the human condition than most of the pundits of your age. Or my own age. You had a cause, but no pulpit, a grievance, but no voice.

You weren't the only one who had questions about citizenship for the native New Mexicans. Colonel Price himself had doubts. In February 1847, he said that the belief that New Mexicans were favorably inclined to the United States government, and presumably United States citizenship, was entirely erroneous.

Both you and Price hit the nail on the head, *amigo*. Many New Mexicans did in fact spurn American citizenship. At war's end, hundreds of New Mexicans opted to remain citizens of Mexico and many moved south to Mexico. The Mexican government gave them land grants south of the Rio Grande and they opened farms and established a number of new towns there.

Of course, you didn't know this. Your problem at this point is not what New Mexicans will do with their political allegiances. Your problem is what decisions you must make now that will define the rest of your life. And Morita's.

I returned to my desk, sat down and picked up the journal.

CHAPTER 5
Bless Me, for I Have Sinned

John Henry sat at his accustomed place in the cantina, against the wall, with a clear view of the bar where Morita must appear as she picked up drinks for patrons. She never failed to turn toward him, knowing that he watched.

Sometimes, waiting for José to pour drinks, she smiled and lightly tossed her head, or raised an eyebrow, or pulled a shoulder back to tighten her dress and emphasize her breast. The candlelight hardly extended to his dark corner and all she saw was a shadow. But she knew he watched.

Indeed he watched, though his vision this night was slightly blurred. He stared into his wine glass. It was his third, more than he usually drank, and this one was almost finished. He picked up the glass and swirled the liquid, tipped the glass up and emptied it.

Morita served three vaqueros in the far corner, fended off their playful flirtations and walked to the bar. She moved the empty glasses from her tray to the bar, spoke to José, then looked toward John Henry's table.

The shadow was not there. She walked to his table and he was not there. She looked around. Perhaps he had joined a friend but she looked around again and did not see him.

He was gone, and he did not tell her. A moment of irritation was followed at once by concern. She looked toward José. He shrugged his shoulders.

*****

John Henry walked in the center of the dark street. Adobes on each side of the road were silhouettes, their edges outlined by pale moonlight. Two old men leaned against a house, bent toward each other, talking softly, puffing on their cigarros, a filmy grey cloud about their heads.

He stopped, listened. He had never known Santa Fe to be so still. No sounds, no movement of air. A dog barked in the distance. He looked in the direction of the sound as if he could see it. Then all was quiet again.

He closed his eyes and inhaled deeply. He smelled the sweet fragrance of lavender and catnip, then the smells of cooking and the pungent odors of manure and decay and mildew. It was a mixture that was Santa Fe.

He remembered evenings like this at home. He had often sat on the porch after supper, listening to the silence. The more he listened, the more the darkness was filled with sound. The sharp chirp of a nighthawk. A rustling in the brush behind the barn, maybe a fox or a possum. The distant lilting whistle of a whip-poor-will, followed by the repetitive taunting imitations of a mocker that seemed to be sitting on top of his head. Soft sounds from inside the house, someone walking, dishes being put into the cupboard. And then silence.

It seemed a lifetime since he had left his Missouri home. Would he see it again? He closed his eyes and squeezed them shut.

Laughter erupted from the interior of a dark adobe on his left. He opened his eyes and looked aside. The face of a young girl appeared in the open doorway. She looked up at him, smiled and withdrew into the darkness. He walked on.

Reaching the road that bordered the plaza, he stopped. The square was empty. He had been at the plaza at all hours of the day and night and had never seen it empty. He shivered and pulled the serape tight about his shoulders.

Walking into the plaza, he stopped in the center when he heard the bleating whinny of a nighthawk. He searched the treetops for the singer and saw nothing but the dark leafy mass.

A rumble of thunder sounded overhead. He walked across the plaza, his head down. The breeze quickened, a few large raindrops pelted him, and he was running. By the time he reached the portico of the church, rain fell heavily and a sharp wind blew the rain against his back. He leaned into the doorway, away from the wind. The door nudged open an inch and he pushed inside.

The door closed behind him with a muffled thud, echoing softly in the cavernous chamber. He looked about, his eyes adjusting to the dark interior. He was alone.

The nave was dimly illuminated by a candle on a table at the back beside the font and another at the altar. In what appeared to be a small chapel on the right side, midway from entrance to altar, a tray of offertory candles shed some light, though most candles had burned down. Two or three sputtered and died as he watched.

He wavered. He looked toward the altar, and his head spun. Turning to leave, he clenched his eyes and turned back to face the altar which seemed to beckon him.

He walked slowly to the center of the nave and looked around. He had noted the absence of benches when he attended services with Morita before leaving with the army for California. There were still no pews and he was surprised. He thought the presence of the victorious Yankees would have influenced the Mexicans to alter the church to the American style, at least to add benches.

He saw the confessional outlined against the dark wall on the left and walked to it. The confessional was made up of two connected compartments, each with its own doorway covered by a curtain. Morita had explained that the penitent sat in one compartment and the priest sat on the other side.

He pulled the curtain of the penitent's compartment aside and stepped in. A small opening in the interior wall was covered with a lattice and closed with a sliding door. A crucifix hung above the lattice. The only furnishings were a narrow chair that almost filled the compartment and a kneeler on the floor against the interior wall. He sat in the chair.

He had always been intrigued by the Catholic practice of confession. Raise hell, confess in the little box, and all is well. When he had raised the point with Morita, she had been hurt and angry and would not speak to him until he apologized. I was just joking, he had said, and she had given him a lecture on humility and consideration for the beliefs of others.

He had admitted that he was ignorant of Catholic belief. He had never really told her what he thought of the Catholic faith and indeed, religion in general. He knew that if he were to be with Morita the rest of his life, he must learn tolerance and know when to keep his mouth shut.

But he was alone now in the confessional. He knelt and frowned, leaned his forehead against the lattice. "Bless me, Father, for I have sinned. It has been a hundred years since I last confessed and since then I have—"

"That long?" The voice, soft but firm, came through the opening. John Henry started and leaned back. He saw that the shutter behind the lattice had been silently opened.

"I'm sorry, uh, I just . . . I came inside to get out of the rain and I saw the confessional. I've always been curious, you see . . . I'm not Catholic."

"God sends the rain. Perhaps with a purpose?" The priest chuckled.

"Yes, well. I don't want to take any of your time, padre. You must—"

"As long as you are here and curious. Do you have anything to confess? You must have broken a great number of commandments during that hundred years."

John Henry smiled. "Hmm. Well, no, I don't think so."

"Really? You must be an exceptional young man. You have done nothing wrong? You have not committed any act which could place your mortal soul in jeopardy?"

John Henry frowned. *Am I really having this conversation with a faceless person in a black robe on the other side of a walled enclosure in the middle of the night?* His head spun. *Was it the wine?*

"That depends on how one defines what is wrong, doesn't it?" said John Henry. "Does one confess to doing something that men, some men and laws, define as wrong, when the act is the right thing to do?"

The priest cleared his throat, moved on his stool. "Now this is most interesting. You speak of an act that runs counter to law but which law that runs counter to the teachings of Jesus. Am I right?"

"Well, yes. At least, I think so. I'm not real familiar with the teachings of Jesus. But I know what my conscience tells me about right and wrong."

"There are times when selfish men, or men guided

by national or racial or economic prejudice, make laws that are counter to the teachings of Jesus. Every person must decide how to respond. It is always a struggle, for to oppose the laws of men, one must risk the penalties prescribed by men. God is watching. God will reward the righteous and punish the wicked."

John Henry did not know how to respond. He would like to know this faceless padre. Maybe he will come to his church. Morita would be pleased.

"I wish you had come earlier this evening," said the priest, "before my mind and body grew so heavy. You are a thinker and I would enjoy talking with you again. I think you may have more weighty sins to confess than the usual ordinary transgressions that I listen to each day." He chuckled. "Some of my parishioners seem to struggle to find something to confess or to find something ordinary to substitute for something real and awful. Truth is, we all have serious sins to confess. Daily. I still go to confessional regularly."

"You? Regularly?"

"Oh, yes, every day. Mostly for sins of my youth so grievous that I must ask God's forgiveness every day to cleanse my soul of the wrongs I committed."

"I thought that if you asked God's forgiveness with pure intent and a pure heart, the sin is forgiven, and you have a clean slate. As in 'Go, and sin no more.' "

"Ah, you do know something of the Bible, don't you?"

"I was raised in a devout Baptist family. My daddy read the Bible aloud every evening after dinner. We went to church when we could and I went to Sunday School. But it never took with me, even as a young boy. I think I wanted to believe. All of my friends believed.

"But I'm not a disbeliever either. No one yet has persuaded me that there is a God, or gods. But nobody has been able to prove to me that there is not a God, or gods. I've been told more than once that I'm a coward, balancing on the fence, keeping a foot in each camp as a precaution, hoping for the best."

John Henry waited but no sound came from the other side of the wall. He wondered whether the priest was offended or formulating a response. Or had he dropped off to sleep?

"Does that make sense?" John Henry said.

"Oh, yes. It does make sense. It also shows that you are honest and have strong convictions. It also suggests that your immortal soul is in jeopardy."

John Henry straightened. He looked at the black curtain of the confessional that seemed to hold him inside. He shuffled sideways on his stool, leaned forward, preparing to stand.

"Do you pray?" said the padre.

John Henry settled back on his stool. "No."

"You said you were raised in the church. Did you never pray?"

"Daddy prayed before dinner and asked me to pray a couple of times. I never answered and he gave up. My mother taught me a little prayer that she said I should say every night before going to bed."

"Do you remember it?"

John Henry lowered his head, looked at the floor, then at the lattice. He rubbed his cheeks with both hands.

Now I lay me down to sleep,
I pray the Lord my soul to keep,

The priest joined in, and they recited together.

If I should die before I wake,
I pray the Lord my soul to take.

"I had a parishioner who lived in Missouri," the priest said. "He taught the prayer to me. It's a lovely prayer."

"Yes, it is. Sad." John Henry thought he should say more but he had nothing more to say. He waited. A shuffling came from the priest's chamber.

"Would you mind looking into the nave," the priest said, "and tell me whether anyone appears to be waiting for me? If I were to look, it would appear that I am anxious. A parishioner said she needed to confess this evening but I think she is not coming."

John Henry pushed the curtain aside. He released the curtain and turned back to the lattice. "No, father, the church is empty."

"Good. I am tired and I am going to bed. You must do the same." The sound of a stool or chair pushing back sounded from the priest's side. "You must come again. Perhaps we will have coffee and you will tell me more of yourself and what demons you live with. You said you are not a Catholic but you are a child of God. Vaya con Dios."

John Henry waited. He heard the sound of soft footsteps leaving the confessional. He stood, pushed the curtain aside and stepped out. He saw the priest walking toward the front of the church. His head was down and his cassock billowed as he rounded a corner near the altar and disappeared through a doorway.

CHAPTER 6
Jornada del Muerto

John Henry and Morita sat on the stone porch, their legs outstretched, leaning against the adobe wall. He stared at his hands in his lap, frowning. Morita watched him. He had told her about his nocturnal visit with the padre and she had listened without comment. He said that he was intrigued by this priest and would like to talk with him again. Maybe we will go to a service, he had said. Maybe. She had squeezed his arm and rested her head on his shoulder.

He was quiet now, staring at the sunny courtyard and the wall that enclosed all that he held dear. She turned to him. She could almost hear his brain churning. He had said enough earlier that she knew that he had become increasingly depressed with affairs in Santa Fe.

The town was a cauldron where rumors of rebellion boiled and suspicion of neighbors was commonplace. He felt that eyes focused on him everywhere he walked, an Americano in spite of his vaquero clothing and Spanish that was nearing fluency. He assumed that everyone who saw him on the street knew that he lived with a *mexicana*. He could almost hear their thoughts: who is this Yankee and what is he doing in Santa Fe?

With the passage of time, the *Mexicanos* grew more aware that they were not equals in the new American province and feared that they never would be. John Henry had been hopeful that Kearny's policy of fair treatment of the people would result in a melding of Americans and Mexicans into a harmonious whole. But it wasn't happening and he feared that it would never happen. Two classes were emerging, based not on economics or prospects but on race and national origins.

He lowered his head, closed his eyes. He rubbed his cheeks hard with both hands, looked up, eyes still closed. He opened his eyes and turned to stare blankly at Morita.

She waited but he said nothing. "Juanito?" she said.

"Morita, I see no future for me in Santa Fe. I will always be looking over my shoulder, wondering when finally I will be recognized and arrested."

"You did what is right," she said.

"That has nothing to do with how the army and the American government will see me. All they will see is a deserter. They will say that my reason for desertion is of no importance. Desertion cannot be defended, they will say."

She watched him. And waited. He stared at his boots.

"You would be better off without me. I'll be nothing but trouble for you. I should go away now, while I am still a free man." He took a deep breath, looked up into the branches of the cottonwood that shaded the porch. "I might go to Colorado. Or Mexico. Or Canada."

"Okay, what you say may make sense. Except one thing. If you go, I go with you."

He turned to face her. "No, sweetheart, you must stay here. This is where you belong. It is your home. I will never be able to live a settled life. I will always be on the run. I could not let you be part of that."

Morita glared at him, pursed her lips. "Juanito! Stop it! You talk . . . what you say . . . nonsense! That is stupid talk. We are one person. If you stay, I stay. If you go, I go."

"No, that is not—"

"I kill myself if you leave without me."

"But, Morita—"

"I kill myself!"

He looked long into her eyes, put his arms slowly around her shoulders and pulled her to him, held her tightly, his head resting on hers.

"What am I saying," he said softly. "I could never leave you. I could never let you go."

And yet he did go. Standing at the window, I leafed through the pages of John Henry's journal and found the passages in which he explained his decision not to abandon Morita and Santa Fe permanently.

He had decided that he would continue to live in Santa Fe and take his chances. Someday, he would find a way to state his case, to explain why he had not been able to support this war.

But not yet. Tensions were still high from the Taos uprising and John Henry knew that tempers were such that he could not expect a reasoned reception. So he would leave Santa Fe for a time.

Like every historian and genealogist searching for information, I wished that John Henry had begun writing about his New Mexico sojourn from the time he left Fort Leavenworth, or even from his Missouri farm, but he had begun the journal only after his return to Santa Fe from California. He added comments from time to time about what came before, and these are helpful, but it's not the same as an account of what happened day by day when the memory is vivid and the hands still sweaty.

This frontier farm boy, with only a third-grade formal education, wrote in complete sentences, clearly chronicling his experiences and his thoughts. The writing was more intelligent and more revealing than most of the documents of the period written by university graduates and I had seen plenty of them since I began this search for my ancestor.

Morita had wanted to go away with him but he convinced her that she must stay and carry on as if nothing were amiss.

You coming back, she had said in her throwback English when she was playing with him. Yes, he replied. If you no come back, she said, I find you and cut you throat. He had smiled and swore that he would have to come back now.

He wrote all this in his journal. It's obvious that he enjoyed the exchange and the sentiment. I sure did.

Traveling on El Camino Real that ran between Santa Fe and Mexico City, John Henry and his escort of two vaqueros from Antonio's ranch had seen the occasional horsemen and traders' wagons. Some traveled southward toward Chihuahua, some in the opposite direction toward Santa Fe.

Their route ran through the dreaded *Jornada del Muerto*, the route of the dead man. The hundred-mile track through a dry, flat landscape of lava and scrub mesquite was marked by a complete lack of water, grazing or firewood. No spring, no stream, only a trail of sand and stone. The traveler who strayed from the trail risked being impaled by the thorns of *cholla* and prickly pear cacti. The trio had been warned about the region and carried adequate provisions and water on the two pack burros.

As difficult as it was, the trail was more direct and physically easier on man and beast than the alternatives.

Since passing El Paso del Norte, the road had been empty. Except for the three following horsemen who appeared to be setting their pace to remain barely within sight. One of the sharp-sighted vaqueros had spotted the riders a day out of Santa Fe.

At noon stop on that day, John Henry pulled the spyglass from his pack and trained it on the three men, hardly specks on the back trail to the naked eye. In the spyglass, they materialized as three Americans, judging from their clothing and hats. Their nooning appeared to consist of draining the contents of bottles, likely not water, judging from their erratic behavior.

The horsemen were in no hurry. When John Henry and his companions stopped for the night, the riders disappeared, apparently to a trailside camp. When John Henry and the vaqueros broke camp each morning and set out, the three horsemen soon appeared on their trail.

On one occasion, to test their suspicions, John Henry and his companions stopped at mid-morning for two hours, something travelers on the Camino never did. The followers also stopped and hung back. When John Henry and the others resumed their ride, the horsemen followed, specks on the back trail.

John Henry and the two vaqueros sat their horses on a rising looking down on a wide basin. The land was dry, the vegetation a scattering of sage and mesquite and scant grass. Grazing cattle were scattered in the flat to the distant foothills.

Just ahead, a wagon road snaked down the slope to a

cluster of buildings in the near side of the valley. A large ranch house, barn and outbuildings, corrals and bunkhouse. A windmill and watering troughs.

John Henry scoped the ranch with the spyglass. He saw no movement in and about the ranch buildings. All was tranquil, a quiet tableau. They rode down the dusty road toward the buildings.

The three riders pulled up before the ranch house of Joaquin Vargas. They dismounted slowly, stretched and handed their reins to a barefoot boy of twelve years, clad in white canvas pants and shirt, who had run from the barn at their approach.

"Señor Vargas!" the boy yelled to the house before running toward the corral ahead of the trotting horses.

"Here, taste this El Paso del Norte wine, good wine, not like your weak Santa Fe wine, which we use for cooking." Vargas laughed and poured wine from a decanter into the glasses of his three visitors. They sat on the covered porch in chairs of hand-hewn wood.

John Henry sipped his wine. "I must agree, Señor, but El Paso del Norte wine is not new to us. I have given up aguardiente for this wine." The two vaqueros drank from their glasses and nodded their agreement.

Vargas sat down, took a long drink, closed his eyes and smiled. He opened his eyes and turned to John Henry.

"Mi amigo, you may stay here as long as you like. I admire you for your wisdom and your courage in opposing this war." Vargas's face clouded and he slammed his fist on the arm of his chair, sloshing his wine on the porch floor.

"Damn the Yankees! Sorry, Señor, but what right do they have? They pretend Mexico invaded their territory, Texas, *their* territory, and they answer by invading Mexico and making war on her. Damn them! They have no right!"

The vaqueros looked at John Henry who sipped his wine.

Vargas softened. "Sorry, señor. I am not being a good host."

John Henry smiled. "You have not offended me, señor, and you have said nothing that I don't agree with. The war is wrong and I face imprisonment for opposing it. You are most gracious to let me stay here until the government forgets about me."

Vargas smiled. "You are a good man, a brave man. I am proud to know you. I am glad to know that not all Americans are scoundrels. You may stay here as long as you like. And you may bring your woman. Antonio told me about Morita in his message." He smiled broadly. "If what Antonio says is true, I would enjoy having her here, even more than *you*." He laughed, leaned over and clapped John Henry on the back. "You better keep your woman away from Antonio. He's an old dog but he still has teeth." Vargas chuckled.

"They are here, señor." Tomás, the boy who had met them on their arrival the day before stood in the yard with a companion, Mateo, also twelve. John Henry stepped down from the porch, looked up. The evening sun hovered above the horizon, the sky a silver-blue turning gray, layers of color materializing above the horizon.

"Tell me what you saw," John Henry said.

"They camped last night in a bunch of mesquite in the third arroyo to the north, near the red windmill. We left the ranch before sunrise and hid in bushes and watched them. They were sitting around a little fire, drinking from bottles. There were bottles all around on the ground. They talked loud but we could not understand them."

"I would not be able to understand them, even if I understood English," Mateo said. He smiled. "We were far away from them, but I could smell them anyway."

"While we watched," Tomás said, "they finished drinking from the bottles and threw them into the bushes. They began picking up things from the ground and putting them into saddlebags on their horses. I think they were getting ready to leave, so we ran here to tell you."

"You have done well," John Henry said. "You were careful, you were not seen, and you brought me the information that I need so we can be ready. I am proud of you. You are brave and trustworthy." He shook the hands of the boys. "Now, stay inside tonight."

The boys frowned. "But—" John Henry held up his hand, silencing Tomás.

"There will come a time when I will call on you. But not tonight. Off with you." The boys smiled and walked away, chattering to each other, looking back over their shoulders at John Henry.

*****

The large barn had bays on each side with a wide lane running down the center that opened on each end. Hay was stacked in one side, and stalls for horses and mules ran down the length of the other side. Hazy moonlight dimly illuminated the opening on the north side.

The silence was absolute. Nothing moved. Then three dark shadows glided slowly into the opening, shuffling, bending toward each other, whispering, looking side to side anxiously. Animals in the stalls moved about, disturbed. A horse made a low snorting noise, a sound like a low snore or a purr.

The three shadows materialized as men, dressed in

wrinkled shirts and trousers and shabby coats. They moved slowly, huddling against each other, heads jerking side to side, eyes darting right and left.

A soft sound behind the men brought them around sharply. They started at the appearance of three silhouettes at the barn opening, moonlight describing three men with arms at their sides, hands poised about their hips.

The three soldiers whirled around and made to rush to the opening at the other end. They stopped abruptly. They saw in the south opening three large figures, arms akimbo, poised to draw. The intruders huddled together, scared out of their drunken wits, jerked around, front, back, ready to bolt, but in what direction?

Suddenly, a specter dropped down from the rafters directly in front of the soldiers, yellow slicker flapping. He landed crouching, arms stretched out horizontally, glaring at them, the figure's face a grinning skull.

The three soldiers screamed, whirled around and ran for the north door, bumping against each other in their terror, oblivious of the three figures who had barred the opening but who now stepped aside.

The soldiers continued running across the yard, stumbling, falling, scrambling up and running for their lives.

At the barn opening, bathed in moonlight, John Henry removed the skull. He and the vaqueros laughed as the soldiers ran past the corrals and disappeared over the rising beyond.

John Henry and Antonio sat on the porch, coffee cups in hand. They sipped from the steaming cups, squinting in the morning sun.

"How did they know, these stupid drunks?" Vargas said. He laughed out loud. "I can't stop laughing."

John Henry smiled, then sobered. "I was recognized in the saloon. Our paths must have crossed in Santa Fe before I left with the column for California or maybe on the march from Leavenworth to Santa Fe. I didn't recognize him, but he recognized me, even through my beard and his addled brain. He and his friends must have decided that if the army wouldn't do something about my disloyalty, they would take care of me personally.

"I can understand that. I can understand how soldiers can take this personally, figuring that I ran away from the war, leaving them to fight the enemy while I ran. I understand that. Problem is, who is the enemy? It gets all mixed up."

"Well, at least we know that these three soldiers have had enough of war for a while," said Vargas. He snorted. "I doubt they will talk much about this affair back in Santa Fe."

Vargas upended his cup. "More coffee?"

John Henry shook his head. "No, gracias."

"Now what will you do?" Vargas said.

John Henry hesitated, looked at Vargas, at the barn and the horizon, back to Vargas. "I wish I could end the uncertainty. I just want to live a long life with Morita, have children, become a good citizen, enjoy Santa Fe with all my good friends." He lowered his head.

"For now, I don't know how to do this. So I will impose on your hospitality a while longer."

"You do not impose on my hospitality," Vargas said. "You accept my hospitality that is offered without reservation and with my thanks for your sacrifice."

Vargas stood, clapped John Henry on the back and took his cup. He walked through the door, leaving John Henry to stare at the sandy yard and wonder what was in store for him.

John Henry and the two vaqueros lived in the bunk-house with Vargas's hands. Each morning, John Henry rose at dawn, did a rewarding, hard day's work with men he liked and trusted and they became friends. On one occasion, he rode with four of the vaqueros to El Paso del Norte, a two-day ride, to pick up supplies. One man drove the wagon, the others horseback. The ride and the visit were most satisfying.

John Henry was at peace with himself for the first time in months. He slept well, he worked hard, and he enjoyed the companionship of good friends.

It couldn't last. As content as he was on the ranch of Joaquin Vargas, it could only be an interlude before he had to return to Morita and Santa Fe and the decisions that he must make.

John Henry stood with Vargas at the hitching post in front of the ranch house. John Henry's two companions stood nearby, smoking, holding their horses' reins, talking softly, glancing occasionally at John Henry and Joaquin Vargas.

"My sincere thanks for your hospitality, *señor*. My mind has cleared. I hope affairs in the north are settled. And now I must return to my home, Santa Fe."

Vargas shook John Henry's hand vigorously. "You are welcome in my home anytime. Have a safe journey home. *Vaya con Dios.*"

"*Adios, mi amigo,*" John Henry said. Vargas waved to the two vaqueros and they returned his wave. John Henry and his companions mounted and they set off at a lope.

CHAPTER 7
You Are Mexican in Spirit

The evening sun cast a shaft of light through the doorway into Morita's kitchen, describing a bright rectangle on the floor. John Henry and Morita sat at the table, holding mugs of rich chocolate. John Henry sipped from his mug, lowered it to the table.

They stared at their mugs. Morita waited.

"Señor Vargas invited us to come. I would work for him. He said he would build us a little adobe. We would be safe. I could become a Mexican citizen."

She waited. When he said no more, she said: "But you will not."

"No. I would never be at peace. I would have been silenced. I would never have taken the responsibility for defending myself, for explaining."

"I understand," she said.

He looked up at her. "Am I being rational? Is anyone going to listen? Does it matter to anyone but me? And you. If no one cares, why do we stay? If not Mexico, we could go to Colorado. Why not?" He lowered his head, stared at his mug.

"We could do that," she said, "if you would be happy."

He looked up at her. "Yeah. If I could be happy."

He stood, sighed heavily. He bent down, took her chin in his hand, raised it and kissed her. "There is only one place I am always happy, *bonita*, holding you." She stood and they embraced.

*****

John Henry sat with Andrés and Calixtro at a corner table at the back of the cantina. A single candle on each of the dozen tables dimly illuminated the room. It was quiet this evening. The usual orchestra of two guitars and a violin was absent. Five patrons sat at two tables, talking softly. José held two empty glasses and wiped a table near the bar.

John Henry had hardly tasted his wine. He stared at the glass on the table. His companions had finished their aguardiente. They watched him.

Calixtro stood and walked to the bar, carrying his empty glass. José stepped behind the bar and filled the glass. The vaquero returned to the table and sat down. He took a swallow.

"You are Mexican in spirit, John Henry Jed Weber," said Calixtro. He smiled. "Become a citizen. The government says that we *nuevo Mexicanos* can become American citizens if we wish. But it should work the other way too. You could become a Mexican citizen. Then you would be safe from the American courts." He leaned back, took a long drink from his glass, satisfied that he had solved John Henry's problem.

"I wish it was that simple," John Henry said. "Don't forget that the leaders of the Taos ruckus were Mexican citizens. And you know what happened to them. They were arrested for *treason*. They were tried in an American court and executed.

"No, I would not be safe from prosecution. The government will interpret the law to suit their purposes and the courts will follow along. Truth be known, nobody in New Mexico will be safe until the military is no longer in control and when capable, experienced, open-minded civilians have taken their place. Only then will we enjoy a democratic, classless society."

I read the journal entry again. A democratic, classless society, you say. Good luck, John Henry.

I laid the journal on the desk and picked up a single sheet. It was a photocopy of the front page of the *Santa Fe Republican*, the town's first newspaper, which began publication in September 1847. The page was dated November 13, nine months after John Henry voiced his expectation of a classless society.

I read the article: "How can any American help but feel proud of his country? How much better does he love it after witnessing the poverty, ignorance, and imbecility of another nation?"

I doubt the writer and the editor, possibly the same person, would have been so crass if he hadn't believed that his readers agreed with the sentiment. Another piece in the newspaper commented on the improvements that were sure to come with the infusion of the Anglo-Saxon spirit and institutions.

No, John Henry, a democratic, classless society was not brewing in 1847. A goodly number of Hispanics in modern Santa Fe likely believe that this happy result hasn't happened to this day. Much less mid-nineteenth century.

John Henry, Calixtro and Andrés stood on the bank of the river, shaded by tall cottonwoods. Swollen by recent rains in the mountains, the river coursed through the heart of Santa Fe, providing the water supply for the town and surrounding farms.

Andrés puffed on his cigar, raising a smoke cloud around his head. He withdrew the stub, held it up and looked at it, tossed it into the stream. He leaned toward John Henry.

"The troubles are not over," he said. "There are still people, mostly in the north, who resist. Manuel Cortez—he led the rebellion in Mora, you know—he was not captured when Price caught the leaders at Taos. I know Manuel Cortez. He is a patriot and he will not give up until he is victorious. Or dead.

"I heard that Manuel had gathered some countrymen who want to fight. He enlisted allies among the Comanche and Apache. I heard they attacked an army wagon train and took two hundred horses from them. When the soldiers came after them, Manuel's followers beat them off and the soldiers had to retreat. Victories like this encourage those that wish to fight the Americans. Some men from Santa Fe have ridden north to join Manuel."

"I understand how the rebels feel," John Henry said.

"Patriots, John Henry, not rebels."

"You are right, of course," John Henry said. "I agree with their unhappiness, no, their outrage. But this is only prolonging the inevitable. It will come to no good end." Calixtro and Andrés exchanged a glance. John Henry noticed.

"I hope my friends will not become involved in this," said John Henry. "What could you expect to gain? You cannot defeat the Americans and force them to leave. You can only be jailed or killed. Either way, your families suffer."

Andrés looked at John Henry. "Is honor and dignity nothing?"

"And you, John Henry," said Calixtro, "did you not risk all by deserting and voicing your opposition to this unjust war? Did you think you would win with your protest? Why did you not accept that you must be obedient and be quiet and carry on?"

John Henry was disturbed by the implications of this conversation. He was afraid for his friends. They thought too much. They were too much like him.

John Henry rode with Andrés and Calixtro down the slope on a game trail that wound through a mixed cover of prairie sage and barberry. Scattered cottonwoods in the flat below foretold a stream, though none was visible from the trail.

The three rounded a bend in the trail and saw two men ahead who sat their horses in the middle of the trail. The men wore pistols and had rifles cradled in their arms.

Andrés rode ahead and spoke with them. The men pulled their horses off the trail. Calixtro and John Henry rode past them. John Henry nodded. The sentries nodded, unsmiling, watched them pass.

At the bottom of the slope, the three riders rode through thick, tall cover and heard the soft sounds of a cascading stream. Then they heard the voices, faint, then louder, and laughter.

They rode from the brush into the rebel camp. A scattering of tents and stretched canvas shelters lay in a clearing on the bank of the small stream. Upstream, the flat opened into a wide meadow of bluestem bunchgrass as tall as a horse's belly.

There were forty or fifty men in the camp. They looked up at the three riders approaching. Some smiled, waved, returned to what they were doing, smoking, cleaning weapons, rubbing down their horses. Most ignored the newcomers, content that the sentries would have done their job.

"*Hola,* Andrés, Calixtro!" Manuel called. He had spotted the three when they emerged from the thicket and had walked toward them. "Get down, we will feed you." The three dismounted.

"Who did you bring with you?" Manuel said, gesturing with his head at John Henry. "Did you bring a spy?" He smiled.

"This is Jed Weber, a good friend," said Andrés. "We trust him with our lives."

"Then he is my friend as well," Manuel said. "Welcome, Jed Weber." Manuel extended his hand, and John Henry shook it.

"You know who we are and what we do, Jed Weber?" Manuel said.

"I do."

"And what do you think?"

"I feel as you—"

Suddenly all heads turned upstream at the sound of a bugle. The sound seemed to come from a copse that lay beyond the meadow of tall grass.

"Scatter!" John Henry yelled. "That's the charge bugle! Scatter!"

Some men ran for cover. Others ran to their horses, pulled rifles from scabbards. Andrés still held his reins. He swung into the saddle and kicked the horse into a gallop into the thicket. John Henry had let Remolino's reins trail, and the horse bolted at the rush of men and horses in the clearing.

John Henry ran into the thicket behind him, pulling his pistol from its holster. He crouched behind a thick barberry bush and peered through the cover toward the clearing.

A vaquero galloped alone from the meadow, across the clearing and into the thicket. A sentry, John Henry decided, who had not had time to alert the encampment and now was riding for his life.

John Henry watched the retreating sentry, looked back to the clearing to see Calixtro struggling to control his terrified mount. The horse had reared at the commotion around him and ran across the clearing, reins flying, Calixtro in pursuit. He had just grabbed the reins when he stopped abruptly at the sound of hoof beats.

John Henry saw them. About thirty troopers had rounded a streamside thicket and galloped toward the camp, sabers raised.

Calixtro froze. He dropped the reins, the horse shied and galloped into the thicket. Calixtro looked side to side, searching for an escape. The trooper leading the charge galloped toward him, his saber held high.

John Henry pushed the brush aside, leveled his pistol on the trooper. "Veer off," he said softly, to himself. "Goddammit, veer off."

The trooper bore down on Calixtro. He raised the saber to strike. Calixtro crossed his arms above his head.

John Henry's eyes blurred. He squeezed the trigger, lowered the barrel, fired. The horse's legs buckled, and he collapsed. The soldier sailed over the falling horse's head and tumbled, rolling on the ground, losing the saber. He scrambled up, looked around frantically and ran to the rear. A following trooper pulled him up behind his saddle, whirled his mount and galloped back into the meadow.

A steady fire from the thickets forced the troopers to withdraw. They galloped back into the meadow and around the streamside thicket, the sounds of their mounts' hooves growing dimmer.

They were gone. It was deathly quiet. John Henry exhaled, lowered his pistol, sat down heavily. He struggled to stand, flexed his back, looked below.

Men walked slowly from cover, holding their weapons loosely. They looked around. Two of their compatriots lay dead at the edge of the clearing. Three more dead were found at the edge of the thicket where they were hit and fell. The bodies of three soldiers lay in the clearing.

The trooper's horse that John Henry shot lay on its side, trembling, its head lifted, trying to rise. It nickered softly. A man walked to the horse, shot it in the head with his pistol. The horse's head dropped heavily to the hard ground. Others in the clearing jerked around at the shot, weapons at the ready.

John Henry's eyes blurred. He wiped them with a sleeve, lowered his head and looked at the pistol that he held. Sliding the pistol slowly into its holster, he looked up into the cottonwoods, watched the large leaves fluttering gently in the light breeze.

"You saved my life, *mi amigo.* I will not forget it." John Henry wiped his eyes again with a hand, turned to see Calixtro standing behind him. John Henry nodded, rested his hand on Calixtro's shoulder.

"We need to go," said Calixtro. "Where is Andrés?"

"Yes, we need to go. The officers will not be happy with this patrol. They'll not let it rest." John Henry pointed at the thicket across the clearing. "Andrés rode up that path. Let's get our horses and we'll find him."

Calixtro whistled loudly. John Henry walked up the trail behind the clearing. He found Remolino grazing in a patch of dry grass. He took the reins, patted the horse on the neck and led him down to the clearing. Calixtro was mounted and waiting.

John Henry mounted, and they rode slowly across the clearing toward the path where Andrés had disappeared. Men were scattered about the clearing and the fringes, picking up gear and packing.

Manuel, standing beside his horse and stuffing gear into saddlebags, saw John Henry and Calixtro approaching. He waved to them and they pulled up. Manuel walked over to them.

"Now you see how we live, Jed Weber. We are chased, attacked and our people are killed by the Americanos who think we have no right to live at peace in our country."

"I understand and I am sorry, Manuel. I wish there was something I could do," said John Henry.

"You are one of the good *americanos*, Jed Weber. There will come a time when you will help us." He extended his hand to John Henry who took the hand and they shook.

Manuel waved and walked to his horse. John Henry and Calixtro walked their horses from the clearing up the brushy path. They had hardly penetrated into the thicket when they saw Andrés's horse standing in the middle of the trail, the reins trailing. Andrés's body lay sprawled on the ground under the horse's head.

They dismounted and stood over the body. He was face down, his arms spread. The back of his shirt was soaked with blood. His pistol was still in its holster.

John Henry rubbed his face with a hand. "What a waste," he said. "What a waste."

They gently rolled the body over. The lifeless eyes, wide open, stared at the heavens. John Henry winced. He had been in the army almost a year during a violent war and he had never seen a dead body. Calixtro, tears rolling down his cheeks, repeatedly crossed himself. He kneeled beside Andrés's body and gently closed the eyes.

"We need to go," John Henry said softly. Calixtro nodded. Raising the body to a sitting position, they lifted it, draped it over Andrés's horse's saddle and tied it under the horse's belly and to the saddle horn. They mounted and rode back to the clearing, Calixtro holding the reins of Andrés's horse.

The clearing was empty. There was no evidence it had ever seen an encampment but for trampled grass. They rode up the brushy trail that would lead them to Santa Fe.

CHAPTER 8
The Demise of Jed Weber

"Juanito! Are you crazy?"

Morita leaned into his face, almost nose to nose. They stood in the yard, just inside the gate. She had run to the gate when she heard him ride up. He had hardly tied the reins and stepped inside the gate when she was on him.

"It's all right," he said. "Everything's quiet now. Cortez has moved his people north. The army won't go after them. The army wants peace and quiet. They don't want to incite a new uprising."

"You are crazy! You might have been killed. Or hurt. Or taken prisoner. How would that look? Do you think they would wonder why Jed Weber was in that camp? How did you know where Manuel Cortez was?"

"Calixtro and Andrés told me."

She glared at him, open-mouthed. "They were with you?"

"I was with them. They were going to his camp, and I was curious."

"Mierda! I thought they were smarter than that. I thought you were smarter than that!"

"Sweetheart, it's okay." He touched her cheek.

She batted his hand away. "No sweetheart me!" She glared at him, looked aside. "I can't even talk right." She looked back at him. "Why don't you think about me? What about me? What would I do if something happened to you?"

She softened, drooped, and the tears came. John Henry wrapped his arms around her shoulders and held her. Her arms were limp at her side.

"I'm sorry, *mi preciosa*. You are right. I let my curiosity get the better of my good sense. It wasn't very smart."

She put her arms about his waist, pressed her head against his chest. "You won't do something dumb like that again? Promise?"

"Promise." He lifted her head and kissed her.

He looked into her eyes. "Morita . . . I must tell you. Andrés was killed." Her eyes squeezed shut and she lowered her head, dropped her arms. "We were caught right in the middle of the fight. He was mounted and tried to get away but he was shot in the back. We brought his body back to his mother."

Morita listened to this quietly as if nothing he said could shock her any more. She turned away and leaned on the gate. He put a hand on her back and she turned away.

John Henry and Morita hurried across the plaza toward the church. Morita regularly attended services but it was the first time he had gone with her since his return to Santa Fe from California. He had accompanied her a few times before the march to California but had not been interested in attending since his return. Until now.

John Henry was glad when she told him last evening that they were going to church. He was afraid that she would be too angry and distraught to go anywhere with him. But he knew that she needed to go to church. She said she would pray for Andrés's mother and for the soul of Andrés.

There was another reason. When he told her a week ago about his conversation with the padre in the confessional, he had described it as an interesting experience but only that.

She had been excited about the encounter and believed that he was mistaken, that it was a powerful spiritual experience. She said that he would learn later how important it had been for both of them. This was the first opportunity to go to church since the encounter.

They were late. Fifteen minutes earlier, there would have been dozens hurrying across the plaza to the church, but now, late, they were alone.

John Henry opened the door and held it. Morita bowed her head and stepped inside. He followed and eased the door shut behind him. They stood there a moment, their eyes adjusting to the dark interior, Morita crossing herself, then walked to the center of the nave.

Morita, like most of the women, kneeled, crossed herself again, and bowed her head in prayer. The men for the most part stood but occasionally kneeled, then stood again.

John Henry remained standing. He looked down at Morita. She held her hands in prayer before her, her eyes closed tightly. John Henry touched the top of her head. She opened her eyes and looked up. He smiled. She frowned and returned to her prayers.

John Henry looked around. Nothing seemed to have changed since he had departed Santa Fe with the Army of the West, bound for California. The statue of Christ was still there, protected by a net. Nearby was the doll—it looked like a doll—that was dressed as a priest holding a cross.

The live priest walked to and fro, speaking in Latin which neither his parishioners nor he understood. John Henry wondered whether it was the same priest he had talked with in the confessional. It didn't sound like him but it was late then and the priest had been tired.

The orchestra of violin and guitar at the side of the altar played the same tunes John Henry had heard at Morita's cantina, albeit at a slower tempo.

John Henry had always considered the Catholic faith, religion in general, actually, a great bundle of superstitious nonsense. Yet, for a brief moment, today, watching Morita, he experienced a sensation that he had not felt before. A reverence and calm that told him to think again, to ponder the meaning of faith, to wonder at this widely-held belief in something that he could neither explain nor understand but which many considered central to their lives.

Morita crossed herself and stood. She took John Henry's arm and they walked to the door.

The next time they went to the church, it was dark, and the plaza was deserted. They walked around to the side of the church and stopped at a door of heavy weathered planks under a stone-framed overhang. They waited in the shadow.

One by one, eight of their friends joined them. The old woman, Tía, who lived with Morita, arrived and nodded solemnly to John Henry and Morita.

John Henry knocked softly on the door. He waited but there was no response. He knocked again. They heard a shuffling inside and the latch lifted. The door opened with a squeal from rusty hinges and the priest motioned for them to come inside. Morita and John Henry stepped through the doorway and the others followed.

John Henry and the priest exchanged smiles and nods. He had talked with the padre on several occasions since their meeting in the confessional. They had shared stories of their childhood, education or rather lack of it, their beliefs and prejudices, their anger at unjust laws and bigoted leaders in church and government. John Henry at first had wondered whether he confided too much in this Mexican priest but ended in thinking him one of his dearest friends. He learned his name, Francis.

The sanctuary was dark but for a globe of light coming from the right side of the altar. When all were inside, the priest locked the door and led the group to the head of the nave and into a small chapel at the side. A number of candles illuminated the room.

The priest motioned for John Henry and Morita to go to the front of the chapel and invited the others to sit on the half dozen benches. They took their seats, looking around, whispering to each other.

When all were seated, the priest stood before the altar and raised a hand for silence.

"My friends, we are gathered tonight to join these two young people in holy matrimony. This service shall be known to them and me and you and God. No one else shall hear of it."

He stepped back onto the dais and bade John Henry and Morita to kneel before him.

I held the marriage certificate, yellowed with age and torn at the bottom. The names on the certificate are Morita Carmen Luisa Flores and John Henry Harris. Morita and their friends had tried to persuade John Henry to marry as Jed Weber but he would not have it. I'm through with lies, he had said. I will marry only once and I will marry as myself. My wife and my children will carry my name, not that of an imposter.

They lived in their little adobe, in peace, as he had always dreamed they would. He rode out to Antonio's ranch each morning and worked until almost sundown. He rode back, home, each evening to dinner prepared by Morita and Tía.

After the meal, he walked with her to the cantina where he sat with a glass of wine and watched her. She glanced his way often and they could not mask their love and yearning. Patrons, most of whom were friends, smiled and sipped their wine and aguardiente.

After closing, the two lovers walked on the dusty road back to their little adobe. She clung to him, then pushed him away and danced and twirled, singing a song from the cantina and swinging her sandals, then she turned soft and quiet and took his arm and squeezed. He leaned down and kissed the top of her head.

Inside their adobe, she lit a single candle in the bedroom and placed it on the small table beside the head of the bed. They undressed each other and he sat on the bed. She stood at the foot of the bed, her naked body outlined in the soft glow of the candle.

Then he lay down and she came and lay beside him, their bodies entwined and hands touching and caressing. John Henry kissed her lips, her nose and eyes and wondered why he was so blessed.

*****

I closed the journal. Oh, my, John Henry, you could make a fortune today writing erotic romance novels. His accounts of the nights with Morita were graphic but they also were poetic. I was more impressed than ever with what this country boy could have been with some opportunity and a little luck.

It didn't last. Turns out that Morita and their friends were right. He should have married as Jed Weber, never mind the lie. Somebody, somehow, by some subterfuge or bad luck, saw the marriage register at the church and noticed a name that he recognized.

Or a name he was looking for. Somebody heard about the marriage, became curious or suspicious, and found the register when the priest wasn't about. It wouldn't have been difficult. Priests weren't accustomed to hiding things. Surely no one would violate the sanctity of the church.

Good luck, reverend, if you believe that. Maybe the devout Mexican Catholics who fear the wrath of the Lord wouldn't violate the sanctity of the church, but maybe some Yankee infidel wouldn't be so fearful.

The word spread that one John Henry Harris, obviously an American, was recently married. Since no trader, no civilian, seemed to know a John Henry Harris, the conclusion seemed to be that he must have arrived in New Mexico with the army.

Eventually, it seems that someone in an official or military capacity, recognized the name, and the investigation began. It was rumored that word had arrived from army officials in California that one Private John Henry Harris was absent from his unit and unaccounted for.

When he returned from Antonio's ranch at sundown, two weeks after his marriage, John Henry tied Remolino's reins at the rail beside the five horses tied there. He recognized army brands and saddles.

Inside the gate, he saw the lieutenant standing on the porch. Four privates armed with rifles clustered together in the yard. They looked about nervously, uncertain, awaiting orders.

Morita stood in the kitchen doorway, her arms crossed over her breast. Tear tracks marked her face. John Henry walked through the gate and stopped in the yard before the lieutenant.

"Private John Henry Harris?" the lieutenant said.

"Yes, sir."

"I'm arresting you on a charge of desertion."

John Henry didn't blink. "Sir. May I put some things together?"

"Uh . . ." The lieutenant clearly wasn't accustomed to arresting deserters. "Uh . . . yes, yes. Of course."

John Henry walked through the bedroom door. Morita hurried to follow him but the lieutenant stepped in front of her. "Not you, miss."

She stopped, looked anxiously at him, looked into the bedroom to see John Henry in the darkened interior, holding up a hand to restrain her. She backed away from the door.

John Henry came out holding a small canvas bag. "May I say goodbye to my wife?"

The lieutenant blinked and frowned. "Why, yes, yes, of course."

John Henry took Morita in his arms and they embraced. She held him tightly as tears streamed down her face. He pulled back, kissed her lightly.

"Tell our friends. I will send word as soon as I know anything." He turned to the lieutenant. "Where are you taking me? Will I be permitted to have visitors?"

"Fort Marcy. I don't know about visitors. They should

ask at the adjutant's office at the fort."

John Henry touched Morita's cheek, kissed her, and stepped off the porch. The lieutenant and soldiers followed. John Henry opened the gate, looked back briefly at Morita, and he was gone. The gate slammed closed and Morita sobbed into her hands.

CHAPTER 9
The Commander is God

I picked up a cardboard box from the floor and placed it on the desk. The label pasted to the side of the box identified the contents: *Santa Fe New Mexican/Harper's Monthly.* The newspaper began operation in 1849, *Harper's Monthly* in 1850. The fledgling weekly newspaper and the new monthly magazine were eager for exciting, eye-catching copy early on and included many articles that reported on the stormy years of the Mexican War that preceded their launch by a few short years.

John Henry's trial was still fresh in the minds of most Santa Fe residents in 1849 and 1850. It had been the talk of the town and everybody had an opinion that they were quick to share. Reporters must have interviewed Santa Fe traders and, it seems from the content of articles, one or two writers probably made the trek to Santa Fe for first-hand interviews. Thus, readers got a fresh rehash of the 1847 trial. The articles would have been especially interesting for the newcomers to Santa Fe that had swollen the population in the past few years.

I pulled a stack of photocopies from the box. Some of the articles I had found online but I collected most during research trips to Santa Fe and Albuquerque. I had not spent much time in New Mexico before my interest in my ancestor but now I have a good understanding of the land and the towns and the people.

And I might add that I love the country. Been there so many times in the past couple of years, it's almost like a second home. The Indian ladies selling their jewelry at the Governor's Palace and the plaza call me by my first name.

Colonel Price didn't know what to do with John Henry at first. He had dealt with uprisings and unrest but those problems were straightforward and he knew what had to be done. He had never had to deal with desertion. And this desertion question quickly became a hot issue. He had permitted John Henry to have visitors and the visitors had done a lot of talking.

Here was an eloquent Missouri farm boy who had joined the army to fight for his country. And he had performed according to expectations right up through the invasion of New Mexico and the march to California. He had even been part of the charge on the Californians at the battle at San Pascual, though he was gravely ill at the time. Only after this battle, when he might have been suffering from mental fatigue or amnesia, did he make his move.

Mental fatigue? Amnesia? John Henry, did you offer mental fatigue and amnesia as a defense? Probably not. I don't suppose the authorities recognized or understood, these maladies in 1847. The authorities likely would have thought the private daft if he had claimed any mental condition as a defense. Maybe one of the hard cases would have responded like General Patton in World War II who slapped two soldiers who were suffering from battle fatigue before the condition was recognized as disabling.

Anyway, John Henry's position was becoming crystal

clear to the local public in 1847, as he sat in detention at Fort Marcy. He had been as eager to fight the greasers and wave the flag as any other soldier in the Army of the West until he entered Santa Fe where he found no enemies. The more he saw in Santa Fe, the more his mind opened, and he decided that he could not support a war against a people who had not wronged him or his country.

One part of the public, mostly Mexican, but some resident Americans as well, agreed with his position, that one should not support an unjust war.

This was not the first time that one who was supposed to fight refused to do so on moral grounds. Nor would it be the last time. I wasn't sure what all this had to do with John Henry but I became fascinated with the examples and extent of opposition to war by members of the military.

Throughout the history of warfare, each side has tried to persuade enemy soldiers to lay down their arms, to recognize that they were being exploited by their superiors. Some Mexican leaders during the Mexican War, though John Henry would not have known of them, had openly encouraged American soldiers to desert.

General Mariano Arista had encouraged American soldiers in the opening hostilities in Texas in 1846 to recognize the unjust nature of the war and to desert and become Mexican citizens. I found no evidence that the General's pleas had any effect.

Yet many soldiers did, in fact, desert the American army in numbers. The desertion rate during the Mexican-American War was 8.3%. Most did not leave for philosophical reasons. Some deserted so they could re-enlist and receive a second enlistment bonus. Some deserted because of the miserable conditions in the camps or the treatment they received at the hands of superiors. Others took advantage of the free transportation to California where they deserted with their weapons.

The immigrants were a special case. A large number of recent arrivals in the United States, fleeing famine and political oppression in their European home countries, joined the army out of desperation. Though they found employment, they did not escape the virulent anti-Catholic, anti-foreigner movement called "Nativism" that was sweeping the nation in the 1840s. Many of these recruits began to wonder whether they could fight for a country that, far from welcoming them, persecuted them instead.

The Mexicans tried to take advantage of this disaffection. They encouraged desertion with promises of land grants, money and commissions as officers in the Mexican army. Some American soldiers responded to the overtures but were disappointed later when the promises proved illusory.

The most notable response was from hundreds of disillusioned and desperate Catholic immigrants from Ireland and Germany and other countries who deserted and formed Saint Patrick's Battalion, which fought as a unit in the Mexican army against American forces.

The fate of the battalion's members was mixed. Most of those who were caught by the Americans were executed as deserters and traitors. Those who escaped capture returned to their native lands or became Mexican citizens and lived at peace in the country after the war. The Saint Patrick's Battalion is still revered in Mexico today.

All this is just to say that my ancestor's desertion was not unique in the war. It was unique, however, in Santa Fe in 1847.

It seems that everybody in Santa Fe knew about John Henry's imprisonment and impending trial and talked about it. Respected Mexican citizens in New Mexico weighed in. They had been angry when Price's courts had charged the Taos insurgents, Mexican citizens, with treason and hanged them. Now they came to John Henry's defense, arguing that this soldier should be applauded for recognizing the unjust nature of the war and had protested it in the only way he could, by refusing to take part.

Well. The sentiment is well taken but the argument flies in the face of the official, long-held, unimpeachable requirement that a soldier must obey his commander's orders. He does not have the luxury of deciding whether the order is just. That's what the military mind believes.

Oh, this argument raises so many questions. I became a bit obsessed with ferreting out examples that supported John Henry's stand against unjust war, not always involving desertion.

Lieutenant Joseph Cramer, for example, refused to take part in the Colorado militia's attack on peaceful Indians camped at Sand Creek in southern Colorado in 1864. The militia's commander, Colonel John Chivington, was incensed and threatened Cramer with court martial. When public outrage turned against the Colonel, Cramer was pleased to testify against him.

Should American soldiers have participated in the massacre of Indians at Wounded Knee when they knew it was wrong? Because they were following orders?

Must God-fearing, decent German soldiers posted as guards at Auschwitz take part in genocide? Even when they knew it was wrong? I was following orders, they claimed, when confronted by Allied tribunals.

Should American soldiers in Vietnam have taken part in the massacre at My Lai because they were ordered to take part, even when they knew it was wrong?

Hundreds of young men fled to Canada during the Vietnam War. Sure, some simply didn't want to become cannon fodder but most were resisting being drawn into what they considered an unjust war against a people who wanted only to escape colonialism and form a country.

These examples serve history by illustrating the folly of the I-was-following-orders argument but they would not have impressed the members of John Henry's court martial. They were soldiers themselves. Following orders.

Before tackling the proceedings of John Henry's court martial, I needed to learn what I could of the history of courts martial, particularly as they were constituted and operated in 1847.

I read online sources and bought a couple of books on the subject. I learned at the outset that I could forget what I knew about civilian courts. In courts martial, the commander was in control. There was no jury of the accused's peers.

There were few restraints on the commander. He chose the members of the court, made up of officers under his jurisdiction. Defendants had few rights. The defendant wasn't even guaranteed counsel. It was up to the commander. If the commander decided that the accused should not have counsel, he had no counsel. If the commander decided that he could have counsel, the commander appointed the counsel. There was no appeal to the commander's actions. Nor was there an appeal to the finding of the court.

Punishments were often arbitrary, determined by the bias of the commander. Unlike civilian courts, the defendant was not protected by the constitution. Punishment was not specified or uniform. It was strictly at the discretion of the commander who had convened the court.

In courts martial, the commander was God.

I shook my head at the arbitrary, unfair system that pervaded the court martial system.

Objections to the practice of court martial from the public and politicians were rare. The public placed great faith in the military, believing that it would protect the country and its citizens. Accordingly, they believed that any soldier who violated that trust was guilty and should be punished.

Yet, there were scattered complaints about the arbitrary, unfair treatment of the accused in courts martial. The complaints had little effect until 1846 when John O'Brien, an army lieutenant, wrote *A Treatise on American Military Laws, and the Practice of Courts Martial: with Suggestions for Their Improvements.* I had a copy of the reprint, published in 2009. I had purchased it on Amazon at the bloated price of $32.99. That still rankled me.

In his book, O'Brien called for putting restraints on the power of commanders, establishing more uniform procedures and outlining specific penalties for specific offenses.

I doubt that anyone in Santa Fe was even aware of O'Brien's book at the time of John Henry's trial. It wouldn't have mattered if they had. Congress and the courts, and the public in general, were not impressed by O'Brien's arguments. Those who could change the law chose not to do so. It was not until WWI that there was any substantial change in the practice of courts martial.

Colonel Price was in no hurry to convene John Henry's trial. He rather appeared to wish the whole messy situation would go away. He knew that the proceeding was going to inflame passions on all sides and did not need the distraction from trying to administer the new American territory of New Mexico. But convene he must.

Price's selection of court members ran pretty much according to long-standing army custom. This was to be a general court martial, which required a minimum of five members on the court and a trial judge advocate to present the army's case against the accused.

For this latter post, Price appointed First Lieutenant Joshua Bingham, who had studied for the bar at a Washington law firm before joining the Army. Bingham fortuitously had arrived in Santa Fe with a supply train only the month before the convening of the court.

Upon being told that his first duty in Santa Fe was to prosecute a case of desertion, the sentence for which likely was death, Bingham was aghast. He was a mild-mannered fellow and told Price that he knew nothing of courts martial. Don't worry, Price had told him, this case is cut and dried and will be over in a day or two. He would be given whatever guidance needed from others who had some experience in courts martial. He was assured that the task was perfunctory, required by Army regulations, and would look good on his record. Bingham was more doubtful than convinced but he knew he had no choice but to accept the assignment.

The first person appointed to the court as a judge was Private Andrew Johnstone, a member of the mounted Missouri regiment. Back in Missouri, he was a lawyer. During the early weeks of the Santa Fe occupation, he had organized frequent gatherings at which he explained the origins and nature of the war to soldiers. I recall from John Henry's notes that he attended Johnstone's talks.

On first reading about this appointment, I was baffled. I had read in more than one source that only officers served on courts martial. Then I learned that Price got around this by promoting Johnstone an Acting Lieutenant. Presumably, the temporary promotion would terminate at the conclusion of the trial.

When Johnstone received word, in January, that he had been elected a member of Congress, his zeal and patriotism, and self-confidence and authority, only increased. Some said that his mind closed on the day he received the notice.

The second member appointed was Second Lieutenant Bascom Rogers, a New Yorker and recent graduate of West Point. The Army of the West was his first posting and he was eager to make a name in the military. He was energetic, a by-the-book perfectionist, and full of himself.

First Lieutenant David Lipscomb was the third appointee. Steady and reliable, he was a plodder without imagination, content to follow orders and veer neither left nor right, adding nothing, suggesting nothing. A career soldier who had risen to the peak of his competence, he was destined to retire a First Lieutenant. Whatever his shortcomings, Price would miss him on the drill field and the barracks and assumed that he would return to his customary duties within a few days.

Price was running out of officers that he could spare for the court martial, even for the few days that he expected the trial would require. He settled on Captain William Anderson for the fourth appointee. Reluctantly. Dr. Anderson had been assigned to Price's staff for the march of his Second Missouri Volunteers to Santa Fe and the Colonel knew him only too well.

During the march, the doctor had paid more attention to his whiskey than to his charges. When he did treat them, they often refused to take the medicines prescribed to them, having no confidence in this swiller.

Anderson's reaction to their attitude was swift and malicious. The soldiers under his care were particularly incensed when the doctor in an alcoholic haze said that he would send as many of them to hell as he could.

Price decided that Anderson would be delighted to sit on the court martial where he would be required to do nothing, even listen. He did little else at the post hospital where he was a fixture, like a piece of furniture, and saw only those patients that required little care and whom he could not hurt. Price recently had applied to Washington for Anderson's early retirement.

Captain Robert Steele was the fifth and final addition to the court. Steele was a member of Kearny's staff who had been left in Santa Fe in the paring before the General's departure for California. He had been one of Kearny's most trusted officers and the General thought he would be useful in helping Price run affairs in Santa Fe. As the senior member of the court, Steele would serve as its president.

Since Kearny set out for California, Steele had confirmed Kearny's confidence in him as he had become invaluable to Price. Price had not wanted to appoint him to the court since he relied on him in his office but, frankly, Price could think of no other senior officer to appoint. In any event, he anticipated a short trial and expected that Steele would return to his duties in his office within days of the convening of the trial.

What no one seemed to know at the time was that Steele was a Mormon. He was not an active practitioner and had never professed the faith publicly. Not that he was ashamed of it, he just believed that he could observe his faith privately, in a fashion that would not damage his military career.

All this was altered in Santa Fe. In Santa Fe, he was reunited with his younger brother, John, whom he had not seen for four years.

John had lived in Mormon communities in the East and Midwest that had been persecuted regularly for years. The brethren had moved westward time and again to escape the violence and persecution until Mormon leaders decided to seek a haven in the Salt Lake region.

John was a member of the encampment of migrating Mormons at Council Bluffs when Captain James Allen rode into the camp. John was one of the 513 Mormons recruited at Council Bluffs to form a Mormon Battalion that would become a unit in the Army of the West.

The decision to recruit Mormons was not a hasty one, nor was it a surprise to Mormon leaders. They had been trying to secure some sort of assistance from the federal government in the westward migration after their expulsion from Nauvoo, Illinois, early in 1846.

President Polk was sympathetic. He expressed his friendship for the Mormons and promised that he would not forget that he had received Mormon votes. As a measure of assistance, he suggested that Mormons be inducted into military service.

John and many others, at first, refused to join the group, citing the long-held grievances against American governments and citizens who had persecuted the Mormons. Mormon leaders overruled the dissenters and the Mormon Battalion was formed. The new Mormon force marched westward across the plains to join in the conquest.

It was not long after the Battalion's arrival in Santa Fe in early October that John learned that his brother was here. He had known that Robert was an Army officer but he had lost touch with him in recent years. But here he was and John arranged, through channels, to meet him.

From that point forward, Robert got an earful from John and other Mormons. They told him personal stories of the persecution and humiliation they had suffered for years at the hands of townspeople and governments. Robert knew something of what had happened to his brethren but he had not heard the stories from the inside.

In private conversation between the two brothers, Robert told John about the upcoming court martial. He was of two minds about it, he said. As a soldier, he had to reject desertion as anathema to military order but, as a man, he knew he would be touched by arguments on cause and character of the accused.

Robert's brother was not so conflicted. "I sympathize with the accused," John said. "I oppose this war for different reasons but it all boils down to opposition to an oppressive government. I opposed the formation of the Battalion at Council Bluffs and I was forced into it against my will. I don't blame the elders. They did what they thought best for the people. But I tell you, brother, I will see them, the whole United States, in hell before I will fire one shot against a foreigner for them."

"Take care, John, that no one hears you say such things," said Robert, "not even the brethren. This talk could be seen by some as disloyalty, even treason. I would not wish to have you hauled into a court martial. The poor fellow who is charged in my court is indeed guilty of opposing the war as immoral, guilty of accusing political leaders of deception and avarice, guilty of wishing to be left alone to live a long life at peace with his new wife. But he is not charged with these faults. Or virtues, as they may well be. He is charged with desertion and treason, charges that are much easier to prove. John, you will say nothing to anyone of our talk, remember, even the brethren."

John nodded. "I will be careful. But I will not change my opinion. I do not envy you for your role on this court martial. Pray for guidance, brother. Trust in the Lord."

John left Santa Fe in late October with the Mormon Battalion, bound for California. General Kearny had ordered the Battalion to follow his trail and join his force in the conquest of that distant Mexican province.

Robert had stood in front of the Governor's Palace, watching the Mormon Battalion march by. John nodded to him from the ranks. Don't forget me, John had said that morning before muster, don't forget your Mormon brethren.

Robert would not forget them. He had been drawn into the plight and mentality of the Mormons: persecuted, anti-military, anti-war. He did not share any of this with Colonel Price or the other members of the court.

CHAPTER 10
Justice and Laws Made by Men

Manuel Chaves nodded to the orderly who held the door open for him. Colonel Price stood, smiled. Since Chaves's trial and acquittal, Price and Chaves had become friends. Chaves was a respected leader of the *mexicano* residents and Price had consulted him often.

"Señor Chaves, Manuel, come in!" Price extended his hand, and Chaves shook it. "Sit down, sit down. How are you this fine day?"

"It is indeed a fine day, Colonel. I wish to talk with you—"

"I know why you are here, Manuel—sorry to interrupt—but you waste your time. You must have other pressing matters that need your attention."

"This is the most important matter for me today," said Chaves, "and for anyone who believes in justice."

Price leaned back in his chair, looked to the window and back to Chaves. "This trial is distracting. It is being blown out of proportion. There can be only one result. A soldier may not vacate his post without leave."

"But there are always mitigating circumstances," said Chaves.

"No, not in this case. The regulation is clear."

Chaves pondered, looked at the window a long moment. He looked back at Price, leaned forward.

"Consider," said Chaves. "You are walking on a street of houses. You hear a commotion across the street. You look and you see a man and a woman. The man has a diabolical grimace on his face. He grips the woman by the throat. In his other hand, he holds a knife and he is poised to strike. You have no time to try to reason with the man and you are too far away to restrain him. He is about to kill the woman. You have no choice. You draw your pistol, aim at the man, and fire. You are a good shot, no?" Chaves smiled.

"Rather good," Price said.

"And this is what you would do?"

"Yes. It would be the right thing to do," Price said.

"What if the man and the woman were play-acting? What if they were practicing for a drama that was scheduled to be presented that very evening?"

Price smiled. "I wouldn't have known that, would I?"

"No, but you, nevertheless, killed an innocent man. Are you guilty of murder or would the judge consider the mitigating circumstance? You thought you were saving a life."

"I see your point," said Price, "but it doesn't apply here."

"Why does it not? This young man was doing the right thing, the moral thing, when he protested this unjust war by committing a nonviolent act that did no harm to any person!"

Price frowned. Chaves was a friend but he was becoming a nuisance. Price sighed. "This damn trial. This is not a case of right or wrong. It is a case of law. He broke the law."

"Laws are made by men, *mi amigo.* All men are flawed. Sometimes they make laws that are not just and sometimes the best way to expose an unjust law is to violate it."

"That may be so, but anyone who violates a law, any law, just or not, must be prepared to suffer the consequences."

Chaves slumped. "We do not disagree, my friend. I wish . . . do you have no options? No other way to deal with this?"

"Of course! I could dismiss the charge. Free the prisoner. And suffer the consequences, which likely would be my dismissal from the service, and, if some hard cases had their say, be crucified."

I pulled a bunch of sheets from a folder, labeled "Fort Marcy and Trial." Leafing through the stack, I extracted a drawing and pushed the other papers back into the folder. The drawing, titled "Fort Marcy 1846," pictured a fort such as I had never seen anywhere in the West. Or anywhere in the world, for that matter.

The day after leading the Army of the West into Santa Fe in August 1846, General Kearny ordered Lieutenant William Emory, an engineer—the same Lt. Emory who later introduced John Henry to ancient Indian sites on the march to California—to find a location for a fort. He wanted a strong fortification that would serve as a bulwark against opposition to the American occupation of the town. Kearny declared that the new fort should be named after the Secretary of War, William L. Marcy.

Emory picked a site, a low mesa about 650 yards northeast of the plaza, for its proximity to the town center and its height with a commanding view of the town. Under the supervision of Emory and Captain Randolph Barnes Marcy, the regimental quartermaster and no kin to the Secretary, soldiers and hired laborers built a tridecagon fort, a thirteen-sided structure of adobe walls, nine feet high and five feet thick. The fort was surrounded by an eight-foot-deep dry moat. Dirt extracted from the moat was used in building the adobe walls. Thirteen guns were mounted on the parapets.

Outside the walls, a partially underground powder magazine and a blockhouse of adobe and pine logs for weapons were built. The blockhouse also served to protect the entrance to the fort.

Only a few structures were built inside the fort. Offices, meeting rooms, some stables and sheds for tack. A kitchen and long room that served as a dining hall. A similar long structure that served as a barracks for the few soldiers that were quartered there. In the center, the dusty parade with some few patches of grass and a flagpole in the middle. At the far end of the parade, opposite the gate, there was a vine-covered arbor sheltering a table and half a dozen chairs.

The fort was originally intended to house a thousand soldiers but quarters for them were never built inside the walls. Instead, troops were accommodated in buildings on the mesa nearby and below at a barracks near the Palace.

John Henry was incarcerated inside the fort. Hardly a cell, his accommodation was a cabin of sorts that backed onto a wall. There was so much sentiment in his favor in the town that Price wanted to avoid any implication that he was being treated as a common criminal. John Henry had promised not to try to escape, and Price took him at his word, so he was simply assigned the detached quarters and allowed to walk about the fort's interior without restriction. There would come a time when Colonel Price would regret this liberal arrangement, including the public's access to him.

He was permitted to have visitors. Manuel Chaves visited often and assured John Henry of his friendship and support. He told him about his own trial and commented on the similarity of their cases. He also explained how John Henry's proceeding would be different from his own. He told him what he knew about the members of the court and how to respond to their questions.

Unfortunately, Chaves said, Colonel Price had already rejected his request to appear at John Henry's trial as a witness. Price had responded to his request by pointing out that the law and the war were not on trial; a soldier was on trial.

Chaves said that he had been tempted to speculate out loud that if the judge advocate or the defense counsel called him as a witness, Price would not have the authority to block his appearance. He was tempted but he held his tongue. By this time, Chaves probably knew as much about courts martial as the Colonel.

Price also told Chaves that he suspected that Chaves was using John Henry's trial as a vehicle for publicizing his support for those who had opposed the American occupation, some who could still face trial for their actions, including perhaps on a charge of treason. Price smiled when he said this but Chaves saw no mirth in the comment.

Morita visited John Henry every day, except when illness or work prevented. He often stood at the fort entrance, waiting, looking down the road that led to the plaza. A guard always stood nearby, more for conversation than concern that he might bolt.

On her first visit, Morita had been surprised to see his clean-shaven face. He explained that the sergeant who was responsible for him said that he was still a soldier and should look like a soldier. He had sent a barber to his cabin to shave him.

The gate guards never failed to smile when they saw Morita coming up the hill. They did not interfere when she arrived and hugged John Henry and kissed him. Rather, the guard usually stepped back to give them space, watching all the while, this plain American soldier and pretty Mexican girl. The guard might lean toward them, frowning, trying to understand their conversation, always in Spanish unless they were addressing him.

On one occasion, at the end of her visit, Morita and John Henry strolled over to the gate to talk with Michael, a guard who had become a personal friend early on in his imprisonment. They exchanged pleasantries. Michael smiled at Morita as if John Henry weren't standing beside her.

"Michael," said John Henry, "can Morita stay the night with me?"

Michael frowned, looked aside, confused, looked back at John Henry. "Johnny, you know she can't do that."

Michael turned to Morita, grinned. "You can sure stay with me if you would like that."

Morita took Michael's hand in both of hers, bent toward him in supplication. "Please, Michael, please let me stay with Juanito," trying hard not to laugh.

"I would really like to do that for such a pretty girl," Michael said, "but I would be shot if I did that."

Morita straightened. "Okay, we wouldn't want that to happen," she said. All laughed.

It was so unreal, this imprisonment. John Henry was treated virtually as a guest, not a prisoner. Soldiers and townspeople who were at the fort on business greeted him and chatted.

Most strangers were immediately impressed with

his intelligence and good nature. Soldiers often hovered about him, simply to listen to him talk about anything he wanted to talk about.

Not all shared this sentiment. Some soldiers were furious that this deserter was being coddled and would have preferred that he be shackled and locked up in solitary confinement. A goodly number of townspeople, all Americans, those who wanted to see the new American possession Anglicized as quickly as possible, grumbled that this deserter brought shame on his country and should be punished harshly and promptly.

But these latter were the minority. Most of the town's populace, Mexican and Yankee, either sympathized with John Henry or expressed no interest. Price knew the way the wind was blowing. He had inherited an attitude and policy established at the outset of the occupation by General Kearny. A policy of appeasement. Treat the populace gently and they will be more likely to cooperate in the establishment of the new order.

On a lazy afternoon, John Henry lounged at the open gate beside Michael. When he stood guard at the gate, and this was as often as he could convince his superior that he should be assigned gate duty, Michael and John Henry spent pleasant hours reminiscing about a common Missouri frontier boyhood. An observer would not have seen a guard and his prisoner, only two young men who valued each other's friendship.

Now they looked toward the road that wound down the hillside to the plaza. Two soldiers walked by them and through the gate to the outside. One of them slapped John Henry on the shoulder and smiled.

"Waiting for Morita, are ya'?" the soldier threw over

his shoulder. "She ain't comin'. She told me to meet her at th' cantina tonight." The other soldier laughed.

"I doubt José will let you inside," John Henry called. "You better go to Tules's. She has what you want." La Tules ran an upscale gambling establishment that also provided pretty prostitutes for her customers. At least, that's what John Henry had heard. He had never visited Tules's place.

The soldier stopped and looked back. "I've heard of Tules's and I ain't interested. I'm interested in your little woman. I'm goin' to visit, and you ain't gonna be there." He laughed and turned to go, waving over his shoulder. The two soldiers strolled down the road, talking and laughing.

"What's going on here!" John Henry turned to see Lieutenant Rogers glaring at him.

"Uh, sir, I'm saying goodbye to a couple of friends," John Henry said. "They're going down to town."

"Your friends? Soldiers! By God!" Rogers turned to Michael who stood just inside the gate. Michael jerked to attention. "Why is this prisoner at this open gate?"

Michael looked aside, looked back at Rogers, stammered. "Well, uh, sir, uh, he's allowed to be out and about, I think."

"Well, he shouldn't!" He turned to John Henry. "Return to your cell! Your quarters!"

John Henry stiffened and saluted. "Yes, sir!"

Rogers turned on his heel and stormed off, raising a cloud of dust on the dry parade. "By God!" he mumbled as he walked away.

John Henry smiled at Michael who glanced at Rogers's back. Rogers went inside an office, slamming the door behind him.

John Henry looked at the departing soldiers, now half hidden on the hillside road. "Watch out for the little blade she carries! "John Henry called. "You won't see it until she sticks you!" The soldier waved over his shoulder without looking back. John Henry smiled and watched until they disappeared down the road.

Michael looked uneasily at the office door where Rogers had disappeared. "Johnny, if he comes back this way, I'm going to tell him that I told you to go to your cabin and you told me to go to hell. Then you're in trouble." He grinned. John Henry smiled.

He looked toward the road. It was empty. He wasn't looking for anything or anybody. It was what he did a good part of his day. Watching. Hoping.

A single figure appeared, his head first, then torso, striding up the hill. He was in uniform. His head was down as if he was picking his way on the rough road.

John Henry frowned. There was something strangely familiar about this soldier. The bouncing walk on the balls of his feet, the slight rounding of the shoulders. The soldier looked up.

Brad! It's Brad! John Henry took a step toward the open gate.

"Whoa, Johnny." John Henry looked at Michael who stood beside the gatepost, holding his rifle loosely cradled in his arm.

"Sorry," John Henry said. "It's an old friend."

"He's comin' this way, ain't he?"

Brad arrived. The two friends embraced, pulled away, embarrassed. Brad stepped back. "I'll be damned," he said. "I wondered about you for a long time." He looked at the guard. "He been behavin' hisself?"

Michael nodded. "He's been a good boy. Best duty I ever had, watchin' him."

"Let's go up and sit," said John Henry. He motioned

with his head toward his quarters. He looked at Michael who nodded.

"That's where I live." He pointed toward his cabin. They reached the building and sat on the bench in front.

They looked at each other, smiled. "Be damned," said John Henry. "Okay, tell me."

"Be damned yourself." Brad smiled, took a deep breath. "Well, you know, we took a real licking from the Californians. They're calling it the Battle of San Pascual now. When it was over, the Californians hightailed it and we were sure glad they did. Man, they're not afraid of anything and what horsemen!

"We were a sorry lot and just wandered around the field a while, trying to understand what had happened. The General rode around, telling us to get ahold of ourselves and get moving.

"We collected our dead and wounded and moved into camp where you saw us. I expected to find your body on the field and sure was glad we didn't. I wondered what happened to you and thought I would never see you again. When your head popped through the brush out where I was picking up firewood, I had a real fright. I was so glad to see you. Then you drew back into the brush.

"I watched the back trail and saw you just for a second when you rode from one wood to another. I knew where you was going. I still thought that was the last time I would ever see you.

"After we had set up camp and got some rest and grub, the officers did a count. We took thirty-five dead and wounded. They checked the roster, did a roll call, and everybody was accounted for. Except one person. You.

"We was sent out to look over the field for another body. We searched the plain and the scrub at the edge and back into the woods. Nothing. We looked for tracks leading off the field but there were so many tracks on tracks that nobody could say that any particular tracks was yours.

"When we rode back to camp, I saw this soldier talking with the General. Remember Colonel Cooke sent him ahead from the Mormon Battalion to scout trail and he rode into camp just before the battle? Remember that he was placed in the advance unit with you and me? Remember he asked us if anybody knew somebody named 'Juanito' and said he had a message for him?"

"Yeah. I remember all that," said John Henry.

"Remember you had a hard time convincing him you was Juanito? He told you that he had seen Morita at the cantina and talked with her and told her he was going to California with the Mormon Battalion and that they were following General Kearny's army. Remember he said that she asked him to tell you that she was waiting for you? Remember that you got real agitated and started to pull your horse out of line? I knew you was crazy at that point and that you intended to hightail it for Santa Fe."

"I wasn't thinking too clearly," John Henry said. "My head was splitting and my eyes were burning like fire, but, yeah, I remember. I remember that I was going to race back to Santa Fe and Morita if I had to battle the devil to do it. I remember that Captain Johnston just happened to be riding by and I almost collided with him when I pulled out. He was real angry and ordered me back into line and that was just about all I recall. The charge was a blur and I blacked out."

"You blacked out? What happened? Where did you go?"

"I woke up in a wood up on the hillside. My head was clear. I didn't hurt anywhere. I swear I felt good! I had not been free of pain for months. My horse was browsing nearby, thank god.

"I saw the smoke from your fires and rode down to the thicket near your camp. That's where I saw you collecting firewood. That was a lucky break. Somebody must be looking out for me."

They sat silent, looking out over the fort interior. Half a dozen soldiers stood at the gate, chatting, laughing. None was armed. One slapped another on the back and they walked through the gate to the outside.

The sun had set and fleecy cloud layers colored the sky above the fort walls and the trees beyond.

"Why are you here?" said John Henry. "How did you get here?"

At that moment, Lieutenant Rogers was striding across the parade toward the gate. He looked in Harris's direction, stopped. He stared, hands on hips. He strode toward John Henry.

"Uh-oh," said John Henry softly. He and Brad jumped up, stood at attention.

Rogers stopped in front of the two rigid soldiers. "Harris, do you have permission for this?" He glared at Brad, looked back at John Henry.

"Yes, sir. Private Andrews at the gate let him in. He knows he's here visiting me. I have permission for visitors, sir."

Rogers was livid. "By God, Harris! I would have you in irons!" The lieutenant glared, shook his head, turned and strode toward the gate, kicking up a trail of dust in his wake.

John Henry and Brad sat down slowly, leaned against the cabin wall.

"Nice fellow," said Brad.

"New kid in the neighborhood," John Henry said, "trying to make a name for himself. Just checked in a couple of months ago. He's harmless, I hope." He stared at Rogers, who was talking to Michael at the gate. Rogers glanced back at John Henry as he talked.

John Henry turned back to Brad. "Where were we? Yeah, why are you here and how did you get here?"

"That's the best part. After we reached the coast and joined up with our forces there, we took it easy. Waiting for orders, they said. Hell, we were so banged up, we had to get well and get our weapons in order.

"Anyway, while we're just resting up, a trader comes in from Santa Fe. He had a message from Colonel Price, asking the General if he knew anything about a soldier, maybe a deserter, named, yep, John Henry Harris. Well, the General did know. So he decided to send a dispatch back to Colonel Price, to say that he sure did know about this person.

"I heard that he was going to send the dispatch by a trader, so I suggested to a friend who knew the General's aide that wouldn't it make more sense to send a soldier, accompanied by a couple of Mex scouts, to carry the dispatch. It would get to Santa Fe a lot quicker than by some trader who was busy with pack mules and a herd of horses.

My friend thought it was a good idea and mentioned it to the General's aide. The aide thought it was a good idea and told General Kearny. The aide mentioned me by name. The General also thought this was a good idea and here I am."

"Well, it's good to see you, old friend. I thought that look I had of you through the bushes was my goodbye."

They sat silent, looking at the sky and the dozen or so soldiers strolling, leaning against the fort wall, chatting, smoking, killing time, the principal activity of soldiers anywhere, any time.

"I saw Morita," Brad said. "Me and the scouts rode in yesterday afternoon and I went to the cantina last night. She remembered me and we had a nice talk. I told her everything, everything I've told you. She's sure some woman, Johnny. Don't blame you for doing whatever you had to do to get back to her."

John Henry tried to smile and failed. He looked aside. "Yeah." His response stuck in his throat. He shook his head, looked at his feet.

They sat quietly for a long moment. "You got yourself in a mess of trouble, John Henry."

John Henry pursed his lips, looked at the riot of colored cloud layers in the western sky, darkening as the sun sank lower below the horizon. "Yeah. . . . What about you?"

"The General told me to report to Colonel Price and he would decide what to do with me. When I gave the message to his aide, he told me to take two days off and report back. I suppose they will find something for me to do."

Brad brightened, turned to John Henry. "Tell you what, Johnny! What if I ask to be assigned to duty at the fort here? I could learn everything I need to know about the place and I could help you escape. We could pull it off. We would just—"

"Can't do that, Brad. I gave my word that I wouldn't try to escape."

"Hell, that don't matter. What matters is that you get outta here. Morita said that you and her had talked about maybe going to Colorado. Or to Mexico. Either way, all of this would be behind you, and you could start over. I'm serious, Johnny. We could do this. Hell, I might meet you wherever you go after my enlistment is up."

John Henry turned to look at Brad. He knew that Brad was dead serious and would do his best to do exactly what he described. And he would do it at considerable risk.

"Brad, you're a good friend, better'n any I ever had and hope to have. And I know you would do this. But I can't. If I run now, it would be admitting that I did something wrong and now I'm running from it."

"You did do something wrong, Johnny. You deserted."

"See, that's what I've got to face, Brad. I've got to show them that what I did was right. I refused to take part in an action, a war, that is wrong. How can it be wrong to do the right thing?"

Brad frowned. "I don't know about that. All I know is that in the short time I've been in Santa Fe, I've heard a lot about you and your trial. There's lots of people who are with you but even they worry about what's going to happen to you."

CHAPTER 11
Case for the Defense

"Juanito, I can't sleep."

Morita and John Henry sat on the bench in front of his cabin. A guard leaned against the wall of the adjacent cabin that held the tack of the fort's mules and horses. His rifle rested against the wall beside him. He drew on a *cigarro* and blew smoke over his head. John Henry didn't know him but he seemed a reasonable fellow. With the trial approaching, John Henry was guarded more closely than before.

"Why not?" John Henry said.

"I reach for you in my dream," she whispered, glancing at the guard, "and when I don't feel you, I get scared. And I wake up. I can't go back to sleep." She took his arm and pulled him to her, rested her head on his arm.

"Juanito, I'm tired of all this." She pouted. "I want you in my bed. I want to walk home with you from the cantina. I want to walk in the plaza with you."

"It shouldn't be much longer. I think the trial will begin any day now. That's what the guards say. They say the people are for me and they say the trial should be a short one. It won't be long before we can be together, muchacha.

We'll have some decisions to make."

"Decisions? What decisions?"

"We need to decide once and for all where we will spend the rest of our lives. I love Santa Fe but do we want the memory of this trial to hang over us every day? We could go somewhere new, maybe to Mexico or Colorado or somewhere else? We could start over again where no one knows us. But don't worry about it now. We'll deal with it later."

He looked toward the guard whose head was down and his eyes were closed. John Henry put his hand on Morita's cheek, pulled her head around and kissed her. "Just know that we will be together soon, and don't worry. Sleep all night."

"Okay, you say so."

They sat silent. The sun warmed their legs, their bodies in the shade of the cabin overhang. "You know what I miss?" said John Henry. "Sitting like this on our porch, leaning against the wall, our legs in the warm sunshine, your dress pulled up above your knees. You have nice legs, mi preciosa."

She looked up at him, smiled. "You do too, guapo. Remember when we made love after lunch one day and sat on the porch with no clothes? I saw your legs. And lots more."

She smiled, squeezed his arm, slid a hand slowly down his side toward his legs.

He looked toward the guard. "Don't do that, sweetheart, you're going to get us both in trouble." She smiled and withdrew her hand.

"The first thing I'm going to do when I get out of here is go to the cantina, drink a glass of good wine, or two, or three, and watch you. All evening. Then we're going to walk home barefoot and make love for two days."

"And then we will have a big meal to make up for no eating for two days," she said. "Remember the first big meal that Tía and I made for you?"

He leaned back and closed his eyes. He did indeed remember. How could he forget? It was one of the most pleasant memories of his first days in Santa Fe.

The dinner had begun with bowls of thin soup, then roast chicken cooked with onions, a dish of boiled beef, rice covered with thin slices of boiled egg, tortillas and bowls of frijoles and red chili.

He remembered the first hot chili he had eaten just two days after the army entered Santa Fe. It had almost taken the top of his head off and tears had streamed down his cheeks. The old Santa Fe hands had laughed their heads off. He soon acquired a New Mexican leather throat and now he liked chili which seemed obligatory at every meal.

Morita and Tía's meal also included a large bowl filled with peaches and apricots and bunches of small purple grapes. For dessert, a sponge cake.

"Yeah," he said. "A meal just like that. Now I'll dream about that and lose sleep."

"You don't dream about me?" she said.

He took her hand and held it, looked into her eyes. "I dream about you every night and every minute of every day. I am dying inside. Do you know that when Brad told me that he would help me escape, I considered doing it? I knew that by doing it, I would be with you again and, for a moment, that was all that mattered. But how long could we be happy when I would always know that I had run?"

She touched his cheek. "I know. It's okay." She stood. "Now I must go. I will tell Tía. She will begin planning."

She stood and looked down at him, forced a smile. She leaned down, kissed him, turned and walked toward the gate. He stood and watched her until she disappeared through the gate. The guard also watched, turned to John Henry, smiled.

*****

Father Francis stood at the open gate, talking with the guard. The guard pointed and both looked at John Henry. He sat at his usual post on his bench. Father Francis nodded to the guard, raised a hand, either in thanks or blessing, John Henry could not tell which.

John Henry stood and watched the padre walk across the dusty parade. He arrived and Father Francis took John Henry's hand in both of his.

"Señor Harris, it is good to see you in health. "You are eating well and taking care of yourself?"

"Father Francis. As well as I can. I have little choice here. If I am well, it is because I am being given what I need. I have too much time on my hands."

"Have you had time to reflect on your immortal soul? Have you remembered any sins to ask God's forgiveness for? It's still over a hundred years since you confessed." He smiled.

"Can one ask forgiveness for doing stupid?"

"Ah, the marriage record," the padre said. "I must apologize. I should have guarded the book more carefully."

"No, padre, it's not your fault. I was being vain. I should have married as Jed Weber. Can one ask forgiveness for vanity?"

"Oh, yes. Vanity is an expression of pride, one of the seven deadly sins."

"Then I ask forgiveness for being stupid. Everyone advised me to do what I had advised others to do, forget John Henry Harris and accept Jed Weber. I must seem ridiculous."

"Don't be hard on yourself, Señor Harris. The Lord knows you and loves you. It is written: 'The Lord sees not as man sees. Man looks on the outward appearance, but the Lord looks on the heart.' "

"Thank you, Father. Morita is right. About you. About a lot of things. She is a remarkable woman, you know."

"Yes. And you are a good man, Jed Weber John Henry Harris. When all this is finished, I will be happy to welcome you into the church and the presence of God."

John Henry stood in his open doorway, leaning against the frame. He looked across the parade toward the outside gate. He spent a considerable portion of his day, watching the front gate. Watching for Morita, or lunch, or Brad, or anything or anybody that might occupy his time. The gate was always open until sunset when it was closed. It was opened again at sunrise.

His only occupation, other than watching the gate, was writing in his journal. He usually sat on the bench, the journal resting on his crossed legs, the inkwell on the bench beside him. He wrote with a tight crimped hand, in narrow lines to conserve space.

On this day, he looked up from his journal and saw three men at the entrance talking with the guard. The three looked out of place. They wore black wool suits and black cravats more appropriate for an American city than a foreign province, albeit now flying the American flag.

The guard looked at a paper he held. He nodded and returned the sheet to one of the men. The guard pointed toward John Henry. The men looked in his direction. They walked briskly across the parade toward him.

John Henry stood and waited. When they were still

ten feet away, the leader of the three smiled broadly and extended his hand.

"Mr. Harris, I am so glad to finally meet you."

John Henry took the hand and they shook. John Henry was impressed with the firm grip of the speaker.

"John Henry, please."

"John Henry. I am Steve Burke." He turned to his two companions. "This good-looking gentleman is Kenneth Jackson." Jackson frowned, smiled, shook hands with John Henry.

Burke gestured toward the third man. "The dignified ne'er-do-well there is Jeremiah Bradley." Bradley touched the brim of his hat, stepped forward and, head down, shook John Henry's hand.

"Sorry I can't ask you inside," said John Henry. "There's nothing in there but a bed, one chair and a little table." He looked around. "There's the arbor." He pointed toward the small arbor at the edge of the parade.

The roof of the arbor was a lattice that was covered with lush ivy. Under the arbor were a table and six chairs.

"It's actually for officers but there's no one there and they wouldn't likely chase us since you gentlemen must have permission of the Colonel to be here." They walked toward the arbor.

"Indeed we do," said Burke, as they walked. "I must say that we have his permission because he seemed to want to be rid of us and didn't know how to do that short of agreeing to our request to see you." They reached the arbor and each found a chair and sat.

"I wish I could offer some refreshment," said John Henry, "but I'm a bit short at the moment." The three visitors smiled.

"Not necessary," said Burke. "You are undoubtedly

wondering who are these strangers." John Henry smiled.

At that moment, Lieutenant Rogers, walking toward the offices adjacent to the gate, stopped near the arbor and glared at the group seated in officers' territory. John Henry jumped up. *Why does this man appear so often when I have a guest? It's as if he watches me so he can confront me.*

"Sir, uh, we have Colonel Price's permission."

The officer glared, hands on hips. "You have ten minutes, Harris."

"Sir, but—"

"Ten minutes."

"Sir." John Henry saluted. Rogers returned the salute, turned and marched away, as if on parade.

John Henry sat. He spoke softly, head down. "Prig. He's the junior officer here, in rank and time in Santa Fe. He's already let everybody within shouting distance know that he should be in Mexico in the middle of the fighting. His principal occupation at Fort Marcy seems to be making my life miserable. He's full of . . . himself.

"Unfortunately, I learned just this morning that he's a member of my court martial board. I suppose you know about my upcoming trial. I can't think of any other reason for you wanting to see me."

"My good man," said Burke. "Indeed we do know about your trial. That's why we are here."

*****

This might have been your lucky day, John Henry. These three worthies were among the leaders of the anti-war movement in the States. Anti-war sentiment, rather. I suppose it would be stretching the definition to call the agitation against the war a movement. "Movement" suggests an organization that plans activities, demonstrates and holds rallies in support of a cause. There was some of that but mostly the anti-war activity was more spontaneous and relied on newspaper comment and word of mouth.

I set a handful of photocopies on the desk beside a stack of six volumes on the Mexican War. Each copy had something to say about opposition to the war. I had gleaned material from the books and I had collected useful bits and pieces from internet searches.

When the war broke out, there was an immediate outcry from different interests for different reasons. Anti-slavery forces opposed it because of the assumption that any territory acquired in a war—and the United States surely would win this war—would be suitable to slavery.

Representative John Quincy Adams, the ex-president and adamant opponent of slavery, spoke out fervently against the war in Congress. Members of the Whig party opposed the war. A powerful political force in the 1840s, Whigs believed that territorial expansion would detract from their desire to strengthen the economy by industrialization, not by the acquisition of new lands.

Many leading literary figures, adherents of the Transcendentalist movement, opposed the war on moral principle. A notable member, Henry David Thoreau, was jailed for refusing to pay his poll taxes, which he said would be used to finance an unjust war. The experience inspired him to write his seminal *Civil Disobedience*.

Indicative of the mindset of Thoreau and other anti-war figures, it is reported that when philosopher Ralph Waldo Emerson visited Thoreau in jail, Emerson asked his friend, "Why are you here?" to which Thoreau replied, "Why are you not here?"

Some who spoke out against the war are notable for their opposition only in retrospect. When the congressional representative from Illinois named Abraham Lincoln spoke against the war, he became so unpopular in his home state that he did not even run for a second term. Lieutenant U. S. Grant had serious misgivings about the war. He called the American settlement in Texas and the eventual separation of Texas from Mexico a conspiracy to acquire territory that would be suitable for slavery. He thought the war against Mexico one of the most unjust wars ever fought by a strong nation against a weaker one.

All this is just to say that you were in good company when you decided to oppose this war, John Henry. And that's just the tip of the anti-war iceberg.

"You couldn't have known about me when you set out," said John Henry. "I was arrested only last month."

"Indeed. We didn't leave Missouri to meet you. We'd never heard of you. We came to Santa Fe to investigate how the local Mexican people are faring under the occupation. There are a great number of people in the United States who feel the same as we and we received backing for our journey from like-minded groups and individuals.

"When we arrived in Santa Fe last week and began conversations with the people, we very soon learned about you. Everyone wants to talk about you. You are already famous, young man, and you will be famous back in the country.

"By the way, Mr. Jackson here speaks fluent Spanish. He is a great help in our conversations."

Jackson smiled, frowned. "Passable Spanish, passable. I'm a Missouri merchant and do business with Mexican traders from Santa Fe and Chihuahua. Well, just Santa Fe at present. The Chihuahua trade has ended. The business with Santa Fe has actually increased. But at a terrible human cost."

"Yes," said Burke, "and that's why we came to Santa Fe." He sat up straight in his chair, pursed his lips. "Now to business! We are going to ask Colonel Price to permit us to speak at your trial. We want to show the members of the court that your action in opposing this war is common and part of an historic movement, a recognition among American citizens that unjust war, this particular unjust war, will not be tolerated!"

Burke's heat had risen as he spoke and he ended with a hard bang on the table with his fist. He was almost shouting at the end. John Henry was reminded of a Baptist preacher at a revival meeting.

"I thank you," said John Henry. "I had no idea that there were other people in the country who think like I do."

"Many, many," said Jackson, "all over the country. Some for political reasons, some for economic reasons, but most because they abhor the aggression of a rich, powerful country against a weak, impoverished nation that has not wronged the United States. The war is simply wrong."

"I appreciate what you're trying to do. You might want to talk with Manuel Antonio Chaves. You'll have no trouble finding him. Manuel Antonio Chaves. He is well known in Santa Fe. He has strong views on the trial and has also asked the Colonel for permission to appear at the trial."

"How did the Colonel respond?"

"He told him that he, Chaves, had nothing to say that would influence the court. I don't agree but the Colonel doesn't talk to me."

"Who is this Chaves?" said Bradley.

"He is a leader in the Mexican community. He was an important person in Santa Fe before the invasion and he took part in the fighting. He was arrested and tried for treason. He had an American counsel and, together, they convinced the court that he was guilty only of fighting for his country. The Colonel respects him but still refuses to let him appear at my trial."

Burke frowned, pondered. "I understand better now why Colonel Price was so unfriendly when we introduced ourselves and asked his permission to talk with you. He didn't know how to respond for a moment. He finally said we could see you but reluctantly, I'm sure. Now I wonder how he will respond when we tell him we want to speak at your trial."

"What I'm wondering," said Bradley, "is why the trial has not been convened. Do you know, John Henry? When did you say you were arrested, a month ago?"

"About that. Manuel, last time he visited, wondered about that too. That's Manuel Chaves, who I mentioned. He thinks that the Colonel is busy with other stuff and knows that the trial is going to cause a big ruckus in Santa Fe.

"Manuel said that the Colonel thinks this is cut-and-dried and should require only a couple of days, maybe a couple of hours. Manuel told him that that will not be the case at all if this is a fair trial. He said the Colonel got a little huffy at the implication but agreed finally that perhaps it was not going to be the work of a day. But he wasn't happy about it and that's why he hasn't started the trial."

"Do you have counsel assigned yet?" Burke said.

"I'm not sure that I will have counsel. I understand it's up to the Colonel."

"My God!" said Jackson. "The military court martial system seems anchored in the Middle Ages. The more I hear about it, the more I am convinced that it is designed not to determine whether the accused is innocent or guilty but to punish the accused as quickly as possible!" Bradley laid a hand lightly on Jackson's arm. Jackson glanced at him.

Jackson leaned back in his chair, sighed. "Really, it seems designed more to set an example than to seek justice."

They fell silent, looked across the parade toward the gate, glanced at the sky over the fort walls.

"We must be off," said Burke. "We will find your Manuel Antonio Chaves and see what he can tell us. We will want to hear his version of the conflicts that followed the invasion and anything he can tell us about the welfare of the Mexican people today. And about his trial and his views on your court martial and prospects."

All stood, handshakes and smiles all around, and the three walked across the parade toward the open front gate. John Henry watched them go.

"I will tell you what Colonel Price will ask you at your first meeting with him." The speaker was Manuel Antonio Chaves. He sat with the three antiwar Americans in his parlor. Each held a glass of wine. Their chairs faced the fireplace where a few ends of firewood burned in a low flame over a bed of coals and ash.

Through an intermediary, Burke had arranged this meeting with Chaves. Burke had suggested a meeting at a public place of Chaves's choice but Chaves had insisted that they come to his house.

The three visitors were welcomed at the door by a woman who led them past a reception room and dining room to the parlor. The Americans noted that all of the rooms they passed had floors of hard-packed soil. This was the usual condition for the other homes and shops they had visited in Santa Fe and they were not surprised here. As usual, colorful carpets covered the earthen floors. They had been surprised, on the other hand, on entering the parlor. The floor was of fitted wood planks, one of the few they had seen in Santa Fe.

"The Colonel will ask," said Chaves: " 'What do you have to say to the court that would have any bearing on this trial of a soldier who deserted his post during a war?' You tell me if he doesn't ask you this."

"I would expect it," said Burke. "I can only appeal to his sense of justice. This soldier did what was right. He did the only thing he could do to show his opposition to a war that is just wrong. He risked his life. What more could anyone do than that?"

"I understand. I said the same to the Colonel. And he was unmoved. He said it was irrelevant. The accused broke the law, he will say, and that law is not on trial; the accused is on trial. He will say the same to you. How will you respond?"

Burke leaned back in his chair, exhaled heavily. He turned to look at Jackson and Bradley. They looked blankly at him and at each other.

"But your trial," said Jackson. "John Henry told us about it. Your counsel convinced the court that you were not guilty when all indications were that you would be convicted. Could your trial not be cited as an example, a precedent, for John Henry's case?"

"I wish that were so," said Chaves, "but I fear not. I was a citizen of Mexico fighting for the freedom of my country. John Henry is an American citizen and an American soldier. It is not the same. Nor will an appeal to reason and justice be likely to impress the members of the court. Unless you can come up with another line of argument, I fear that your presentation will fall on deaf ears. If indeed you are permitted to speak at all."

The three Americans stared into the fire. Finally: "What do you intend to do?" said Burke.

"Oh, I will press the Colonel to let me speak. Or I will appeal to John Henry's counsel to call me as a character witness. If John Henry has counsel."

Burke was surprised. "You will? But—"

"I doubt that any but the larger part of the population of the town will be impressed with my argument, but I will try nevertheless." He smiled. "Unfortunately, the populace will have no say in this trial. Yet, maybe God will smile on us."

"I appreciate your seeing me, Captain. I know you are busy with the approach of the trial." Burke sat with Captain Steele on a bench in the shade of a large cottonwood on the plaza.

"Actually, I am not. I am waiting for an opportunity to review the general court martial process in the manual. It seems that General Kearny left a manual here but, so far, no one has been able to find it."

"You have served on court martial boards, though?" said Burke.

"Only on summary boards for minor offenses. Never for such a serious charge as this. Never for a general court martial. Now, why did you want to see me?"

Burke shifted, cleared his throat. "Well. Since you are the senior officer, I take it that you will preside."

Steele nodded. "Yes, it seems that . . ." He looked aside toward the Palace. "Yes, I will preside." He looked back at Burke. "What is your interest in the trial?"

"You perhaps know that my colleagues and I are active in the movement against this war." Steele nodded.

"I would like to speak at the trial to tell of the widespread opposition to the war throughout the nation by people in all walks of life," said Burke. "I want to illustrate that what this soldier did was not original or isolated. That what he did was in tune with a very large population that feels the same as he."

Steele listened, head down. He turned to Burke. "I understand. I might even say that . . ." He stopped, cleared his throat. "No one on the court will dispute that many people oppose the war. But that is not the issue here. The question before the court in not about the nature of the war, the origins of the war, the pursuit of the war, or whether the war is justified or wrong. The question before the court, the only question before the court, is whether the accused deserted. It's that simple."

Burke closed his eyes, opened them. "I have heard that the penalty for desertion in wartime is death. Surely there are options if there are extenuating circumstances. Surely there is some discretion left to the court martial board, especially to the head of the court."

"That's a question that I will explore in the manual. If we can find it."

"And may I speak at the trial?"

"That's another question that I will explore in the manual. As interesting as I find your argument, and I think your argument has some merit, it may not be relevant. I'm afraid I can't give you much hope of an appearance. We'll see."

Steele rose and Burke followed. "Thank you for seeing me," said Burke, "and hearing me out. I will hope for support from your manual." Steele smiled, extended his hand and Burke grasped it.

Burke watched the Captain walk across the plaza toward the Palace. He remembered what Manuel Chaves told him. If the defense counsel calls you as a witness, neither Colonel Price nor Captain Steele can prevent you from testifying.

CHAPTER 12
Court Martial

Manuel Chaves stood just inside the fort entrance. He spoke urgently with the guard. As they talked, he glanced anxiously toward John Henry's quarters. John Henry sat on the bench in front of the cabin. Chaves waved and John Henry stood. The guard nodded to Chaves and Chaves strode, almost ran, towards the cabin.

"Señor Chaves, *mi amigo*, it's good to see you."

Chaves breathed deeply, catching his breath and composing himself. "John Henry, I have the most wonderful news! A stroke of good fortune!"

"Please, sit," John Henry said. They sat on the bench.

"You remember that I told you that I was represented at my trial by Captain William Angney. He was a lawyer in Missouri before joining the army. He is a very accomplished attorney and open-minded and, most of all, Colonel Price respects him. He likes him.

"Well, Captain Angney was attached to Colonel Doniphan's army that left for Chihuahua but Angney became homesick for Santa Fe. He applied for a post that would return him to Santa Fe. He loves this country and hopes to settle here someday."

"How do you know all this?" John Henry said.

"That's the wonderful part! Doniphan agreed and detached him to return to Santa Fe and report to Colonel Price for assignment. Since we had become friends during my trial, he contacted me on his arrival to tell me that he had returned and to renew the friendship.

"Of course, I told him about you and I took the liberty to ask him if he would represent you. He was intrigued by your case and said that he would, if Colonel Price agrees! We talked to the Colonel. He was not particularly happy about it but since he considers both of us his friends, he said he could not turn us down. What good fortune!"

John Henry stood at the fort's open gate and watched the sun set behind the trees that bordered the road down to the town. Candles already illuminated the interiors of some of the houses below. There was no sound but an incessant dog's barking in the distance, then a child's shout from a house at the bottom of the hill.

A figure walked into view on the road, a head that became a torso that became Brad. He waved to John Henry. Brad arrived and clapped John Henry on the shoulder. John Henry didn't know this guard and told him that Anthony Bradford had come for a visit. The guard nodded and Brad stepped inside.

"Let's walk," said John Henry. They walked along the edge of the parade in front of cabins, corrals, storerooms and offices that backed up against the fort wall. There were few people on the parade at this dinner hour.

"I've got no news for you," John Henry said. "Don't generate much news here. What about you? Have you been assigned yet?"

"I sure have. I'm attached to Colonel Price's office,

reporting to his aide. That's Captain Phillips. I don't know what the hell I'll be doin'. Don't know what I can do in an office. Right now, I'm just running errands for him. I think Colonel Price just wants to keep me near so he can ask about General Kearny and California. He's already called me and Captain Phillips in a couple of times and asked me a bunch of questions.

"There's not much I can tell since General Kearny didn't talk to me. All I know about what he was doing is what I saw and heard from my friend who knew the General's aide. And I sure don't know what the General was thinking. But I did keep my eyes and ears open. And right now I'm the only person around here who's been to California. So maybe I can tell them a thing or two."

"Sounds like pretty good duty. I wonder whether it will last to the end of your enlistment. Hope so. If we are still in Santa Fe when your time is up, maybe I'll convince you to stay in New Mexico."

"Yeah, maybe." They fell silent and walked.

"Hate to tell you this, Johnny," said Brad, "but you've probably guessed. I'm going to be called as a witness for the prosecution at your trial. The officer in charge of handling the Army's case, what's his name, Lieutenant Bingham, has an office at the other end of the Palace from Colonel Price, and he sent word for me to see him. I went over and he told me about me being in your trial.

"I told him I was a friend of yours and didn't really want any part in all this. He thought that was pretty funny. He said that I had no choice in the matter and that he wouldn't ask me to express any opinions, just to tell the truth when he asked questions. When I didn't respond, he got all serious and said that if I didn't answer and answer truthfully, I could get in a whole mess of trouble."

"Don't worry about it, Brad. You need to do exactly what he said. I expect he will ask me questions as well if I am called to testify. All we need to do is tell the truth. Both of us."

Brad relaxed, looked at John Henry and smiled. "I wish I felt as good about this as you do."

Before tackling John Henry's court martial, I needed to know something of the process. I had read about courts martial in the twentieth century, mostly World War II and since, but I needed to know how it was constituted and pursued in 1847.

The sources were hard to come by. Writers of relevant documents did not have twenty-first-century readers in mind. They wrote for the military readers who were accustomed to the jargon. I consulted *General Regulations for the Army of the United States 1841.* Hard going and mostly stuff that might have been useful for officers in the service in 1841, but I found some bits and pieces that shed some light on the court martial process. But little useful on the composition of the court and the routine of the court martial process.

I found some helpful information in accounts of the mutiny trial of John Charles Fremont, convened in November 1847, only a few months after John Henry's trial. A biography of General Kearny, Fremont's accuser, was most interesting in showing how an accused and excellent counsel can turn the tables and put the accuser on trial.

In Fremont's trial, Kearny was a witness and had no counsel. Fremont and his brilliant counsel discredited Kearny, the accuser, by asking him hard questions, some irrelevant, that Kearny nevertheless agreed to answer. While not himself on trial, Kearny came out the loser.

The court found Fremont guilty of mutiny and sentenced him to be dismissed from the army. Members of the court nevertheless recommended that President Polk exercise clemency because of his previous service.

Polk was sympathetic to Fremont and accepted the verdict but remitted the penalty. He ordered him released and returned to service. Fremont was outraged and resigned. He remained sufficiently popular in the public mind that he could become a candidate for the United States presidency in 1856.

Too bad you didn't have an opportunity to use this strategy, John Henry. You didn't have an accuser, as such, unless the army can be called an accuser. The most interesting point in Fremont's trial for your case is the possibility that a guilty verdict need not result always in the usual punishment.

I admit to a certain prejudice about Fremont. I get ticked every time I see him called "The Pathfinder." He found no paths. He followed known trails and almost always had local Indian guides who knew the country well. When he didn't have Indian guides, he got lost. But right now I'm looking for descriptions of court martial procedure, not stoking my biases.

I wrote to the National Archives and Library of Congress for the records of actual court martial cases during the Mexican War. There must have been many cases but apparently they were not recorded beyond a listing and a sentence or two of description. On the other hand, John Henry's trial aroused so much interest at the time that it was still being talked about and written about for years to come. I found plenty of comment on his trial but little on the content of other trials of the period.

Colonel Price couldn't put it off any longer. He decided finally that he must convene the court martial and get it over with. They had been unable to find the court martial manual but the Colonel had sat on two general courts martial and was confident that he could give any help to Steele that he required. Necessity superseded caution, at least in Price's mind.

The Colonel called Captain Steele to his office and, together, they agreed on the date: April 12, 1847, a Monday. Price still expected that the trial would be finished in a couple of days.

Day 1: The room set aside for the trial was the largest inside Fort Marcy. It had a plank floor and plank walls. The room had only two windows, both on the western wall which provided ample light in the afternoon and but weak illumination in the morning. The wall opposite the windows backed up against the fort wall.

At the front of the room, the five members of the court sat behind two small rectangular tables that were pushed together. Facing the officers, John Henry and Captain Angney, his counsel, sat behind a small table. Lieutenant Bingham, the appointed judge advocate, sat at a similar table at their left. A second chair beside him was unoccupied. A single chair was placed before the windows, facing the center of the room.

A dozen chairs were arrayed in a row at the back of the room, presumably for witnesses and spectators, though none were occupied on this first day.

Colonel Price had not been inclined to welcome visitors. He had initially even rejected Morita's request to attend but he thought it over and relented to avoid an uproar from the townspeople.

As late as this first day of the trial, Price was still mulling the request from the three antiwar activists and Manuel Chaves to attend. He believed that they had nothing useful to the trial and would be a distraction, perhaps a nuisance. He hoped Captain Steele was so inclined, though he could not be sure.

The Captain had been strangely reticent in conversations lately about the trial. Price realized that he could not prevent anyone from testifying if the judge advocate or the accused's counsel called a particular person as a witness. Pressed for time and burdened with other tasks, Price had finally thrown his hands in the air and left decisions on visitors and witnesses to Captain Steele, a circumstance that troubled the Captain.

Captain Steele glanced around the room, cleared his throat. He was obviously uneasy. Conversation died and all looked at the captain.

"We will follow the required procedure in this trial but it is my intention that the proceeding be informal and no one should be hesitant to speak at any point. Just so there should be no confusion, however, please ask my permission to speak." He looked around the room. The other four members of the court nodded or looked blankly at him.

That's what Steele said but he was still unsure what exactly the required procedure was. The manual that described court martial procedure had never been found. None of the officers appointed to the court had ever sat on a general court martial board and Steele was uneasy about proceeding. He had appealed to Colonel Price to put off the trial until the manual was found or until higher authority had been consulted but Price was adamant. "Get this thing done!" he had said.

Steele continued. "The members of the court, including

the five officers acting as judges and the judge advocate and defense counsel, have executed a signed oath to perform the duties required of them during this trial. The documents are on file in Colonel Price's office."

"Captain Steele, may I speak?" said John Henry. Everyone in the room looked abruptly at John Henry as if to say: how dare the accused interrupt these proceedings? The members of the court looked at Steele. The Captain pondered a moment. Not an auspicious beginning.

"You may," said Steele.

"Sir, I have been advised by my counsel that I can challenge any member of the court," said John Henry.

The other four members of the court, puzzled, glared alternately at John Henry and Angney, then looked to Steele.

"Is that true?" said Captain Anderson.

Captain Steele frowned. "Yes," he said without taking his eyes off John Henry.

Anderson flinched. He knew that he had not been appointed to the court for his knowledge of military justice and assumed that his position was precarious. As Price had expected, Anderson had been delighted with the assignment but now he saw the few days' respite from the post hospital in jeopardy.

"Who do you challenge?" said Steele.

John Henry shifted in his chair. "Lieutenant Rogers, sir," said John Henry. Rogers stiffened, looked abruptly from John Henry to Steele.

"Your reason, your justification for the challenge?" said Steele.

John Henry looked at Angney who nodded. John Henry avoided Rogers who glared at him. John Henry looked only at Captain Steele.

"Sir, ever since I arrived, the lieutenant seems to

have gone out of his way to make it difficult for me. His attitude seems to suggest that he cannot be impartial on my case here."

Rogers jumped up and leaned forward over the table, fire in his eyes. "By God!" he said. "You are a prisoner! You deserted, and you act like you're on a holiday! You come and go as you wish in the fort! You have visitors! Why do you—"

"Lieutenant, please sit down," said Steele calmly. Steele, at first, was inclined to let Rogers say his piece but decided to intervene to prevent Rogers's disrupting the court or bursting a blood vessel. The lieutenant's face had grown increasingly flushed and saliva had spewed as he shouted.

Still fuming, Rogers sat down slowly, never taking his eyes off John Henry. John Henry did not look at him and this seemed to increase his anger.

Lieutenant Lipscomb looked uneasily at the other members of the court. He appeared embarrassed. Or puzzled. He wasn't sure what to make of the affair. It was his first court martial. He had never even sat in on a court martial as a spectator.

Steele pondered. He tapped a pencil on the table. "The decision is not mine. This rests with the authority who convened the court and that is Colonel Price. I will take this up with him." He stood.

Rogers was beside himself. He glared at Steele. "You're really going to take this challenge seriously."

Steele ignored Rogers or he seemed to. "The court is adjourned until tomorrow at 9:00 a.m. Lieutenant Rogers, stay, please."

The members of the court, all but Rogers, stood and Steele watched the three officers file out of the door. Others in the room followed. John Henry and Captain Angney were the last to leave.

When the door closed, Captain Steele, still standing, faced Rogers. Rogers stood. "Lieutenant," Steele said, "the challenge is permitted by Army Regulations. You are recently from the Point and you should know this. Henceforth, control yourself in this courtroom, and do not challenge my authority. Is that understood?"

"Yes, *sir*," said Rogers, loudly accentuating the "sir." That's what he said but he still fumed. Steele noticed. Rogers remained standing at his place, whether in defiance or awaiting orders was uncertain.

"Dismissed," Steele said. Rogers picked up his hat from the table, clamped it on his head, adjusted it vigorously side to side as he strode to the door and opened it abruptly. He pulled it shut.

A soldier reined his horse in hard at the Governor's Palace. He dismounted hurriedly and tied the reins to the hitching post. He strode into the building, stopped at the desk of Colonel Price's aide.

"Yes?" Captain Bingham said.

The rider inhaled deeply, catching his breath. "I'm a guard at the trial at the fort, sir. I have a message from Captain Steele. The message is urgent for Colonel Price."

The aide put up a hand, either willing him to wait or calm down or catch his breath. The aide stood and walked to the door behind him. He knocked and opened the door, went inside. He returned and held the door open. The horseman nodded and went inside.

"Yes, what's happening? What is this urgent message?" said Price. The Colonel was not happy to receive a message from a breathless Fort Marcy guard. It could only mean trouble.

"Sir, Captain Steele said to tell you that a crowd of people has gathered outside the fort entrance."

Colonel Price frowned, sighed. "A crowd of people. What are they doing?"

"Just standing there. Real quiet like. Just looking. Really strange."

"Hmm." Price looked through the window toward the plaza. "How many people?"

"About a hundred maybe."

Price stood and walked to the window. "God," he mumbled under his breath. "When will this end?"

"Sir?"

"Nothing. Return to the fort and come again in a couple of hours. Or sooner if something happens that I should know about. Tell Captain Steele."

"Yes, sir. Sir?"

"Yes, what is it!" said Price. The soldier jumped at the sharp response.

"Sir, the trial has been adjourned for the day. Captain Steele is coming down to talk with you."

Price closed his eyes and rolled his head. "All right. Dismissed." He opened his eyes in time to see the soldier salute. Price returned the salute. The soldier did an about face and almost ran to and through the door. The aide closed the door.

"Just standing there, you say?" said Captain Phillips to the guard. The soldier stopped.

"Yeah. Yes, sir."

"Strange," said Phillips.

CHAPTER 13
A Good Man

Morita and John Henry sat at his cabin. She held his hand in her lap. Soldiers passing glanced at them. Some glared, others waved. Most ignored them. The couple had become a familiar twosome, sitting side by side on the bench at the front of the cabin.

"I didn't expect to see you this early," he said. "How did you know to come?"

"I came up with the people this morning. When I walked across the plaza, everyone was walking this way. By the time we reached the fort, there were fifty people and more kept coming. I think there must be a hundred fifty now. They are still there. They will stay until sunset."

"What do they do?"

"They wait. They pray. They are your people, Juanito. Our people. When all this is over, you will be the most well known person in Santa Fe."

"How did you know the trial was adjourned?"

"This afternoon, the soldier named Michael saw me standing with the people. He called me over and he told me the trial had been adjourned for the day. I asked him if I could see you. He said he didn't know about that. He looked behind him and all around and told me to hurry and come in. Michael is nice. I like him."

"Yes, he is a good friend. Most soldiers, most Americans, are good people."

They were quiet. They looked above the western wall at the sky that displayed a riot of color as the sun dropped lower. She squeezed his hand, laid her head on his shoulder.

He tensed and she looked up at him. She followed his gaze across the parade. Lieutenant Rogers stood near the door to an office. He stared at them.

"Sit up straight, *muchacha*, and scoot away from me," said John Henry, not taking his eyes from Rogers. "Let's not give the prick any reason to make you leave."

She frowned, looked intently at Rogers. "I think I will ask Calixtro to kill him. He would do it for me. What do you think of my idea, *guapo*?" still staring at Rogers.

"I think that would not be a good idea, sweetheart. What would I do if they traced the deed to you? Then I would have to kill anyone who laid a hand on you and how could I do that when I am held here? Hmm?"

"Maybe I will let him live for now." She had not taken her eyes off Rogers, who still stared at them. "Maybe he will be sent to lead a patrol against the Navajos and I will ask a Navajo friend to kill him."

John Henry had a hard time keeping a straight face. "If I laugh when I am staring at him, *muchacha*, he will explode. So be quiet."

"Okay." They watched until Rogers turned and entered the door behind him. Morita took his arm. She looked at him. "Juanito?"

He looked down at her upturned face. "What?"

"I love you."

He glanced around. No one was looking their way. He

leaned down and kissed her. "I love you, sweetheart. Now go home. It's going to be dark soon."

She smiled, squeezed his arm. They stood and walked toward the gate in the gloom.

Day 2. John Henry and Captain Angney sat at their table, leaning toward each other, talking softly. Lieutenant Bingham scanned a paper that lay on his table. John Henry turned around and saw Morita, the three antiwar activists and Manuel Chaves sitting in the row of chairs at the back of the room.

Brad sat in the chair at the end of the row. He looked directly at John Henry. John Henry smiled, a hint of a smile, and Brad nodded. John Henry turned back to the front when the outer door opened.

The five members of the court filed in, pulled out chairs, scraping on the wooden floor, and took their seats. Captain Steele looked right and left at the other members. He cleared his throat, glanced about the room.

"Order, please," said Steele. "We adjourned yesterday to consider the challenge of the accused to the participation of Lieutenant Rogers in this trial." Steele looked down at a file of papers on the table before him, absentmindedly, nervously, shuffling the papers. "The challenge is rejected. The trial will proceed." Lieutenant Rogers leaned back in his chair, looked at John Henry, smiled.

Steele looked up. "Lieutenant Bingham," he said.

Bingham rose and stood behind his table. "This case is clear and indefensible. All that need be proven is that the accused left his post without permission and that he had no intention of returning. That is to say, he deserted. This in the midst of a war that still rages in the south." Bingham nodded to Captain Steele and sat down.

"Would the accused please stand?" said Steele. John Henry stood.

"Private John Henry Harris, how do you plead to the charge of desertion?"

"On the advice of my counsel, sir," John Henry said, "not guilty."

"You may sit." John Henry sat, glanced at Captain Angney. Angney nodded.

Bingham stood. He placed the paper he held on the table. "I call Private Anthony Bradford to testify."

Brad stood and walked to the chair in front of the windows. He looked nervously at Captain Steele and the other judges, then at John Henry. John Henry looked at Brad without any sign of recognition.

The bailiff walked over to Brad. "Private Bradford, raise your right hand. Do you promise to tell the truth, the whole truth and nothing but the truth, so help you, God?"

"I do."

"Sit, please," said Bingham. Brad lowered his hand and sat.

"Private Bradford, did you march to California last year with General Kearny's army?"

"I did. Wasn't much of an army, just a hundred men."

"Just an expression. His force. His unit. And were you a close companion with the accused during that march?"

"Yes, sir, I was."

"Did the accused ever say or indicate that he had thoughts or plans to leave General Kearny's force during the march to California?"

"Well, sir, he said that he didn't think he could take part in this war because it was wrong and if he took part, he would be doing wrong and—"

"Just answer the question. It's not a hard question. Did

Private Harris ever say or indicate that he planned to leave General Kearny's force without permission?"

"Yes, sir."

"Explain. When did he say this?"

Brad fidgeted, glanced furtively at John Henry. "Well, the night before we were going to attack the Californians—we shared a tent—he woke me up in the middle of the night and said he was leaving. He had been suffering terrible with bad headaches and he said when he decided to leave, his head cleared, and he knew it was the right thing to do."

"And did he in fact leave?" said Bingham.

"No, sir, about that time the call to horse sounded. The General had decided to get an early start and so everbody was running around the camp like crazy. He couldn't leave."

"Did he at some point later make to leave?"

Brad frowned. "Well, uh, maybe. When we was lined up waiting for the charge bugle, he whipped his horse out of line without no order to do that."

"And did he then leave?"

"No, sir, right at that time, Captain Johnston was riding by, and John Henry ran smack into him, almost knocked him off his horse. The Captain was right angry about that and ordered John Henry back into line."

"What happened next?"

"We charged the Californians and got our asses whupped."

Lieutenant Lipscomb and Dr. Anderson guffawed. Both immediately sobered and looked at Captain Steele who stared at them, tight-lipped. Lipscomb nodded to Steele and Anderson raised a hand, both gestures an apology of sorts.

Bingham glared at Lipscomb and Anderson. He turned

back to Brad. "All right. Did you see the accused again, after the battle?"

"Yessir. We was camped in the middle of this open flat and I saw him at a considerable distance riding through some dark woods at the head of the valley."

"In what direction was he riding?"

Brad looked furtively at John Henry.

"Don't look at the accused, Private Bradford. Look at me. You swore to tell the truth."

"Yeah, sir, I know. That's what John Henry said too."

"That's commendable. Now, in which direction was he riding?"

"He was riding toward the back trail, where we had come down from our last night's camp."

"So he was headed east."

"Yes, sir."

Bingham walked to his table and picked up a sheet. He walked back to Brad and showed him the paper. "Did General Kearny give you this paper to deliver to Colonel Price?"

Brad glanced at the paper. "I can't say for sure. I didn't read it. It was sealed. But if that's the paper his aide gave me, then I did bring it to Colonel Price."

Bingham turned to the judges. "I can assure you that this is the paper that Private Bradford delivered to Colonel Price."

Steele looked at the defense table. "Captain Angney, do you concede that this is the letter from General Kearny that the witness delivered to Colonel Price?"

Angney pondered, frowning, looked at Brad a moment, then at Captain Steele. "We do so concede for now so the trial may proceed but we reserve the right to question its authenticity later if circumstances suggest otherwise."

"Oh, for God's sake!" All in the room looked abruptly at Lieutenant Rogers. Rogers, flushed and fuming, glared at Angney.

Captain Steele stood slowly. He looked at the wall above the line of chairs at the back of the room. "We will adjourn for thirty minutes. Please return promptly. Thirty minutes." All in the room stood, looked at each other, puzzled.

"Lieutenant Rogers, stay, please," Steele said, picking up some papers from the table, without looking at Rogers. Rogers turned toward the windows, closed his eyes, pursed his lips.

All in the room but Steele and Rogers stood and made their way to the door and passed through. Brad was last in the file and closed the door behind him. Steele waited for the door to close. He turned to Rogers who stared through the window.

"Lieutenant." Rogers turned abruptly to face Steele. Rogers stood slowly. "Where do you think you are, Lieutenant? The club? The union? The quadrangle? By God, you are sitting on a general court martial! This is the last outburst that I will tolerate. One more, and I will remove you from this court, it will go on your record, and you may even see yourself charged!"

Rogers lifted his chin. "Sir, Colonel Price—"

"Colonel Price is not running this court! I am running this court! Forget that at your peril. You're still wet behind the ears, Rogers. You are an apprentice! If you want a career in this army, you had better get your head on straight. Learn to watch and listen."

Rogers glanced casually aside, blinked slowly, looked back at Steele. Steele noticed.

"This is your last chance," said Steele. "Be the officer

that the Point trained you to be. You know what is expected
of a member of a court martial board. I expect you to
restrain yourself, listen to witnesses with an open mind,
and be a model, not a distraction. Is this understood?"

"Sir," said Rogers softly.

"Is this understood!"

"Yes, sir," said Rogers, without enthusiasm. It was obvious to Captain Steele that the lieutenant was obedient,
but hardly repentant.

"Order, please." Captain Steele placed the sheets that he
had been shuffling on the table, his usual nervous opening.

The members of the court and others were seated.
Brad slumped in the witness chair, looking about. All
in the courtroom looked at Captain Steele, wondering
whether he would now reveal something of the conversation that he had held during the recess with Lieutenant
Rogers. He did not.

"Lieutenant Bingham, resume, please," said Steele.

Bingham rose, picked up a paper from his table.
"Thank you, sir. I wish to comment on the content of
this letter, addressed to Colonel Price. The letter is signed
by General Kearny.

"When Colonel Price received information that a person who resembled Private Harris had been recognized
in Santa Fe, he wrote to the General to ask whether he
had any information on the status of Private Harris. The
General replied that he did indeed.

"At the end of the battle with the Californians, the
General had an accounting done of the members of his
force. They accounted for every member, living and
dead, except one. That one was the accused, Private
John Henry Harris. The General had the valley and the

adjoining woods and hills searched and there was no sign of Private Harris. No live soldier, no wounded soldier, no body. There could be only one conclusion. Private Harris was alive and he was gone. He had deserted." Bingham held up the paper. "This letter will be on file in Colonel Price's office for anyone's perusal."

Lieutenant Bingham returned to his chair and sat down.

"Captain Angney, do you have questions of the witness?" said Steele.

Angney stood. "I do."

"Private Bradford. Did Private Harris ever say anything that would suggest what he thought about his country?"

"Yes sir. He said he loved his country. He said something like that lots of times."

"Did you ever see any sign that he had a hard time dealing with how he felt about this war?"

"He said he thought about it all the time. He said it was tearing his insides out. On the one hand, loyalty to his country and to his soldier pards and, on the other hand, not wanting to support a war that was wrong. I think it was that worry that made him so sick with bad headaches that made him black out sometimes. He blacked out a number of times during the march and the doctor had to tend to him."

"So he said that the war was wrong. Did he ever elaborate? Did he explain what he meant by the war being wrong?"

"He said that Mexico didn't do nothing wrong. It didn't attack the United States. It didn't steal anything from the United States. The United States invaded Mexico anyway. That's what he said."

"You said that when your unit was in line, ready to attack the Californians, Private Harris's horse was wheeling out of line. Could the horse have been spooked and wheeled out of line on its own, without any action on Private Harris's part?"

Brad brightened. "Yeah, uh, yes, sir, it could've happened that way! That could've been what happened."

"Or Private Harris could have felt the runs coming on from a plate of bad beans the night before?" said Angney.

"Yeah, it could've been that too!" Brad was enjoying this too much.

"Let's get back to the Californians. When Captain Johnston led the charge on the Californian horsemen, did Private Harris take part in that charge?"

"Yessir, he did. He drew his sword just like the rest of us and charged just like the rest of us. Well, not just like the rest of us. He was sick as hell. I think he was blind sick at that point."

Angney consulted some notes that he held. "You said that you later saw Private Harris 'at a considerable distance riding through some dark woods.' At a considerable distance in dark woods. Are you sure that was Private Harris? Could it have been somebody else? A Californian, for example? Could you have thought it was Private Harris because you were looking for Private Harris?"

"Yes, sir. Now that you say it that way, I'm not sure it was John Henry at all." Brad heaved a great sigh.

Angney faced Captain Steele. "That's all I have for this witness at the moment." Angney returned to his chair, glanced aside at John Henry.

Brad looked at John Henry. John Henry nodded ever so slightly. He had never taken his eyes from Brad during his testimony.

"You may step down, Private Bradford," Steele said. Brad stood and walked to his chair at the back of the room. Morita smiled, and he sat beside her.

"Thank you, Captain Angney and Lieutenant Bingham. We will adjourn for lunch and resume at 2:00 p.m.

At 2:20 p.m., Captain Steele spoke to the assembled court. Except the court had not fully assembled. It was twenty minutes past the announced time for the afternoon session when the officers filed in. Counsel and witnesses were sitting in their accustomed places, and the judges took their seats. All but Captain Anderson.

The good doctor was nowhere to be seen. When he did not show up at the usual gathering room for the court members, Captain Steele had sent two soldiers to look for him. They returned after fifteen minutes to report that he was not in the fort.

But there's one more thing, one of the soldiers said. A guard at the gate said that Captain Anderson had passed through the gate at 11:45 this morning, walking down the road toward the town. The guard said that Dr. Anderson had not returned. Steele did not share this bit of news with the court.

"Regulations require a general court martial board of five officers," said Steele. "Since the fifth member of our board is absent, we cannot proceed. We are adjourned until 9:00 a.m. tomorrow."

Steele learned later that Dr. Anderson at 2:00 p.m. was involved in a lively discussion at a popular cantina on the question of whether masturbation really caused insanity.

"Shall I dispatch a unit to the fort to supplement the guards?" Captain Phillips said. He stood before Price's desk. The colonel stared at the window, frowning. "The crowd is still growing. They have been quiet, so far, but it is unnerving. Shall we disperse them, send them back down the hill? We could also put up a barrier at the bottom of the fort road. That would not stop them from climbing the hill some other place but if they do that, that would suggest intent, and we could take further action."

Price leaned back in his chair, still looking at the window. He turned back to Phillips. "No, let's not antagonize them. So far, they have been intimidating but peaceful. But you have a point. The people go down the hill each evening at sundown, you say?"

"Yes, sir."

"Send fifty men up to the fort at midnight tonight. Then send up an additional fifty each night until the trial ends. These troops will stay in the fort until further assignment. The fort officers will have to find rough accommodation for them inside the walls. Also, instruct the officers of the troops billeted in the plaza barracks to have their men ready at all times."

Day 3: John Henry and Captain Angney and Lieutenant Bingham sat behind their respective tables. Morita, Brad, Chaves and the three antiwar partners sat in the row at the back. All stood when the five members of the court martial board filed in, pulled chairs back and sat behind their table.

Dr. Anderson was noticeably nervous, his eyes darting about the courtroom and cutting back and forth among his fellow judges, all of whom ignored him. Except Acting Lieutenant Johnstone who looked at him with a smirk that could only be recognized as contempt. The look did not go unnoticed by Anderson.

"Lieutenant Bingham," Captain Steele said, "do you wish to commence?"

"I yield, at the moment, to Captain Angney," Bingham said. Steele nodded.

"Captain Angney," said Steele.

Angney stood. "Thank you, Captain." He turned to Bingham. "And you, Lieutenant." Angney turned to face the board. "I have explained earlier that I reviewed military law before being dispatched to Santa Fe, in case I should have an opportunity to practice my profession during my term of service. I erred in not bringing the latest army publications on the subject, but, as I have mentioned before, I have copious notes.

"One of the developments that I found particularly interesting in my research was the growing interest in military circles and the general public in permitting presentations in courts martial on the character and motivations of an accused. I understand that this tendency is so pronounced that the revision of the manual for courts martial, now underway, almost surely will include this provision.

"Since Captain Steele announced on the first day of this proceeding that this trial would be informal, I beg to be permitted to introduce information of this sort, testimony on the character of the accused and background on his actions."

Lieutenant Lipscomb frowned, turned to Steele. "Can we do that?" Captain Steele stared at the wall.

"I should think we cannot," said Acting Lieutenant Johnstone. "We are bound by the procedures outlined in the current manual for courts martial."

"I should think we can decide what to admit by a vote of the board or a declaration by Captain Steele," said Anderson, glaring pointedly at Johnstone. "Since I have not seen a manual of courts martial and I'm not a lawyer, I don't know what the hell court martial procedure is."

The four board members looked at Captain Steele.

Steele slumped, stared at the windows. He wished with

all his heart that he was not sitting in this room, taking part in this trial, bearing on his shoulders the burden of decisions that must be made, decisions that weighed on questions of right or wrong and ultimately on whether this good man who only wanted to live in peace with his wife would live or die.

He sat up and faced front. "Proceed, Captain Angney."

"Thank you, sir," said Angney. "I call Manuel Chaves."

Chaves stood and walked to the chair at the window. He did not sit. He faced the five officers of the court. The bailiff swore him in.

Angney stood behind his table. "Señor Chaves, do you know the accused well enough to be able to comment on his character and cause, that is, on what motivated him to act as he did?"

"I do," said Chaves. Angney sat down and nodded to Chaves. Chaves remained standing.

"I thank the court for permitting me to speak to the character and cause of the accused," said Chaves. "I do not contest that the prisoner left his post without permission. I contend that the departure was logical and justified."

Captain Steele leaned over the table, his eyes fixed on Chaves. The other members of the court looked at Chaves and settled back in their chairs. They knew about Chaves's case and knew what to expect from him now.

"In all countries," said Chaves, "the findings of past trials are important in assessing the meaning and findings of later trials. When American soldiers invaded New Mexico, I fought them. I was a citizen of Mexico, fighting for my country against an invading foreign power. I did what everyone here would agree was the right thing to do. I risked my life to fight for a cause, freedom of my country.

"Private Harris did the same. He believed in a cause,

justice. He believed that he had an obligation to do what was right, to oppose an unjust war. Just as I risked my life to fight for a strong moral cause, so Private Harris risked his life to do the same."

Captain Steele was genuinely interested and listened to Chaves. The other members of the court alternately looked at Chaves, looked over his head, looked out the window, glanced idly about the room, often stopping on Morita. Chaves was either oblivious of their lack of attention or chose to ignore it. He focused his delivery on Captain Steele.

"I was arrested and accused of treason," said Chaves. "During my trial, my counsel argued that the United States, far from punishing me, should be applauding me for standing up for a just cause, defense of my country. So the United States should applaud Private Harris for opposing this unjust war of a strong nation against a weak country that had not wronged the United States and which is still emerging, even today, from the turmoil of its own revolution against an oppressive European imperial power, just as the United States has done.

"Private Harris's case is not so different from my own. I ask you to apply the principle evident in my trial and the judgment in my trial as you consider your judgment in his case." He paused, looked from Steel to Angney.

"Lieutenant Bingham, do you have any questions for this witness?" said Captain Steele.

"No questions," said Bingham.

Steele looked right and left at the members of the court. "Does anyone have a response or a question for Señor Chaves?"

Acting Lieutenant Johnstone leaned forward from his position at the end of the long table, looked at Steele.

"Yes, I do, Captain," said Johnstone. Steele nodded.

Johnstone turned to Chaves. "An interesting bit of history but your case has little resemblance to that of the accused. At the time of your arrest and trial, you were a citizen of Mexico; the accused is a citizen of the United States and an American soldier. Further, you argue a moral question which is not acceptable in a court of law, including a court martial. We are concerned here only with the question before the court. Did the accused desert or did he not?" Johnstone looked at Captain Steele, leaned back in his chair.

"Any other questions or comment from the board?" said Steele. When no one responded, he turned to Chaves. "Thank you, Señor Chaves."

Chaves nodded to Captain Steele. As Chaves was walking to the back of the room to resume his seat, the outside door opened a crack. A face appeared in the opening. Every head in the room turned to the door.

Bingham stood. "Ah, Captain Steele, so sorry for the interruption. I have a message that pertains to the question before the court."

Steele nodded. Bingham waved to the face to come in. The soldier came in a step, nodded nervously to the room, walked quickly to Lieutenant Bingham. He handed a note to Bingham and whispered to him. Bingham nodded, mouthed a thank-you. The soldier withdrew almost at a run and closed the door. All looked back to Bingham.

"Sorry. Thank you, sir," said Bingham.

The interruption, seemingly inconsequential, had raised the tension in the courtroom. Now everyone relaxed and looked at Captain Steele.

Captain Angney stood.

"Captain?" said Steele.

"May I proceed?" said Angney.

"Yes, please," Steele said."

"I call Robert Burke," Angney said. Burke stood and walked to the witness chair. The bailiff administered the oath, and Burke sat down.

"Mr. Burke, please tell the court how you came to be in Santa Fe and how you know the accused."

Burke leaned forward in his chair. "My two colleagues and I are active participants in the movement against this unjust war, a movement I might say is widespread, popularly supported, and growing in momentum every day. We were encouraged and sponsored by some of the leading lights of the movement to go to Santa Fe to learn how the native population of the conquered province fared under the occupation by the invaders."

"Mr. Burke," said Captain Steele. "You are not speaking to a gathering of people that you would like to convert to a cause. Please just respond in plain language to Captain Angney's questions without the politics."

"Yes, sir, sorry," said Burke. "I . . . get carried away. I feel that strongly. I will respond plainly." Steele nodded.

"Carry on," said Angney to Burke.

"On arrival in Santa Fe," Burke said, "when people learned who we were, they could talk of nothing else but Private Harris. We applied for permission to visit him at the fort which Colonel Price kindly granted. We have talked with Private Harris a number of times since then."

"What can you tell the court that will have some bearing on this case?" said Angney.

"I can only add to Mr. Chaves's testimony. This war is unlike any war that has ever been pursued by the United States. There are tens of thousands of Americans who not only do not support this war; they actively oppose it.

These are loyal Americans who love their country and will fight for its freedoms against attack from any foreign power. But they do not support a war of aggression by their own country against another country that has not committed any wrongful act against the United States!" Burke's heat and volume had risen and he had to resist the impulse to shake a fist.

"Mr. Burke. Please," said Steele.

Burke clasped his hands, nodded repeatedly. "Ah, sorry, sorry. . . . What I wish to say, to impress on the court, is that far from being an isolated case, Private Harris's attitude toward this war is not out of the ordinary at all. He is in step with an attitude that permeates American society. That is, the view that every person should stand up for right, to oppose the pursuit of an unjust war, to show by whatever means possible, at whatever risk, that this wonderful country has been wronged by the greedy passions of a few of its political leaders!" Burke's heat had risen again and he held up a hand to Steele in a gesture that said, there I go again, sorry.

"I end with an endorsement of Mr. Chaves's comment about the accused. Private Harris is one of the gentlest, brightest young men I have ever met. He loves his country passionately and he loves Santa Fe. He wishes to make his home here in this new American province with his wife, a daughter of the country and a fine woman. He has harmed no one. He has only praise for the way the army has treated him.

"I plead with the court to release this fine young man, this good American, to his wife and the good people of Santa Fe."

Steele looked up and down the line of officers. "Does anyone have a question or comment for Mr. Burke?"

Lieutenant Johnstone raised a hand. Steele frowned, pondered, nodded to him.

"Only that this testimony is not testimony at all. It is political protest posturing and has no bearing on this case. I hate to beat a dead horse but the war is not on trial. Private Harris is on trial. The issue is not the morality of the war. The question is desertion." Johnstone leaned back, a sure signal that he was finished.

Steele looked up and down the line of officers. He saw no evidence of anyone wishing to speak and turned to Burke. "You may stand down, Mr. Burke. Thank you."

Burke stood, nodded to the court, and walked to his seat.

"Thank you, gentlemen, we will break for lunch and resume at—"

Lt. Bingham jumped up. "Captain Steele, sorry to inter-rupt. May I request an adjournment until late afternoon?" Everyone in the room glared at Bingham. What now?

"The reason?"

"Ah, I need to look for a witness."

"A witness. All right," said Steele, "we are adjourned until 4:00 p.m. today."

CHAPTER 14
Mitigating Circumstances

The room buzzed with more lively conversation than usual at the reconvening of the court. Captain Steele picked up the stack of papers on the table in front of him and shuffled them.

"Order, please." The room fell silent at Captain Steele's voice. All were in their usual places except for three newcomers, a soldier in uniform who sat beside Lieutenant Bingham and Calixtro and another man who sat beside Morita in the back row.

Bingham, frowning, had watched Calixtro and Morita from the time they came through the door till they reached their seats at the back.

"I see you have found your witness, Lieutenant," said Steele. Bingham turned around abruptly.

"Yes, sir," said Bingham.

"Proceed."

Lieutenant Bingham stood. "Thank you, sir. The defense has presented testimony that comments on the character and motivation of the accused. I beg leave to do the same."

"Proceed," said Steele.

"I call Private Adam Bidwell," said Bingham. The soldier beside him stood, looked down anxiously at Bingham. The Lieutenant gestured to the witness chair at the window. Private Bidwell walked to the chair. The bailiff stepped over and swore him in.

"Sit, please, Private Bidwell," said Captain Steele. Bidwell sat, looked anxiously around the room.

"Private Bidwell," said Bingham, "were you part of a patrol that engaged a group of insurgents on the morning of March 20 of this year?"

"Yessir, that's the date you said."

"Yes, well." Bingham glanced sideways at Captain Steele and back to Bidwell. "Yes, that's the date shown in the record of the patrol's action for that day. On that day, did you participate in the cavalry charge on the insurgent camp?"

"Yessir."

"Were you fired on from the insurgent camp during the charge?"

"I sure was. I thought I was dead."

"Did you get a good look at the person who fired on you?"

"I sure did. I wasn't but thirty or forty feet from him and I was looking him right in the eye. I was looking right down the barrel of the pistol that he had pointed at me."

"Do you see the shooter in the courtroom? If you see him, point to him."

"That's him, right there." Bidwell pointed at John Henry.

"Thank you, Private, you may step down." Bidwell stood, looked around, walked to his seat at the back. John Henry looked up at him as he passed, but Bidwell avoided eye contact. Bingham returned to his chair.

Captain Angney stood.

"Captain Angney?" said Steele.

"Sir, I would like to present a witness who will testify to the action introduced by the previous witness."

Bingham turned sharply and glared at Angney.

"Proceed," said Steele.

"I call Calixtro Menendez." Calixtro stood, looked down at Morita who smiled at him. He walked to the witness chair, followed by the man who had come into the courtroom with him. The bailiff swore Calixtro and he sat. His companion stood beside him.

"Sir," Angney gestured toward the man standing beside Calixtro, "this is Carlos Ruiz. He will translate for the witness."

Steele nodded. Angney turned back to Calixtro. "Calixtro Menendez," said Angney, "were you present at the action described in Private Bidwell's testimony?"

"Yes, sir, I was."

"Was the accused, John Henry Harris, with you?"

"Yes, sir. We rode out from Santa Fe together, Andrés Pico too."

"Were the three of you part of this group, called 'insurgents' by the judge advocate?"

"No, sir."

"If you were not part of the group, how did you happen to be there?"

"We was just curious. A friend in Santa Fe told me where they were camped and we rode out to have a look, just to look."

"Did the accused encourage you to join this group, indeed any group that was active in fighting against the American position in New Mexico?"

"No, sir! He always told us not to get involved in any resistance. He told us to accept that the Americans had won and they were not going to go away. He never encouraged anybody to fight against the Americans."

"All right, now back to the camp. Were you involved in any way in the actual battle?"

"Well, only that I was trying hard to get away. When the bugle sounded and the soldiers charged the camp, I was in the clearing trying to mount but my horse spooked and ran away, and this soldier is charging me with his sword raised. He was looking me right in the eye. I put my arms over my head because I thought that sword was going to cut me in two."

"He was looking at you right in the eye? He was not looking at John Henry right in the eye?"

"No, sir, he was looking at me, deciding where he was going to part my hair. I don't think he even saw John Henry. John Henry was behind some bushes."

"And why did his sword not cut you in two?"

"Because John Henry shot the soldier's horse, and the soldier went rolling. John Henry saved my life."

"The accused shot the horse? You mean he was aiming at the soldier but missed and hit the horse?"

"Hell, no—sorry, sir—if he had meant to shoot the soldier, he would have shot the soldier. John Henry is a good shot. I've seen him shoot and he can hit any target dead on. He wouldn't miss a target as big as a man at that close range."

Angney looked at Steele. "Thank you, sir. That's all I have."

"Lieutenant Bingham?" said Steele.

"No, sir." Bingham glared at Angney.

"We will adjourn and reconvene at 9:00 a.m. tomorrow," Steele said.

John Henry, you're lucky that Michael was on gate duty when Bingham's man announced at the gate to a knot of soldiers that he was in a hurry because he was looking for a soldier who was part of the action at the insurgent camp and did anyone know where he could find Adam Bidwell. Also that Michael had the presence of mind to call Morita from the crowd at the gate and tell her what was going on.

Your luck held when Michael caught you and Lieutenant Angney on the parade during the adjournment. The lieutenant thought the conversation between you and Michael highly unusual but he stood back and did not interfere. Why would a defense counsel interfere when his case could take an upturn at this new development?

Calixtro and his interpreter had arrived with Morita for the 4:00 p.m. court session.

At this point in the trial, John Henry, you must have felt quite lonely in the courtroom and in your cabin. Actually, you were in good company. Desertion was common in the army, in the Mexican War and for decades after. You would have been surprised to know that in the Mexican War, 6,825 men, nearly seven percent of the American army, deserted.

And it didn't improve after the war. Hell, desertion in the western army was the thing to do. In the years between 1867 and 1891, a total of 88,475 men in the western army deserted, more from boredom than conviction. That's one-third of the men recruited by the army during that period. Some of the deserters were caught and tried but I was surprised to find that the death penalty was not the usual result.

The commander of one western fort had so many troops desert or try to desert, about a quarter of his force, that he couldn't execute all of them. To do so would have been more a measure of his lack of control over his soldiers than on their loyalty.

So he had the deserters branded with a large letter D on the hip, assigned them hard labor, and welcomed them back into the unit. He told them that the punishment was in lieu of execution and he would be watching them carefully. No second chances.

This practice of branding as an alternative to execution was not new in the last half of the century. John Riley, the Irish-American who deserted the U.S. Army and became the chief founder and leader of St. Patrick's Battalion in the Mexican War, was captured near the end of the conflict along with scores of his comrades. While many of the rank-and-file in the Battalion, all deserters from the U.S. Army, were executed, Riley was not.

General Winfield Scott, commander of American forces, declared that since Riley had deserted before the declaration of war, regulations dictated that he could only receive the lesser sentence of whipping and branding. He was lashed in the plaza of San Jacinto until his back was in shreds. Then he was branded with a two-inch letter D near his eye.

I shook my head. Stories like this remind me that human beings are only animals with an elevated ability to communicate and calculate, nothing more.

But back to my research. The more I looked, the more I became aware of the many alternatives to execution for deserters. I picked up my copy of *General Orders of the War Department*, published in 1863. I opened the volume at a bookmark and read that a convicted deserter "shall suffer death, or such other punishment as, by sentence of a court-martial, shall be inflicted." *Such other punishment*, meaning that other punishments were an option.

I put the book on the desk and picked up a half dozen

sheets stapled together that I had printed from an online copy of *Courts-Martial of the U.S. Army.* I tried to buy a copy but couldn't find one. Probably for the best. I'm collecting a horde of expensive old books that I'll have no use for once this research is done.

Anyway, the book has lots more stuff than I need. But I did find some intriguing comments. One passage tells about a particular Army commander who "does not believe that trial by general court martial is necessary or desirable in every case where the administrative charge of desertion has been made against a very young soldier who has been in the military service but a short period of time. . . . If it appears that the soldier has future potential value to the service, trial by general court martial should not be recommended." Meaning that the offense perhaps should be tried in a lower court, say a summary court martial, which could not assess the death penalty.

All well and good but these last pieces were written after 1847 and would have no bearing on John Henry's case. In 1847, there were few fine points of the law on desertion being discussed. In any event, the point about being restored to duty would not apply to John Henry since he had no intention in remaining in the service. Course, if it were an alternative to execution, he might well have given it some thought.

I am reminded of a movie I saw a while back. About a man who had the ability to go back in time and change something that would alter the course of events. If I had that ability, I could have shaken up that courtroom. Hell, I would have blown them away with my arguments and John Henry would have been freed at once and become famous.

What nonsense, and I haven't even had my front porch G&T.

Day 4: Captain Steele looked around the room. It was strangely quiet. Lieutenant Bingham bent over his table, studying a document. Captain Angney and John Henry leaned together, whispering softly. Manuel Chaves and the antiwar three sat in the middle chairs of the back row. Morita and Brad sat at the end of the row.

Colonel Price and Captain Steele had rejected dozens of requests from townspeople to attend the trial on grounds, perhaps justified, that there simply was no space for them in the courtroom. It was a convenient explanation. Price and Steele knew that Chaves and the three activists kept the townspeople up to date on the court's proceedings but they wished to avoid increasing the public clamor that surely would be the result if spectators from the town were admitted to the proceedings.

"The court will come to order," Steele said. Everyone looked up. "Lieutenant Bingham, we are ready for your closing comment."

Bingham stood. "Thank you, sir." He picked up the paper from his table, laid it back on the table. "The case against the accused is clear and simple. A soldier is required by his oath to follow orders. What chaos there would be if every soldier were permitted to weigh options in response to every order issued. A soldier has a duty to his country and its citizens, to his fellow soldiers and to himself.

"We have heard testimony that Private Harris was part of General Kearny's force that marched to California to take part in the subjugation of that Mexican province. We have heard testimony that Private Harris expressed his intention to leave the command and return to Santa Fe. We heard testimony further that Private Harris was seen riding toward the back trail, the trail that leads eastward. Cross-examination suggested that this might not have been Private Harris. Whether it was or was not Private Harris is of no consequence since Private Harris appeared later in Santa Fe. Once in Santa Fe, he changed his name to avoid detection.

"While his action in leaving his post in California illustrates his unwillingness to do his duty as an American soldier, he returned to New Mexico and took part with insurgents in an action against the United States Army, his part almost resulting in the death of an American soldier.

"There can be only one verdict in this trial. The accused left his post without permission. He had no intention of returning. He is a deserter." Bingham walked around his table and sat down.

"Captain Angney," said Steele. Angney rose, looked down at John Henry, walked around the table to stand in front of it, and faced the judges.

"We have heard the Judge Advocate's comment about the duty of the soldier. What greater duty is there than to do what is right? Private Harris did what he knew in his heart was right. He opposed a war that he knew was wrong. He opposed it in the only way he could. He refused to take part.

"Some say that his refusal to take part, to do his duty as a soldier, is proof that he does not love his country. To the contrary, his actions are evidence of his deep love for his country. He is devastated that the reputation of his country has been soiled by its aggressive action against a weak, peaceful neighboring state.

"Some counseled him that he is a soldier whose responsibility is to follow orders and leave the political decisions to the politicians. He rejects this notion. He does not believe that a wrong can be justified by the defense: I was following orders.

"Private Harris is no coward. He could have fled to Mexico to make a new life for himself and his wife. He would have been called a hero by Mexicans. He could have done that, but he chose to stay and defend his actions, to explain why he had felt so strongly about this war that he put his life at risk.

"We have heard testimony that though Private Harris did not support his country's subjugation of New Mexico, he nevertheless urged his Mexican friends to accept the result, to accept the reality that the United States had won and was here to stay. He encouraged them to find their way in the new order."

Angney looked up and down the row of board members. The officers were awake, apparently alert and appeared to be listening. Whether they were impressed or amused was hard to read in their faces. He picked up a paper from his table.

"In closing, I wish to introduce a plea for your consideration. I read from General Regulations for the Army of the United States, 1841, article 230: 'If mitigating circumstances have appeared during the trial, though they may not be considered in determining the sentence, still they may afford adequate grounds for recommending the prisoner to mercy.'

"Mitigating circumstances indeed have been presented, showing that the accused acted honorably in pursuing the only course open to him in his opposition to what he believed to be an unjust action by the United States against a country that had not wronged the United States. If the law requires you to find him guilty of the charge of desertion, I appeal to you to acknowledge that he acted out of a strong moral conviction, that he has injured no one, and plead that you exercise mercy in granting him a release to his wife and the community. He loves Santa Fe and will be a devoted and useful citizen."

Angney nodded to the judges, walked around his table and sat down.

Captain Steele adjourned the court, to reconvene at 9:00 a.m. the following day.

CHAPTER 15
Easy, *Guapo*, Too Tight

John Henry slouched on his bench. He leaned against the cabin wall, his legs stretched out and crossed. Morita rested against his shoulder and held his arm with both hands.

"I think we are nearing the end," said John Henry. "I can't imagine that anything more can be said that has not been said, anything useful, that is." He shook his head. "A lot has been said that is not useful or even relevant."

"What means 'relevant'?"

"Anything that has something to do with the trial or with me," he said.

"Am I relevant to you, Juanito?" She looked up at him, smiled.

He bent down, kissed her on her forehead. "Yes, *muchacha*, you are relevant to me. Everything you are, everything you say, every breath you take, is relevant to me. I will show you how relevant you are to me when I get out of here. We will never be apart. I will keep you in sight every minute of every day and night."

"Even when I go pee?" She laughed.

"Well, maybe not there."

They looked across the dusty parade where a couple

of dozen soldiers at the opposite wall stood and sat on benches, chatting and smoking. Another knot of soldiers stood at the wall near the front gate. Others walked about on the parapet above. All held rifles cradled loosely in their arms.

"Look." He pointed at the sky above the western wall. It was just beginning to display the layers of color that John Henry had come to look forward to each day. They watched as the colors deepened and the cloud layers changed in shape and tint.

"Captain Angney has been brilliant," he said. "It was a stroke of luck, him coming back to Santa Fe. And how fortunate to have Señor Chaves as a friend and supporter."

"I saw Señor Chaves today," Morita said, "outside with the people, just before I came in."

"How many people today?"

"Señor Chaves said at least four hundred. I think the soldiers are very nervous. But the people began to leave when I came in. I didn't know the soldier at the gate. He did not smile when I came in."

"I think Colonel Price is afraid that something is going to happen. Every morning when I look out and when I walk across the parade to the courtroom, it seems that there are more soldiers than the day before. I think more soldiers are coming in each night and staying."

They sat silent, watching the changing sunset. Now the clouds seemed to boil, dissipate, reappear and change color and shape.

Morita gripped John Henry's sleeve and pulled him closer. She looked up at him.

"Juanito?"

He looked down at her upturned face. She looked into his eyes.

"Juanito?"

"Yes." He frowned. "What, *querida muchacha* sweetheart?"

"Juanito . . . I'm going to have a baby."

His eyes opened wide and his jaw dropped. "What! You are? Are you sure?"

"I am sure." She took his hand and held it to her belly. "Maybe you can't feel but I have missed my bleeding and Tía and the old woman who has birthed most of the babies in the barrio said that I am going to have a baby."

John Henry took her in his arms and held her tightly. "Sweetheart, that's wonderful!" He pulled back and looked into her face. His eyes misted over. "Wonderful. I'm going to be a daddy!" He hugged her again.

"Easy, *guapo*. Too tight."

He released her, took her face in both hands and kissed her lips softly, pulled her to him and held her loosely, resting his head on hers.

"A baby. Oh, what a wonderful world we're going to show our son." She looked up at him, frowning. "Or daughter," he said. She smiled.

"We'll keep him, or her, in our bedroom for a while. Then, maybe, we'll build another room next to our bedroom with a door between the rooms. I'm sure some of our friends will help. I'll bet somebody has experience with building. Never thought of it, never had any reason to think about it. But now . . ." He smiled broadly. "Or maybe we'll finally decide to move to Colorado or Chihuahua. What decisions we will have to make!

"And when we get settled with this one, we'll get busy on a little sister or brother." He pushed a hand under her rebozo and touched a breast through her dress. She wriggled and pressed against him.

"Juanito, would anybody notice if we went inside for a few minutes?"

He smiled. "I'm afraid they would, *muchacha*. And you'd make so much noise they would come running to see if you are okay."

"I am not okay, Juanito. I want you in my bed."

"Soon, sweetheart. We are almost finished here. Maybe tomorrow. Or the next day."

A movement at the gate caught his eye. The guard was waving. "Time to go, *mi guapa.*" They stood and walked toward the gate.

Day 5. At the fort's front gate, a crowd of townspeople had gathered by sunup. More trudged up the hill and, by midmorning, they numbered more than five hundred. Most were Mexicans but there was a scattering of Americans as well.

The people stood quietly for the most part, though some talked softly with neighbors, all eyes fixed on the open gate. More came, walking slowly up the hill, alone, in twos and threes and larger groups, and joined the others, watching the front gate, waiting.

Four guards stood at the open gate, rifles cradled in their arms, watching the people.

In the courtroom, all members of the court were in place, waiting for Captain Steel to open the proceedings. Steele looked over the room and up and down the line of judges. He picked up a stack of papers, shuffled them, a movement that even he recognized as a nervous tic. He laid the papers on the table, faced the room.

"We have heard evidence on the question before the court and we have heard the closing arguments by the judge advocate and counsel for the defense," said Steele. "The court will now vote on the charge: Is Private John Henry Harris guilty or not guilty of the charge of desertion?"

"Captain Steele," said Angney, "before the court votes on the question of guilt, may I speak to a point that could have a bearing on the vote?"

The five officers looked at Angney, registering in turn surprise, puzzlement, a hint of anger.

Steele leaned back. He inhaled and exhaled heavily. "All right. Yes."

Angney stood up behind his table. He looked about the room, then back to Steele. "Any findings of this court will be invalid because the court is not properly constituted."

Steele lowered his head. He was exhausted and this was the final straw. "What are you talking about, man?"

"Only commissioned officers may serve on a general court martial. Lieutenant Johnstone does not satisfy that requirement."

"He was appointed Acting Lieutenant by Colonel Price who convened this court," said Steele. "I think you know that."

"The acting appointment does not satisfy the requirement as a commissioned officer," Angney said. "Further, removal of Lieutenant Johnstone from the court leaves only four commissioned officers and five members are required for a general court martial."

Captain Steele looked at the wall over Angney's head, then back at the counselor. "What is the source of your information on the subject?"

"Sir, you know that I am a lawyer. I have mentioned that when I volunteered for service, I studied the 1841 General Regulations for the Army, the latest edition, in case I should be asked to exercise my profession while I was in the service. I also read from other documents that described military law and the court martial. I took notes, which I brought with me to Santa Fe. All that I read that commented on the general court martial state clearly that only commissioned officers may serve. Some of the documents specifically state that acting officers may not serve."

Captain Steele winced, clenched his eyes and lowered his head. He looked like a man in agony. Indeed, he was. He did not relish the role that had been cast upon him. He had never been quick to judge in his personal or professional life and he wished with all his heart and soul that he was not a part of this tribunal.

Since his conversations with brother John and the brethren in the Mormon Battalion, he had been depressed, struggling with memories of their accounts of oppression and punishment for belief that ran contrary to what a powerful majority in the country considered the norm. He had lost sleep, tormented by a growing conviction that he had abandoned his faith and his brethren.

He raised his head and looked at Angney. "Do you have a copy of the 1841 regulations in your possession?"

"I do not," said Angney.

"Is there a copy in Santa Fe?"

"Unfortunately, there is not. At least, I have not been able to find a copy. I have looked."

"But you have your research notes with identification of your sources?" Steele said.

"Yes, sir. I have. You are welcome to review them, if you wish."

Steele looked toward the window, seemingly wishing for deliverance from this dilemma and this counselor and this court.

"I will take it under advisement. The court is adjourned until . . . my call."

Captain Steele stood rigidly, almost at attention, before Colonel Price's desk. Steele was uneasy, shifting from one foot to the other. Price stared at the window, then at Steele.

"I've never heard of this," said Price. "Why is this happening! Why did I agree to let that goddam busybody serve on this court!" He looked again at the window. "Damn." He looked back at Steele. "What do you think? Is Angney to be trusted?"

"Yes, sir, I believe him. I think that he has reliable notes that say what he says they say. If we proceed, our verdict could be overturned."

Price stood and walked to the window. He looked out to the plaza. He turned back to Steele. "I don't think so," said Price. "Am I correct that there is no appeal to the verdict of a general court martial?"

"That is my understanding. But if the court is not properly constituted, then technically there is no finding, no verdict." Steele shifted from foot to foot. "Sir, would you consider an indefinite adjournment until we can clarify this question? Or we could . . . if we look at Captain Angney's notes and decide that the court is not properly constituted, we . . . you could dissolve the court and appoint a new court. The work has been done and a new court—"

Price grimaced, held up a hand, palm outward, looked hard at Steele. "Do your duty, Captain." Steele waited. But Price said no more.

"Sir," said Steele. He saluted. Price did not return the salute. He only stared at Steele. Captain Steele turned and walked from the room.

CHAPTER 16
The Book is Closed

Day 6. At dawn, the crowd outside the fort's gate numbered over six hundred. The people stood quietly, though they edged closer to the gate than usual. It was the first time the gate had been closed. A rumor had circulated in the town on the afternoon of Day 5 that the trial appeared to be nearing an end and, now, they waited.

The Army had no choice, of course. John Henry was found guilty when the court reconvened at noon on Day 5, and he was executed at first light the following day, Day 6.

There could be no discussion now about the composition of the court, no pondering alternatives to execution, no consideration of a humanitarian release to his wife and the community. The trial was finished and the book was closed.

When Captain Steele adjourned the court on the morning of Day 5, he had told members of the court and counsel to stay in the fort and be ready for his call to reconvene. Witnesses and guests left the fort and were not notified of the reconvening.

I held the photocopy of the article from the *Santa Fe New Mexican* that told about the execution. No one had been permitted to leave the fort from the reading of the verdict on Day 5 to the completion of the execution on Day 6. So there had been no announcement and no witnesses were present at the execution. Colonel Price had decided against the usual hanging, fearing that the sounds of the construction of a gallows would inflame the crowd standing outside the gate.

The crowd had no hint of a verdict or an execution until they heard the rifle volley inside the fort.

Morita, standing with the crowd outside the closed gate, recoiled as if the rifles had been aimed at her breast. She dropped to her knees. Holding her face in her hands, she sobbed, her body shaking convulsively. Tía and friends touched her, supporting her, stroking her hair.

The crowd of townspeople knew what the rifle fire told. They groaned and shouted, angry shouts, as they moved toward the wall. Guards on the parapets above held their rifles at the ready. Smoke from the discharge of the rifles in the courtyard rose and swirled above the fort walls.

The shouts and muttering from the crowd dissipated, then turned strangely silent as the people stared at the wall and the guards above. The guards glanced sideways at each other, uneasy at the eerie quiet that had settled over the crowd.

Then it was over. In twos and threes, the people turned from the fort to walk silently down the road to the town.

Morita stood at the gate, alone, quiet, her face pressed against the rough timbers. Tear tracks marked her face and her eyes were dry. She had no more tears. Tía and two others stood nearby, waiting.

Morita stayed at the gate until darkness closed in, and she let Tía put her arm around her and help her down the hill to the town.

John Henry Harris was buried in the fort cemetery at midnight. Morita learned of the interment the next day when a rider from the fort gave her a message from Colonel Price's aide.

*****

There's little left of Fort Marcy now but a memory. I visited the site on one of my earliest research trips. It's a park today, the 6.5-acre Prince Park. No walls or buildings remain. Earthen mounds faintly trace the outline of the fort's foundations. Slight depressions encircling the foundations suggest a defensive ditch, perhaps the moat, where defenders could fire on attackers. Interpretive signs erected by the city and the National Park Service tell the story of the fort.

Fort Marcy was never involved in defending Santa Fe. The post cemetery in 1847, had as many as 300 new graves, the victims of fever, measles and lack of medical attention in general. None apparently died of military actions unless the Taos uprising could be considered a military action. John Henry's body was laid to rest with the casualties of that conflict. These also had died for a cause.

Near the post cemetery, Governor Charles Bent, Captain H. K. Burgwin and Albert G. Wilson are buried, all of whom were victims of the Taos rising.

Actually, the fort had begun to deteriorate and its usefulness curtailed even before John Henry was incarcerated here. By late 1846, most of the artillery and personnel had been transferred down the hill to the military facilities near the plaza. Only a few offices and personnel remained at the fort.

Fort Marcy saw some little use during the Civil War and was abandoned in 1868. The death knell for the fort came in 1887, at the hands of fortune hunters. A horde of old coins, some as old as 1726, were found at the base of the walls. This led to a frenzy of digging that toppled the walls. The foundations are now buried under the landscaping laid out in the 1960s when the town created a park on the site. The view of the town from the hill is still most pleasing.

Morita would not be consoled. The light in her life was extinguished and she had only shadows now. She visited John Henry's grave every morning and every afternoon. She sat on the ground, crying softly, rocking back and forth, back and forth. Tía and friends wanted to accompany her but she said she needed to go alone. They shook their heads and did not insist.

The only person to accompany her to the grave was Father Francis and on only one occasion. When he saw her in the street and asked her if he could visit the grave with her, she had burst into tears and apologized for not coming to him. He had assured her that he understood and that he simply wished to offer his condolences and his blessing.

They walked up the hill to the fort cemetery and she showed him the grave. She was surprised when he said that he had visited the grave already. She sat on the ground beside the grave and grieved, rocking back and forth, as if she were alone. He knelt beside her and prayed silently.

The peace she had felt with Father Francis did not last as her dark mood returned. She stayed in her house most of the day, lying on her bed, staring at the ceiling. Or sitting on the porch, where they had sat so often, staring at the dusty yard.

She walked alone to the cantina each afternoon and waited on tables as usual but with no warmth and no greeting that should be a part of the service. Patrons who knew her and had known John Henry understood and spoke softly to her but patrons who did not know complained to José about this sullen serving girl.

José spoke gently to her, apologized for doing so, and explained that he had a business to think about. She listened, head down, and said nothing.

On the few occasions that she went to the market to buy food for the kitchen, she found it hard to concentrate on what she needed, how much she needed and what she should pay. She had always been a shrewd bargainer but now she simply accepted the asking price and paid it. The seller usually was surprised and sometimes offended when she did not engage in the give-and-take of buying, the usual practice.

She stopped caring. About herself, her appearance, her contacts. She often walked barefoot in the streets, ignoring the greetings of passersby, her mind blank. Her dress was soiled, her hair uncombed. It was only with much urging that Tía was able to persuade her to bathe.

At other times, memories flooded back and her mind raced. Sometimes she smiled, then she sobbed until she had no more tears.

On one day, she sat on the bank of the river, staring at the shallow stream coursing below, and her mind cleared. She knew what she must do. She loved Santa Fe, the only home she had ever known but it no longer held her.

She would go to John Henry's parents. She would talk with them about her life with John Henry and she would grieve with them. If they welcomed her, she would have her baby, their grandchild, at their house. When she made the decision to go, she felt a heavy weight lift from her body and a lightness in her soul. She would go home, his home.

*****

Morita sat beside John Henry's grave. She arranged the handful of wildflowers she had placed under the head-stone. Her eyes were dry and she smiled as she told him about her plans. *I am not leaving you, my heart. I'm taking you with me. Our child will be born at your home and you'll always be with me.*

"Morita." She turned to see Steve Burke and his two companions standing there, hats in hand. She stood and walked to them.

"We're sorry to intrude," said Burke.

"You don't intrude," she said. "Thank you for coming. I want to ask you something." She told them about her decision to go to Missouri, to the home of John Henry's parents, to have their child there, and to live with his parents. If they would have her.

"That is a very big decision," said Burke. "You are sure you want to do this? Your friends are here. You have known only Santa Fe. Your life is here."

"I must do this. I have no life here, not now. I will die if I stay here. I am already haunted by dreams of death. After I made this decision yesterday, I slept last night for the first time since . . . it happened.

"I asked you to see me because I want to ask your help. I don't know how I will go to Missouri. Can you tell me how to go? Who do I talk to? I want to go with a traders' caravan but I don't know how to arrange it? Can you help me? I want to go now."

Burke, Jackson and Bradley looked at each other. They glanced at her, back at each other. Burke nodded, followed by nods from the other two.

"Can you help me?" Morita said.

"Yes, we can indeed," said Burke. "We are making preparations ourselves to leave Santa Fe. We have arranged transport in a caravan leaving for Missouri next week, five days from now. We will ask the captain if you can come with us. Would you like that? We have bought two wagons for our transport and there will be ample space."

Morita's hands went to her face. "*Muchas gracious!* Yes, thank you. I would like that. I can be ready to leave tomorrow! Today!"

"Well, not so fast," said Burke, smiling. "I must talk with the captain. I'll see him this afternoon and let you know."

She took Burke's hand in both of hers. "Thank you. Thank you." She wiped her eyes with a hand. Burke and Jackson and Bradley smiled and bowed to her.

CHAPTER 17
Home to Missouri

A group of loaded wagons behind mule teams was bunched up on a dry flat above Santa Fe. Other teams pulling wagons moved slowly up the road from the town toward the assemblage.

Burke and his two partners and Morita stood beside their two wagons. The two hired drivers lolled at the heads of their mule teams, talking and smoking. The partners had bought the wagons not just for transportation but for commerce as well. They had talked it over and decided that they should take advantage of the opportunity to engage in a little business, pooling their resources to buy the wagons and mules and trade goods.

The partners had been trying to arrange a return to Missouri since the end of John Henry's trial and had been disheartened to learn that traders customarily did not leave Santa Fe for the eastward journey until early autumn. They were delighted when they learned that a small caravan would set out in June for an unusual summer crossing.

They had worked through a Santa Fe merchant who helped them buy the wagons and teams and trade goods. Most of the wagons in any caravan bound from Santa Fe to Missouri were loaded with sacks of gold dust from placers and mines near Santa Fe and silver bullion from the mines of Chihuahua.

The three partners' modest funds would not permit them to engage in that trade, so they had to be content with a cargo of furs, wool and coarse Mexican blankets. They rationalized that these goods also would provide better comfort for riding and sleeping than specie.

Morita walked away from the wagons, looked back toward the town. She had been anxious to leave, even excited about the coming journey. It would be the first time she had gone more than ten miles from her home.

She sagged, and her eyes misted. *What am I doing, Juanito? I am leaving Santa Fe, and I will never see you again. I will have our baby, but I leave the place where we were so happy. I will never visit you again in the cemetery. I will never again sit beside your grave and talk with you. But Father Francis said that I would take your soul with me, and you will always be with me.*

I said goodbye to our friends last evening, and they cried with me. I asked Tía to come with me, but she cried and said she could not leave the land of her ancestors. She said she would die before she was out of sight of Santa Fe. I cried with her, and I can understand. But, Juanito, I would die if I stay. I could not go on as I have since you went away.

"Morita." She turned to see the three partners standing beside their wagons. "It's time," Burke said. Their two teamsters sat on the wagon seats, lines in hand, waiting for their employers and pretty passenger to board.

Burke had introduced her to the drivers earlier. Gary, a gangly youngster who smiled shyly, whipped his hat off and bowed to her, and Charlie, a grizzled, dried-up hard case who frowned and said nothing. He had hardly taken his eyes off her since first learning that he would drive her wagon.

Morita walked over and climbed into the back of the wagon and sat on a pile of blankets. Burke climbed up on the wagon seat with Charlie, Jackson on the other wagon seat with Gary. Bradley climbed into the back of Gary's wagon. He was content to be jammed into the clutter of his photographic paraphernalia.

The teamsters shook the lines and moved into the string of wagons that had snaked up the incline away from the town and toward the bunched collection of wagons. Morita looked back at the town, receding gradually. She watched until the wagon reached the crest and rolled across and the tears came.

She knew that she would never see Santa Fe again. A hole had opened in her heart that would never be closed.

I stood at the window, holding a photocopy of an article from the August 15, 1849 issue of the *Chicago Star-Telegram*. I chuckled at the extraordinary luck of this amateur sleuth—that's me—in tracking down this piece. It's a write-up based on the newspaperman's interview with Steve Burke in Chicago. The same Burke who led the delegation to Santa Fe and befriended James Henry and helped Morita go to Missouri. How the reporter found Burke is not explained.

During the interview, Burke told about his meetings with John Henry and with Chaves. He also commented on the proceedings at the trial and his conversations with friends of John Henry and Morita and other townspeople. He told how Bradley had repeatedly asked to take pictures at the trial and as often been turned down. He described the end when the three activists had stood with the townspeople outside the closed gate, heard the shots and watched the smoke from the rifles lift, thin, and disappear.

Bradley did take pictures of the fort and the crowd outside the gates during the trial. I have made inquiries about these pictures but no one seems to know where they are if they still exist. I alternate between anger and anguish that Bradley was not permitted to take pictures of the trial. What a treasure all these pictures, those that were taken and those that were not, would have been for posterity and for me.

The newspaper article comments on the eastward journey of the three partners. Interestingly, it does not mention Morita. Maybe Burke was shielding her. Maybe he thought telling her story would be intruding.

It does mention that Bradley again slowed their progress with his incessant requests to give him time for pictures. On one occasion, Bradley exclaimed loudly at the beauty of the prairie and insisted they stop. He busied himself pulling his camera and gear from the wagon while his partners watched the wagon train moving toward the horizon. The three companions were frightened to distraction when four mounted Indians rode from behind a hillock and were on them in a moment.

The Indians stopped at the wagon, then saw Bradley standing nearby behind his camera apparatus on its tripod. They rode over to him and one dismounted. He looked at the camera from all sides. Bradley lifted the cloth hood and pointed at the viewfinder. The Indian bent and looked. He saw the image in the viewfinder and jerked upright. He looked back at his companions, grinned, said something to them.

The other three dismounted and walked over, looked into the viewfinder. They jerked back at the image they saw, spoke to each other, laughed. Bradley smiled at what he interpreted as enthusiasm.

He became the quintessential photographer. He pushed and pulled the four into position for a photo. They alternately frowned, grimaced, smiled, sobered, and Bradley snapped.

The Indians walked back to Bradley. One patted Bradley on the shoulder. Another grasped the tripod in his arms, lifted it and walked toward his horse.

Bradley cried out as if his child were being kidnapped. The Indian looked at him in surprise. The other Indians apparently persuaded their companion that they had no use for the apparatus. He frowned and set it down. Bradley steadied the camera apparatus, spread the legs of the tripod, nodded to his benefactors.

The Indians looked at the wagon train ahead, barely visible on the trail. The partners followed the Indians' gaze and looked nervously at each other.

The apparent leader of the four spoke to Burke: "T'bacco," he said.

Burke smiled and walked to the back of the wagon, out of sight of the Indians. He motioned for Morita to lie down and pulled a blanket over her. He dug into a sack and pulled out a small bag. Walking back around the wagon, he handed the bag to the Indian who took it and nodded. None of the three Americans smoked but they had been cautioned to have a supply of tobacco ready for just such a confrontation as this.

The four Indians mounted and rode at a walk down the back trail. The Americans learned later that this foursome was part of a largely peaceful Cheyenne band that often approached isolated wagons to ask for tobacco or trinkets. However, if there were loose mules or horses for the taking, that was a different story.

The *Star-Telegram* article added a lot of information about the trial that John Henry would not likely have known at first hand. At least, the article included material that did not make its way to John Henry's journal. His hours were pretty well occupied during the course of the trial and he had less time than usual to devote to his journal.

The picture that Bradley took of the Indians has never surfaced. Too bad, Mr. Bradley. You might have produced one of the first photos, if not the first, of western Indians.

Early on, when I began working on John Henry's story, I was puzzled when I first looked at his journal. The crisp handwriting that clearly was John Henry's was followed by entries in Spanish, then entries in rough English, like in a child's hand. This English in the different hand improved over time.

It became obvious soon enough. Morita had carried the journal with her when she left Santa Fe. She probably carried it as a keepsake but about halfway to Missouri, she began to write in it. She continued to fill the pages to the end of the journal. And through four additional journals that continued for years longer.

She wrote not only about what happened to her during those years after leaving Santa Fe, she also wrote in considerable detail about her time with John Henry in Santa Fe. Her grammar and spelling were not always correct but she wrote clearly and passionately. I'm not ashamed to admit that I got pretty teary more than once as I read her narrative.

I wonder whether John Henry had read his journal to her. I wonder because her entries show the same talent for telling it like it is. Like the story about the randy teamster.

Morita's first entries in the journal were in Spanish. When I asked Benny, one of my *Latino* cowboys, to translate it for me, he read a few pages while we sat in the rocking chairs out on the porch. It was hot that day and I made us some ice tea. He read a couple of pages and looked up at me with wide eyes and a big grin.

"This your grandma, did you say?"

"Yeah, well, my great great grandma."

"Wow, she's some woman."

"I've come to that conclusion. What does it say?"

It seems that Charlie, the teamster who drove the wagon that Morita rode in, had the hots for her from the beginning. She had noticed his stare more than once but passed it off as curiosity, an interest borne out of lack of female contact, or maybe from bashfulness. She tried to be nice to him but he was curt and withdrawn. This didn't keep him from staring.

One evening, when the caravan stopped at the bedding ground, just about sundown, the three partners and Gary jumped down from the wagons and hustled away to do their business. The usual thing for Santa Fe travelers was to do their business just about any place convenient downwind from the encampment. But Morita's presence caused them to modify their practice. If there were a bush in walking distance, half a dozen men would huddle behind it. If there were no bush in sight, they would walk a bit further and pretend they were invisible.

Morita customarily waited in the wagon until the men returned before she walked out to relieve herself. On this occasion, the partners and Gary were hardly beyond shouting distance when Charlie jumped down from the wagon seat, hurried around to the back of the wagon and climbed in. He crawled on top of her, one hand on her mouth and the other fumbling with his belt and pants.

Then he recoiled with a sharp cry. He rolled off Morita and sat up. He held his stomach with a hand.

"Son of a bitch!" he said, "what . . ." He looked at his hand. It was filled with blood that dripped on the blanket.

"You bitch! I'll—"

"You'll nothin', Charlie." Four hands grabbed him by the shoulders, pulled him roughly from the wagon and dropped him to the ground. The two men had run over at the driver's first shout.

Charlie looked up wide-eyed at the traders. "I'm stuck, boys! She stuck me!"

"Well, ain't that too bad, Charlie. She shoulda killed ya," said the big trader who had reached the wagon first.

The second trader, the caravan captain, looked down, a look of pity or contempt. "Git over to Foley. He'll fix you up. You'll walk the rest of the trip. Or you can hoof it back to Santa Fe, if you like. Maybe the Comanche will give you a horse to ride. Or not. Now git up and git out of my sight."

Charlie struggled up and hobbled away, holding his hand at his stomach and groaning.

The captain looked into the wagon. "Are you okay, missis?"

"I'm okay. Thank you." He looked at the short blade that she held.

"Take care of yourself, you hear?" he said. "I really think you can do that." He smiled. "Sorry about Charlie. He ain't the sharpest knife in the drawer. He won't bother you no more. I promise you that."

Thereafter, Charlie walked at the rear of the caravan, eating dust. At the evening camp, he sat outside the circle of wagons, watching the encampment. No one paid any attention to Charlie and no one invited him to have supper with them.

On the third day of Charlie's banishment, he dragged, falling farther and farther behind. Morita watched him from the back of her wagon.

That evening, she walked out to him where he sat on the ground, a good hundred feet from the nearest wagon. He shivered from the cold. Morita handed him a blanket and a plate of beans and biscuit. He looked up at her with a blank face, took the blanket and plate without a word.

The following evening, she took him a plate and sat beside him. They talked, and he thanked her for the supper. Morita's act suggested to the traders that he was forgiven and they began talking to him. Burke even rehired him to drive Morita's wagon again. Kenneth Jackson had never really gotten the knack of driving, even with the repeated instructions from Gary.

From that point forward, Charlie joked and laughed with the partners and became Morita's companion and protector. He was more bluster than belligerent but he got his hackles up anytime somebody looked twice at Morita.

*****

At the end of one particular day that seemed like every other day, the wagons of the caravan were drawn up at dusk in two parallel columns. Traders had built a few small fires beside wagons to ward off the cold, heat coffee water and to prepare the evening meal. Men squatted around fires or strolled about the site, drinking coffee and eating from tin plates.

The captain stood behind the last wagon in the column with Burke and Morita and half a dozen traders. They looked down the back trail at a small campfire a couple of hundred yards away. At this distance in the dark, nothing else could be seen except a shadow when a figure walked in front of the fire.

"What do you make of them folks?" said the captain. Two riders leading a pack mule had been following the caravan since catching up three days ago. Except they didn't catch up. They rode a couple of hundred yards behind the caravan during the day and camped at the same distance at night. Their fire was kept burning all night.

The captain had sent four men back to check on the horsemen a couple of days ago in daylight, but the two riders had galloped away with their mule before they reached them. Nobody felt threatened by the followers but curiosity was getting the best of the captain.

At noon stop the next day, Morita stood behind her wagon, looking through John Henry's spyglass at the two strangers who had stopped the usual two hundred yards behind the caravan. She lowered the spyglass, still looking at the strangers, pushed the tube into itself.

She walked around her wagon to the back. Pulling a blanket aside, she dropped the spyglass into a bag. She felt around in the bag, pulled out a small knife, the same she had used on Charlie. She laid the knife on the bedding, pulled the blanket over the knife.

The next morning before sunrise, the captain organized two parties of three men each to investigate. The first party was to ride out in a wide circle to the left and come up behind the followers' camp. The other party was to ride a bit on the right to flush the two men leftward where they would run into the outriders.

It wasn't necessary at all. The two men didn't move from their night's camp when they saw the three riders on the right approaching. They stood beside their fire and beckoned the riders to come in.

The three horsemen dismounted, shook hands with the men at the fire and accepted cups of hot coffee. They squatted around the fire circle, sipping from the cups. The three riders on the left came into camp and the two followers apologized for not having enough cups for them.

The two men broke camp, packed up the mule and rode to the caravan with the others. When they came up to the wagons, the captain walked over to them. They dismounted, holding their reins and talked with the captain. Morita and Burke watched the group from a distance.

The group broke up and the two stragglers began to walk away, leading their horses and mule. One of the men turned. He saw Morita at the moment she saw him.

It was Captain Steele. He stopped, stared at her a long moment. He handed his reins to his companion and walked to her. His companion remained where he was, holding the reins, watching.

"Mrs. Harris, I . . . I didn't know you were in this caravan." He looked at Burke. "Mr. Burke." Burke nodded.

"What are you doing here? In civilian clothes," said Burke. Steele looked at Morita. He glanced at Burke, then back to Morita.

"I . . . may we talk later? This evening? The captain has invited us to ride with the caravan," Steele said. Morita stared at him, unblinking.

"Yes, we will be here," said Burke.

Steele bowed slightly, took a few steps backward, turned and walked to his companion. He looked back over his shoulder at Morita. The men walked their horses around the wagon column.

The three partners and Morita sat together on the ground at their fire. Steele and his companion sat opposite them.

"I got little sleep for weeks following the trial," Steele said. "I could not focus. I avoided Colonel Price until he called me in and reprimanded me. He told me either to check in at the hospital or snap out of it.

"Then John here appeared. He is my brother. Well, he didn't appear. He sent a man to my office to tell me that he was here, in Santa Fe. We met outside town. He had ridden in just the day before. From San Diego. He was a member of the Mormon Battalion."

Burke turned to John. "Was? Your enlistment couldn't have been up. You deserted."

John didn't blink. "If you like. I left. I assumed that the Battalion was going to be ordered into battle and I wanted no part of it. I had a job I didn't like. I quit. Found some Americans in San Diego who had the same opinion I had of the American military and they welcomed me. In fact, they sympathized with the Californians. They didn't fight with them but sympathized with them. They had adopted the California lifestyle and said the Americans will ruin everything now.

"They introduced me to some Mexicans who were going to drive a herd of horses and mules to Santa Fe and they agreed to take me on. They didn't ask questions. So here I am." He was silent a moment, looking into the fire. "I'm the happiest I've been since I was forced to leave my brethren at Council Bluffs."

The group was quiet, watching the flames of the dying fire.

"And you, Captain Steele?" said Burke.

Steele straightened, leaned forward, stared into the fire. "When John showed up, everything fell into place. My mind cleared. I knew what I had to do. We are going . . . away."

"So," said Burke. "You also deserted."

Steele stared into the fire. He inhaled deeply, exhaled. "Yes," said Steele, "I deserted. There is no other way to say it. I deserted." He looked at Morita whose head was lowered. She appeared on the verge of breaking down.

"Mrs. Harris," said Steele. "I am so sorry. I am so dreadfully sorry. I wish with all my heart . . . I beg your forgiveness but I do not expect it."

"With all due respect, ma'am," said John, "your husband should have left when he had the chance. You could have gone to Mexico. They welcome deserters there, I hear. I hear he was a smart man. You could have had a good life there."

"John," Robert said softly, staring into the fire.

"He was a man of strong convictions," Burke said. "He was convinced that what he did was right. He believed that when he explained why he did what he did, others would understand, and right would win out."

John smirked. "You expect the army would listen and do what's right?" he said with some heat. "They won't. They won't even think about it. They'll follow orders."

"That will do, John," Robert said softly. He straightened, flexed his back. "We must go." He looked at Morita. "I will regret my part in . . . what happened every day of my life. I will pray for you and for the soul of Private Harris."

Morita raised her chin, lowered it and stared at Steele. She said nothing.

He stood. John looked up at him and stood. Robert nodded to all those seated at the fire and the brothers walked away into the darkness.

Morita walked around to the back of her wagon. She reached inside, lifted the edge of the blanket, opened her rebozo and pushed the knife she held into the bag. She pulled the blanket over the bag.

A week later, Robert Steele stood with the captain at first light as traders were hitching teams and packing for the day's departure. John stood behind Robert, holding the reins of their horses and the pack mule.

"Where to, Mr. Steele?" said the captain.

"Ah, we're heading out to . . . uh—"

"We're going to Texas," said John. Robert and the captain turned to look at John. "Should be some opportunities there now that Texas is part of the United States. We hear there's lots of wild cattle for the taking."

"South? You sure?" said the captain. "You'll ride right through the middle of Indian country before you reach Texas. If you reach Texas."

"We'll be fine," said John. "Don't you worry about us."

"Okay, you say so. I hope you get there with your hair on."

Robert cut his eyes at John. He touched his hat to the captain. The two brothers mounted and rode off the trail, heading southward into the plain. The captain watched them go. Other traders standing nearby also watched, chatting and chuckling. One shook his head.

John, you're not only a deserter, you're a damn liar, not that I blame you under the circumstances. Texas, indeed! Everyone in the wagon train knew by now that you were Mormons and they knew exactly where you were going.

As soon as they were out of sight of the caravan, the brothers turned a hundred eighty degrees and headed north where they joined the Mormon migration to Utah. They were going to the Mormon sanctuary in the valley of the Great Salt Lake.

I'm not guessing. I was curious and did a little research. Mormons wanted to found a state, Deseret, within the United States so they could choose their own leaders rather than be organized as a territory that would be governed by Washington appointees. Add polygamy to the mix and it was all downhill from there.

Washington declared the Mormons in rebellion and dispatched an army to force the issue. Having suffered persecution from Americans for decades, the Mormons believed that the United States Army now was intent on nothing less than annihilating them. The Nauvoo Legion was organized in 1857, to oppose the army's invasion of the Salt Lake Valley.

John Steele would not fight for the United States in the Mexican War but he would fight for a cause he believed in. He joined the Nauvoo Legion and was one of the few casualties of the short and mostly bloodless war. He proved with his life that he was not a coward.

I found no evidence that Robert Steele, lately an officer in the United States Army, was part of the Mormon resistance. Purely by chance, I saw a document telling about a trading party that departed the Salt Lake in summer 1856, bound for Oregon. The document stated that the party was led by a former army officer who exercised exceptional leadership qualities during the journey. Captain Steele? Perhaps. I didn't pursue the story. Not relevant.

Morita had the last word on Robert Steele. She wrote in her journal after the Steeles left the caravan that she had not decided whether she wanted to see Captain Steele in heaven or hell.

CHAPTER 18
His Father's Son

Yeah, Benny, she was sure some woman. Benny said that Morita's journal was going to be good reading and he would be happy to translate the Spanish for me. He said that he should be able to get on it pretty soon and would bring it back as soon as he was finished.

Oh, no, I told him. That journal is not going to leave my sight. That's worth more than my weight in gold. I told him that his chores now included an hour or two at my desktop every day, translating. Or he could dictate the translation to my cell phone and I would do the typing. He laughed and said that he could do that.

Before reaching Missouri, Morita had switched to English in the journal. Benny said that the Spanish was well written, grammatical and with good spelling.

The early English entries were a chore to read as it must have been a chore for her to write. She seemed determined and must have asked for help from her three companions for her composition improved quickly. She would lapse into Spanish, occasionally, when she wanted to be clear on a particular point, but then she would switch back to English. She kept writing in those journals for years and eventually could write better English than me.

*****

The caravan pitched camp on the outskirts of Independence. The three partners drove into the town and sold their goods for a modest profit. They also sold one wagon and a team, keeping the best wagon and strongest mules.

On this last evening, the traders drank to everyone's health and caroused till almost dawn. Next morning, the traders struggled from their beds and said their goodbyes. After their minds had cleared satisfactorily, they collectively set a date in early fall for the next Santa Fe departure.

As the camp was breaking up, the three partners scurried about, talking to traders, asking for help. They had promised Morita that they would take her to John Henry's parents' farm, and though they had talked with traders during the trip about Missouri and the towns hereabout, they were anxious to get any last-minute information the traders could offer.

Problem was, they didn't really know where the parents lived. Morita knew that John Henry had invented the farm near Franklin to go along with the invented Jed Weber. So John Henry's real home wouldn't be near Franklin.

John Henry had talked with Morita about the farm where he grew up, and he had talked about the countryside, but she could not remember him mentioning any particular town that was associated with home. When he talked about the country, he had named towns and what had happened in them, stories that others had told him about visits to towns but Morita had never made any attempt to sort the towns out in a landscape.

When she was listening to the partners talking to a

couple of traders, she heard the name of a town: Clinton. And she remembered. John Henry had said that he enjoyed going into Clinton on occasion with his daddy to pick up supplies. His parents' farm must be near Clinton.

Morita told the partners and they were able to get good directions to the town. They were advised to stock up on provisions in Independence since Clinton was more a crossroads than a town.

Clinton was southeast of Independence, not too far. They could reach it in less than a week. Morita was elated at first, excited, then she was terrified. What will they think of this girl, this Mexican, bringing the news of the death of their boy, their only child?

John Henry had received only one letter from his folks. He had written to them on his arrival in Santa Fe in August 1846. He received their reply when he returned from California the following February. He wrote to them after the wedding but would they have received that letter? The closer they came to Clinton, the more anxious Morita became. Will they still be there? What will she do if they will not have her?

As they approached the town, they stopped people on the road to ask. The first two people they asked did not know them. I'm not from these parts, they had said.

The third person they asked replied that he sure did know them. "Yeah, they're still there, about five miles south of town. Cain't miss it. We'll, you cain't miss it if you know what you're looking for.

"On the road that goes south from town, just past the creek, look for two big pecan trees on the left hand side of the road and a buckeye at the edge of the meadow. Just before you get to these trees, take the little road, not much bigger than a trail, into the woods on the left side. Bout a half mile takes you to their place. Cain't miss it."

Burke shuddered at the can't-miss-it assurance. He had heard this before and knew from experience that it usually meant that the speaker traveled more on instinct than landmarks.

Clinton indeed was just a wide place in the road. One general store, a feed store with a livery in the back, a two-story frame building bearing a sign which announced that it housed a café and had rooms available. Adjacent, set back from the road, was a substantial, neat Clinton First Baptist Church.

Burke shook the lines and the wagon rolled down Clinton's main street, its only street, and headed south.

Clinton. I've wondered about that since first reading Morita's journal. Wonder if I'm related to Bill. No, that's Arkansas. Well, his folks might have come from Missouri. Must look into that.

I cannot fathom Morita's feelings as the old Santa Fe Trail trade wagon rolled down the dusty woodland road toward a meeting with John Henry's parents. What would she say? Hello there, I'm your daughter-in-law, Mexican by the way, come to tell you that your son is dead, and I want to live with you and have my baby here. Is that all right? Not likely those words but she must have rehearsed what she would say as the meeting grew closer and closer. The terror increased until she thought she could not catch her breath.

It was all for nothing. When the wagon pulled up in the yard and she crawled down to stand beside the wagon, his mother saw her through the open front door. She called, "Honey, come around here," and her husband came running from around back, thinking something was wrong, and they came to her and took her in their arms and cried, for they knew what her coming alone meant.

The three held each other close, sobbing in each other's arms, loath to let go, as if letting go would be the end of it. But they finally did let go, stepped back, wiping eyes and looking at each other, trying to smile. Then John Henry's mother took Morita in her arms again and held her while his father stroked the mother's hair.

They pulled away again and Morita introduced the three partners and the parents. The partners told how happy they were to meet John Henry's parents and what a fine young man he was and they would be on their way.

James and Alma said that they would do no such thing. They must pull the wagon into the yard for the night and they must have supper tonight and breakfast tomorrow before leaving. James didn't wait for a reply, but just un-hitched the team, took the mules' lines and led them to the corral. All three partners expressed their profound thanks because they were bone tired and nothing would suit them more than a home-cooked meal.

While James tended to the mules, the partners unloaded Morita's things and repacked the wagon for the morning departure. Alma and Morita worked and talked in the kitchen, stopping what they were doing at times while Alma listened to Morita, then returning to the fixings.

After dinner, after the partners had thanked Alma and James again and retired to their beds in the wagon, James made one last check on the stock and went to bed. Alma and Morita sat in their chairs before the glowing embers in the fireplace, talking softly, brushing away tears, smil-ing at a story from childhood and another about a sunny afternoon sitting under the covering of an adobe porch.

John Henry's parents welcomed Morita as their daughter. Morita's stories of her days with their son brought laughter and tears and helped them come to terms with his loss. They had kept John Henry's room as he left it, expecting, hoping, that someday he would return. It was her room now and it was in this room she had her baby.

With Alma's help and the assistance of a neighbor who had birthed most of the babies in a ten-mile radius, she had a healthy son she named James Henry after his father and grandfather. His grandmother was so attentive to the baby that his grandfather told her to let his mother hold him occasionally.

She did hold him, of course, and was loath to let him out of her sight. During solitary walks in the fields, behind the house, with the growing boy, Morita spoke to him in Spanish and, in the evening, sang songs that had been sung to her by her mother and Tía so many years ago and so far away.

James Henry's grandfather also was very attentive to his grandson. He walked with him in the woods, telling him the names of trees and showing him the small animals that populated the undergrowth. When he was older, James taught him to stalk game, to shoot straight and to kill only animals that were needed for the pot.

When James Henry was older still and asked his grandfather why he didn't have slaves like his friends' parents had, the grandfather explained why no man had a right to own another man like he owned horses and mules. The first time James Henry told his friends that owning slaves was wrong, he got a good thrashing.

James Henry grew in years and wisdom and strength and was not reluctant to give a thrashing of his own when he was provoked. He had not forgotten the lesson learned from his grandfather about the dignity and worth of all men and he volunteered to join the Union Army when he turned seventeen.

James Henry's grandparents were aghast at his decision to go to war. But his mother did not object. She said his father would be proud and would not stand in his way. We don't object, said his grandparents, but he is so young. He is a man said his mother.

When it was time for him to leave, Morita stood with him in the yard. She hugged him and placed her hand on his cheek. "Vaya con Dios, my son," said Morita. "Never forget me. Never forget who you are. Come back to me."

So he left. He didn't want to make it hard on his grandparents, surrounded as they were by neighbors who mostly supported the Confederacy, by joining a Missouri Union force, so he volunteered for the 11th Illinois Cavalry. His grandparents had heard too much about the carnage of this Civil War and expected never to see him again. Morita assured them that he would survive. In her own room, at night, she knelt and prayed.

James Henry joined the Illinois unit in time to be wounded in an action near Vicksburg in late 1864. Some of the fine fellows he had come to know died of combat or disease but he survived. At the end of the war, he was mustered out and returned to Clinton with a limp that he had the rest of his life but never slowed him down.

James Henry became a regular hand on the farm. He learned about horses and crops and pigs and chickens but he was most intent on learning how to care for the dozen cows that his grandfather raised for the beef market. In the evenings, he walked with his mother through the woods and they talked about Santa Fe and his father.

Most of the neighbors didn't take kindly to this Yankee living amongst them and they let him know it. He decided that beating two or three of them to a bloody pulp would not increase his popularity, so he controlled his words and his temper. His only real friend was the Baptist preacher but even he counseled James Henry that living with James and Alma could turn the locals against them as well.

The neighbors liked James and Alma well enough, especially now that James's opposition to slavery was no longer an issue. But the locals could not forget that this Yankee was living under their roof.

So James Henry began to think about the future. Maybe it was time to move on, find his own place and his own way. He had been thinking about cattle and Texas ever since he settled with his grandparents. He had heard in Clinton about the herds of cattle being driven north from Texas on a trail just a few miles west of town. He rode over one evening and sat around the campfire with cowboys who planned to sell their herd in Sedalia.

The cowboys were happy to talk with this local who wasn't trying to turn them and their cattle around. It seemed Texas longhorns, a hardy breed that wasn't bothered by blizzard or drought or cactus, carried a tick that didn't infect the longhorns but did infect the soft local cattle. So Missourians and Kansans tried to turn the herds back by force, thereby endangering longhorns and cowboys in the process.

The cowboys told John Henry about the great numbers of wild longhorn cattle that roamed the empty places in Texas. Anybody with a good horse and a hot branding iron could become a cattleman, they said.

James Henry was enthralled and he was hooked. He figured it was going to be harder than the cowboys suggested but he knew this was what he wanted and he knew he could bring it off.

With the savings that he had hoarded, James Henry bought a good wagon, two stout mules and a sleek riding horse. The drovers had described the horse he would need to work wild cattle and he was lucky to buy a horse that fit the description. The seller was a Texas cowboy who planned to settle down in Franklin with a pretty girl he had met and made his case on his last drive. If she was still single and still agreeable to his plan.

James Henry and Morita said their goodbyes to his grandparents early on an overcast morning that mirrored the mood of the four. They tried without success to hold back the tears and James Henry promised that they would return to visit before too many years had passed. Everybody in the conversation knew that this was unlikely but said nothing.

James Henry drove the team from the yard to the dusty road, Morita waving as the tears came, the parents waving from the yard until the wagon rolled around a turning and was swallowed by the dark woods.

*****

James Henry was lucky to throw in with some other folks driving five wagons to Texas. The three families were headed for the sizable community of Fort Worth. Sizable for Texas. This group had moved together to Missouri just three years ago, planning to settle there. They decided that they had made a bad choice and were returning home.

James Henry and Morita said their goodbyes a few miles north of Fort Worth. He said that they had decided to have a look at Jacksboro. They would settle there if they liked what they saw.

"Jacksboro?" said the leader of the family group. "Didn't I tell you to avoid Jacksboro?"

"Well, it sounds like good country with a lot of wild cattle and not too many people," said James Henry.

"Yeah, it's all that, but watch out for the people. They're a strange lot. But if you insist in going, I'll wish you good luck. You'll need it."

Strange lot, indeed. The man had told James Henry about the addle-brained, wrong-headed people in Jacksboro who made up the majority of the population in one of the few Texas counties that voted against secession. James Henry decided that he would get along just fine with the good people of Jacksboro.

James Henry set about making good on his dream. He bought a sizable spread for a fair price from a widow woman who had lost a husband and two grown sons in the war and wanted to move to Fort Worth to live with a daughter there. The place on the banks of the west fork of Keechi Creek had good pasture and some scattered woods.

He built a log house that Morita made into a home. Never mind that the timber and sod ceiling dripped wet and spiders on occasion. They were together and they were home.

James Henry hired two drifters who would become his regular cowboys. The three rode miles in all directions, catching and branding longhorns that were as quick and elusive as jackrabbits and thick as fleas. At the same time, he added to his acreage by buying bits and pieces from neighbors who were less resourceful or had decided that this solitary life was not for them.

At the end of ten years, James Henry was the leading rancher in the area, in acreage and animals. He had a comfortable ranch house built that Morita managed and to which locals gathered for fine dinners and good conversation.

James Henry and Morita and their nearest neighbor were frequent guests in each other's homes. The Hewletts had moved to Texas about the same time he and Morita arrived. They had come from Georgia and the neighbors had some lively discussions about the war and its sorrowful passions. The differences were always smoothed over by good manners and good wine that James Henry bought on infrequent trips to Fort Worth.

It wasn't just conversation that James Henry sought with the Hewletts. He took a strong fancy to their pretty daughter, Vera. With their permission, he courted her and after the passage of but six months, they were married, with the blessings of the three parents.

In precisely nine months, less ten days, from the date of the wedding, a son was born. The timing has been occasion for questions and a snicker or two. James Henry asked Morita if she minded that he name the boy John Henry. It will be wonderful, she said. He will be my second John Henry. Ever since then, we have referred to my grandfather as John Henry the second. A daughter, Priscilla, was born a year later.

James Henry prospered. He continued adding to his acreage and herd and improved his house and outbuildings. He lost a beef now and then to Indians but he was spared the raiding that plagued some of his neighbors. He figured that this was due to the fact that one winter in the middle of a blizzard, he had invited a half dozen near-frozen Comanche hunters into his barn and fed them.

John Henry the second grew to manhood and became his father's top hand. Priscilla married Walter, the handsome son of James Henry's Jacksboro banker. Walter wanted to work cattle rather than clerk in a bank and he was soon working alongside John Henry the second.

A true Harris, John Henry the second soon decided that it was time to find his own way in a new country.

CHAPTER 19
Home to West Texas

West Texas was long since quiet and in the first year of a new century John Henry the second decided to move west.

Morita declared that she had moved enough and stayed with great granddaddy and Vera in Jacksboro. John Henry the second had been gone but a year when his daddy, James Henry, was stricken by a partial paralysis in his left side. He was hardly able to leave the house and required considerable care. By this time, Priscilla and Walter had moved into a house on the ranch. Priscilla looked in on Vera and Morita every day and was a big help.

James Henry declined steadily and soon was bedridden. Morita was constantly at his side. She talked with him about the good times, growing up on the Missouri farm, walking in the woods, stopping to search for a singer in the treetops.

Sitting by his bed, Morita sang to him in Spanish, childhood songs she had sung to him when he was a toddler. He smiled and sometimes joined in, then stopped, breathless.

When James Henry passed on to his reward, Morita withdrew into herself and hardly spoke. She stood before the window hours at a time, staring into her past. Priscilla tried to comfort her, tried to share her grief. She put her arm around her grandmother's shoulders while Morita stared through the window and said nothing.

Later, outside on the porch, Vera held her daughter and cautioned her to give her grandmother time. Vera knew that Morita had to sort through memories and find peace.

One morning when Vera was in the kitchen preparing breakfast, Morita came in, smiled, reached into the cupboard for dishes and began to set the table. Vera knew that Morita had worked it out and had come home.

Morita and Vera persuaded Priscilla and Walter to move into the large ranch house. They let their house to the ranch foreman who was delighted since he had plans for the pretty daughter of the Jacksboro feed store proprietor.

John Henry the second kept in touch with frequent letters. Since moving west, he had worked on a large ranch near Lubbock. He was not unhappy with his lot but he longed for his own place. With help from his mother and Walter, now managing the home ranch, and Walter's father, the Jacksboro banker, John Henry the second bought a spread near Sweetwater in west Texas. Walter advanced him a herd of breeding stock and he launched his ranch.

John Henry the second was fortunate to enjoy wet seasons and mild weather in the early years and his herd increased. The ranch grew in size with the purchase of chunks of acreage that adjoined his.

In spite of his preoccupation with the ranch, he was not immune to the charms of the daughter of a close friend who lived two ranches south. John Henry the second married Janice and within a year, my father was born. Carrying on the family tradition of confusing the genealogical charts, they named their son James Henry. He was thereafter called James Henry the second. A daughter, Margaret, came along less than a year later.

Daddy grew to manhood on the ranch, the only life he knew and the only life he ever wanted. When he took over management of the ranch, he continued to enlarge the acreage and herd. He added a horse breeding program and produced some of the top registered quarter horses in west Texas. He married Emily, the daughter of the preacher at the Sweetwater First Baptist Church. My sister, Debra, was born a year later, and then there's me, born ten months after that.

I last saw Grandmama Morita at her home on the ranch near Jacksboro. It was the only time I really remember her. I was only four. We drove up to the house where wagons with teams still hitched and a few pickups and cars were parked on the road, in the driveway and in the yard. Daddy had to park the pickup a good walk from the house.

Daddy started to knock on the front door but a long-faced relative I didn't know opened the front door before he could knock. The relative and Daddy exchanged nods. Mama and Daddy and Debra and I walked into a bedroom crowded with cousins and uncles and aunts, relations I didn't remember seeing for a long time, some I didn't remember at all. They all got real quiet and looked at Mama and Daddy and Debra and me when we came into the bedroom.

Daddy pushed Debra in the back toward the bed where Grandmama Morita lay, covered with blankets and a white bedspread up to her chin. A white lacy cap covered her hair. Debra stood there by the bed a full minute, then reached up and touched Grandmama's hand. She turned and smiled at Debra. Debra smiled and walked back to Mama and hugged her leg.

Daddy pushed me in the back over to the bed. Grandmama Morita turned her head toward me and smiled a little smile. She extended a shriveled, bony hand to me and I took it.

"*Hola, mi calabacita,*" she said in a small voice.

"*Hola,* Grandmama."

She squeezed my hand ever so slightly, then pulled her hand back slowly. She crossed her arms over her chest and stared at the ceiling. I saw a tear, just one, roll down her temple to her neck. Daddy turned me around and we walked through the door with Mama and Debra.

It was the last time I saw Grandmama Morita. She died that night. She was 105 years old.

We went to her funeral two days later. After the service at the Jacksboro Baptist Church, I stood in the pew alone while Mama and Daddy and other family members lined up to file past the open casket for one last look at the remains and to say goodbye. You need to see her and say goodbye, relatives had told me, or you'll never be able to accept that she is gone.

I was told later that I was a bright child and, even at four, I could understand all they were saying but I wasn't buying it. At least, not at Grandmama Morita's funeral. I had learned my lesson.

Just a month before her funeral, we had gone to the funeral of my old Uncle Buddy in Sweetwater. He wasn't really my uncle but that's what I had always called him. He was just a good family friend. Uncle Buddy had always played with me and joked with me and I loved him very much. I had walked with the family to the front of the church to view the remains—they always called the dead body the remains—and I had been shocked.

He was dressed in a brown suit and a white shirt and tie.

I had never seen Uncle Buddy in a white shirt and tie. The remains had a fine haircut and had been shaved and was all powdered up and smelled like Uncle Buddy had never smelled. Uncle Buddy had always smelled of tobacco and sweat, never sweet like this.

It's the only image I have of Uncle Buddy today. Not the funny, grinning, playful old Uncle Buddy. Just dressed up, powdered pink remains.

When Mama and Daddy joined the queue to walk past Grandmama Morita's casket, I stayed in the pew by myself. I have never viewed another dead body at a funeral to this day.

When I think now of Grandmama Morita, I see the sweet face of the old woman who smiled at me and said, *"hola, mi calabacita."* Hello, my little pumpkin.

Daddy told me years later that, at that last visit with Grandmama Morita, Walter had caught him out on the porch and told him that a few days ago, a few days before she died, he was in the barn about noon and heard Morita's voice. Thinking she was talking to him, he walked out and there she was in the yard, standing in the shade of the big oak, there beside the glider, just talking away in Spanish.

She would pause, laugh, talk some more. She sat down slowly, a little rickety, in the glider. She kept on talking, laughing, swinging her arms like she was sort of punching somebody gently, all the while gliding slowly back and forth, back and forth.

Carlito was working in the hayloft and Walter asked him to walk over to the porch to try to understand what she was saying. Didn't mean to eavesdrop, Walter told Daddy, just curious.

Carlito did a roundabout walk to the porch where she

couldn't see him and edged over to the banister and listened as Walter watched. Morita kept up her chatter, talk, laugh, frown, listen.

Carlito, sober-faced, looked over at Walter, then backed away from the banister and did his roundabout return to the barn.

Walter smiled. "What's going on?"

Carlito did not smile. He had a long face. "Who is Juanito?"

"Ah. That was her husband. He . . . died too young."

"I don't want to listen no more. That was a private conversation with Juanito." Walter nodded and he and Carlito went back to what they were doing.

Walter worked in the barn until sundown. On his way to the house, he saw that Morita was still in the glider, her head back on the headrest and leaning sideways. Walter walked over, thinking to wake her up and walk her in to supper.

He couldn't awaken her. He picked her up, surprised at how light she was, and carried her to her bed. As soon as he and Priscilla got her settled, he telephoned the doctor. That evening, he telephoned all the kin to tell them that they should come see her as soon as they could get here.

CHAPTER 20
All Good Things

I closed the journal and laid it gently on the desk. Opening the top drawer on the right side of the desk, I picked up a small padded box. Donie used to keep her rings and earrings in it. I stood and walked to the window.

Opening the box, I took out the picture, holding it carefully at the edges. It was a daguerreotype, black and white, clear and sharp. It was sealed in a protective glass cover with strips of paper coated with some sort of mucilage. I tilted the picture toward the light from the window.

In the picture, a young man sits stiffly in a straight-backed chair, dressed in a wrinkled uniform, staring grimly at the camera. He holds a book in his lap. A young Latina stands beside him, her hand on his shoulder, her lips pursed, seemingly suppressing a smile. The photographer would have told them to be still, don't smile! Every time I look at the picture, I expect the girl to burst into laughter. She wears a simple light yellow cotton dress, a gray rebozo around her shoulders.

I turned the picture over. Written on the backside in a clear hand: John Henry and Morita, Fort Marcy, 1847. The hand is not John Henry's. Probably Morita's. I have seen her handwriting from her later years and the writing on the back appears to be the same. I turned the photo over to look at the images again. Two young people in their prime.

Until I saw the picture, I conjured up images every time I read a passage from John Henry's journal. This vigorous youngster from a Missouri farm, raised by hard-working parents, devout Baptists, who taught him the virtues of truth and a belief in the essential goodness of man.

And this young woman, a child of privilege who was denied nothing by doting parents, who lost her parents and position early in her life and had to make her own way in a demanding, male-dominated culture. The photograph confirmed the images of two strong, resilient young persons that I had imagined.

The picture was a blur as the tears came. I had never cried over any picture, any memory, except when I thought of Donie or saw pictures of her. But I don't mind admitting that I blubbered when I first saw this picture. I still have a hard time looking at it.

I might never have seen it. It was buried in a small box of odds and ends that had come to me with the papers from my granddaddy. I doubt he ever saw it. At least, he never said anything. Maybe he saw it and didn't make the connection. Nor did I when I first saw it. I shudder when I think that Granddaddy or somebody else might have thrown it out when cleaning and getting rid of old stuff.

The picture was made by Jeremiah Bradley, the anti-war activist who appeared with his two colleagues at Fort Marcy in 1847. I did some research on Bradley and I was flabbergasted.

Bradley had served as an apprentice to Joseph Pennell who had been associated with Samuel F. B. Morse who had, in turn, learned about the mysterious practice of photography from the master himself, Daguerre.

Bradley had worked under Pennell alongside another apprentice named Mathew Brady. When Bradley was ready to strike out on his own, his interest ran to recording images in nature. He was enamored with the paintings of artists who would later be called the Hudson River School and wanted to record similar images in the West with the camera. That's why he was quick to join his fellow anti-war activists on their trek to Santa Fe.

He dismayed his companions at the start by filling their wagon with his unwieldy apparatus and delaying their progress with his incessant requests to stop so he could record a particular view. On repeated occasions, the two partners fidgeted as they watched the other wagons in their train moving away while Bradley set up his gear, adjusted, readjusted, finally finishing with a flourish and packing the gear in the wagon. Then the whipping of the mules, looking side to side for Indians who often threatened lone wagons on the trek to Santa Fe, until they caught up with the other wagons.

Too bad about you, Jeremiah. When you left Santa Fe and returned east, you decided to become a pharmacist instead of a pioneer in the new field of photography. You might have become the photographer of the West or the Mexican War. You might have become the forerunner of your co-apprentice, Mathew Brady, who later became famous as the visual chronicler of the Civil War. Too bad. History doesn't remember pharmacists, Jeremiah.

Since photography was a distraction rather than a profession, Bradley showed his pictures only to friends. These small-minded people saw them as oddities, images recorded by a box, much as images were captured by the artist's brush.

The people who might have understood the significance of the pictures never saw them. Bradley's three children were not interested in their father's odd hobby and the pictures remained in boxes in closets and attics for generations. Except for a few scattered remnants, all of his pictures have been lost.

Unfortunately, John Henry made no mention in his journal of the occasion when the picture was made. Strange, for it wasn't every day that one had his picture taken in 1847. I'm sure it was the first time he had even heard about the practice of recording images with anything other than a pen or brush. I wonder whether he ever saw the picture.

I have no idea how or when Morita received the picture. Did Bradley give it to her in Santa Fe? Or did he give it to her at an evening campfire on the trail, fearing that he might cause her grief rather than joy? Maybe he promised to send it to her at John Henry's parents' place. However she received it, his parents would have looked at it with surprise and broken hearts.

I showed the picture to the owner of the best camera shop in Lubbock and asked him how to take care of it. He was dumbfounded. He said I had a treasure and asked me all about it. He said I had one of the earliest examples of daguerreotypes and said it belonged in a museum.

That led me to start thinking about what to do with all the stuff I had accumulated in my research. Stuff in my head and materials I have collected. Doc says I should write a book. Doc Edwards, the local Sweetwater doctor, retired now from doctoring, who runs cattle on the spread just north of mine, has written a bunch of books about his ancestors that first came to Texas about the time mine did. Our families have known each other for three generations.

Doc says that I have an obligation to write a book so people hereabouts and throughout the country will know something about the opposition to the Mexican war from a very personal point of view. He says he'll help me with crafting, proofing and submission. I don't know about this. Sounds like a lot of work. We'll see.

And then there's the materials. Doc said that I need to put them somewhere other people who are doing research on the same period will have access to them. He said that I should put it all in there, even my notes and jottings. Really? Would people want to see that stuff? He said that they sure would.

Maybe I should put the materials somewhere. Son Paul would accept the stuff if I offered it to him. He wouldn't want to hurt my feelings. But he would store it somewhere and it would be lost till a grandchild or somebody else found it in an attic or cellar. If it didn't get burned up in a fire first.

I went with Doc to a convention in Lubbock last June, a group called Western Writers of America. He was right at home since he is a good writer and has published a bunch of books. He could talk with them about writing from the inside.

I felt pretty small and insecure. But the G&Ts and red wine at the bar and receptions loosened my inhibitions and I had some pretty good conversations. Some of the people there who weren't too full of themselves even listened to me and seemed interested in what I was doing.

During the course of the convention, we visited the Southwest Collection at Texas Tech. It was nice to be back on campus, lots of changes since I was here last. Doc has done research here and introduced me to the curator. When Doc told him what I was doing and that

I had amassed a horde of materials, the curator became positively ecstatic.

He said that they would be delighted if I would give my materials to them when I was finished with them. Or even before I was finished. He said they would organize the stuff and catalog it and it would be even easier for me to use. Don't know about that since I know where everything is in my study. But it might be interesting to see if anybody else would find the materials useful. I told him I would think on it.

I sat with Doc in the rocking chairs on the front porch one evening, watching the sunset and listening to the breeze in the cottonwoods. I sipped my G&T and Doc drank from his beer bottle. I have tried many times without success to civilize him by encouraging him to try my excellent G&Ts but he is unmoving. I don't drink, he always said, beer is food.

I didn't even offer a G&T this evening. Just got a beer from the refrigerator and handed it to him. Neglected to open it and he had to go back to the kitchen for an opener. I yelled at him where to look for it.

I rocked slowly, staring at the front fence. I was spent. Depressed. I had never felt so empty with no energy and no ambition. I looked up at the sunset, the lacy cloud layers turning twenty pastel shades, and even that didn't stir me. I glanced at Doc's empty chair, realizing how impolite I had been to make him open his own beer.

Doc returned from the kitchen and sat down. I apologized for my rudeness and my mood. Doc laughed out loud. I was surprised at his response and was on the point of saying something really rude.

He reached over and clapped me on the knee. "Don't

worry about it, Olin. Happens all the time. Any time somebody finishes a research project that he's been totally absorbed in, that has occupied his time and his thoughts every minute of the day, the usual result is deep depression. You'd think the result would be elation but it never is. You are drained, depressed, empty.

"It passes. It finally dawns on the researcher that he has finished and he is satisfied. He's glad he's finished and he's ready to start putting it on paper or moving on to that other topic that has been rocketing around in his head for months. Now he gets energized and moves on."

"Yeah, I guess that's about it. I never thought I would get to the point that I could decide that the research is finished." I sat up straighter. "But I guess you're right."

He leaned over and patted my knee again. "Course, you aren't actually finished on this one, are you? Not yet. You still got to write the book." He smiled, took a long drink from his bottle, pointed it at me. "And don't forget. I'll help. Just ask."

We sat quiet, glass and bottle in hand, watching the sun sink below the horizon and the sky darkening. The wind picked up and papers blew past in the yard. A large tumbleweed rolled and bounced on the road in front of the house toward the barn.

"Be damned," said Doc. He leaned forward in his chair. "I hadn't seen a tumbleweed in years. I must be gettin' old."

Large drops of rain sounded on the tin porch cover. The wind increased and papers and rain blew horizontally across the yard.

I told Doc that he better be on his way, that he's sure to get soaked, as it is. He agreed that it was time to go. We stood, shook hands, and he was gone, running to his pickup, shielding his glasses with a hand. He opened the pickup door and hopped inside, slamming the door. I heard the engine start, he backed up, and headed out of the yard to the road. I watched his lights until he rounded the corner and knew he was rolling down my road toward the county road.

I stood on the porch until the blowing rain chased me inside. This was sure some fierce storm. I went into the kitchen, felt the coffee pot. It was still warm. I took a cup from the cupboard, the one that Doc gave me last month. On the side, the words: *Write On!* I smiled, poured the coffee and sat at the kitchen table, watched the rain pelting the windows.

Yeah, it feels good to reach the end of a satisfying task. And it was well done if I say so myself.

And this tops it off. I picked up the letter from the table and re-read it. I had received it just this morning from the United States Army Judge Advocate General. It had taken them three months of cogitating to reply to my letter.

The Army finally agreed that John Henry's conviction was dead wrong. Oh, they didn't say that the finding that he was a deserter was wrong. They just admitted that the court was not a legal court.

John Henry, you and your counsel got it right. Private Johnstone could not serve as a member of a court martial. Never mind that Price promoted him to the temporary rank of Acting Lieutenant. He wasn't a bona fide commissioned officer. So the Army, in 2016, threw out the 1847 judgment. John Henry was not legally a deserter.

Bit late for John Henry.

Course, if the Army had decided that the court was not properly constituted while he still lived, they would have tried him again at a proper court martial and found him guilty again. It still matters that they threw it out, for me anyway.

Forgot to tell Doc about the letter. I'll tell him in the morning, bright and early. He'll be real interested.

Now to bed. Next week we start putting all this stuff into the book. Doc says it'll be a bestseller. Hoo-ray, Doc. Write on!

EPILOGUE

Doc stood in the yard, looking at Olin's house. Only there was no house. It was a pile of kindling, broken pipes and scattered chimney stones. Half a dozen men, Olin's hands and other friends, climbed about the wreckage, searching. They didn't really know what they were looking for, just anything that should be salvaged.

The ambulance had taken Olin's body away at first light. They had responded quickly to Doc's 911 call and reached the house in less than twenty minutes.

Doc turned to Cindy who stood beside him, staring at the remains of her childhood. She reached for Gail and put an arm around her shoulders.

"It wasn't much of a twister, as Texas tornadoes go," said Doc. "It must have touched down right on top of the house. It didn't cause much damage in the county. My house wasn't touched and I saw little damage on the drive over here."

Doc shook his head. "I never believed in premonition but, now, I don't know. Did your daddy sense something? Why else would he have insisted that I take all his research materials home with me last evening? Why had he handed me the letter addressed to the curator, describing the donation of his papers to the university?

"We had just finished loading the stuff in the pickup last evening when the rain started. Good thing I had the cover on. We had plans to take the materials to Texas Tech today. I was going to pick him at first light. We planned to have breakfast on the drive up.

"Did he tell you that we went to the campus last week and made arrangements?" She shook her head. "He gave the Southwest Collections curator a letter telling about his intention to donate the materials. The curator asked us to go out for coffee, said he needed to get some stuff done.

"While we drank our coffee at the Starbucks just off campus, Olin told me that he was going to take me at my word, that I would help him write John Henry's story. I told him that I would be delighted. In fact, just last week, I submitted a finished manuscript for a novel to my publisher and I haven't begun work on the new book short of pondering and outlining. I told him I would have plenty of time to work with him on his John Henry project. I was enthusiastic. This book was going to be a good read and a major contribution to the history of the Mexican War, especially to the anti-war movement.

"When we finished our coffee and walked back to campus, the curator showed us a locked display cabinet on the wall beside the door to the reading room. Behind glass, there was the picture of John Henry and Morita and a photograph of your daddy displayed side by side. The curator said that he was going to have the daguerreotype resealed in a new protective frame but he wanted to show us where the photos would be permanently displayed.

"The curator had asked your daddy some time ago to give him a picture of himself that he could use if he decided to donate his materials to the college. Olin had made a fuss but agreed to have one made. The picture that he gave the curator was taken by Barbara with her cell phone. I think you know Barbara." Cindy nodded.

"It's a good likeness and I told Barbara so but it's incomplete. I can't see through that cowboy shirt to his heart. He was a good man, Cindy. I'm gonna miss him."

"Me, too," she said, hugging Gail beside her.

"It grieves me that he won't write John Henry's story now," said Doc. "But it's a story that needs to be told. If it's okay with you, I'll write it from his materials. Including the last paper in the collection. Just before you pulled up, one of the cowboys working through the rubble handed me a crumpled, wet sheet that he had just found. It was the letter from the United States Army Judge Advocate General that I told you about.

"Cindy, I'm going to write your daddy's book. Will you help me?"

"I will," she said. "And I'll tell you this, what I was going to tell Daddy. I have decided to retire at the end of this school year and move up here. Gail will be close by at Texas Tech." She paused, looked at the wreckage of the house. "This was supposed to be a surprise. He didn't even know we were coming. We stayed at a motel in Sweetwater last night."

Tears welled up in her eyes and she turned to Gail. They held each other. Doc put his arm around both women.

Cindy wiped her cheek with a hand. She looked back at the ruined house. "I'm going to rebuild this place. I knew every inch of it and I'll rebuild it."

"I'm real glad to hear it, Cindy. You've got a good foreman and I'll give you all the help I can. Just ask. If you want to stay on the place while you're building, you can borrow my travel trailer. I'd be real happy if you would do that. Will you?"

Cindy smiled. "Doc, you're an angel if heaven has big ol' burly angels. I'm going to take you up on the offer. And you may regret offering help before we get this house built and I learn all about running this ranch."

"Not likely. I'll clean up the trailer and have it over in a couple of days. I'll give you a call when it's ready. Here's my card with my telephone numbers." He pulled out his wallet, extracted a card and gave it to her.

She pulled a small case from a jacket pocket, took out a card and gave it to him. "Here's my phone number and address. We'll be coming up weekends as often as we can."

"That's good. Just let me know when you're coming. I want to take you to Texas Tech and show you your daddy's collection. We'll be spending lots of time there while we are writing this tome." He walked to his pickup, waving over his shoulder.

As he climbed into the pickup, he waved again, and Cindy and Gail waved. They watched him pull away onto the road and disappear around a turning.

Gail put her arm around her mother's waist as they walked toward their car.

"Mama, tell me about Grandmama Morita."

AFTERWORD AND
ACKNOWLEDGEMENTS

At the end of my book, *Santa Fe mi casa*, John Henry rides eastward, leaving California's valley of San Pascual behind, bound for Santa Fe, *a casa*. This book, *If I Should Die,* carries the story forward.

Research for the first book was useful for this sequel but I incurred new debts as well. For leads on courts martial in general and on Mexican War cases in particular, I thank Paul Hutton and Durwood Ball at University of New Mexico. Johnny D. Boggs helped with both courts martial and data on Santa Fe. Rachel Adler, Archives Bureau Chief at New Mexico State Archives, provided information on courts martial in the archives. Gregory Maggs, Professor of Law at The George Washington University Law School, helped me with the intricacies of military law.

Thanks to Tomas Jaehn, Librarian, Fray Angélico Chávez History Library, New Mexico History Museum in Santa Fe, for help with Santa Fe materials in the library's holdings. Eleanor Bernau, Archives Coordinator at the *Santa Fe New Mexican,* provided information on this early

New Mexico newspaper.

My thanks to Candy Moulton, Executive Director of Western Writers of America, for permission to let Olin and Doc attend the 2015 convention of WWA in Lubbock. I am grateful to Jennifer Spurrier of Southwest Collection, Texas Tech University, for accepting Olin's donation of his papers to the Collection.

Joanna Smith provided interesting pictures and information on old Fort Marcy. Merrilee Miller and Andrew Miller, attorneys, assisted with legal terminology and courtroom procedure. My thanks to Mickie Flores, Magdalena Hernandez, and Lilia Becerra-Quintor for help on Spanish dialogue. Mickie, Maggie and Lilia tried to teach John Henry proper Spanish but the gringo still made mistakes.

Thanks to the Pacific Critique Group for their comment on the manuscript. I'm particularly grateful to Daniel Hobbs for his careful reading of the story and spot-on suggestions and Jennifer Hoffman's assistance with formatting.

Finally, my profound thanks to Steve Turner, aka Doc, a walking repository of all things early west Texas, particularly anything related to cattle ranching.

Since I can't blame anybody else for the errors in the narrative, I'll have to accept full responsibility. The errors are all mine.

IF YOU LIKED THIS,
YOU MIGHT LIKE: COFFIN JACK:
A WESTERN DUO

ONE-EYED COFFIN JACK IS A DEADLY MAN.

Coffin Jack is a dark souled assassin that does not possess much; he lives alone with only feral cats for company in his isolated shack in the mountains and barely ventures down to civilization except when he gets the call.

Joined by his now partner, Lowell Devereux – a naive reporter who was unceremoniously thrown into the path of Coffin Jack while seeking uplifting stories to inspire the readers back east – the two are out prove all that they are capable of. Their wild journey takes them across country to confront a series of deadly challenges and plunge into an esoteric nightmare that transforms the pair. From there they are taken on a trail through the darker side of the Old West where factions differ and it is a new enemy they must face...

A tongue-in-cheek Western with all the blood and thrills of a regular rough ride, or as Coffin Jack might say, "Ya gotta own a pinch of salt for this one."

Coffin Jack: A Western Duo includes – Deathdealer and Gravedigger.

AVAILABLE NOW

ABOUT THE AUTHOR

Harlan Hague traveled a circuitous road to western lit-erature. A native Texan, he earned business degrees at Baylor University and University of Texas and worked in management for four years before receiving his enlight-en-ment and switching career and field to teaching history. He earned a further two degrees, the last a Ph.D. in history from University of Nevada, Reno. He taught United States history, American West and the environment at San Joa-quin Delta College and summers at Cal State Stanislaus and University of Oregon.

While teaching, Hague wrote a few dozen history ar-ticles on the American West that published in scholarly journals. He turned to writing books and, in the process, received a number of academic and professional honors and grants, including National Endowment for the Humanities.

Since turning to books, Harlan Hague writes about people searching for redemption and fulfillment in the West, running from their demons, leaning on others. He likes endings that close with a sigh and a question. His books have won several awards in national competitions. His screenplays, mostly based on his books, have earned some notice and are making the rounds.